For Lisa & David,
Truly hope you enjoy the book. Best Wishes,
R.T. Anders
3-25-04

One-Sided Doors

R.T. Anders

Joanne P. Geisler – Editor

Michael Csontos – Illustrations, Cover, Author Photo

Printed in Victoria, Canada

This is a work of fiction. Names, characters, places, and incidents are either the product of the author's imagination or used fictitiously. Any resemblance to actual persons (living or dead), events, or locales is entirely coincidental.

Note for Librarians: a cataloguing record for this book that includes Dewey Classification and US Library of Congress numbers is available from the National Library of Canada. The complete cataloguing record can be obtained from the National Library's online database at: www.nlc-bnc.ca/amicus/index-e.html

ISBN 1-4120-1567-7

TRAFFORD

This book was published on-demand in cooperation with Trafford Publishing.
On-demand publishing is a unique process and service of making a book available for retail sale to the public taking advantage of on-demand manufacturing and Internet marketing. On-demand publishing includes promotions, retail sales, manufacturing, order fulfilment, accounting and collecting royalties on behalf of the author.

Suite 6E, 2333 Government St., Victoria, B.C. V8T 4P4, CANADA
Phone 250-383-6864 Toll-free 1-888-232-4444 (Canada & US)
Fax 250-383-6804 E-mail sales@trafford.com
Web site www.trafford.com TRAFFORD PUBLISHING IS A DIVISION OF TRAFFORD HOLDINGS LTD.
Trafford Catalogue #03- 1944 www.trafford.com/robots/03-1944.html
10 9 8 7 6 5 4 3 2

This book is dedicated to the memory of my sister
Melvina Mae Mackinder

Acknowledgements

I extend my deepest gratitude to my editor, Joanne P. Geisler, who stuck with me throughout this entire endeavor. Her wit, guidance, comments, knowledge of the English language, and attention to detail are greatly appreciated. Any errors remaining in the text, (from pesky last minute changes or flashes of inspiration), are without doubt my own.

The amazing talents of Michael Csontos produced the book's beautiful cover and meticulously detailed inside illustrations. I'm sure my readers will appreciate them as much as I. He even took the "author's photo", to wit, I hold him completely blameless for the results.

I'd also like to thank my friends who live in Victorian Estates for their support and encouragement during the undertaking of this effort. Special recognition goes to Marie Peshenka, Reesie Wilson, and Eleanor Brainard for uncounted dinner-party invitations where they generously shared delicious food, a circle of acquaintances, and sparkling conversation.

Thank you all.
R.T. Anders

<u>Author's preface to the 2361 edition (Gregorian Date) *</u>

Since I am considered by some as a time traveler of renown, the powers that guide the academic world approached and requested that I write a pre-selected text concerning my exploits. Therefore, I had advance knowledge this book would become required reading for students embarking on a career in <u>Timeline Distortion Recognition and Repair</u>. In sympathy with those despising yet another typical dry memoir and mission log collection of my contemporaries operating in the last 40 to 50 years, I attempted to enhance the obvious and create an adventure.

In promoting the element of surprise for factual deeds already performed, it became necessary to manifest the supposition that at least one character be a native from the reasonably recent past. I arbitrarily selected the male protagonist, which, in retrospect, seems the logical choice. To maintain some semblance of peace and tranquility amongst my peers, I cast myself as the character from these neighboring annals of time. In conclusion, my objective, and my hope, is to transcend the mundane, while enlightening, making at least one bit of rote learning more enjoyable.

As an aside, the publisher will transmit the full text, minus this preface of course, to an associate who by choice has remained in the past. The book will be printed under the guise of a work in the genre of science fiction, (an obsolete term – now called future fiction). The purpose of this exercise is simply their desire to participate in the celebration at the turning of the last millennium. Imagine if you will, the impact on the world if this preface were in fact not deleted. The purchaser would realize that instead of a new work by a current author, they would be buying a manuscript not prepared and written until another 360 years in the future.

A poignant example of why such extreme care and diligence must be maintained when dealing with the aspect of time. REMEMBER IT WELL.

Good luck in all your future endeavors, even if they're in the past.

Cordially,
R. T. Anders

* 61.321 Sol System Standard Date

"When you sit with a nice girl for two hours, you think it's only a minute. But when you sit on a hot stove for a minute, you think it's two hours. That's relativity."

- Albert Einstein

Prologue

Dr. Thomas Hughes had finished his free-weight workout and exhausting run. Now, after a shower, he stood relaxing on his mountain home's deck, enjoying the quiet and gazing up into an inverted, shifting bowl of night sky. The sides were formed by the gently swaying seventy-foot ponderosa pines, while the dark, false, infinite bottom was liberally sprinkled with scintillating luminous points.

He found the sight awe inspiring. Such speculative scenes always caused him to inwardly reflect and consider the minuteness of one's existence. In a relative sense, life lasted only a second, allowing enough time for nothing more than the futile attempt to explore a single grain of sand.

Tom's body began to slowly sway with the rhythm of the soft enchanting music flowing from his home's interior. He chuckled, as the remembrance of a five-item childhood list tiptoed into the present, tapped a shoulder, and deftly positioned his musing within a shimmering, gossamer web of carefully selected memories.

Ever since Jurassic Park was first viewed, he'd wanted a pet T-rex, which was number one. The closest thing to date had been a six-foot green-iguana named Pookie-Oogly. Entries two through four ... anti-gravity, time travel, and matter teletransportation ... had been significantly anomalous interests for a child. They stemmed from an early fascination of physics. His current work had directly led to the accomplishment of item two. He felt confident the future would supply answers to three and four.

Perhaps it was ironic that the first four items could actually come to fruition if enough time were allowed, although none of his friends had believed this possible. Whereas, the fifth and final item, love, which most people took for granted, proved to be the most elusive. Nonetheless, it had been added to the list when he was at the impressionable age of sixteen. His smile faded to a frown.

Her name was Shannon, and coincidentally, had been in his first hour physics class. Tom closed his eyes and concentrated. He could still envision her soft, smoothly curled hair blushing with the color of a sunlit-beach, draping down over one side of her lovely face. Shannon's eyes seemed to have witchingly fabricated their own distinctive shade of vibrant blue. Whenever she entered a room, it seemed brighter and warmer. Her smiles urged him to write reams of poetry. Perchance if he had ... things would be different, but would they have turned out better?

They had chatted on several occasions, and Tom never felt more alive than when he made her laugh. He had even walked her home a few times. Once, she reached out and touched his hand. But sadly, he had never been able to ask her for a date, because self-esteem was a non-existent support platform for him. So, it became love at a distance, and in the end, he moved around the classroom until the hearth that flamed with the passions and dreams of his affection ... was hidden from sight. In retrospect, it would have been totally unfair, and unrealistic, asking her to join him in his world, yet at the time, he was unable to even conceive fusing into hers.

Tom's parents had purchased an older home that had been built in nineteen fifty-three. When the house was updated and converted from oil to gas heat, the two-hundred-fifty-gallon oil tank in the basement across from the furnace was removed. He had claimed the alcove of vacated space and built a lab. A waist-high bench extended down both sidewalls and spanned the area between. Shelving was erected to cover the back.

From the time of his earliest recollections, his mother and father had argued almost every night, forcing him to retreat deeper into an already insecure psyche. The lab became the only world that provided solace. He was nine when it was built. By his twelfth birthday, it was equipped with everything a college lab could offer, except for an analytical balance and a gas Bunsen burner. The first was too expensive, and the second his parents forbade because they thought the responsibility was greater than a child his age could appreciate. That was as laughable then, as now, since even as a child, he had handled responsibility better than the two of them combined.

Tom matured with the permanently ingrained opinion that some people should never bear children, especially ones who reproduce just because they're physically able. To them, it's almost a badge of adulthood honor. At first, the child is proudly displayed, but joy becomes burden, and is then consigned to a psychological attic, flanking the rest of their temporary ... forgotten treasures.

A sudden pang of guilt accentuated the fact he wasn't perfect either. After all, the love interest of his young life had gone to the senior prom alone. The stinging reminder perched on his shoulders, weighing them down like a permanently attached one-hundred-pound albatross with steel claws. It refused to be shaken.

His jaw muscles were clenched, starting to ache ... eyes squeezed tightly shut, beginning to purge briny drops ... hands drawn into tight fists, which beat lightly on the deck's top rail. Running to escape the past constantly drove him harder and faster into the future. Finally, drifting slowly back toward reality, he relaxed and managed to shake off the maddening excursion into a realm of supposedly unchangeable yesterdays.

A break occurred in the music, and the voice of a radio announcer carried through the open door, warning of an approaching storm. It triggered the memory of his search for lunch through practically non-existent kitchen staples. He decided to go out for a late dinner, then stop at the all-night grocery for supplies.

Reclusive living in a forest certainly had peace and quiet advantages, but it was a challenge driving down the side of the mountain at night on a passageway requiring four-wheel drive even in good weather. Still, regardless of the rigorous ride, it would be gratifying to get out of the house and provide his brain with a rest while doing some strictly recreational reading. Once he traversed the two mile stretch of treacherous dirt road and reached the two-lane blacktop, the remaining five-miles to the city limits were rather serene. Denny's was the destination. In a town this small, it was the only after-hours restaurant that served food, without drunks and smoke on the side.

His hide-a-way retreat was located in the Bradshaws just south of Prescott, Arizona. Inside, the glass-door wood stove emitted a soft wavering glow of light, comforting warmth, and the sound of crackling manzanita. It was late October, and the Gambel oaks had shed their leaves with the tannin leaching into the soil and evaporating. Combined with the surrounding forest of pines, it gave the air a heady, pungent odor. Deep inhalations almost made you dizzy.

To the east, Spruce Mountain was silhouetted against the rising three-quarter moon, while in the ravine below ... a whippoorwill started its early evening serenade. Singing was the last thing Dr. Hughes had on his mind. Scientific journalists had recently labeled him the Rosetta stone of modern physics, yet he felt life had become nothing more than a large stationary boulder, upon which was growing a suffocating moss mat.

Impulses raced through his neural network gathering and collating information, deciding if this was a feeling of self-pity, but a negative answer flashed on his private display-screen of self-awareness. Tom had consciously convinced himself that life was fine; it was probably his personal outlook that needed adjustment. A change was definitely needed, but his cognitive reasoning process couldn't supply any hints as to source or implementation.

Perhaps a chance encounter would provide the answer.

"There once was a lady named Bright,
Who traveled much faster than light,
She departed one day, in a relative way,
And returned on the previous night!"
- Anonymous

Chapter 1
Getting To Know You

When the alert indicated this particular restaurant was a probable destination, Khattyba Bright had left the motel, driven to the town's only Denny's, and waited. The reconnaissance team had deterred her contact until it could be attempted in a public place because they lacked a complete report on Dr. Hughes' mental stability. It was simply an attempt to keep the unidentified risks at a minimum.

The photo-ID and fact-filled portfolio lay next to her on the car seat, but its presence wasn't required. His bearded, mustached face, dark blond hair, sky colored eyes, and five-foot ten-inch physically-fit frame were indelibly etched in her memory. They had briefly conversed on the phone seventeen years ago, but she was confident Dr. Hughes would never make the connection between that sixteen-year-old girl, and the woman she had become.

Kate spotted Dr. Hughes' late-model, white Chevy pickup as it turned into the parking lot. She waited a few minutes after he parked and entered the building's side door, then exited the vehicle she had borrowed from a librarian friend. Kate stopped, mentally revising her plan of introduction. She unlocked the car and quickly scanned the pile of books on the back floor. Following a bout of disappointing frustration in selection, one was finally chosen at random.

The hostess exchanged greetings with Dr. Hughes, then automatically led him to one of his favorite spots. She took the drink order and said a waitress would be with him soon. Tom preferred the back wall by the kitchen because there were only two booths, which commanded minimal customer traffic. Otherwise, he had a tendency to people watch, which he considered an amusing diversion, but detrimental when concentration was required. Except for the occasional hello, the servers could be ignored without missing anything if he didn't look up. The waitress arrived and took his order.

"Fried chicken salad, no onions, French on the side, and a dinner roll instead of toast. I have a decaf with cream coming. Thanks."

After entering the restaurant, Kate joined with two other team members already seated at a table. They disclosed where Dr. Hughes was sitting and suggested an order had been placed. She was advised to remain and talk with them until it appeared his meal had been completed.

When dinner arrived, Tom's ever-present companion, a book, was set aside. He didn't like anything on the chicken and bacon pieces, so they were eaten first; dressing was then added to the remaining salad. Anyone watching would probably think the actions strange. When he finished, a waitress cleared the table and refilled his drink. The book was resurrected.

Almost a cup of coffee later, Tom sensed, more than saw, someone standing nearby. His head slowly swiveled left and caught sight of two perfectly shaped legs, clad in nylons, extending downward into black, high-heeled shoes. This was definitely not the waitress with another refill.

His eyes reversed direction and manipulated like a racecar trying to stay on a curvy road. They maneuvered up past the hemline of the dark skirt, around the hips, encircled the front of the waist, and onto the satiny white blouse.

Tom's upward gaze bumped over the buttons, pinched between the petite breasts, crawled the curl of the shoulder length auburn hair, and finally dropped into the deepest, Caribbean green eyes he had ever seen. It was his most enjoyable trip in a long time.

He softly, almost reverently, spoke the first word that came into mind. "Wow."

Kate smiled. "Pardon?"

He felt his face flush. "I'm sorry ... you took me by surprise."

Her smile widened. "The hostess informed me this was the reading corner. Would you consider sharing? In my opinion, this seems like quite a redneck area, so I doubt most guys care if they ever see a book, let alone read one."

From the time he was a small child, teachers had always alleged being an avid reader would pay big dividends. Maybe they were right. Tom tilted his head and read the title from her book's spine aloud. "The Ten Best Positions For Mutual Sexual Pleasure." He teasingly inquired, "Is that a precursor of what I can expect?" Some old forgotten recipes began to cook.

Kate's eyes slammed shut and her teeth clamped. She was so embarrassed she felt hot enough to melt and disappear into the floor's carpeting. She would never forgive herself for overlooking the detail. Her mind screamed, 'Come on! Think of something!' Finally, she managed to blurt out, "It's a friend's ... she wanted a second opinion before giving it to her husband."

Tom raised a hand and motioned towards the seat across from him.

When she inquired about his current read, he explained it was a probable fictional work about time travel. Kate's brows knitted together as she stared into his eyes. "Why do you say it's only probable? I'm confident that on this date, time travel did not exist."

Tom noted the specific reference, in past tense, with curiosity. He hung his head and smiled, then looked up and echoed her words. "Exactly. In this day and age, time travel doesn't exist. But, presume for a moment you are a traveler from the future, come back, and just for fun, write a book about your adventures. It could be for money, although I'd find that unlikely, or perhaps just a childish prank.

Imaginably, the world of the future has become so terrible, or just plain boring, the only place for a sense of humor is in the past. Whatever the reason, since everyone would assume it's fiction, you could say anything within the realm of possibility ... and no one would suspect," he looked around and gave her a wink, "except for people like you and me."

Kate nodded. "Like looking for a shadow in the shade."

The comment took him by surprise; he considered it an admirable comparison. She slid her book onto the seat and suppressed a smile, while thinking she might actually borrow it to glance through. "I assume you're reading for pleasure, not business."

He shrugged. "Actually ... both. The book is fun, but the idea is part of my work. I was a physicist, and I still do physics, but not in an official capacity. My esteemed colleagues thought my interpretations of time and space were a bit extreme and put me out to pasture at the ripe old age of thirty.

They referred to me as bleeding edge, undisciplined, wild, and even a little crazy. I thought I was simply, imaginative. What they wanted was leading edge, controlled, and investigative. A cute little house-trained puppy, on a leash.

Deception was never my forte and I openly admitted to stepping on toes, but damn it, apologies were issued afterwards. Nothing was done purposely, or out of malice. Those bastards, my supposed friends, chose to come after me with single-minded aforethought and were completely determined to inflict as much pain as possible ... and they succeeded. My name is spoken more often at social gatherings than in the scientific circle, and my title may as well be senior toilet tester. The only place I still put physicist as my occupation is on the back of an IRS 1040."

Kate frowned. "Is a title that important to you?"

"Outwardly, no. But deep inside, I feel part of me was mandated excised, and it wasn't malignant. Did you ever call a master chef a cook?"

"No."

"Try it sometime. Just beware of flying pots and pans, and if he picks up one of those big knives ... run."

She decided to nudge the topic train back on track. "I've dabbled in the sciences myself, especially physics."

"Ah. I don't suppose you're familiar with, for instance, Lorentz transforms?"

With a feigned look of surprise, she leaned forward and tilted her head to one side. "You must mean the mathematics that transposes the coordinates linking two or more spatial frames of reference in relative motion to each other. Those particular formulas reveal that the observed difference between a defining characteristic at rest, and its prime in motion, grows asymptotically as the speeds involved approach a significant percentage of light."

It took him a long moment to realize his mouth was hanging open.

Kate pulled a hand-held display from her purse and continued. "I have a report ... Thomas Edward Baker, age 34, born March 29, 1979. You have a tested IQ of one hundred fifty plus, not quite genius level, so you weren't able to completely detach yourself from society, which, psychologically, left you in limbo.

You graduated high school at sixteen, though you barely passed English because you were too shy to speak in front of a class, college at nineteen, and obtained a Ph.D. in particle physics at twenty-two. That same year, you changed your name to Thomas Einstein Hughes. When asked for a reason, you stated Einstein was your philosopher's stone for scientific thinking and Howard Hughes was your 'ne plus ultra' archetype for getting things done. You became an MIT fellow at twenty-five. At twenty-seven ..."

The waitress interrupted. "More coffee, sir?"

Tom pushed the cup toward her. "Yes, please ... thank you."

“Oh, excuse me, sir, I've been looking for that pen.”
The errant pen Tom had been twirling while reading and rereading the print was handed to the waitress. Once it was out of sight, he realized even the color couldn't be remembered for certain, let alone the words.

Kate restarted her delivery, upset at having lost its momentum. “At twenty-seven, your continued research in the direction of your doctorate thesis on quantum chromo-dynamics won you the Nobel prize for discovering the graviton. It was nicknamed metamorph because it alternates existence as particle or wave, depending on its current complement of quarks. This dual nature made it more elusive than the tau neutrino. A year later, its antiparticle was ascertained. Work started on top-secret government projects developing temporal displacement devices ... you lovingly called time machines. Concurrently, projects to exploit and address the graviton were initiated."
She looked up and they locked eyes. "With all the activity you were generating, you must thrive on having several fires around the iron."
Tom's mind was being hammered numb, so he didn't even challenge the misquote, making his response more reflexive than conscious effort. “I only hold one at a time in the fire, the rest remain just close enough to stay hot.”
Their visual embrace was broken; she returned to her tirade. "You became unruly, pressing faster and harder while others were just trying to stay abreast.
At thirty, as you mentioned, you were dismissed when your fellow particeps criminis began to fear for their lives during several experiments. Private backing came to the rescue and you've been working at ultra-secure facilities ever since.
You're single, overly sensitive, socially inept, and at times, probably certifiable. I know who you are, and I'm intimately familiar with your work. Bleeding edge is just one term a small mind would tend to associate with people they can't possibly understand. I've never considered myself a small-minded person. I would suggest you don't either."

As the verbal barrage ended, Tom gave her an eyebrows up salute, and realized this was one of those times when it felt like you were riding a bike so fast your feet fly off the pedals. No matter how you struggle, it requires a certain amount of time to get things back in sync. Until you do, you're helpless. For the moment, he was capable of only one thing ... asking a stupid question. "What's that gismo you keep looking at ... a personal organizer?"
Kate chuffed. "This gismo is a solar-powered, sound-activated, multi-functional, self-programming, self-updating, display/interpreter/recorder wireless communications device ... with alarm."

With only one foot back on a pedal, his comeback wasn't as effective as desired. "Oh."
Tom finally managed to reconnect his mouth with his mind. "I'm not sure you know who I am, but you certainly know a lot about me. Stage center, enter the Sisters W."
"Sisters W?"
With a grim stare, he fired a vocal retaliatory salvo. "Who are you? What do you want? Why me? Why you?"
Tom expected a mollifying reaction. Her unwavering stoical expression unbalanced him even further. Kate crooked her finger, drawing him closer, and

they leaned together over the table.

She put her mouth close to his ear and whispered, "I'm afraid I've been toying with you, Dr. Hughes. I know a little more about the workings of nature than you might imagine. I majored in Timeline Distortion Recognition and Repair, and have a minor in physics and also psychology, with an emphasis on intellectual aberration. I'm something you've only dreamt about. The book you're reading could be about my adventures. I literally edit history.

For purposes of conversation, and your amusement, you may call me Miss Bright. In time, I will answer your questions. I believe that's what you refer to as 'a play on words'." She steepled her fingers, waiting to see what effect the exposé would have on him.

His expression emulated the blankness of a freshly cleaned chalkboard. Tom grinned, and finally laughed at the reference to the namesake in an old poem about traveling faster than light with which he was familiar. Upon seeing her cut-diamond visage, he knew she was serious. While nervously shifting position, he fought to regain some semblance of mental equilibrium by quickly recounting the conversation, and understood there were several possibilities, each with its own probability.

One, she was angling for project information for his old government friends. Who else would make him more willing to let down his guard, than someone purportedly from the future? What could he possibly tell her, she didn't already know? That sounded hot, it was given a fifty share.

Two, his backers instructed her to engage him in casual conversation to scrutinize the level of his loyalty. That could be pretty warm too; it'd be something they'd do. Give number two a thirty.

Three, she's young, but too old for a college sorority razing, although it could be a cult or club initiation. But, it didn't feel right. Give it a five.

Four, maybe she's just a nice, intelligent, attractive lady looking for a friend. Yeah, and I'm a firefly just waiting for some kid to pull my butt off and stick it on his model car's headlight. Ten percent.

Five, any minute someone with a large butterfly net will walk in looking for her ... probability ... say five.

That left number six, everything she said was true. Probability ... atomic.

According to his flawlessly performed statistical survey and execution of several higher math functions, there was a minimum eighty percent chance of divulging something crucial if he wasn't cautious.

Course of action ... continue the fun, remembering to gingerly test each thought before serving it on the tongue, and watch for subtle trip lines of mental land mines.

Tom shrugged. "Would you care for something?"

"Just water."

He flagged the waitress. Her drink arrived. They talked for almost two hours.

Kate collapsed against the seat back ... exasperated. "I don't understand your obstinate view that's so defiant to the concept of a closed universe."

"Partly, we're arguing semantics. By coincidence, you've also discovered my life long nemesis. I refer to it as my one-sided door syndrome." Tom spread his hands. "Let's assume this room is the cosmos. It contains substance within a bounded domain. You discover the door is the farthest extension of matter. It ends there. My contention is space continues opposite the other surface, unless the door was one-sided. Explain how it's conceivable not to have a reverse, and I'll concede the possibility of finite expansion. In other words, show me how space can end."

Kate closed her eyes, and weighed a response ... eventually stating, "It's late, Dr. Hughes, I promise to try and prove it tomorrow."

Tom skeptically accepted her words. "Okay, it's a date." He added in a lighter frame of mind, "One thing I know about space, some has developed in my stomach. Will you join me for a dessert?"

Kate checked her machine's display while the request was considered. "That does sound tempting."

Reaching into her purse, she retrieved a small container, extracted two pill-sized capsules, and placed them on the table.

Tom studied the objects. "What are those?"

She pointed to each. "The pink is Dutch apple pie; the white is vanilla ice cream."

"That's a disgusting idea."

Snickering, she thought, 'If he only knew', but verbally replied, "It's just a joke."

The real thing arrived and was consumed by both.

Kate tried to suppress a yawn, but was only partially successful. "Good evening, Dr. Hughes, I must be going. Is your home at eleven acceptable?"

Tom nodded. "That'll be fine. Good night, Miss Bright, I'm looking forward to tomorrow. Considering your wealth of information, may I assume you know where I live?"

"Yes, finding it will be no problem."

That was somewhat of a surprise, since after first purchasing his property, it had taken him almost a week acclimating to the ride. Tom conjectured about this woman from wonderland, then added, "It was nice meeting you, say hello to Alice for me."

Kate briefly debated and finally countered, "If you enjoy interesting tales, wait until you see what's at the end of the rainbow." She was pleased with the rapport they had established, but as expected, discerned he believed the truth to be a façade. However, she also discovered it was fun hiding in plain sight. Kate realized the negative data concerning Dr. Hughes' personality appeared to be in question.

Tom took a last sip of coffee and watched her walk away ... chiding himself for his thoughts.

"To know that which before us lies in daily life, is the prime wisdom; what is more is fume, or emptiness, or fond impertinence, and renders us, in things that most concern, unpracticed and unprepared."

- Milton

Chapter 2
Facing the Facts

Tom managed to pop one eye open and squint at the clock. It apparently read ten something, his eye unable to finely focus without the aid of an extra lens. He fumbled for his glasses atop the nightstand.

After finally getting to bed, he'd lain awake for awhile, thinking about the conversation with Miss Bright and the subjects that had been addressed. Time travel, matter teletransportation, super-strings, closed time-like loops, the grandfather paradox, gravity lifts, Grand Unified Theory, essentially the whole gambit of issues confronting the frontier of physics.

His body's innermost recesses were informing him that at the moment, the most pressing problem in the universe was getting something to eat. He pulled on his clothes, wobbled down the short staircase, and entered the kitchen. Expecting Miss Bright soon, breakfast was fast and simple.

The table had been cleared and the cereal bowl was being placed in the sink, when they made their presence known. Tom finished his orange juice with a couple of swallows and realized physics would have to wait a short time longer, because the squirrels wouldn't. They could be heard running around on the deck looking for a handout. The nuthatches, along with Mr. and Mrs. Raven, were probably there, too.

He fetched a few slices of bread, crossed through the living room, and somewhat cautiously opened the door. The coast was clear, there weren't any animals near the entry. Tom walked out and began tearing the bread into pieces. With a shudder, he stopped and stared. Somehow, he found himself in the house again.

He chuckled and then mumbled, "Guess I'm a little more tired than I realized." He commenced to try again, and ended up in the house once more.

Now, there wasn't anything to snicker about.

Tom eased back towards the open door, stood there, and slowly advanced a hand until it was passing over the threshold. With wide eyes and a sudden puff of air, he sprang back, unable to believe what had just been experienced.

As his hand advanced through the plane of the doorway, the front of his fingertips appeared and were coming back in! It was like putting his hand into a mirror, and at the juncture of flesh and glass, the image projected outward.

He gathered his wits and courage, finally managing to try again. Tom extended his arm out slowly, completely to the elbow. First - fingertips, then the hand, followed by the bulk of his arm, advanced into the room. Standing there seeing, but not completely believing, he rotated his arm, and the incorporeal hand turned with it. With practice, an elbow could be grasped using the hand on the same appendage.

Tom surveyed the vicinity for Miss Bright, thinking this must be her proof of how space can terminate. It must be a local barrier set up for demonstration purposes. The parameters of the field must be adjustable depending on the setting of - what? Some machine? It was altogether fascinating, yet the outside world was also still visible. She had shown how space could end, but his nemesis lingered intact.

Deciding to try another tact, he picked up a chair and threw it against one of the windows. The inside pane was destroyed, but the outer one endured the onslaught. The chair penetrated the glass, then entered a reflecting space and reversed direction ... the chair and shards of glass remained inside. His intellect deduced that the field must completely surround the home's exterior. Meanwhile, the scientist in him was busy contemplating at what level this effect was being produced.

He walked back to the entrance and slowly pushed his face through ... at first ... not noticing any difference. Abruptly, his outward view changed to one of looking rearward ... into the house. Tom lowered his gaze and winced upon realizing he was looking at his own back, finding the whole situation deeply unsettling. He stepped back, closed his eyes, relaxed, and forced slow deep breaths while trying to regain his composure.

Tom stood physically inert, but his mind was a raging storm. All the evidence obviously proved Miss Bright was from the future. He had always known this would occur someday, but never in his most cherished fantasy did the hope exist it would happen to him. He chuckled, mentally reenacting last night's pointless exercise in probability and statistics.

After a short time, he felt better and called out, "You certainly have a way of making your point, Miss Bright. You must also have studied theatrics, because I'm most impressed. Please come in so we can talk. I'll put the coffee on."

When Kate entered, he was in the kitchen. She stopped and observed the shambles. "I've heard of small storms but this must have been an excessively violent micro burst."

He plugged in the coffee maker and leaned out towards the living room. "Well, my eccentricity is well documented and I'm sure that's somewhere in your report. Besides, I suspect I won't have to worry about the house much longer."

Kate tucked his comment away for future reference, and replied, "By the way ... I believe 'put the coffee on' ends with a preposition. Shouldn't it have been, 'I'll put on the coffee'?"

Tom frowned. "Are you always so ... complex? What do you do for entertainment, pull the second hand off clocks?"

The lady became quite animated, waving her arms like a bird that forgot how to fly. "Me! You're the one who won't be satisfied until every secret of the universe is bagged, tied, and labeled with your own personal monogram."

"Careful, Miss Bright, I know we talked a lot last night, but this could be the start of an actual conversation. And ... for your verbose, but misbegotten information, I can be just as content with the simple things in life. Give me a small block that'll turn eight-five, a close-ratio four-speed, a five-eighty-six rear gear, and I'm a happy guy."

A decidedly concerned and quizzical expression formed on her face while staring at her portable device's display. Tom couldn't pass up the opportunity for a tease. "What's the matter ... bad news from home? Don't tell me, the sun just winked out and that thing can't run on batteries."

She pulled what was evidently a wireless micro-receiver from her ear and checked it. "It's just static. That means the machine's interpreter is confused. My, um, device, can translate any human language including most sub-dialects and colloquial expressions, but it hasn't a clue as to why a small block of something with the dimensions five by eight, together with the numbers four, and five-eighty-six, should make you feel so elated."

For some impish reason, that pleased him to no end. "The coffee's ready, so I'll let you stew over that little tidbit while I get the cups. Do you use cream and sugar?"

Kate shrugged. "I don't know. I've never had coffee."

Tom stopped in his tracks, snorted a laugh, and shook his head. He thought about all her exacting and sometimes strange responses. "I'm sorry, but I have to ask. Have you ever dated a guy named Spock, or maybe he's some relation? I can picture the two of you flitting about the universe ... dropping in on a multitude of civilizations. As they begin laying their technology and knowledge at your feet, you both hold up a hand and say, 'we just want to know if you have any Red Pop'."

His stress level had been building awhile. When he saw the look on Miss Bright's face, and her only reaction was a long, slow blink, the dam broke. It started with a chuckle, quickly became an outright laugh, then turned into a wild boyish giggle.

Tom slid down the cupboard's front with tears streaming from his eyes. He saw her become alarmed and pull a small canister that resembled pepper-spray from a pocket, having no doubt hers would be more effective. He slowly waved his hands in surrender, then wiped the wetness from his face. "You don't need that ... honest. Whew, I guess I just needed to release the tension. I'm sorry if I alarmed you."

Tom's face turned notably somber ... his eyes downcast. "My tomorrows seem rather dubious ... at best."

Kate retrieved the thought she had stored earlier. "Is that why you said you wouldn't have to worry about the house?"

"Yes."

Kate pursed her lips. "What makes you imagine I mean you any harm?"

"I doubt your intentions are predisposed towards violence, but it's a long shot you made the trip to find out how you take your coffee."

She sat on the floor across from him and leaned against the refrigerator. "Being closer to the ground lowers the center of gravity, thereby enhancing one's calm and stability. Beginning now, that might become very important."

"You're about to be brutal."

"When discussing dessert last night, you mentioned not caring for toppings that were overly sweet."

Tom forced a small smile. "Asked and answered. Okay, kiddo, spill da beans."

"I'll give you a choice of two versions ... 'Through the Looking Glass' or

'Magical Mystery Tour'. Pick one."

He laughed. "Magical Mystery Tour, please. Thanks for the comic relief."

"You're welcome."

Kate consulted her device, and then commenced. "Everything we've discussed to this point, you've experienced as part of your life. Presently, I will begin describing events that only we of the future know transpired.

As for the Sisters W, there's no change in what I revealed about who I am. The only difference is that now, I trust, you believe me."

He nodded. "Most emphatically."

"What I want ... is to smooth over a rather bumpy part of history. Not that this old earth hasn't survived rough roads before, but to be completely honest, and it may or may not be obvious, the adjustments we make are for the benefit of the future, not the past. We make no claim to be benevolent, but we also try our best at avoiding any additional harm.

Just before the turn of your last century, the world experienced an end to the cold war between the United States and the Soviet Union. In truth, it was only de-escalation, but it was definitely a step towards peace. There were many skirmishes between the smaller powers, but these were heavily monitored and if the need arose, could usually be controlled.

Most political and military eyes were focused on China. It had formidable nuclear capabilities, and a combination of long and short-range delivery systems. They could also pack potent biologics into their warheads. In reality, China would be a much more dangerous adversary if they kept an aggressive act totally conventional. Even if the U.S., Europe, and Russia joined together, they couldn't manufacture enough bullets to kill three billion, swarming foot soldiers. China could achieve victory through sheer numbers. The other super powers would have to hold their nuclear and biological weapons in check for fear of slaughtering their own forces.

Surprisingly enough, history will show that although a threat, China wasn't the problem. They were much too intent on controlling their population and seeking to maximize their business relations with the West. They knew this was best for them politically and economically, and to their credit, they successfully achieved a slowly declining population growth rate.

The totally unexpected culprit that literally brought the world to the brink of a war, which, between the release of nuclear and biological agents, would have wiped life from the face of the planet, was, drum roll please ... the United States. The very same self-proclaimed defender of freedom loving peoples everywhere.

However, in its defense, as you stated in your own last night, nothing was preplanned. This wasn't the brainchild of a demented military fanatic, or some right-wing governmental splinter group in league with the third world. In fact, both the military and governmental leaders were unwitting pawns, drawn in by a sequence of unprecedented events, which in the end, they turned to their full advantage, of course. Most world dignitaries, even in aggressor nations, demonstrated forbearance with the problems of the U.S. when they were behind closed doors, but in public, they were inflexibly harsh. If it hadn't been so tragic, it would have been amusing ... a regular worldwide circus.

Most similar situations arise from the ashes of dismal failures. The ironic twist is that the problems, and world pressure to solve them, resulted from a string of brilliant scientific successes that occurred so rapidly the world couldn't gather its collective breath while absorbing their impact on society.

Generally speaking, these accomplishments were brought about by the efforts of one man. Would you care to hazard a guess?"

Tom looked to her with the first hint of understanding in his eyes. "That would certainly soothe the ruffles of Sister, 'why me'."

"Before I continue, Dr. Hughes, I'd like to express my admiration for you as a physicist, and now that I've met you personally, as an individual. You're certainly not the uncaring, selfish egomaniac I was prepared to expect. Unfortunately, our forward observers, by design, are not allowed to get too close while a subject is under study; they must remain incognito by the very nature of their work and status. They are trained to generally gather data on situations and the masses, not directly from individuals. Why are you laughing?"

"Are you familiar with the term 'oxymoron'?"

"Yes."

"You give someone you send back in time a title of forward observer, and fail to see the humor?"

"Oh ... it's really quite amazing. I've worked with that term for years and failed to make the connection. I guess it's because we have a tendency to always think in the present tense, no matter 'when' we are. See, this goes to prove you do have a preoccupation with titles."

She held up one hand, signaling for him to wait, while the other went to an ear, adjusting the receiver. "I've been notified, that according to simulation of your thought patterns, there's a 93.7 percent probability that your last statement acted as a trigger and now you have at least two questions. I will attempt to answer them before you even ask."

Tom shrugged. "Probability theory isn't exactly high on my list right now, but go ahead, thrill me."

"The first is no. We, as yet, are unable to visit our future. Trigger word was forward. The second answer is also no. We, again as yet, have not found a situation where times arrow is reversed and history flows backward. Trigger was back. Obviously, it wasn't just the words. The statement in its entirety, flow of thought, inflection, and of course, your own knowledge base were all involved. How'd we do?"

He had taken a number and now it was his turn to wear the dunce cap. "Has anyone ever said you are one very scary lady?"

"No. Not that I can recall."

Tom opened a drawer, grabbed a pencil and paper, scribbled something, then spoke aloud, "Ydal yracs yrev eno era uoy."

Kate pressed against the cupboard. "What is that?"

"You are one very scary lady ... backwards. I didn't want the comment to appear obvious."

"I see. Was the 'not' obvious comment a compliment or criticism?"

"You're the one with the crystal ball. You tell me!"

"Humph, I see that sarcasm is also one of your traits. Now, Dr. Hughes under glass ... comes the interesting part."

"Hey, I haven't been sitting here exactly bored."

She smirked and forged ahead. "After detecting the graviton, your newly acquired knowledge led to several other finds in quick succession. One of these was a million-caret gem ... the first tachyon type particle. It is the very foundation for time travel and superluminal message systems."

He sat up, wide-eyed. "Wow, I found that! I am good."

"Please exercise some constraint, Dr. Hughes ... don't make me retract what I said earlier."

"Sure, but do you realize what a discovery that is?"

"My entire career is based on it, remember?"

"Oh yeah, sorry, I just got excited ... please ... continue."

"While you were preparing to make the announcements, the U.S. National Security Council assumed control and placed the military in charge of the entire operation, under the guise of eminent domain. You were placed under house arrest.

Alas, enough information was prematurely released that other countries became alarmed, even America's allies. Rumors propagating rumors generated problems for the U.S. almost geometrically. The world was aware of the graviton and its anti-particle, yet because the discoveries were unearthed in house, so to speak, all information regarding these finds were easily confiscated and concealed. But, there were still enough cold war contacts in place that data continued to flow with little delay.

The anti-graviton made gravity lifts possible. The military could position these devices anywhere and use their natural stealth capabilities to place satellites, or warheads, in orbit without the telltale effects of a conventional launch, thereby making detection virtually impossible. The most condemning rumor alleged that by exploiting the graviton's properties, the U.S. had developed a procedure to manufacture micro black holes. Using a silent, undetectable anti-gravity lift as a delivery system, think what a weapon that would be. Panic buttons were being punched with sledgehammers.

It appeared the only way of drawing back from the cataclysmic abyss was to cast a blood offering. Because of data deliberately leaked by the government, you were considered by the world to be in charge of all developments, including weapons, so you became 'the' designated pressure-relief valve.

Behind closed doors, the decision was made to charge you with treason under the laws of the National Security Act. It would be the biggest pre-staged exhibition in history, presented solely to prevent the turning of launch keys. The U.S. government and military wanted the world focused on your trial.

High-ranking officials worldwide knew what the U.S. was attempting, and while personally offended, they nevertheless considered it good politics. Plans were drawn up for information sharing through joint projects, and one by one ... the fires of negative opinion were ultimately extinguished.

The press was coerced to intentionally slant the news, creating a monster, so the world masses would picture you as the mad scientist of all history. Your tribunal was dragged out as long as possible to keep heating world opinion, although the definitive outcome had been determined the same night you were ordered brought up on charges. The unanimous decision handed down by the judges deemed that you were to be executed before a firing squad, and have the event broadcast on global television. When the press learned about this little bit of showmanship, even they were stunned. The U.S. wanted to make the event as visible as possible, so their actions against you would be viewed in a positive light."

Tom just stared. "I don't understand. It sounds like I was just doing was my job."

"That's correct. You must understand, Dr. Hughes, no one from my time blames or holds you responsible for this nightmarish turn of events. We view you as having been surrounded by a pack of wild slavering dogs, snatching bits and pieces from your plate whenever someone tugged your sleeve and caused you to look away.

We've made several small alterations to the timeline between our now and your now in preparation for the final commutation involving your, shall we say ... terminal disposition. In addition to being in constant contact with the planning specialists, computers, simulators, and of course local observers, I'm also empowered with fairly broad discretionary actions. It's time for me to answer the question you're asking yourself most often since the beginning of this evaluation."

"Is it live, or is it Memorex?"

"This seems like a rather inappropriate time for a demonstration of your spontaneous wit, Dr. Hughes."

"Sorry ... nervous reflex. I guess the question you're awaiting is, what are you going to do with me?"

"Obviously, we've come back before you detect the other particles and their related issues are generated." The next piece of information was critical; she made sure he was looking directly at her for maximum impact. "It's been determined that if you die now, the discovery of the other particles will be spread over sufficient time so their impact can be absorbed without creating any associated problems. These breakthroughs will be based on your notes and papers left behind. The fact they are published worldwide generates the certainty many more scientists will be involved, thereby eliminating a U.S. monopoly and its attending grievous sentiments."

She noted his stunned expression with satisfaction. "If I tell you that disappearing will accomplish identically the same task, will the color come back into your face?"

"Is that a subtle way of saying I should pack my toothbrush? You really know how to get a guy's attention."

"Unfortunately, it's the only way to complete the project. We've simulated the situation until we thought the computers would melt."

"When you toggle your anti-humor switch off, you can be a real stitch, Miss Bright. By the way, do you ever undo a change?"

"No. For all practical purposes, figuring the logistics is impossible. The computers refuse to touch it. They cite a dangerously high probability of creating a closed time-like loop."

His gaze wandered around the kitchen while considering the statement. "True. You'd become immortal. But, constantly repeating one short segment of your life would be a hell of a way to spend eternity."

"That's why we plan, think, re-plan, and rethink before we even consider initiating a change."

"Just out of curiosity, what if I refuse to go with you?"

Her look indicated that would not be a wise choice. "Is there anything else?"

"Actually, yes." Tom reached over and took her hand.

Kate's eyes opened a little wider and her body tensed slightly, but otherwise she remained in the same position.

He touched the skin on her hand, then carefully examined an arm.

Her expression was questioning, then finally became quite startled. She excitedly jerked her hand free. "You think I'm an android!"

Unabated, he replied, "Well, yeah, the thought has crossed my mind."

"Thank you very much! You ... you unappreciative boor. I'm the one who argued to convey you forward. Most of the others judged it'd be more expedient if you had an accident."

"Hey look, princess, if I'm going to have every atom in my body sliced, diced, and microwaved, I think I have the right of taking at least a minimum of precautions. I'd like to know that someone, not something, is convincing me to take the meat-grinder express. I'll bet it's a lot simpler bouncing a machine around the universe in a hail of photons, than a piece of flesh and blood. I want to believe there's a chance I'll exit over-easy, not scrambled."

She only offered a corrective comment. "We use tachyon class particles, not photons."

"Whatever!"

After a short time, their hard stares began to soften like two scoops of ice cream in a high-power microwave. Tom assumed a conciliatory repose and spoke first. "I'd really like it if you'd walk with me. I could use a friend to talk with, right about now."

Kate smiled a show-all-your-teeth smile. "Me, too."

Tom grinned back. "This is strictly a gut feeling, but I trust you."

"An unjust acquisition is like a barbed arrow, which must be drawn backward with horrible anguish, or else will be your destruction."

- Jeremy Taylor

Chapter 3
Second Thoughts

Tom helped Kate get to her feet, then peered out the kitchen window and noticed the sky had become completely overcast. "The weather center warned a front would be moving this way. It appears to have arrived. I'm going to run upstairs for a second, I'll be right down."

He descended the stairs pulling on a light jacket, remarking, "You'd better grab your coat, too. It's cooled off since the sun went in."

She slipped her coat on as he finished donning his. They were walking toward the front door when he unexpectedly stopped, staring at the exit with a worried expression.

She laughed and playfully poked him gently in the side. "It's okay, the field is down, I disabled it before entering."

Tom turned and faced her. "No, it's not okay."

"Why?"

"Because if we go out there without any treats for the animals, we won't make it off the deck alive."

The remark startled her. "They didn't seem dangerous or aggressive when I was out before."

Tom softly laughed at her naive sincerity. "No, not really dangerous. It's a figure of speech. They're just so used to me feeding them that they get confused when I don't. What's the animal situation in your time?"

She thought for a minute. "They exist only in remote areas. Animals were banned from the cities years ago, even domestics, especially the dogs. They became too much of a noise pollutant. People have electronic pets now.

Once common diseases were under control it was obviously undesirable to have the animals re-introduce them. Fleas and ticks were the most troublesome.

Larger animals no longer exist on earth, but luckily for the conservationists, the space colonies were established before all the species became extinct. There are several thousand frozen ova and sperm samples of most breeds stored off-planet. When humankind finally reaches other planetary systems, perhaps the animals can be re-introduced on suitable worlds. It'd be tragic if that part of the world's legacy disappeared forever."

While listening, he had returned to the kitchen and gathered a horde of goodies. A half loaf of bread from the counter, two full loafs from the freezer, and all the Twinkies and nuts he could find.

She was startled by the result of his collection. "Do you plan on feeding all of that to them at one time?"

"Why not? It would just spoil in the house. Believe me, all of this will be gone by tonight. What isn't eaten, will be tucked away someplace.

I was going to restock my supplies last night after dinner, but forgot about it following our meeting and conversation. Good thing I didn't, huh?"

Kate nodded. "Strange how things work that way sometimes."

Tom walked near a window adjacent to the deck. He looked out and chuckled. "Yep, they're all there. Would you get the door, please?"

As soon as the door cracked open, a squirrel came running through. Kate screamed and jumped back.

Tom slowly shook his head. "It's alright, that's only Veronica. She's rather pushy. Don't worry, she'll follow us when we leave."

He used his foot to swing the door open wider. "C'mon out. Here, take a couple slices of bread, break it up, and throw it around."

His hands were full, so he pointed with an elbow. "The other squirrel over there is Betty, she's tame and gentle. When you're done with the bread, grab a Twinkie and feed it to her by hand."

Two ravens in a nearby tree flew to the far side of the deck railing and began their raucous call. There were at least a dozen nuthatches flying back and forth over their heads. She stood mesmerized as another four squirrels were seen headed for the deck.

Both ravens hopped down and began waddling toward her. She backed against the railing and looked to Dr. Hughes for help. He saw her distress and threw some bread between her and the ravens. They cocked their heads and eyed him, then started gulping down the bread.

Tom gave her a somewhat sheepish look. "I'm sorry, I didn't realize this would upset you. Go back inside if you want. They'll all be busy eating in a minute and then we can take that walk."

Kate gazed down and saw Betty sitting with one paw on her shoe, looking back up at her. "No, I think I'm okay now. In all honesty, I've never been this close to an animal before. I've only seen them in holographs, but you're right, Betty does seem docile ... and patient."

Opening the Twinkie, she stooped and offered the squirrel a piece. The animal took it in her paws while positioning her tail up over her body and head.

Tom found it amusing to watch her interact with the animal. "That's her friendship pose. When they do that, it signals the other squirrels they are just minding their own business and offering no threat."

Betty sat eating her Twinkie, seeming very contented. Tom scanned the deck and noticed the other animals were at ease with Miss Bright, too. "It's interesting. The animals sense you mean them no harm. Usually, if anyone else is near when I feed them, they're very skittish ... not so with you. That's a compliment from them."

Kate looked up ... pleased by the remark.

He looked past his truck at the small building on the other side. "By the way, if you need to use the facilities, that's it."

She rose and checked in the direction of his gaze. "I presuppose 'facilities' in this case means the lavatory?"

"You assume correctly."

She displayed her puzzlement. "Why outside? Isn't that inconvenient?"

"Yes, and it's intentional." He issued a short laugh. "Imagine what it's like on a cold winter night. The point is, when I come here I usually want to be alone. Someone may come up for awhile during the day, but once they're informed about the outside bathroom, almost no one ends up staying overnight. However, I have a secret. Come with me."

Tom led her back into the house, up the short flight of stairs, and opened a door. "This used to be the inside bathroom. It's a small space, so I turned it into a storage room, but look back here." He opened a split storage door with shelves, revealing an entry behind, which led into another room. "If no one is around, I usually leave it open so it's more practical."

Kate walked in and scanned the newer bathroom with shower, sink, toilet, and mirrored wall. "This is nice."

He pointed to a set of rungs affixed vertically in the wall. "Take a peek up there."

She climbed the unconventional ladder and found an entrance into a spa room on the roof. The center was about seven feet high, with the apex sloping sharply down to four-foot redwood walls that were mostly windows. There were several screened and shade covered skylights built into the ceiling.

Kate retreated down the steps. "It's no wonder you keep this part of the house a secret. You'd probably never get anyone to leave once they saw it."

As they turned to leave, she noticed another door on the back wall of the bathroom, but she didn't remark about it.

They walked out through the house and onto the deck.

Tom gathered up the remaining treasure trove of food, supported it with an arm and one hand, and offered the other to her. "C'mon let's walk."

She looked at the bundle of provisions and then back to him. "Are you expecting an entourage?"

It took a second for the question to register. "Oh, the food. There's a small clearing where I turn the truck around just down the road. I'll dump the rest there."

They walked down the steps leading from the deck to the ground and then past the truck parked about fifteen feet from the house.

She eyed the outside bathroom structure. "Mind if I look?"

"No, go ahead. I keep it clean and supplied since it's handy if I'm working out here, or for the somewhat unwelcome guest."

Kate opened the door and looked inside. "It's actually much nicer than I imagined. But, I agree, it'd be very unpleasant coming out here in the middle of the night."

Tom chuckled. "That's the idea."

When they reached the clearing, he emptied the remaining packages. Tom noted her watching while he stuffed the empty plastic wraps in a pocket. "I hate litter."

She nodded in agreement. "Do you have any particular destination in mind?"

He indicated a general direction with a nod of his head. "Yeah, I thought we'd wander over to my outdoor think-tank. I have a five-acre parcel, which is bordered on three sides by national forest. The next hill over is still part of my property. From base to summit, it's about a three hundred foot rise.

There are two paths. One goes straight to the top along one side. The other winds up and around like the threads on a screw. The peak is quite rough from weathering and erosion, but there's a flat spot in the middle. I have a round padded seat that affords a three hundred sixty degree view of the surrounding country. Considering you're probably not used to the altitude, the round-a-bout path is more apropos."

They started down the road. She walked with her hands clasped behind, he with his inserted in front pockets, his thumbs hooked through the belt loops. The first few minutes passed quietly, each content to observe the scenery.

Tom broke the silence. "You realize, your interesting little demo answered my question, but failed to resolve my dilemma. First - it was artificial. I'm curious if a field like that could ever be generated naturally in the environment.

Second - the barrier that effectively acted as an invisible doorway ... was just that, invisible. I could still see the world on the other side. Therefore, though space inside the house terminated, outside it obviously didn't."

She nodded. "I knew you wouldn't disappoint me."

"Hmm, what do you mean?"

"I was wondering when you would get around to that."

Tom chuckled. "Well, my plate has been rather full as of late. You can take full credit for that"

"Remember, it was, as you say, a demonstration of how space could end, not a definitive answer to your question. Look at it this way, it'll give you something to work on in the future."

He laughed. "Is that another play on words?"

Having meant it as an innocent remark, it took a moment to catch his meaning. "Oh, no ... I meant it just as stated."

The conversation fell flat, lapsing into a somewhat awkward silent interlude. After walking a few minutes more, he looked over at her. "What about the fourth sister W? Why you? Did you volunteer, was your name pulled out of a hat, or maybe you knew you couldn't resist my charm? How does one get involved in altering the events of the universe while beaming around through time?"

Laughing, she replied, "I think I have an answer you will appreciate, probably said best in the words of your own twenty-first century." She cleared her throat and proclaimed in a deep voice, "According to the advertising safety council, 'I'm a professional, don't try this at home'."

His laugh demonstrated his appreciation. "Pretty good, Miss Bright, I like that. I like it a lot."

Her eyes beamed back at him. "Thank you, but I'm sure you realize how important it is if a timeline is going to be altered, that you're sure of all your facts. Most of my work is just plain, dry research. It so happened that late twentieth-century history is a hobby of mine. When the computer collated all the requirements with available personnel, my name floated to the top.

It had also been quite some time since I'd been on a field operation. When I first heard of the project, I practically held my director for ransom at a chance to be on the team." A moment later, she laughed at some private thought.

"What's so funny?"

Kate explained. "I was just thinking about some of the contests we had in graduate school. They're equivalent to some of the engineering competitions held in your time at MIT and Cal Tech.

Students are formed into teams and given a problem to solve, and the winner is whoever comes up with the cleverest or most innovative solution. The answers are not always practical, but it's the spirit of the competition and teamwork that count.

We had different categories in simulating timeline changes. One of my team members won the funniest change award. She simply substituted an ingredient in a cooking recipe, changing what called for a teaspoon of baking powder to one that used a teaspoon of gunpowder. The judges called the result, 'explosive'."

"How did you fare?"

"I'm sure you've seen pictures of Napoleon. Do you remember his stance with one hand inside his coat?"

"Yes, sure. Why?"

"One of our assessment categories required simulating the subtlest change, which in turn created the biggest divergence from actual history.

My project involved Napoleon and which hand he held inside his jacket. It started when I was browsing through some old books and came across a painting of him. On nothing more than a whim, I simply switched which hand was held within the jacket and ran a simulation through history, not really expecting to find any appreciable difference. In reality, the result was extremely surprising.

Apparently, during one occasion when Napoleon was at a university talking with other students, he and a Russian began arguing. They were standing facing each other, and as it happened, the Russian was left-handed.

The Russian pulled a knife and tried to stab Napoleon. It became a matter of timing. Since Napoleon's right hand was already in a defensive position inside his jacket, he was just able to deflect the knife away from his body without suffering any harm. But, during my simulation, all other variables remaining the same, the Russian would have succeeded in killing Napoleon, because now the right hand would have come from a much lower starting position and wouldn't have had time to deflect the knife. Because of this, Napoleon dies, and several years later Russia successfully invades France and annexes it to the motherland. All of history for the entire world is changed, hinging on the fact that Napoleon stood with the opposite hand inside his coat. For that, I won the award." She looked to him, awaiting comments.

"Very impressive, that's a fascinating dissertation. It's easy to understand why you won. It makes me wonder how many instances like that occur everyday, probably millions of times, and they go completely unnoticed. An 'X' number of elements combined 'Y' different ways. Maybe we should forget about time and just relive the same day over. Each day would evolve differently based on just the subtle changes each person makes without any conscious awareness, or effort. An almost infinite number of January 1st occurrences. The party animals ought to love that."

Kate was listening, but had no idea where he was going with his diatribe. It sounded like complete and utter nonsense. "I don't wish to be rude, Dr. Hughes, but is there a specific point you're seeking to achieve?"

He pursed his lips and thought for a couple of seconds. "Well, yes there is, but I suppose it did sound like rambling. I'm deciding on how best to inform you about something you probably won't like hearing."

They were almost to the point where the paths leading up the next hill separated. She walked along expectantly. Tom stopped upon arriving at the juncture. "This place is as good as any to explain. I think our futures are like these two paths, they go in different directions."

She looked along one path, then the other. "Actually, a poor example, Dr. Hughes. These paths start differently, but, as you mentioned, end up in the same place."

"Touché, Miss Bright. Except in this case, no point is awarded. You know what I mean."

Kate frowned. "You've changed your mind about going. The simulations were correct, I've been expecting it."

"I view it as never having had a choice. It seems like my mind was being made up for me. I'm extremely curious about something. Even with the chaos I supposedly created, the world powers obviously didn't destroy life on earth. Why is it necessary to change the order of things? Maybe, knowing what I do now, I'll just skip the country when things get hectic."

"Think about what you just said, Dr. Hughes. You, would in fact, be changing the outcome of history. The pressure valve previously available would be missing, and according to simulations, after a massive global confrontation, life on earth would indeed end."

"Okay, let's assume I believe my life is worth giving in trade for the work I will accomplish before its end. I live alone, who'd miss me. The only two places I'm happy is here at home, and buried in my work at a lab.

You alluded to the fact yourself ... discovery of the tachyon is one of the most important scientific finds on record. Now you're asking me to give it up. That should be my choice. Where does that leave your logic at this point?"

Her face took on a pleading expression. "There's more to the story than I told you. I was hoping to manage without the gruesome details."

"I thought I could trust you, was I wrong?"

Kate shook her head. "No. I haven't lied to you, but some things were purposely omitted."

"Lying by omission is still an untruth."

She sighed. "I promise to fill in all the particulars, then hopefully you'll understand. Shall we continue our walk?"

He gazed up the trail. "I hope you didn't somehow signal someone to be waiting at the top. I don't want anyone to get hurt, because I'll definitely have friends with me." The look she returned, plainly indicated she was mildly startled, and somewhat hurt. "It would seem, Miss Bright, we could use a little time to ourselves. I'm going up the direct trail, why don't you use the other. I'll meet you on top. I'm sure you'll contact your team, and personally, I don't want to hear the conversation."

Tom turned away and started up the hill, while she stood there watching his figure gain altitude. She thumbed her comm link and began a verbal trek of her own.

Kate breeched the top, pushed a pine bough aside, and saw him sitting on the padded bench. She bent over with her hands on her knees and began catching her breath.

Tom noticed her difficulty and became concerned. "Are you okay? I forgot that you're not used to this. We are at seventy-five-hundred feet, and it does take some time adjusting to the thinner air."

"I suppose ... you actually ... enjoy this?"

He laughed. "And you didn't? That's what you get for beaming all over the place."

Kate walked over to the bench, placed her right foot on the seat, and massaged her calf while issuing a soft moan. Tom examined her leg and grinned. "Does it mention somewhere in your report that I'm a leg man. Is that the reason for this little show? Not that I mind."

Finished with the right, she switched legs. "Do you mean, as in one who enjoys the sight of shapely woman's legs, or as in when you're eating a chicken?"

He chuckled. "That's good, Miss Bright, you're learning, and in this case the answer is yes to both."

"With me as the subject, what would your considered opinion be in response to the first instance of the question?"

He studied the left leg, which was still propped on the seat. "First, it's a complex curve. I suppose a case could be made for a section of an ellipsoidal plot, but on the other hand, if the shin were taken as the directrix, and using a focus of about two inches, it might ..."

A soft punch to his arm interrupted the analysis. "That's not what I wanted to know. Start over."

Tom studied the leg again. "Alright, let me try this. When I first saw you standing next to my table last night, the thought that rambled through my mind was, 'those might be the nicest looking legs I've ever seen in my life'."

His gaze drifted to her eyes. "Unfortunately, that's not what we came up here to talk about."

Kate smiled. "No, but I wish you could have let me enjoy the moment."

Tom grinned. "Who knows, maybe if you can convince me to go, there'll be more flattering comments in the future."

"Then I'm going to try hard." Looking left, then right, and not seeing anyone, she finally checked behind, asking, "Where are your friends?"

"They're right here." Reaching behind inside the jacket, he pulled a nine millimeter semi-automatic pistol from the waistband of his pants. "These are my friends, Smith & Wesson, together with fifteen of their subordinates."

Kate raised her eyebrows. "I see that you picked up more than your coat from upstairs." She seemed disappointed. "Do you think you need that?"

Tom sat with his eyes and the gun directed at the ground. "I'm not sure what to think anymore, Miss Bright. You tell me."

Sensing his dark mood, she sat near him and placed a hand on his arm. "Let me fill in the earlier omissions, and after that, if you decide not to go, no one will try and force you. You have my word, and the guarantee of the entire team. We'll find a way to work around it somehow."

He nodded. "Okay, you have the dirt floor."

She produced a folded piece of paper from her pocket. "I'd like to read an excerpt from the testimony of a young man named Chester Higgins. An investigative reporter recorded it forty years after your death. Higgins was one of the ten members of your firing squad and given full immunity in exchange for his deposition. All the squad members were between the ages of eighteen and twenty-one, and belonged to the National Guard. Higgins was from Tennessee."

> ... and we all wondered why Dr. Hughes was kept in his cell and not allowed to attend his own trial. So's one night I slipped in [he knew the guards on duty] and talked with him [Dr. Hughes]. He wasn't any monster, he was nice. He hadn't even had a chance to talk with his lawyer. All he had done was invent some stuff and they [the government and military] took it all away from him. He said he was just trying to make the world a better place and make it easier for people to get

> along. I told all this to the other guys [National Guard members] and we started asking questions. We were told to shut up and mind our own business. This was on a need to know only basis and we didn't need to know anything. They [the ranking officers in charge] said we were to just do our duty or else we'd end up in the brig the rest of our lives. They [ibid] also threatened our families. So's none of us wanted to shoot Dr. Hughes, but we had no choice. On the day we shot him [Dr. Hughes] most of us closed our eyes when we pulled the trigger. Four of us missed completely. The other six shots hit him, but only in the arms and legs, some of them just a graze. We figured we done our duty so we was off the hook. A doc came over to pronounce him [Dr. Hughes] dead and he [the doctor] had a tiny needle with some stuff in it. He saw Dr. Hughes wasn't dead, just unconscious, so he went to give him the shot, but most of it was spilled when the reporters pushed in trying to get pictures. I heard the doc tell some VIP he didn't get enough in. They [Doctor on duty and staff] said Dr. Hughes was dead and had him carried off. Later on I talked with some other guys [guards in closed door meeting, guards in morgue] and they said the VIP's had a meeting and were trying to smuggle Dr. Hughes to some secret site where he could continue working but the rest of the world would never know about it. They [VIPS] said they couldn't lose because if Dr. Hughes got out of hand or wouldn't work they'd just kill him. How could they get in trouble if he [Dr. Hughes] was already dead? All this time, Dr. Hughes was layin' on a slab in the morgue in one of those cubbyholes. The guys [morgue guards] said Dr. Hughes came to about ten minutes after they [morgue attendants] slammed the cubbyhole door. They [medical staff] hadn't even given him [Dr. Hughes] any painkiller. According to the guys [guards] in the morgue Dr. Hughes screamed for almost thirty minutes before going quiet, and that he had slowly bled to death. His [Dr. Hughes'] face was all twisted and warped. There were bloody fingerprints all over inside the cubbyhole. It wasn't a very nice way...

"That's the worst of it Dr. Hughes, but there are many other details of the trial and subsequent actions if you want to hear them." Kate folded the paper and replaced it in a pocket.

"Thank you, Miss Bright, but that won't be necessary. I appreciate the chance you took by allowing me to decide. You must have been pretty sure of yourself."

"No. I was certain of you and your integrity."

Tom rose and walked to a small point overlooking a valley. Far below, a doe was walking with a fawn trailing close behind. At that moment, he wished he were that fawn ... innocuous, protected, driven only by instinct, with its whole life yet to come. His only crime was a burning desire to create and discover, and yet, like any artist, he had paid for his innocence with the disapproval and ridicule of others.

Kate could feel his pain. She rose, walked over, and stood next to him. Her hand brushed his and they took hold ... his other still held the gun. Without turning, he asked, "When do we need to leave?"

"You can take a week to get organized, if you want."

"How does tomorrow sound?"

"That's fine with me. Are you sure it's enough time?"

Tom finally turned and looked at her.

"It's more than enough. I'd go today, but it'd be nice spending one more night here, and say goodbye to my animals in the morning. I'll miss them, they've been good friends. It doesn't sound like I'll be around many animals anymore."

"That's probably quite true. People make a concerted effort to avoid animals in my time ... at least on earth."

He remembered the gun and studied it. "I've never even fired this particular weapon, but I'd like to take it. It'd at least be something familiar to have around, but mostly because it was a gift from an especially good friend. Will that be a problem?"

"No, I think I can get it cleared."

His gaze returned to her. "Are you returning to town?"

"Yes, it's still early, but there are preparations to be finalized. Why?"

"I'll drive you. I'm hoping you'll agree to spend my last evening here with me. We could have dinner, then I'd make some popcorn and put on a movie. By the way, do you like to dance?"

"Yes, but it's been a long time, and we'd probably have to allow for synchronizing our steps."

"There are certain selections of music I've always wanted to play while dancing with someone special, but the opportunity simply never arose. A lady who's about to completely change my life should appropriately qualify. Would you like to try?"

"I'd be honored. May I ask who performs the music?"

"The Lettermen ... it's an early 1960's group. Musically speaking, everyone says I was born about twenty years too late. One song in particular, 'The Way You Look Tonight', has always been my favorite. Were you intending to leave from this location tomorrow?"

"It's certainly desolate out here. However, in this instance, that would be an advantage. Why do you ask?"

"I don't want you getting the wrong idea, but if you decide to stay, I have a back bedroom where you'd have complete privacy, and if you ask nicely, I'll even let you use the indoor bathroom."

Kate flitted her eyelids. "Well, if I get to use the indoor bathroom, how could I possibly refuse?"

They laughed, then turned and left together.

"Persons extremely reserved and diffident are like the old enameled watches, which had painted covers that hindered you from seeing what time it was."

- Walpole

Chapter 4
Last Night At Home

After dropping Miss Bright off at her motel, Tom went grocery shopping one last time. It made him wonder what shopping would be like in the future, or if one needed to shop at all.

They had agreed on a light dinner and his special salad, so he picked out two six-ounce New York cuts, two Idaho bakers, French bread, iceberg lettuce, red cabbage, carrots, cucumber, kiwi, green grapes, and a bag of organically grown cherry tomatoes.

Tom also planned to open a bottle of Special Reserve Merlot he'd been saving for an auspicious occasion. A friend who owned a small private vineyard in Washington State had sent it to him about three years ago.

He made one additional stop before returning for his passenger.

Kate brought out a small bag, presumably containing a change of clothes and other personal items. Tom watched as her team members loaded equipment into the truck bed and covered it with a tarp. He also noticed she didn't have the previously ever present 'hand held device'. "What happened to the toy you always carry around?"

At first, the question didn't register. Then it dawned on her to what item Dr. Hughes was making reference. "Since the mission is officially approaching completion, I traded my field recorder for my personal one." Her left wrist was offered for examination. "This is WD7 ... wrist device model seven. The latest model is fifteen, but this one and I are kind of old friends, so I keep it."

"If they ever produce a model forty, there's going to be some sort of patent infringement lawsuit filed."

Kate tilted her head. "I don't understand."

He just grinned. "Never mind. But, if it really is an old friend, you should call it something like 'sport' or 'ace' instead of WD7. That seems cold."

She nodded. "Hmm, I'll keep that in mind."

The team members announced everything was ready. They shook hands all around, then Tom and Kate climbed into the truck and headed back towards his mountain. As they drove along, he couldn't help thinking about his home in the wilderness. "Out of pure curiosity, would it be possible to find out what's on my property in the future?"

"That seems like a logical request. I'm sure the records computer would be able to assist you. If you're thinking about having another place like the one you have, I suppose it's possible, but almost everyone lives in the cities."

Tom grumbled, "Almost everyone lives in the cities now, but that's not where I want to be. If I could beam between the city and a home in the woods, I'd be delighted."

She shrugged. "Then we'll have to see what we can do."

He lightly tapped the steering wheel. "Oh, I almost forgot. There's something about tonight."

"Yes?"

"No shop talk. I'd just like us to enjoy dinner and the movie, and if you wouldn't mind, maybe you'd tell me a little about yourself. I'd like that a lot. Does that sound agreeable?"

"It sounds like an exceptionally affable evening, thank you, and since you mentioned it, what's the film's subject matter?"

"The one I have in mind was released back in the 1990's, its entitled 'The Butcher's Wife'. According to the story, there was a race of beings in the very early days of the earth that lived an almost idealistic life. They were always happy. The spirits that ruled the world at the time were jealous, so they split the beings into two parts, becoming man and woman, and separated them by time and distance. Supposedly, the meaning of true love is when the original halves, called split-a-parts, manage to find each other again, and you never know when or where it might happen. I thought you'd enjoy it, but if not, I have almost a thousand others from which to choose."

They had reached the turnoff onto his dirt road. Each rode sheltered in their thoughts as he navigated the remaining distance to the house. Tom contemplated whether he'd ever see anything like the beauty of the mountainous forest again. Kate enjoyed seeing a small deer herd and watching some javelinas rooting for a mid afternoon meal. He slowed as he approached the last turn, expecting some of the animals to still be packing food away. To his surprise, they were already gone, and so were the goodies.

Tom chuckled. "Well, they got it all. They're probably sleeping and patting their full little bellies. That's by far the most food I've ever given them at a single feeding. I've always made being around them a kind of fun time, and usually just fed little snacks. I realized I might leave here someday, so didn't want them to become dependent on me."

After carrying the groceries into the kitchen, he showed her the area situated behind the bathroom. "I saw you notice the door earlier and wondered why you didn't ask about it."

"I didn't want to seem overly inquisitive and thought this would be a likely location for the other bedroom."

If actions and facial expressions were any indication, either her neck or shoulders appeared to be causing her some discomfort. "Turn around, let me take a look." Tom gently poked and prodded for a minute. "What do you have under your skin ... ropes?" After a short time, he finally managed to massage most of the tightness away.

She gingerly moved her head in small circles. "Thank you. That feels much better. I'm afraid these last few days have taken their toll on me, too. I just remembered, I have a bathing suit from using the heated pool at the motel. Would you mind if I took a shower and relaxed in the spa afterward?"

"No, not at all, I'll just add it to your bill. But, you really don't need a suit. Although I'd probably be tempted, I promise not to peek." He walked over to the closet doors. "There are a few good friends that use the house when I'm going to be away for a while. I keep some guest bathrobes in here ... in fact, this one has never been used." It was tossed onto the bed. "There are towels in the bathroom and upstairs in the spa. I'll start the salad now. Give me a yell when you're finished and I'll throw the steaks on the outside grill. Enjoy." He walked out of the room and closed the door behind him.

The shower had felt good, but the spa was terrific. Kate dried off, wrapped a towel around her head, slipped into a robe, and padded out to the top of the stairs. "Dr. Hughes, I'm finished."

His head poked around the corner. "Good timing, Miss Bright, everything is just about ready, except the steaks. How do you like yours?"

"I always set my auto-cooker to medium."

"Auto-cooker?" He shrugged. "Okay, medium it is."

She gazed down at her mode of dress. "I'm sorry, I suppose I look ridiculous."

"No, Miss Bright. You look like someone who just stepped out of a spa. The heat is on low, so you have about twenty minutes."

With that, he disappeared back around the corner; she turned and walked toward the bedroom to dress.

When Kate walked down the stairs, she got halfway and stopped, slightly stunned. The table was set with plates, silverware, food, wine, candles ... and fresh flowers. "I wish you hadn't gone to this much trouble, Dr. Hughes."

Tom looked up from his work and grinned approval of her attire. She wore a simple, one-piece red jump suit, with sublimely contrasting orange and blue striped socks. "I'm used to microwave dinners or eating in restaurants. This is my last night at home, Miss Bright. What better way to spend it than with good food, pleasant, comfortable surroundings, and an absolutely lovely guest?"

He pulled out a chair, nervously waiting as she crossed the room and was seated. Tom somewhat awkwardly explained the contrivance of his preparations. "For the salad, there's Thousand Island, Tangy French, Ranch, Italian, and my favorite ... Cherrie Burgundy Poppy Seed. Try a dab of each if you like. We certainly don't have to worry about wasting them."

He quickly pointed out the other available condiments and sautéed mushrooms. Eventually, they settled down to an enjoyable meal while Vivaldi's 'Four Seasons' played softly in the background.

Their conversation started easily with the usual small talk, but soon she took a different approach. "I suppose by telling you a little about myself, it'll also fill in another gap concerning my being a part of this mission.

We are comrades in isolation, Dr. Hughes. Your withdrawal from society was a classical manifestation of your guilt resulting from the conflict between your parents. A mother who was ... there, and an alcoholic father that called you everything but son, and although suffering little physical abuse, your level of intelligence magnified the feelings of displaced responsibility for your parents' self-generated misery."

At this point she hesitated, and he knew she was mentally editing before continuing, both aware that her soft under-belly was being exposed. He wondered if Miss Bright was considering more purposeful omissions. The realization softly slapped him that she would reveal additional information only when it felt comfortable, an altogether too familiar mode of expression that was also well understood by Tom. A wrong word now and her conversation would probably turn to nothing but good books and maybe a future weather report, so other than refilling her wine glass, he carefully maintained his silence as she seemed ready to continue.

"After much debate, the World Council sanctioned a project, which, with hindsight, they might never have allowed. Twenty children were conceived in vitro and implanted into surrogate mothers. Following their birth they were raised without any association of a parent figure. Their guides were rotated on a variable schedule so no patterns of expectations were developed. The children received direction, counseling, education, friendship, and a comradery developed amongst them.

The focus of the experiment was to produce children with a strong sense of independence, confidence, and self-reliability, while avoiding the traumas induced by sibling rivalry and other familial conflicts. In those aspects it was a complete success. These children were lacking, however, in a reasonable ability to interact socially outside the group or within the general population.

To answer the obvious question in your eyes, yes, I was one of TheTwenty. I have no idea who my biological parents were. The word 'love' was something we only read about, and seemed to exist solely outside our group."

Tom squirmed in his chair as her words came uncomfortably close to home. His parents had never once mentioned loving, or even liking him, for that matter. He was beginning to feel a strange kinship with this lady.

Kate had stopped, thinking Dr. Hughes was about to ask a question. When he didn't, she resumed her story. "As it turned out, almost all of us were perfect for time travel teams. Except for the group itself, there was no concept of 'belonging', we wouldn't miss anyone and no one would miss us. We used to think we were created just for that purpose, but research into the planning and implementation of the project proved that it had been executed along only the guidelines and goals originally proposed, and that they had been honorable in intention. In the end, only a few actually became travelers. The rest assumed support positions.

For reasons I won't divulge at present, the project was abandoned when we were twelve years old, and then we were indoctrinated into the regular education system. By the time I was in high school, they proclaimed me well adapted, although at the time I didn't understand what that was supposed to mean. I remember my first dates as a disaster, since I didn't know what I was looking for and certainly had no idea what to expect. When I was sixteen I volunteered for another project." She drained her wine, set the glass down, and looked at him. "But that, Dr. Hughes, is another story."

The conversation turned to more mundane topics such as comparing the music, movies, and science of their respective times.

Concerto for 'Bassoon and Strings in C major' was just beginning as Tom initiated the cleanup. "I'm just going to let these soak for now. I'll throw everything into the dishwasher after breakfast." He looked around the interior of his home and then back to her. " I don't want you thinking I'm some sort of fanatic on cleanliness, but it'd seem a shame to leave the place a mess."

"I noticed earlier that you swept up the glass." She rose and helped him straighten up the kitchen. "That was truly a treat for the palate, Dr. Hughes. Thank you very much. I'm looking forward to the movie, but if you don't mind, I'll eschew the popcorn."

In an attempted comic gesture, he pressed his fingers against his lips and puffed out his cheeks. "I believe we are in complete agreement on that accord, Miss Bright."

Tom walked to the entertainment center and turned the stereo off, while switching on the TV and VCR.

Kate moved and stood by the fire, feeling the warmth on her outstretched hands. "I don't know of anyone in my time who has a real fireplace, it's really quite beautiful, and very entrancing."

"Maybe I'll be the first." He picked up the remotes and sat on the couch ... playing a mind game trying to guess where she'd sit. A moment later, she sat near him, but not too close. He pushed 'play' and then fast-forwarded past the previews and commercials. The evening passed in quiet appreciation of the film, with each of them, now and then, adding a comment or expanding on a fine point.

He pressed 'stop', then rose to put the film in the re-winder. "Almost every time a VCR breaks, it's during a fast rewind, so I use one of these little gems. They're only about five bucks anywhere and last a long time. It's much better than replacing a VCR, especially when they keep getting harder to find, making them more expensive every year. I'm afraid my equipment and tapes are becoming extremely antiquated"

"No need to worry about that in the future, everything's on laser discs."

"I'm sure your units are smaller, faster, and the data is more densely packed, but we've had similar storage media since the late 1990's. There are some models that even predate those. I simply don't want to replace all my tapes. I've always told myself I was going to copy them to DVD's, but just haven't managed doing it yet. So ... does the box-step still exist three hundred years from now?"

Kate nodded. "It's still the basic slow dance step. I guess some things will never change."

"That's probably lucky for me." He slipped the album entitled 'A Song For Young Love' onto the turntable.

She rose and watched it spinning on the platter. "These exist only in museums, and it looks like an original vinyl pressing."

"It is. It's the first album by this group I came across. I've always wanted to transfer my LP's and 45's to DVD's, too, but that's just another thing I haven't done ... now it looks like I'll never get the chance."

It looked like a game of double charades as they attempted to position for the first dance. The first few songs were tough getting through, but by the time 'Blueberry Hill' from side two finished, they were dancing like a couple that had been married for years.

"Dr. Hughes, I have danced very little, and you indicated that you were 'extremely rusty', so I'm somewhat amazed at the melding of our rhythm. I realize I'm probably pressing my luck, but would you mind replaying side one again? Then if you don't mind, I think I'll call it a night."

"I'm pretty amazed myself, Miss Bright, in fact, flabbergasted may be a better term. However, I'd be delighted at another turn around the rug with you. In risk of spoiling the evening, I must confess ... I've never been more comfortable with someone."

"Thank you, Dr. Hughes. Rest assured, the feeling is mutual."

As side one replayed, it was accompanied by a muted shuffling of socks on the carpet. Afterwards, Tom shut off the stereo and carefully put the record away. He turned off the lights, leaving the room lit solely by the fireplace's flame ballet. "Let me add another log and I'll see you to your room."

Her wait was made in quiet anticipation.

He led her up the stairs and through the storage/bathroom combination, stopping outside the bedroom door. They stood there looking into each other's eyes and smiling. They leaned a little nearer and Tom timidly spoke.

"We need to be exceptionally cautious of the inverse square law concerning the distance between the center of two bodies. You know what happens when that interval begins decreasing."

Her eyes said, 'Kiss me', but her lips said, "I thought we weren't going to talk shop?" She winced at how sharp her voice had sounded. It had meant to be a tease, but his eyes flicked to the floor as he began backing up.

"You're right, I'll be more mindful of my own rules in the future. Good night, Miss Bright, I'll see you in the morning." He turned and walked away.

Kate's mouth opened to say something, but her vocal response was cut off by an emergency over-ride from her subconscious. 'No, if you encourage him now he'll only follow your lead, if you want more, he must make those decisions for himself.' She slowly closed her mouth ... then quietly shut the door.

Tom wasn't seen gathering up some things, one of which was the remaining half bottle of wine, and exiting through the front door.

"If you have built castles in the air, your work need not be lost; there is where they should be. Now put foundations under them."

- Thoreau

Chapter 5
Phantasy Physics

Tom awoke with a start, and then found himself temporarily disoriented by the surroundings. Sleeping on the padded seat atop his think-tank hill was not all that uncommon, but the partial hangover was something relatively rare. He'd hardly had anything to drink for years except for an occasional single glass of wine with dinner when the mood struck him.

In reality, on a ten-point scale, this hangover should only register a three, but since he hadn't slept well, it was briefly impacting like a seven. He grunted himself into a sitting position and took in the morning, thankful that most of the storm had blown over. Tom finished blinking the sleep from his eyes, then picked up the bedding, flashlight, and empty wine bottle, as he headed for a home that was not long to be.

Tom approached the house and noticed none of his friends were around. Of course, the sun was barely up, and they knew in their own way from past experience, he was not an early riser. He couldn't help chuckling while thinking maybe they didn't want to see him after the workload of food they had stowed away yesterday. Upon entering the house, he saw Miss Bright sitting on one of the dining table side chairs and attempted to test her mood. "Good morning ... I was wondering if you'd be up."

There was no response, so he replaced the flashlight on a wooden shelf by the door, dumped the bedding on the couch, and walked toward the kitchen with the bottle.

Kate stopped him en route by reaching out and putting a hand on his arm. "Dr. Hughes, before anything else is said between us, I'd like to apologize for the closing stages of last evening. I think you've come to understand I can be quite terse, sometimes even brusque, during a conversation.

Considering the mental trauma you've experienced in the last thirty-six hours, you've been a perfect gentleman, and last night, a most gracious host. It's important to me that you fully comprehend my intention when I made the comment about 'shop talk'. It was meant to be expressed as a congenial repartee, but was ineffectually executed. I perceived the injury in your eyes. Unfortunately, at the time, I couldn't discern a reply to nullify my error. Please ... forgive me."

Tom spun the bottle in his hand during her discourse, watching the label repeatedly blur past. "Thank you, Miss Bright, that's a load off my mind. I thought the evening had gone well, too, and felt you had enjoyed yourself. I know I did. I'm glad it was apparently just a moment of miscommunication.

Obviously, we're not very good sailors, because although the waters weren't exactly uncharted, it seems they were nevertheless unfamiliar, for both of us. I'll consider it a closed case if you will. Now, excuse me while I lay this dead soldier to rest."

He walked into the kitchen and stowed the bottle in the trash, noticing there weren't any additional dishes in the sink. "I take it you've not eaten?"

"No. I thought I'd wait for you."

Tom grinned. "Hooked on my cooking already, huh? That could be a fatal mistake because, believe me, last night was a once in a blue moon affair. How do you feel about bacon and poached eggs prepared in a microwave?"

"It's probably about the same as an auto-cooker. That's the only way I know how to cook."

"An auto-cooker sounds interesting. I hope you'll tell me more about it."

"Don't worry, you'll see one soon enough."

He laughed. "Between the two of us, we'd probably give a nutritionist a heart attack. Okay, I'll tell you what. I've got a bread knife and cutting board around here somewhere. How about if you slice some of the leftover French bread for toast, while I get the rest of the meal started?"

She saluted and smiled. "Aye, aye, captain."

Breakfast was cooked and eaten without any major mishaps; the table was cleared, and the dirty plates were loaded into the dishwasher.

Afterwards, Tom stood by the windows overlooking the deck.

Kate had moved to the couch and was finishing a glass of orange juice. She smiled while watching him. "Are you looking for your animal friends?"

He nodded. "Yes, but I have a feeling they'll take the day off. Actually, I was speculating when the rest of your apparatus is going to arrive."

"All the equipment is already here. I brought everything we need in the back of your truck yesterday."

Tom looked startled. "All I saw were some tubes and ring-shaped things. Are you telling me ... that's it?"

"That's everything. As soon as I finish my juice, I'm going to set it up. I don't suppose you'd be interested in helping?"

"No. Of course not ... why would a physicist want anything to do with a time machine? What are you, nuts? Swallow that juice and let's go!"

He was out the door and down the steps before she stopped laughing.

Kate caught up with Tom as he stood next to the bed of the truck, practically drooling.

"Dr. Hughes, has anyone ever told you you're like a little boy with new toys?"

"Well ... yes, but I like being like this. Why, do you think it's wrong?"

"It's not a question of being right or wrong. It's just that I imagine some people wouldn't accept it as being appropriate behavior for a grown man. Personally, I think it's refreshing."

Tom smirked. "Great. Then let's get these things out of here and you can show me how they work."

"Okay, you take a tube. I'll start with a ring, and we'll assemble them one at a time."

"Roger. Where do you want them?"

Kate scanned the area for a moment. "How about in that clearing, just down slope from the deck?"

"Fine with me." Tom lifted one of the white cylinders, measuring about 5 feet long and 5 inches in diameter. "Hey ... this is heavy, what's in it?"

"The tube is a support structure, but also contains other components. I'll explain later."

He observed as she carefully examined the first ring, as if it were dangerous even to touch. "Would you rather I carry the rings, too?"

"No, thank you. I'm just checking the section-display labeled 'POWER' to make absolutely sure it's in the 'OFF' mode. They're perfectly safe to move with the power 'ON', but in that case, only if it's handled by the outer edge. I prefer to move them with the power off, that way I don't need to worry about it. These should be in a disabled condition by default, but I always check."

Tom watched her carefully lift a ring out of the truck bed. "What happens if you put your hand through the middle with the power on?"

"Are you familiar with the phenomenon, 'spontaneous human combustion'?"

He nodded. "That sounds familiar. I'm sure I've even read an article or two concerning the subject."

"Then all you have to do is think about the consequences."

Tom looked at the ring-shaped object with renewed respect. "Wouldn't it be dangerous to have around children, or anyone else for that matter if they simply became curious?"

"The power supply shuts down automatically to a stand-by mode after a short delay, unless the module is actively in use. It requires a password to initiate the power sequencer. It's really quite safe. In fact, there are several passwords and setups that need to be entered and completed before the device becomes active.

A self-destruct procedure is also in place, in case one gets stolen or left behind for any reason. Most of the components are made of a special material that has a form of memory. If the self-destruct is activated, the whole mechanism forms into a ball and melts down into a powdery substance ... without heat."

They reached the clearing. Tom rested the equipment on one end, looking to Miss Bright for instructions.

She pointed. "See the black grip assist that runs around the tube about six inches from one end?"

He nodded. "Yes."

"That's the bottom. Twist the grip clockwise until it clicks. A set of tripod legs will extend, then just set it vertically on the ground. The tube is called the Main-Body Housing or MBH. The ring is termed a CCC, short for Circular Component Collection. You'll probably be disappointed, but the entire time transport mechanism is simply known as a Time Modulated Transceiver, or TMT."

"These aren't built by some large computer company are they?"

"No, why?"

"Computer companies form acronym central, those guys would love these things just for all the letters they could string together." Tom examined the relationship between the ring and tube structure. "Okay, I assume the ring slides down over the tube, probably display surface up?"

"That's correct."

"What keeps it in place? I don't see any fasteners ... just three tab stops."

"There are six platinum-plated sensors around the ring's inner circumference. They are all redundant, even though each sensor mates only with a specific section of the ring. If the ring were somehow attached incorrectly, the resulting reaction would be equivalent to a 5-megaton thermonuclear device detonating when the unit became active.

Therefore, any one of the sensors can detect an incorrect positioning of the ring. They will inhibit the magnetic latches and connection of the wireless circuitry until it is properly relocated. If none of the sensors are operable, then the TMT will never attempt to activate. There's a location marked 'Mate Ring' near the top of the post. Press on that spot and the 'ready' indicator next to it will illuminate. After that, slide the ring down over the tube and it will automatically orient itself into position. Don't force it. Once engaged, the magnetic latches will prevent it from moving."

Kate watched as he performed the task. "Everything looks good. Congratulations on assembling your first time machine."

Tom noticed another black line around the middle of the tube. "What's the purpose of this second grip assist?"

She shook her head. "It doesn't really have a function. It's just a seal that allows the tube's top half to turn independently of the bottom. That allows the direction of the scan lens to be automatically fine-tuned. Okay, lets get the rest ... one at a time, please."

The remaining three pairs of components were assembled in the same fashion. Tom wondered if something was being overlooked. "Why four units?"

"In this case, because we'll be beaming to a fixed installation site, two of the units are spares, strictly for backup and an added safety factor while we're in the field. The team director insisted I have them, so I didn't argue.

If we were beaming someplace where a permanent TMT station didn't exist, then we would use the extra two units for leap-frogging to our destination, which is termed 'alternate leading'. One TMT could easily convey both of us, but we generally don't do that, again, simply for the safety margin.

During an alternate lead, we would initially use two of the units as primaries for transporting the remaining units to the target destination. Then the secondaries already in place would receive us, and lastly, the primaries would have their destination matched with the originals."

Tom held up a hand. "Hold it. How do the TMTs left behind get transported?"

She grinned. "I was really hoping I could sneak that past you for now." Following a deep sigh, Kate continued. "This is going to be quick and dirty. We're probably less than an hour from my future where you'll be able to sit in front of a computer and ask all the questions you want. First, TMTs are quantum devices. What do you remember about Schrodinger's cat?"

Tom let his eyes roam for a minute before responding. "It was a philosophical attempt at explaining the fundamentals of quantum reality. A cat inside a box could be alive or dead, but the reality of either didn't exist until the outcome was observed. Therefore, the cat could be neither alive or dead, or even both simultaneously." He pulled at his chin. "Are you saying TMTs can be both passive and active at the same time?"

Kate nodded. "Yes ... but obviously only for an instant. Actually, there are two methods by which they can be transmitted. It depends on whether just a change in time is performed, or spatial displacement is also involved. Both techniques utilize something called 'N-dimensional quantum flux', where 'N' has a minimum value of eight for a TMT." She flashed a hand. "Don't even ask about the equations. You'll definitely have to wait for those. They're much more complex than I want to even think about. Is that enough for now?"

He smiled. "Sure. I'll let you return to your semi-packaged dissertation."

"Thank you." She pretended to wipe her forehead and then pointed to the machine. "Each TMT is physically identical to the next, so the only change required is within its programming code. All components of the same model TMT are also interchangeable. Jump programming is originally set at master control, but can be modified in the field if necessary, or as required."

Tom looked at the assembled units. "Are these units ready to transport?"

"The assumable answer is 'yes', but the safe answer is 'no'. The TMTs need to be powered up and have their programming verified and matter bank levels checked. Powering the units up automatically causes an internal self-check to run against all components. I believe in your time it's called a POST, Power On Self Test. A similar procedure occurs in our equipment.

Would you like a tour of the individual parts? I can only give you an operational overview and limited explanations of each component. If you want details, and I'm sure you do, you'll need to talk with the engineers who work in the labs and product design."

"I'm all eyes and ears, Miss Bright. Please ... lead on."

"As alluded to before, there are six sections composing the ring. A neutrino generator, tachyon generator, scan processor, power supply, trace-element matter bank, and control functions ... including cesium clock, safety interlocks, and CTL detect. Each section interfaces through the primary memory bank within the main-body housing. The MBH also contains a launch and detect system for an environment probe.

Again, as in our discussion about alternate leading, probes are only used when portable TMTs, such as these, are being sent to a destination where a permanent TMT station is not installed. The probe consists of a specially tagged tachyon stream. Upon retrieval, the probe can be examined and certain environmental factors can be deduced by imposed changes in the stream.

Basically, we look for airless environments or solid targets, including living matter. If any of these are detected, the target position is adjusted, and the procedure is repeated. Since the probe consists only of tachyon type particles, the targets are never subjected to harmful invasions.

I believe the neutrino and tachyon generators are self-explanatory. The scan processor contains a three-dimensional holographic laser projector/scan-lens system. Its single purpose is scanning/destroying the subject to be transferred. A signature map ... is something wrong, Dr. Hughes?"

"Did you say destroy?"

"Yes, but technically I should say convert. It's the only practical way to circumvent the Heisenberg uncertainty principle. Are you familiar with the computer term 'Non Destructive Read'?"

Tom nodded. "Sure, it means you can read data out of a storage position as often as required without disturbing the original contents."

"That's because you can access the existing data without changing it. As you know, Heisenberg, along with the laws of quantum physics, will not allow us to do that with subatomic particles, so consequently the only way we can 'read' the data is by converting it from mass into energy."

"What happens to all the energy?"

"Some of it's absorbed and used to energize the ongoing scan process. That's why the power supply is so small in the ring; it's only used to activate the electronics and initiate the scan. I'll cover what happens to the rest later.

The subject undergoing teletransportation stands, or is placed on a mat, and is outlined with a charged neutrino field. Anything within the field, from the mat up, is literally disintegrated by the lens system. As each particle is converted, it gives off a specific energy signature identifying its elemental constituents. The signatures are simply mapped to three-dimensional space, and because the procedure takes place literally at the speed of light, time stops, and hence is not a factor.

However, since relativity forbids us sending matter at, or faster than, the speed of light due to its infinite increase in mass, we instead send just the map in the form of modified tachyon class particles. A tachyon can have a plus one, minus one, or zero spin. The alternate spin names, forward and backward, were chosen to coincide with the direction the tachyon will travel in time."

"I had pretty much predicted the plus and minus spins in my own research, but the third spin is a surprise. Does zero spin imply something akin to a stasis field?"

"Clever deduction, Dr. Hughes. I wondered if that would catch your attention. I think you can well imagine what that would mean to life forms traveling on a starship. Of course, we don't have starships, yet, and we have only begun experimenting with the zero spin, but it's there for future use.

To conclude, the map is superimposed on the tachyon stream, one signature position per tachyon, and sent on its way. The disintegration phase is that simple."

Tom shook his head. "I see the TMT, and I hear your words, but it's still hard to believe. You're discussing technology that's over three hundred years ahead of me, yet it sounds like a conversation over coffee about a cross-town shopping trip. My questions are breeding like some out of control bacteria."

Tom looked around and spotted a nearby tree stump, walked over, and sat down to think this through. After all, he wasn't sure if he even knew this woman's real name. Could this all be just a fantastic play act? What if she did work for the competition? His elimination would certainly be a feather in their cap. If they got hold of his written notes and computer, they would almost have carte blanche on many future developments, including the tachyon.

But why the ruse at all? Why not just shoot him, steal the information and be done with it? And yet, what about that field she generated? That was real; he had experienced it first hand. There was no equipment in the world that could have performed that task. However, it would be the ace they'd need up their sleeve for enticing him to step inside some sort of high-powered beam. Maybe they wanted, or needed, it to look like an accident ... or even suicide. His gaze swung up to meet hers, and found a smile across her face.

"It's time, Dr. Hughes."

Tom instantly felt his heart rate jump. "Time for what?"

"It's time to convince you that what I've said is factual. I can read the doubt in your eyes. Your second crisis of disbelief was predicted, and was expected just about now at this juncture in a four-dimensional model composed of cause, effect, and space-time. Stay where you are, and watch."

Kate walked to one of the TMTs and touched pressure sensitive marks on the control section of its ring. Her slow nod indicated an acceptance of the settings. The direction of the scan-lens was adjusted until it was approximately perpendicular to a line between the two units. She walked to a second TMT and performed the identical procedure.

Kate returned to the first TMT and positioned herself directly in front of the lens, approximately five feet from it. Her wrist device gave an audible countdown. On the tick of zero, a dazzling glow enveloped her entire body, then the area immediately returned to a normal light setting. She turned towards him. "Safety feature number one, I'm not standing on a transfer mat."

His gaze fell to the ground by her shoes, confirming the absence of anything unusual. "Is one of these mats a highly complex mixture of future compounds?"

She laughed. "Hardly. They're literally made of any scrap material that's currently available at production time. The only thing that makes them special is a micro-thin layer of iridium. You're probably aware that's an extremely rare earth element, so it's the perfect delineation between ground zero and whatever is being transported."

Kate opened a door on the nearest TMT tube, extracted a rolled sheet of material, placed it on the ground at her original position, stepped on, and restarted the countdown. Another flash ... and then an untold number of barely visible lines shredded her body like bullets passing through paper. It was easily the most amazing thing he had ever witnessed, making the extraordinary experience of yesterday seem commonplace. There wasn't even any smoke. Then it dawned on him ... there wasn't anything, including no Miss Bright.

Kate checks the settings on a Time Modulated Transceiver

"The wise man has his foibles, as well as the fool. But the difference between them is, that the foibles of the one are known to himself and concealed from the world; and the foibles of the other are known to the world and concealed from himself."

- J. Mason

Chapter 6
Resetting The Clock

Tom's quiet wait became nerve racking. Kate's second TMT finally emitted a stunning burst of light, and the system that fabricated her vanishing act operated in reverse. There stood Miss Bright, who turned, spread her arms, and issued a simple, "Ta da."

Tom had no memory of standing up, but abruptly realized his legs were wobbling, so sat back down and breathed a deep sigh of relief. "I thought for a minute something had gone wrong. I expected you to appear at the other TMT instantaneously."

Kate grinned. "I thought you'd appreciate a little suspense, so I added a five-second delay. You seemed to enjoy the theatrics yesterday."

"I liked this one about as much as having a piano fall on my head. That five seconds seemed like five hours."

She smiled coyly. "Hmm, it sounds like you were worried about me, Dr. Hughes."

Tom blushed. "Well, if something happens to you, who else will pay for my window?"

She flicked her eyebrows, then bent down and picked up the mat that Tom now noticed had transmitted with her. It was spooled and replaced in the tube. "Any questions?"

"Ha! How many do I get?"

Kate smiled. "Let's try them one at a time."

"When you reintegrated, there was a rushing of air, almost a wind. What caused that noise?"

She considered for a moment. "Before I answer, I need to know what you remember about the elemental constituents of the body."

Tom shrugged. "Do you mean muscle, skin, bone, and other such items?"

"No ... as in proportions of oxygen, carbon, hydrogen, etc."

"Oh. In that case, I only remember if my body gets bumped hard, it hurts."

Kate nodded. "Uh huh. Remind me to never let you adjust the physiological settings on a TMT. Okay, let's start with basics. The body is composed of about twenty-four elements. Oxygen, hydrogen, and nitrogen make up 77.8%. Why drag heavy, bulky bottles of gases around when what we need is readily available in the atmosphere? That's the second most important reason we check for airless environments before we transfer, the first should be obvious."

Tom just nodded.

"The wind noise you heard was the TMT inputting air for extraction of the required elements to reintegrate my body. Add carbon, from the carbon bank, and the body is 96.3% complete. All other required elements come from the trace element matter bank located in the ring. Both matter banks are enclosed in an electrostatic bottle to prevent accidentally drawing substance from the equipment itself. Material being stored is charged with the same polarity as the bottle, and discharged upon exit.

Now I'll complete our earlier discussion about the conversion process. During the disintegration phase, energy not required from the exchange process to drive the scan is utilized in powering the tachyon generator. Any excess mass that's produced can be used to partially recharge both the carbon and trace element matter banks. A fully charged carbon bank can hold one hundred pounds. The TE bank is fully loaded with twenty-five. When sent to us in the field, they carry sixty and fifteen pounds respectively. That's why the tubes are so heavy.

I'm about five foot five, weighing one hundred fifteen pounds, so I require twenty-one and a quarter pounds of carbon, and four and a quarter pounds of trace elements. Permanent installations of public MMTs have large carbon and TE banks, along with oxygen, hydrogen, and nitrogen reservoirs that are constantly replenished from an outside air source. Considering they only transfer in real time, a tachyon generator isn't required. Next question."

Tom frowned. "Let's back up a second. You've always been talking about TMTs. What's an MMT?"

"Sorry ... didn't mean to mislead you. An MMT is a Matter Modulated Transceiver. It uses neutrinos instead of tachyon particles to carry the superimposed map; therefore it doesn't travel forward or back in time.

Imagine if the general public was allowed to change the timeline at their whimsical call. The world and perhaps our whole solar system would be nothing but a chaotic shambles."

Tom lightly stroked his beard. "Alright, here's one even science fiction writers don't want to tackle. Do you believe in the human soul?"

She studied him for a few seconds. "I think I know exactly where you're going with this. If the soul exists, what happens to it during the transfer, especially since we literally destroy the human body? Am I correct?"

"One hundred percent on the mark."

"The answer everyone finally agreed upon didn't involve any equipment or scientific thinking per se, it was strictly an exercise in theology. When we speak of the soul, we must also consider the belief in God, since they are invariably linked. However, even in theology, the concept of God is a binary. He either exists, or He doesn't.

If He doesn't, then the entire question of what to do about the soul during transmission is futile; the very question ceases to exist. However, if God does exist, then He knows the mind of humankind, its potential, and direction. Therefore, our view of the soul has become simple. Anything God doesn't want man capable of achieving, then in fact, we believe will not come to pass.

Please don't think of this answer as being flippant. As you mentioned, even in your time, the question was in the back of people's minds. When the MMTs, and then TMTs were first conceived, the question of what would happen to the soul became front-page news, and hotly debated for years. This was long before even the first trials with inanimate objects were attempted.

So, in conclusion, simple as it may be, if God exists and He didn't want us capable of moving through time, or even moving from place to place as we do, we would be stopped. Since we can beam anywhere on the planet, even through time, we feel the issue is resolved either way. In answer to your question, 'since it's allowed, God has it covered'."

"True, it's simple, but it does make sense ... just one more example in the law of parsimony. Do you know what item was the first to be successfully transmitted?"

Kate nodded. "Yes ... a single grain of sand ... and if I were a betting person, I'd wager it was probably the most intensely studied object in the history of science. It was examined with fine-tooth combs you can't even imagine, but once the transfer had been proven letter perfect, testing proceeded at a relatively rapid rate."

"What was the final test before they sent a person ... a chimp or maybe an ape?"

"No. Chimps, apes, and several other animals were sent before trying a human, all successfully, too, but the last attempt before man was a species of fern. Each human cell, except gametes and some blood cells, contain forty-six chromosomes. Ophioglossum Reticulatum contains twelve hundred sixty. It was basically surmised that if such a complex organism could make it, we'd probably transfer easily ... at least physically.

The big question was the mental aspect. The animals passed all their lab and physical tests, but they could only tell us so much. Could we still think, would we remember? Everyone held their collective breath on those questions. But, in the end, it worked, and the outlook of the world changed overnight." Kate watched, as Dr. Hughes seemed to absorb every word, but noticed he still appeared confused. "Is something wrong?"

"We haven't discussed the reintegration phase completely, but I believe I'm on the same page with you. The demonstration, however, has raised a serious question for me in conjunction with what was said about sending a TMT to a destination that didn't already have a TMT in place.

Since the TMT receives the map of a subject being reintegrated, and supplies the matter, how is assembly possible if a TMT isn't already in place to receive it? It'd be like sending a TV station signal to a location where there wasn't any receiver, yet you're saying you could still successfully build a screen image."

"This is one of those rare situations where quantum rules are a great advantage, instead of a hindrance. They allow for conditions where energy spontaneously changes into mass at constant predetermined levels, essentially the same as an electron neutrino. This procedure only works for inanimate matter, that's why an MMT or a TMT must be on site before animate objects can be transmitted.

While research teams were working on the Grand Unified Theory, they discovered that tachyons reaching a specific lower energy level would reliably transmute into a mass particle of the same element. Further experiments confirmed this process could produce all elements, although as the element became more massive, it required an arrangement of additional tachyons. If you think about it, the results are consistent with other quantum based laws.

The element produced was primarily a function of the tachyon particle's beginning and ending energy states. These components were combined into what is characterized as a matter inducement matrix. Another factor influencing the procedure was time, except in this case ... time is thought of in terms of distance.

If you want to produce hydrogen, for example, you start with a tachyon with X amount of energy that travels over Y distance, where again, distance is considered real time. At a fixed XY point it transmutes to hydrogen, in every instance. The beautiful part of this progression lies in the fact that other XY values can also induce hydrogen. A different combination of X and Y will generate helium, lithium, or some other element, but at some fixed increment, hydrogen will be produced again.

Therefore, by incorporating time into the matrix, all elements can be theoretically synthesized at essentially an infinite number of occurrences in the table, although currently, most of these energy levels are beyond the scope of our equipment. To actually induce a single atom of hydrogen at a specific distance, just select the matching X value, which is its initial energy state, from the XY set of coordinates in the matrix.

You are aware, of course, that energy is packed in discrete packets, or quanta, which by its very nature often induces an error in the reintegration location. We've found that all elements will still induce as predicted if assembly takes place within approximately ten nanometers of the projected position.

Once a probe determines a specific point within a three-dimensional coordinate system as the locus for the reintegration site, then it must also convey the distance each tachyon will be in motion. Then it's just a fundamental task of using the signature map, particle by particle, as an index into the matter inducement matrix, applying the result as a locus of points around the integration site, and finally, reassembling whatever was transported.

This will ensure that although we have a possibility for error, the exact same amount of offsetting displacement will apply to the entire subject being transmitted on an equal basis, thereby guaranteeing all components will integrate successfully around the designated reintegration site."

Tom slowly shook his head. "Wow, I have no idea what to say. It all sounds logical, but so extremely complex. I shudder to think of all the opportunities that exist where something can go wrong, and yet, I've already witnessed a successful demonstration with my own eyes. For now, I certainly have no choice but to accept your word."

Kate's wrist device issued a series of short beeps. She checked it and informed Dr. Hughes it was her project director, excused herself, and walked away to process the message.

When Kate returned, she found him sitting on the same stump, apparently deep in thought again. "What's bothering you now, Dr. Hughes?"

"There are times I forget my humanity, Miss Bright. What's worse, I sometimes apply that same lack of feelings to my friends. Today, you were the teacher and I the student. It's been a while since I've performed an introspective examination. I don't like what I've been finding. Before we go, I plan on leaving a note addressed to my friends and associates. Basically, it'll be an attempt to reconcile some of the hard feelings we've exchanged."

"I don't want to appear as 'Big Brother', Dr. Hughes, but for the sake of the timeline, may I read it when you're finished?"

He was annoyed at first, but quickly realized the request made sense. "I understand."

Tom walked to the house and composed his apology, while Kate processed the request sent by her director.

Tom strolled back towards Miss Bright, noticing she had changed back into a skirt, blouse, and high-heeled shoes. He found her examining some scorched spots on the ground where two of the TMTs had been. "What happened?"

"My director asked me to download some programming into the spare TMTs and then observe any unusual occurrence while he tested a new jump sequence with them. The only logical explanation for these markings is a tremendous release of energy, which is not normally associated with the TMTs.

All I know for sure is that whatever results the test was supposed to produce, it was apparently successful as signified by his last message. It puzzles me, however, considering the fact it was double encoded and decipherable only by my personal communications device.

I want to give you an injection, Dr. Hughes. It'll help alleviate the jump's effects. It's only an air gun so you probably won't feel anything, just hear a little hiss. Before we actually make the jump, our direction and destination will be cleared and checked. During the jump itself, our progress will be monitored and recorded.

It's all standard operating procedure, even though there hasn't been a malfunction in one of these units in almost forty years. I believe you can rest assured ... they are quite safe. May I see your note?"

Tom handed her the letter and stood quietly aside as she read.

"These are kind words, Dr. Hughes. Guilty or not, you seem to be accepting blame for most of what happened. Your friends should be pleased. Now that you've written this, there are a few other items I'd like to show you. Compare your latest note with another that I have."

Tom scanned hers. "It has my signature. Where did you get this?"

"It's a copy of a note you wrote after finding out your originally designated fate. I couldn't tell you about it before because the timeline may have become corrupted. I might have inadvertently influenced the contents of your latest message, thereby causing a change or omission in some important piece of information you chose to leave behind, which in turn, might have radically changed history.

We couldn't take the risk. As it is, they're almost identical. That's quite remarkable. In truth, I suppose it's only logical, since whatever circumstances existed that prompted you to write the original, are obviously already in place at this point." Kate withdrew another document from her pocket. "Here's another newspaper article you might like to see."

Tom took the paper and unfolded it.

> UP Newswire – Chicago – 12 June, 2017
> For his participation in discovery of a particle called a Tachyon, Dr. Taylor Judson has been selected to receive the Nobel Prize in physics. According to physicists, this particle opens the door to the possibility of traveling in time. Dr. Judson was quoted as saying he would accept only if his former friend and colleague, Dr. Thomas Hughes, would share equally in the award. Dr. Judson stated that without the efforts and information obtained by Dr. Hughes, this discovery would have been delayed by several years,

> possibly decades. Dr. Hughes will be the first to receive the award posthumously.

She accepted the paper as he handed it back. "I suppose it's evident why this couldn't be shown to you before either.

If you're ready, put your current note in the house where you want it found. When you come back, I'll administer your injection and we'll leave."

He took his newly-written correspondence, placed it in his home, and returned. "By the way, Miss Bright, why the reversion to your dressy attire?"

"I understand there's a special reception planned. This is the only semi-elaborate clothing I have with me. I used your outside lavatory to change. I assumed you wouldn't mind."

Tom shook his head. "No, not at all, but I think you look nice either way."

Kate smiled. "Thank you. Incidentally, I had some help figuring out that puzzle about the 'small block' and accompanying numbers. Apparently, at one phase in your life, you must have enjoyed working with automobiles and internal combustion engines, because according to my friends in this time, that's what they deduced from your rather cryptic wording."

Tom chuckled. "I guess I can't get anything passed you. At the time, you were holding all the trump cards, and I was just trying to deal myself back into the game."

Kate laughed. "Well, it certainly worked. I should have realized if anyone could confuse my equipment, it'd be you.

Are you prepared for the future, Dr. Hughes?"

Tom took a long, last look around, gave her an anxious smile, and finally offered a pensive, "Okay, kiddo ... let's get the hell out of here."

Kate dispensed the drug. The TMTs were checked and prepared; both participants were positioned on transmit mats. The countdown reached zero and there were two simultaneous flashes of light. Tom and Kate disappeared. A soft pop occurred when the air rushed in to fill the now vacant spots where each body had stood.

Following the final shimmer, Betty poked her head out from a nest on the upper branches of a nearby tree. She was mute witness to the ominous fact that when the second set of TMTs followed, they left the same scorch marks as the earlier machines.

"The bravery founded on hope of recompense, fear of punishment, experience of success, on rage, or on ignorance of danger, is but common bravery, and does not deserve the name. – True bravery proposes a just end; measures the dangers, and meets the result with calmness and unyielding decision."

- La Noue

Chapter 7
Chicken Little Attacks

Tom's vision returned, allowing him to watch the surroundings spin by as his knees buckled, and his body slumped toward the ground. Stars were observed that didn't belong in a daylight setting. When his voice seemed like it might work again, his thoughts were succinctly expressed. "Oh ... my ... God. Did I miss something, or did the sky actually just fall on me?"

Kate suppressed a laugh and knelt by his side. "I'm sorry, Dr. Hughes, honestly. I certainly take no pleasure in your misery, but the expression on your face is quite humorous." She arose. "Don't worry, the disorientation and melancholy will quickly pass."

With an effort, he managed to prop up on one elbow and take a first look around. There was nothing to see but tall fern plants. Could this be one of the remote spots she had mentioned, perhaps as a soft indoctrination to his new world? She appeared to be aimlessly wandering, yet investigating, as if something were amiss.

"Correct me if I'm wrong, Miss Bright. Didn't you say the shot you administered would moderate the jump's effect?"

"With hindsight, it would probably have been more accurate to say the aftereffects would be reduced."

"This is reduced? You're stating that without the shot, it's worse?"

"Without the preparation, you'd be bedridden for at least a day, maybe two."

"Please tell me this isn't the normal mode of travel in your time."

She noted the concern in his voice, but could only offer the truth, which would probably prove to be disappointing. "We use transference more than sidewalks. It's generally used everyday by almost everyone on the planet, and off-planet, too, for that matter."

Tom thought about her last comment, displayed a troubled expression, leaned back, and examined the brilliant clear sky. There was something flying in the distance with strange looking wings. It seemed quite large, but there was nothing close enough to put its size in perspective. He returned to their conversation. "So, I assume calling a taxi is out of the question?"

"Sorry." She walked over and offered him a hand. "Want to get up?"

He experimentally flexed his legs and arms, preparing to stand. "Yeah, I think so."

She gave a tug. He allowed her to help more than necessary. The procedure was executed somewhat clumsily and they bumped, not completely by accident.

He looked down, she up. They stood toe to toe scanning each other's eyes. Kate finally turned away. Tom's mind raced. He took a step, planted a foot, and then started pivoting around it. "Whoa! What's happening?"

She spun back, threw her arms around him, and he seemed to stabilize.

He decided to add a slight body shake for good measure.

Kate pushed away, holding him at arms length. Her eyes narrowed. "Really, Dr. Hughes, you frightened me for a moment. A residual cerebral dysfunction is possible, but extremely rare."

Fawning innocence, he lowered his head and looked at her over the top of his glasses. "Do I get any points for admitting I liked being held by you?"

"No. You're acting like a child." She spun away again, faking a cough to cover her huge smile. They each scanned the area. She pointed. "How about starting over there?"

Tom brought up a hand, shaded his eyes from the sun, then sighted down her arm to find the target. "It looks like a wide and recently used path. With luck, maybe it'll lead us to a familiar landmark."

As they started off, he observed her flicking looks back and forth. "You seem to be ill at ease, Miss Bright."

"Around you?"

He puffed out a laugh. "No. I mean with this area."

His gaze took in an abundance of pristine nature ... a wide area covered with low ferns, rugged, barren, jagged peaked young mountains, and oddly shaped trees ... nothing like what he'd expected. There was even a volcano in the distance. It was belching great clouds of white smoke he hoped was mostly nothing more than water vapor.

Tom continued to observe her actions. He knew something was really bothering her and, that fact, in turn, bothered him. He halted. "Is something wrong? Did the transfer malfunction?"

"No, the transfer worked flawlessly." Kate stopped and faced him. "If Frank solved his raster pattern problem, this may be his way of welcoming me back, and you to the future."

"Who's Frank?"

"A team member of mine. His prime domain of expertise is holographic projectors. They work fine until he tries creating scenes with large-scale backgrounds. Then the landscape appears to waver, fade, or become ... splotchy." The expression on her face indicated it almost caused physical pain using that definition, but somehow it must have proven to be the most accurate. "No matter how fast a CPU he couples with the projector, it can't handle the massive amount of data it has to manipulate."

Tom tilted his head and gestured with an upward palm. "He only uses one CPU?"

"Yes, but you must understand, we have processors running in the multiple terahertz range."

He shook his head. "It doesn't matter, I don't think CPU speed is the problem."

With arms akimbo, she appeared as if lecturing a small boy. "And I suppose, without examining the machine, programming, or any other aspects of the procedure, you profess to know the answer?"

Tom looked away, then back. "Well, excuse me for breathing your air. If you'll cool your jets, I'll explain. What I'm suggesting is that Frank has the same problem Morbius had in 'Forbidden Planet'."

"Oh ... is that a technical manual encompassing the support or rejection of various opinions regarding matter projection?"

He laughed, wiping a spot of moisture from his eye. "Oh, man. No, it's a Sci-Fi movie. Morbius was a character that had a seemingly unsolvable problem because he was just too close to deduce the answer. It took a fresh view from someone not previously involved, to solve it. The answer was there all the time."

Kate squinted and gave him an icy stare. "I see. You're comparing a twenty-fourth-century scientific project, run by a man who is nothing short of sheer genius, with a twentieth-century science fiction film?"

He slowly waved his hands and answered in a softer voice. "The path to the solution is the same. Bear with me. I'll bet the difficulty is caused by insufficient data-bus pipeline speed and a shortage of level one memory cache. I've run into this problem on dozens of projects.

Input/output processing usually depends on a physical mechanical device. No matter how fast it seems ... it takes an eternity processing data relative to the speed of a CPU. Therefore, the real bottleneck is getting data to or from a CPU, not processing it. If he used multiple projectors, maybe one per view, each with its own processor, then tied the data into a master syncing CPU, it'll avoid overrunning the burst speed of the channel connecting them together.

It's like moving water between two one-hundred-gallon reservoirs using only one pipe and a single pump. No matter how much the pump can handle, the pipe is the limiting factor and by just adding a larger pipe, at some point the pump becomes inadequate. Put multiple pipes and multiple pumps between the tanks, and the problem will go away. I admit that's an oversimplification, but the principal is the same. By the way, I have a question for you."

"Yes."

His eyes bored into hers. "What if this isn't Frank's doing?"

She became apprehensive and avoided his visual accusation. "Then we're in big trouble."

"I distinctly heard you say, 'the transfer didn't malfunction'."

"That's correct. It didn't. If it had, you and I wouldn't be having this conversation. We'd be galactic flotsam."

"Then ... what?"

"Someone changed the programming."

"Frank?"

"No, Picus."

"Great. Is this another guy?"

"Yes. Picus works in master control during time jumps. He's the director who has access to all programming and can override almost any function in case of an emergency. He's also the person who performed the experiment with the spare TMTs before we jumped. I would never have thought this possible of him. The most worrisome part is that he can mask changes so they appear spontaneous."

"If you took an educated guess, which person is it ... Frank or Picus?"

"I'd have to go with Picus."

"Reasoning?"

"The transceivers aren't here, they were recalled after the jump, and my wrist device is displaying a visual alarm indicating a lost signal. It's also locked in full automatic recording mode. I can't alter the setting. None of that happens during a straightforward holographic event. Following a jump, one of the updates upon arrival, is the resetting of wrist devices and TMT clocks to relative date and local time. You'd better get a grip, Dr. Hughes. Unless the transceivers were also programmed to give false data, we're smack in the middle of the Jurassic Age."

Tom did a double take. "You mean, dinosaurs, and stuff like that?" He began to look around in earnest.

Kate replied somewhat sarcastically, "Yes. Stuff like that." She laughed softly. "Of course, if we want tangible proof, we'll have one of the brutes bite you ... if it hurts, then we know this isn't a hologram."

Tom grinned. "What's really scary about that remark is it sounds like something I would say." He continued, more hopeful than believing. "Well, when it's discovered, they'll send a rescue mission. Our progress, direction, or whatever, must have been monitored. You explained that before we jumped."

"True. But Picus could misdirect or simply erase the entire operation."

"Everything? What about backups?"

"Picus has passwords to access everything."

Tom stumbled and sat on the ground. "We're in big trouble."

Kate walked a few more steps, and then froze. She stooped down into the plants and made frantic 'come here' gestures with her hands.

He rose into a crouch and caught up. "What now?" She pointed. Tom's mouth dropped open. He simply stared for almost a full minute before he could speak. "Well, uh, say now, that's no problem. Nothing to get all worked up about. I'll bet that Stegosaurus and I are old friends before the day is out. Besides, according to research, it's a plant eater. As long as we stay out of the way, it'll probably leave us alone." Tom moaned and sat down with his head in his hands. "Perhaps I'd been better off opting for the firing squad."

After a minute he stood back up, staring. His demeanor turned deadly serious. "If this is the Jurassic, then we don't want to follow that path."

She frowned. "Why not?"

"Have you ever experienced a premonition, Miss Bright?"

"I suppose I've had an encounter with something that comes under the heading of a similar phenomenon. Why do you ask?"

"I've seen this exact same scene in a movie. I'll bet dollars to doughnuts that path is a game trail."

"So? It'd make traveling a lot easier, isn't that why it's a trail? Even the animals have enough sense to realize that."

Tom nodded with a tight-lipped smile before he dropped the bomb. "True. The predators realize it, too."

Her eyes widened. "Oh."

He kept his eyes on the Stegosaurus, but asked what would seem to be the next logical question. "So, what did you do, starch this guy's shorts or something?"

"Not exactly."

Tom turned back and faced her. "Okay ... then what ... exactly?"

She picked a long-stemmed fern and casually examined it. "I don't think this was done because of me, at least not directly. I believe it's a way of getting back at you." Her eyes floated back to his.

Tom threw his arms in the air, spun around, and then faced her again. "Oh, well, that explains everything. I've never seen him, met him, or even heard of him until three minutes ago! What the hell are you talking about?"

Kate bounced her hands. "Shhhh. Not so loud. Let's not forget our friend over there. We have no idea how sensitive its hearing is or how little noise it takes to alarm the animal. Sit down, I'll explain."

Tom looked around and laughed. "You want to sit down, here, in the middle of an area where we can't see more than ten feet in any direction, and discuss your personal problems with Picus? If we had a TV and an electrical outlet, perhaps you'd want to catch up on the soaps while you're at it!"

"We're well off the game trail and I'm sure if something big comes this way, we'll hear it." She growled, "Besides, if we talk quietly, it may help to calm our nerves ... then we can logically decide our next move."

"Right ... why not?" Tom took a second look around, sat down, and tried to make himself comfortable. He patted the ground near him. "Let's sit close so we can whisper. Is that alright with you?"

"Perfectly."

Tom grinned. "Hey, too bad there isn't a phone, we could have something delivered. I could really go for a pizza."

Kate laughed. "Now, that's one thing I love ... I mean, like about you ... your sense of humor."

"Ah, ah, ah. The love word slipped out first. I hope you understand ... it's completely within the realm of possibility ... we may die here. So, let's make a pact to tell the truth, and only the truth ... ad infinitum. How about it?"

She looked him directly in the eyes. "I've never lied to you," and offered to shake hands.

Tom hesitated, then took her hand and kissed it.

She blushed. "Well, that ... surprised me."

He shrugged. "Me too."

Tom lay back, supported by his lower arms. Kate was on her knees, resting on her haunches. She opened her mouth to speak, but was interrupted by a vibration and quick, heavy, padding feet. Kate stretched her torso, spotting the disturbance. She relaxed. "Oh, it's only our friend running off."

Tom shook his head. "That's not good."

"Why not?"

"The Steg sounded like it was in a hurry. I doubt if it was trying to catch a bus. An animal runs like that only when it feels threatened. It must have sensed a predator in the area."

He was studying her blouse when they heard a roar. Instinctively, they both dropped flat to the ground. She maneuvered close. A few feet away, there was a particularly tall clump of ferns, which would afford cover, yet allow a view in the noise's direction. He motioned her to stay put and crawled over to the lush stand of concealing flora. Tom checked the sun's angle, removed his glasses, inserted them into a hard case, and shoved it inside his shirt. He rose slowly and scanned the distant tree line.

Kate had scooted closer. "See anything?"

"No, not yet. There's a thick stand of trees and some dense foliage on the far side of the path. Whatever made the noise must be hidden inside."

She followed his line of sight, looking down. "What are you staring at?"

"My pants and your skirt are both dark colors, they blend well with some of this soil. My brown shirt goes with the clumps of dried leaves." He shook his head. "But, I couldn't help noticing that orange blouse of yours. Its brilliance might prove to be a real problem."

Kate frowned, then brightened. "It's reversible." She pulled the bottom out and flipped it over. "See, there's a tan colored liner."

Tom nodded. "Good. I'll keep a lookout for whatever made the racket while you become boring." He turned back and scrutinized the tree line.

She talked while changing. He heard fear in her voice. "You realize it's your turn to save me. I successfully rescued you from your original fate."

He supposed an argument could be mounted against that point, but didn't say anything. Kate curled up against him and softly cried. She was totally out of her element, not that he felt exactly at home. He gave her something to do.

"Miss Bright, see if you can tell if that's an opening in those rocks close to where the Steg was standing. I removed my glasses because I didn't want to chance the sun reflecting off the lenses and drawing attention."

She stayed behind him and levered up just high enough to gain a view. "Yes, there is a passage into the rocks. I can't tell how deep it goes ... or if anything is already in there."

He compared the sun's position relative to the treetops. "The sun should be setting soon. I suggest we sit tight for now. When it's dark we'll use the vegetation for cover as far as we can, then make our way across the open flat to that passage. We'll deal with whatever may be in it when we enter."

Tom swung his gaze back toward the trees and jerked at the sight awaiting him. Standing there in all its glory was what looked like a T-Rex. As he watched, it kept raising its nose and sniffing the air. Feeling him jerk, Kate peered over his shoulder and gasped. Realizing their closeness was a comfort, she pressed against him and whispered in his ear, "What do you think it's doing?"

"It's casting for a scent." He wet his finger and held it in the light breeze. It was coldest on the side opposite the Rex's direction. "Damn, we're upwind of it. Still, we're about a thousand feet away, maybe it smells something else," not believing it for a second. With her in such close proximity, it was now obvious she was wearing a light scented perfume. He laid his face against her hair. "Hey, kiddo, I just got plan 'A'. Do you have any of your perfume with you?"

"Yes, why?"

"Get it out."

She dug into a pocket and produced a small round tube. "It's a mini-spray."

Her hand was shaking a little, so he steadied it while visually checking the vial. "That ought to work. Spritz a little more on yourself and then do me. I want us to smell like anything but something edible."

Finally, she smiled again. "That's pretty clever, Dr. Hughes. A meat eater certainly has no interest in wild flowers." She randomly misted her skirt and blouse, and then did his shirt and pants.

Tom turned half towards her. "I don't want to be gross, but shoot some under my arms. Do yours, too."

When she finished, he looked away. "Um, this is personal I know, but it's important. Are you in your period?"

Kate seemed oddly surprised by the question, but simply replied, "No."

He nodded. "That's a break. No matter how faint the odor may be, it's easy for an animal to detect, especially for a rogue male. I think that's what we have here."

They leaned together and silently watched the Rex. About five minutes later, it stopped checking the air, then circled back into the trees. After watching the development, she leaned away and patted him on the back. "It looks like your idea is working, Dr. Hughes."

Tom took a deep breath, then turned to face her. "Yeah, it seems to have lost its interest." His gaze fell to her legs.

She followed the direction of his eyes. "You really are a leg man."

He grinned. "Yeah, but this time I'm looking at your shoes. I was going to say something earlier but I forgot during the excitement. You need to take them off and tuck them in your waistband. The heel will prevent them from slipping so they won't be in your way. When we get to the crack in the rock, I'll try and break the heels off. You'll be better off in flats, even if they are slanted. Besides, I don't want you ruining the chance to sell my memoirs."

Kate hung her head and thought for a minute. "Okay, I give up. Why in the world would my wearing high-heeled shoes interfere with the sale of a book?" She put an arm on top of his shoulder and rested her chin on it. "This had better be good."

He put his thumbs together and shaped a square with the flat of his hands. "Just picture it. The publisher calls. He says 'Great stuff, Dr. Hughes, except for the part about the lady outrunning a T-Rex in high-heels. That was a bit much'."

She brought her hands to her cheeks and animatedly exclaimed, "Gosh, you're right, how inconsiderate of me."

They bumped shoulders and laughed. She scooted back and lay on her side, resting her head on an arm. Kate closed her eyes and expelled a sigh of temporary contentment.

Tom had turned back and was checking on their latest acquaintance, when there was a thrashing behind him. He spun around, saw that she was up, and had begun screaming at the top of her voice. He hung his head and frustratingly muttered, "So much for Plan 'A'."

Tom jumped up to determine the problem. She pointed at her leg. There was a snake wrapped around it. It didn't appear to be biting, just hanging on for simple survival. The hair on the back of Tom's neck stood up ... he froze. The Rex roared a second later. Tom whirled.

A huge beast broke through the tree line and started running their way. Tom's mind became mush and his single burning desire was for enough time to formulate Plan 'B'. He abandoned trying to think and simply reacted. Tom screamed his apology as a fist flew through the air. He caught her limp form and half laid, half threw it behind a large clump of ferns.

Tom ran toward the crack in the rock, knowing he'd never make it. The primary goal now was to draw the Rex away from Miss Bright. It was strange what started rambling through his mind. The Rex canted from side to side as it ran, reminding him of a loud chicken with a big head.

The self-preservation part of him chimed in, ridiculing his idea, 'chickens don't have six-inch teeth'. His foot slipped a little in the soft, moist soil ... a mental light came on. "Alright you big chump, let's match brawn against brain and see who wins. Plan 'B' coming up."

Tom changed direction, running directly at the Rex. He sucked in as much air as he could hold, letting out a roar of his own. It sounded pitiful. The Rex responded. Tom tried to boost his own bravado. "Show off!"

He knew it was an optical illusion, but swore the Rex doubled in size with every ten feet they got closer. Here it comes, wait for it. Wait ... wait ... wait ... NOW!

Tom planted his left foot and dove to his right. Out of the corner of his eye, he could see the monstrous head come down and around. The Rex's teeth snapped shut next to Tom's left ear and he felt a tug on his hair, then he was rolling and sliding over the stony ground. Sharp edged rocks slashed through his shirt and pants.

The Rex lost its balance; momentum carried it tumbling. It ended up skidding on a shoulder and one side of its face. Tom scrambled up and shook his fist. "That'll teach you to mess with the laws of physics!"

He started a shuffling, sideways run to the rock, but kept one eye on Rex. The animal lay there for a minute breathing hard; it had been a long charge.

Rex lifted its head in the direction of Miss Bright. Tom halted. He searched around in the failing light, gathered a couple of rocks, and threw one at Rex. It fell well short. He scolded himself. "More angle, Tom, more angle."

Another rock flew. It hit the Rex in the back of the head causing it to whip around. The Rex's eyes caught the last rays of the sun, reflecting a fiery, blood red death stare. It chilled Tom's spine, but he waited to see if the beast would come after him again. The Rex was up, running, and closing the gap almost before Tom had a chance to register the action. He spun and ran, realizing too late, the Rex hadn't been running flat out before.

The mysterious passage loomed closer and Tom fervently hoped the Rex would slow instead of risking slamming into the rocks. It would buy him precious seconds. Scant steps before reaching the opening, something bumped Tom over to one side. He sidestepped to correct, but a shoulder clipped one ragged edge of the opening, spinning him around on the way in. His head smashed against a low hanging protrusion just inside the darkened portal. The blow caused him to stagger back toward the waiting Rex.

Dizzy, confused, and hurt, he fell part way out of the rocky sanctuary. A mouth full of teeth began its descent. Tom laughed in his semi-delirious state. His last conscious thought was a question. Who'd eat him first, the Rex, or the animal inside tugging on his foot?

Tom narrowly escapes from the Tyrannosaurus Rex

"Life is thick sown with thorns, and I know no other remedy than to pass quickly through them. The longer we dwell on our misfortunes, the greater is their power to harm us."

- Voltaire

Chapter 8
Reincarnation

Thomas Einstein Hughes was somehow dreadfully cognizant of his death. His consciousness floated, sans body, in a swirling vapor of indescribable proportion and density. He considered it amazing that his thought process had apparently remained the same, but was confident it would surely change.

Since time probably didn't exist here, the metamorphosis would seem instantaneous. One 'second' he would be helpless; the next would bring him complete understanding and functionality within his new environment.

Tom believed an angel would soon appear and act as his guide. Just seconds later, a dim figure appeared and broke the featureless gray. He concentrated and it grew clearer, but there was no angel, no tunnel ... and no bright light. A shade of blue coloring appeared in the center of his vision, and began to spread. It was beautiful. With earthly eyes, he would have cried. The image slowly stabilized, and eventually came into focus.

Part of him was disappointed. The blueness was nothing more than a piece of sky, visible through an opening in the top of a cave. His sluggish rationality was fighting against an onerous mental current; it was slow going.

Tom's body experienced a spasmodic reflex when he realized life was still held within. How could that possibly be? The Rex's teeth flashed in his mind's eye. He winced and pushed back; there was a soft lump behind.

Tom tried to relax and take a personal inventory.

First up, only the right eye was working, but by moving it back and forth, he also thought the left eye could be felt pressing against its eyelid. His left arm was pinned against something and he couldn't see it with just the one eye because his head was unable to swivel in that direction.

He attempted to move his right arm and nothing happened. Tom gazed down at his right shoulder. After staring for a moment, he slowly closed the eye and fought to keep from choking on the bile churning in his stomach. There was no arm. The shirtsleeve ended in a bloody rag. His breaths of ragged gasps gradually began to slow. He reopened his eye and started to resurvey the rest of his body. The right leg was gone below the knee, while the left appeared intact. The upper left side of his torso remained a mystery.

In an effort to find calm, he tried piecing an explanation together. Following a short interval, a plausible story took shape. An animal in the cave must have yanked his body into the opening. His right arm must have fallen back, exposed, and the Rex tore it off. The other animal must be smaller, being able to enter the cave, and it must have sated its lesser appetite with just his lower right leg. Why didn't he bleed to death?

Abruptly, he remembered saliva could sometimes act as a coagulant. The animal must have licked the wounds, which staved off the bleeding. It would also inadvertently ensure it of at least one more fresh meat meal. Tom realized his body was nothing more than leftovers in a take-home box, and that this wasn't life after all; death had just been postponed.

The early morning light from overhead became partially blocked, interrupting his thoughts. There was a loud sniffing sound. Tom looked up and knew he'd recognize that nostril anywhere. It was the Rex. He cringed, closed the one good eye, and jockeyed his position ... trying to become part of the rock wall.

Tom jerked as something fell into his lap. He looked down and found a mat of bloody, auburn colored hair. He squirmed and screamed while gawking at Miss Bright's head. The cave walls began to swim and fade. Tom coughed and spat out the rancid bile he had managed to keep down before. The head appeared to be moving of its own accord. His mind whirled, and then mercifully, he passed out.

Kate's eyelids fluttered. She lifted her head and watched him loll against the wall and become still. The screaming had caused her ears to ring.

Her last recollection was being hit out in the field. Before thinking, she punched him in the arm, then began massaging her jaw. An instant feeling of guilt came over her as she realized he must have somehow saved her life.

She groaned and rose to examine him. His left eye was glued shut with blood that had run down from a shallow wound above the ear. His right leg was folded back under the thigh and buttocks, and the right arm was pinned behind his body. The right side of his head and shoulder were badly scraped and somewhat grisly.

Kate managed to shift his weight, which released his arm, then worked on freeing the leg. She was thankful for a rip in the bottom of her skirt, because it wouldn't have been possible to tear off a piece without it. She laid him down and placed the piece of fabric under his head.

Kate found a puddle inside the cave and used a section of Tom's shirt to cleanse his face and wounds.

After a short time, Tom's drowning conscious came up for air. The first feeling he had was the pricks of a thousand pins and needles in his right arm and leg. Even before opening his eye, he thought about the amputees' stories he had read discussing feeling the presence of missing limbs. It existed only in the mind and was termed phantom pain. Tom expected this was a first-hand experience.

The cool damp cloth felt wonderful on his face; his eyes finally opened wide. He immediately noticed the plurality of vision. His depth perception returned, too. Tom moved his eyes and they settled on the angel. She didn't look so great. He blinked to clear his vision but it didn't make her look any better, and now, it was obvious her wings were missing.

His voice cracked, but the words spilled out, "Are you an angel?"

Kate leaned down and kissed his now clean forehead. She whispered, "If it makes you feel better, I'll be anything you want."

"A child can ask a thousand questions that the wisest man cannot answer."
- J. Abbott

Chapter 9
Puzzles

Kate left Tom to rest and started exploring their new home. There were several small alcoves where animal droppings were found, but each recess was presently empty. The cave they currently occupied was only a minor frontal notch compared to the much larger cavern behind.

Just inside the rear main opening was a deep, clear pool off to the left. A stream flowed into its shallow end. Upon examination of the streambed, she found many rocks with hollowed centers that would serve as cups or dishes if necessary. Kate picked out a rock cup, filled it with water, and cautiously wafted its scent toward her nose. It had a faint mineral odor, but after a sip, it seemed to taste fine.

She wished she had a field test kit, although at this point, what choice was there? At least they didn't have to worry about PCB's and the industrial runoff of the twentieth century. Her stomach began rumbling, so she refilled the cup and took a meal tablet. She checked her skirt pocket and found it contained enough food pills to last the two of them perhaps a week.

Kate decided to check back on Dr. Hughes after an hour of investigation, filling two cups before leaving their water supply.

She found him sitting up. "Well, I'm somewhat surprised to find you awake. The possibility of a concussion really had me worried."

"If you happened to get the license plate of that truck, I'll file suit and we'll be set for life. I remember the Rex bumping me just before reaching the opening, rebounding off the walls, hitting my head, and the Rex about to eat me. After that it's a complete blank. When I first awoke, I thought I was somewhere in the afterlife. It's obvious now the Rex didn't get me, so I really owe you one for pulling me out of danger."

She returned a quizzical stare. "It couldn't have been me that saved you. As far as I'm aware, I was still laying out in the field ... unconscious. I assumed you must have come back at some point and carried me into the cave."

Tom furrowed his brows. "One of us has got to be wrong. Are you sure you didn't wake up?"

"Positive. The first thing I remember after you punching me, was waking up in here, with us dumped into that corner like a pile of dirty clothes."

He arose and they stood there staring at one another, each thinking the other must be mistaken in their recollection.

Kate broke the mood by setting one bowl down and reaching into her pocket, withdrawing a food tablet. "Here, swallow this and wash it down with some water."

"What is it?"

"It's the nutritional equivalent of an average meal." She couldn't help but laugh. "I have Dutch apple pie and vanilla ice cream for desert if you're interested."

He recognized the referral. Tom smiled and shook his head.

"Oh, ouch ... that was a mistake."

Finally, he ingested the pill and emptied the cup. "That tasted pretty good, is that second one for me, too?"

"Yes, I thought you'd be thirsty. I'd have brought more, but I'm only a two rock woman."

He laughed while draining the second cup, practically choking because of the comment.

Most of the day was spent exploring, becoming familiar with the area and what resources might be useful. The remainder was spent gathering and carrying some of the tall fern fronds for bedding. Kate did the bulk of the collecting since every time Tom bent over he started to get dizzy, although by day's end, he noticed a definite improvement. Even so, she would only let him stand watch and do some of the carrying.

One of the smaller niches off the main corridor in the cave had been floored with greenery for use as a lavatory. They even managed to find some driftwood and kindling. Tom spotted some rock that might be flint. Either way, it sparked when struck. By evening, a comforting fire was built offset from under the opening in the cave's roof, in case it rained. The hole was a perfect vent.

Kate searched through the assortment of pills in her pocket. "Would you care for a snack before bedding down for the night?"

"What's on the menu?"

She scrutinized the tablet. "I'm not sure, I think it's similar to vanilla cake with chocolate frosting."

"Don't have any potato chips and dip, huh?"

"Sorry."

Tom patted his stomach. "Actually, I'm not really hungry, so I think I'll pass. But, thanks for asking."

Kate moaned as she stretched. "I'm going to use the facilities before retiring. I'll be back in a minute."

He called after her, "Don't blame me if the seat's up, I used the outside toilet."

Upon returning, she put some additional pieces of wood on the dwindling flames, softly kicked Dr. Hughes in the leg, then snuggled down against him.

Tom stared at the top of her head. "What was that for?"

"You know I like the grass unwinding to the right, not the left."

He lightly touched his forehead. "Oh, sorry, I'll try and remember."

Kate emitted a low snarl. "Ha, I think you did it on purpose."

"You're correct, I like hearing you growl."

Both needed the laugh.

She checked over her shoulder. "How are you feeling?"

"Much better, thank you. I was almost afraid to lower my head, but it seems okay now. Please don't think I'm complaining, but the future isn't exactly what I expected."

The criticism brought a gentle elbow to his ribs.

They were laying on their sides and fit together like spoons. His arm was draped over her stomach. She reached down and covered his hand with hers.

Tom shifted position slightly to get more comfortable. "Hey, kiddo, I've got some questions for you. Before the Steg took off and everything gravitated downhill from there, I think you had just started explaining why this Picus character wants to get back at me.

Also, last night you mentioned something about volunteering for a project when you were sixteen and said 'that was another story'. That really has me curious. I'd like that clarified if you feel comfortable enough. I'd also like to know what you think our chances are of being rescued ... good or bad.

Lastly, have you given any more thought as to which one of us saved the other? Not that it matters, it's just bugging the hell out of me, not being able to remember. I'm starting to wonder if that bump on the head was worse than I thought."

After a lengthy silence, she squeezed his hand. "That's a lot to confront at once. I need some time to think. If I promise to try and cover the ground sometime tomorrow, would that be satisfactory?"

"Okay, I'll let you off the hook for now, just don't forget."

Kate nodded in agreement as Tom added the final statement of the evening. "I hope the neighbors leave us alone."

Shortly following his remark, as they fell asleep, both were puzzling over the answer to the same question.

A soft ray of light fell across Tom's eyes. He awoke and found the moon shining through one of the holes above. What shocked him was its size. Then he remembered that earlier in earth's history, the moon was much closer. It had to be since the earth was spinning faster. It was all just a function in conserving the law of angular momentum concerning a two body planetary system. There was something else different, but it remained just beyond his threshold of perception. It was poised on the tip of his mental tongue, but try as he might, he couldn't taste the answer. He turned over and tried going back to sleep.

Minutes later, he stared back up. Tom smiled, because what had eluded him before was now obvious. Copernicus was shifted far from its normal position. His scientific curiosity was sated. He breathed a satisfied sigh and closed his eyes, realizing the movement would be hard to detect, especially over a short period of time, but apparently in the Jurassic, the moon was still rotating more than exactly once each orbit.

"Among so many sad realities we can but ill endure to rob anticipation of its pleasant visions."

- Giles

Chapter 10
Solutions

Kate awoke at first light and arose to relieve herself in the improvised lavatory. Since it was so early, and deciding more sleep was necessary, she sat next to Dr. Hughes and maneuvered his head onto her lap when she returned.

He woke briefly, turned on his side, smacked his lips, mumbled something, and then fell quickly back into a deep sleep. Kate didn't last much longer.

The sound of someone humming buoyed Tom's conscious-self closer to the surface of awareness. He watched through bleary eyes as a bulky man dressed entirely in white walked past the opening of their alcove and continue down the cave's main corridor. Thinking this had to be a dream, or a delusion induced by his head injury, he simply turned on his opposite side and slept again.

Only another hour passed prior to Tom's bladder prodding him back awake. He fluffed the pillow, shifted his head, and pulled the blanket tighter around him. His eyes popped open. Close to the pillow was a neat pile of clean clothes. All the newly acquired items were inspected as if totally alien.

He made the decision to wash before donning the fresh attire, but remembered the condition of his head, so gingerly elevated his body into a standing position. Tom walked to the cave's front opening and cautiously peeked out around one corner, then the other, ever watchful for their large friend with all the teeth. The one outside wall curved back in on itself, so he checked that location, too. There was nothing to be seen in any direction ... no Miss Bright either.

Mother nature was now urging him, so Tom reentered the cave with the inside lavatory becoming the immediate goal. He turned the corner into the small recess and stopped in his tracks. There in front of him, was a toilet, sink, and what appeared to be a water recycling system. As silly as it seemed, it was somewhat disappointing not to see a shower. At that instant, Tom wasn't sure if they were being rescued, or vying for the cover of Cave Beautiful.

With a quiet laugh, the thought occurred to him that maybe the outside area should be rechecked for a newly acquired address and a mailbox. Tom raised the seat and thankfully alleviated his internal pressure.

Having finished with the first order of the day, he noticed the sink even had a soap dispenser. He washed his hands while slowly tossing his head from side to side, trying to work out the kinks from the night. It was a relief not to feel any pain or dizziness. As he exited the small room, he remembered to lower the seat, thinking that was one hassle they could do without.

Tom stood quietly in the main passageway, listening for any telltale noise. A low murmur could be heard in the direction of the large cavern in back. He pivoted in that direction, making it the next objective. As he neared the large portal, the murmuring resolved into at least two separate voices, one of which was identified as Miss Bright's.

When Tom entered the huge open space, the voices became silent and two faces turned his way ... hers, and the one belonging to the man in white. Tom couldn't help but chuckle, because the newcomer strongly reminded him of the character, Otho, in the movie "Beetlejuice".

He was tall, perhaps six feet, but his body was round, probably tipping the scales at about 240 pounds. His square face, dark hair and eyes, and hard-set jaw made him look pompous, exuding an air of obvious self-importance.

Both men noticed Miss Bright move and purposely position herself strategically between them. Only the man in white knew why. An easily discernable tension was in her voice. "Dr. Thomas Hughes, I'd like to introduce Dr. Jiaan Picus." Picus flinched at the mention of his name, peeking around Miss Bright to observe the reaction. It didn't appear well received.

The smile that had been on Tom's face flipped and formed a snarl. His eyes narrowed and his face flamed red with anger. "I wouldn't harm you for the world, Miss Bright, so I think you should move aside. There's a little matter of risking our lives that I'd like to discuss with Picus."

As Tom approached, his intellect wondered if the strategy that fooled the Rex would work on Miss Bright.

Kate extended her hands, pleading, "It was an accident, Dr. Hughes."

He couldn't help but recall one of her proudly hailed statistics. "After forty years without a malfunction, I find that unlikely."

Picus harrumphed, "I thought you said he wouldn't act like an enraged Neanderthal."

Kate became as busy as a referee in a tag-team wrestling match. "You're not helping things, Dr. Picus."

Tom had stopped and considered listening to Miss Bright's explanation, but Picus' inflammatory comment pulled the firing cord on his cannon of fiery emotion. To Kate's complete surprise, Tom charged directly toward her. At the last instant before collision, he head faked right, then spun and went around her left side with all the finesse of a halfback on a touchdown run.

He lowered his shoulder and caught Picus in the stomach. There was a heavy expulsion of air as they both tumbled into the pool. Picus was having difficulty moving. The blow must have stunned him. Tom pulled Picus up, holding him by his suit.

A surprisingly loud shout came from behind them. "Stop! I've had enough of your combined male attitudes! Dr. Hughes, release Dr. Picus immediately."

Considering the position Picus was in, Tom didn't think that was a truly good idea, but with a smile, he obeyed the command. Picus fell back into the water and started splashing around trying to regain his footing.

Tom stood there with his arms spread out, and innocently as possible simply offered, "I just did as instructed, boss."

Kate stomped a foot and frantically waved her hands in the air. "Oh, I capitulate!"

Tom finally offered a hand to Picus who, under the circumstances, gladly accepted. "Alright, Picus, I'll take time and listen to your story, but it had better be good, otherwise we'll continue the current conversation at another time... if you get my drift."

Picus wasn't sure he understood the statement's full meaning, but nodded enthusiastically, temporarily agreeing to almost anything so his hand could be freed from Tom's vise like grip. Picus stumbled exiting the pool and dropped to one knee on the mud bank. Tom noticed the suit not only looked completely dry, but when Picus stood, the wet mud fell off without even leaving a mark.

Kate scowled at Tom. "Don't you have anything to say to Dr. Picus? I told him you'd understand."

Tom gazed at Picus while fingering the suit. "Nice material."

Kate rolled her eyes and expelled a heavy sigh.

Tom gestured apologetically with his hands. "Look, Miss Bright, this isn't exactly all my fault. If you would have tried explaining the situation before you just blurted out who Picus was, I might have been able to contain myself. You knew how I'd feel when I first met him. As I recall, you weren't exactly thrilled by his actions either. Besides, his remark didn't help things. So, how about if we all just start over and see how it progresses."

Picus appeared fully recovered except for his wet hair. "I'm all for that reasoning, Kate. Admittedly, it was a delicate set of circumstances."

Tom's gaze switched to Miss Bright. "Kate?"

"Yes. My name is Khattyba Bright. Please ... call me Kate."

"Dr. Khattyba Bright," Picus corrected.

Tom chuckled. "How about if the first thing we do is drop all the formality. It sounds like a healthcare convention. From now on, I'm just Tom, and if there are no objections, I'll refer to you as Kate and Jiaan. Is that an acceptable beginning?"

"Actually, if you don't mind, Tom, I prefer 'John'."

"Fine ... John it is."

Picus pointed to the rocks. "Let's sit ... and I believe the first order of business is for me to explain what happened. I've already started telling Kate this whole unfortunate incident is the result of a miscalculation. However, in all honesty, since I willingly took the risk, the blame must rest directly with me.

Kate's mentioned you've been told about the twenty individuals raised without the benefit of a family. Because of that, we, meaning TheTwenty, feel like we're all brothers and sisters, and have a tendency to look after one another, sometimes rather fanatically, I'm afraid.

When it was confirmed you were being brought forward in time, everyone was thrilled. To meet the one person most responsible for the origin of time travel would truly be considered a privilege."

Tom was signaling Kate. "Sorry, John, I'm not trying to be rude, but I'm hungry as hell and just want to ask Kate if she has any of those food tablets left."

John shook his head. "Where are my manners? I don't believe any of us have eaten, and I did bring an auto-cooker. I propose we comfort ourselves with food and drink, relax, and discuss our situation as civilized life forms. Do I hear any abstentions?" He smiled. "No, I didn't think I would."

Tom held up a finger. "Yes, I remember ... I believe it was Doran who said, 'A good dinner sharpens wit, while it softens the heart'."

John was visibly impressed. "Well articulated, Tom."

Unspoken words passed between Kate's and John's eyes that were impossible for Tom to miss. Something else was going on that obviously involved him ... and it made him uneasy.

John wheeled the auto-cooker near their stone seats and brought up the menu screen. "Alright, the chef is now accepting orders. Tom, in a sense, you're the guest of honor. What would you like?"

"Anything?"

"Anything you want."

"Scrambled eggs with a light dash of pepper, bacon, hash browns with margarine, decaf coffee with cream and sugar, and an orange juice ... please."

"Kate?"

"Make that two, except replace the coffee with milk."

"You are both making this almost too easy; I was hoping to show off what I can do with one of these machines."

Tom silently hoped John would do a better job with the auto-cooker than the TMTs.

John's fingers flew over the touch pads and a minute later he remarked, "The food is ready so fast it almost seems anti-climatic to say, 'Come and get it'."

One of the storage compartments held plastic utensils including, to Tom's surprise, stir sticks. Everyone picked up their plate of food and pulled up a rock, so to speak.

As Tom scooped up another forkful of food, the comment had to be made, "This is completely synthetic, right?"

John's mouth was full, so Kate fielded the question. "Nothing but a collection of separately stored molecules. Everything is simply combined on a preprogrammed ratio, although certain variables can be adjusted to suit the individual's taste.

The molecule containers can be re-supplied any time day or night, in any quantity, right up to the limit of the machine. I don't know of anyone who doesn't have an auto-cooker; in fact, all living spaces constructed in the last hundred years have been equipped with built-in units."

Tom smiled at Kate. "Well, I guess this answers the question about our being rescued."

John pensively looked away. Tom caught the action. "Uh, this is a rescue mission, is it not?"

John's gaze swung back. "The long term answer is 'yes', but the short is 'not immediately'. Because of what I attempted, some uniquely important information has surfaced. Kate told me you know we've been unable to visit our future. This new data may shed some light on why we have been unsuccessful.

We've found that going into the past requires less energy than returning to the future. Why ... we're not sure, but the percentage difference has always been slight. Of course, compared to coming this far back, our previous travels have been a relatively short distance ... as measured in time.

The reason I sent you into the past in the first place is two fold. One, I simply wanted to flaunt our technology, which I assumed you'd enjoy.

Two, and more importantly, I wanted the chance for the three of us to talk alone, undisturbed."

As obvious as the question might appear, Tom still felt compelled to ask, "Wouldn't an empty office somewhere have served as well?"

John stared intently into Tom's eyes. "If the answers I was looking for hadn't been satisfactory, you would have been left alone in the far distant past, with only the supplies and equipment necessary to keep you safe and healthy."

Tom rose and took a step towards John. "What did I ever do to you?"

“This has nothing to do with me. It’s all about Kate.”

Another step. “Okay, what did I ever do to Kate?”

“It’s not what you’ve done, but what you might have done.”

Tom looked Picus square in the eyes and balled his fists. “Look, John, I admire the fact you’re so willing to defend Kate, but I’m getting real tired of twenty questions. Please make your point, or I’m really going to lose my temper.”

John looked at Kate, then back to Tom. “I take it she didn’t tell you about her little encounter with you before?”

Now Tom was really confused. “I’ve no idea what you’re talking about, John, not a single clue.”

“Wait a minute, John. I think it’s my turn to do a little confessing. I’ve been trying to tell you about this, Tom, but the timing was just wrong. Last night you asked about the ‘that’s another story’ comment I made at dinner. Here’s what happened.

I told you I was interested in the latter half of the twentieth century. When I was sixteen, a team was formed to take a trip incognito into the 1990’s. I had read about you in books and realized you would have been in your last year of high school in 1995 through 1996. It seemed like an excellent opportunity to learn about you first hand.

You were attending the school in Royal Oak, so I became enrolled in the neighboring Birmingham school as a transfer student. One thing about time travel, it’s easy to supply needed paperwork. Your best friends at the time were Ted, Charles, and Karl. Do you recall the girls Ted and Karl were dating at the time?”

“Give me a sec.” Tom’s eyes searched the cavern. “One was Brenda, the other was called Boots ... I never did know her real name.”

“Boot’s name was Nancy,” Kate explained. “Both girls went to Birmingham, right?”

“Yes.”

“I was acquainted with them. They became one of my sources to learn about you. One day Ted and Brenda were at the local restaurant near Normandy road and Woodward Avenue. Ted was making a phone call inside. Brenda went in to join him and jumped up on the counter by the phone. When she did ...”

Tom’s face lit up. “The counter broke! It fell on the back of her right calf and cut it. We all went to my house because it was closest. I carried her into the bathroom and made her stand on the toilet lid with her leg over the sink so I could clean it with an antiseptic. I thought it was bad enough a doctor should examine it, so drove her to the emergency room at the community hospital. They must have told you about it the next day.”

“Actually, I was at the restaurant when it happened. Nancy told me where you were all going and gave me your phone number. I went home, waited a couple hours, and then called to see how Brenda was doing. You answered the phone and when I found out she wasn’t there, we ended up talking anyway. Do you recall the event?”

“Yes, I think so ... your name was Janet! In fact, we talked for quite a while. I distinctly remember I liked listening to your voice. It was sensitive and compassionate. No wonder you know so much about me, but I still have no idea what John is talking about.”

Kate took a deep breath. “Okay, here it comes. Because of who you’d grow up to be, and the kind, pleasant way you were when young, I developed a schoolgirl crush on you. There, I've finally confessed.

I think John was worried I'd fall in love with you, and you would turn out to be a cad and break my heart. In all honesty, I had no fear of that happening because of the negative data we received about you and your personality. After all, your friends did have you removed from your earlier positions. Nice people generally don't have that done to them, especially by their associates.

When I first met you at the restaurant in Prescott, I was prepared to shred you into confetti, but you fooled me. You turned out to be nice, and you've been even nicer ever since. I constantly thought of what John had warned me about and kept my guard up, but now, I'm thoroughly convinced I want to keep seeing you."

"So, you had John bring me back to the Jurassic just in case I turned out to be a total cad. Isn't that a little extreme ... to say the absolute least?"

John shook his head. "No, Kate didn't know anything about this; it was all my idea. She would have never agreed.

Continuing with my story, we shouldn't be in the Jurassic, because the machines were programmed to transport you toward the Mississippian Epoch of the Paleozoic. Game would have been easy to catch, the temperatures were moderate, and there weren't any large carnivores. Unfortunately, the TMTs required much more energy than forecast, and fell about two hundred million years short of their goal.

Since what I was doing was completely illegal, not to mention unethical, I overrode all the warning flags in order to engage my program as coded. When the fail-safe code deduced the energy shortage, it took the first pair of TMTs as far as possible, then reintegrated them.

The program in the remaining TMTs that transported the two of you was updated to reflect the change, and even though Kate could have been transported back further because she massed less, she wasn't because the original programming had the two of you traveling in tandem, so that criteria was honored.

I originally expected at least a week to determine the results of trial runs. I presume I would have easily found all the discrepancies given time. When I heard the two of you were coming back in only one day, I panicked and pulled the safeties because I was convinced I knew what I was doing. It was shortly after the second set of TMTs was energized that I found the error.

When I realized what part of history you integrated into, I immediately sent one of my aids to check and report on your condition. At first, things didn't look that bad, but then you had the encounter with the Tyrannosaur and I thought you'd both been killed. I'd have obviously been responsible.

Larry, my aid, was in the cave when you hit your head and fell back. He pulled you in. After the beast left the area, Larry retrieved Kate and carried her into the cave, putting the two of you together, then contacted me for instructions. Therefore, although not humorous at all, this has been a comedy of errors ... all mine."

Tom had managed to calm down as he listened. "Even assuming all of this is true, why can't we go back?"

John continued once more. "That's what the new data is all about. Going forward in time over long distances uses much more energy than previously thought necessary. Until now, the maximum distance we've traveled back has been a scant five hundred years. As you re-approach your original timeline, energy is used at an ever-increasing rate. It's also directly proportional to mass. The more massive an object, the more energy it consumes during transfer."

"John, I assume you're speaking figuratively. By more massive, you mean more atoms, therefore a larger signature map, more tachyons to contain the map, thereby requiring more energy. I hope that's right, otherwise you've completely lost me."

"Yes, that's correct. I apologize. I didn't intend to confuse you. It's interesting that the further back in time you travel, the required energy level drops as you get farther from your initial timeline.

Larry came directly here as you did, even though he had to pass through an additional three hundred years. Of course, compared to one hundred fifty million, that was an insignificant increase.

The underlying importance is that in order to get back, he required six alternate-leads with me sending him full matter banks at each stop. The TE banks were never used as much, but the carbon was depleted at every instance."

"What about all the stuff you've had sent back? The cooker, sink, toilet, etc.?"

"Those things are extremely low mass. They're manufactured with silicon aero gels and reinforced with carbon fiber materials. Strong, light, but extremely brittle, so don't slam the toilet seat or it might splinter.

All of those items could probably be sent back to our time on one matter bank. The water recycler was sent empty, of course, and only weighs twelve pounds total, including filters. I, on the other hand, weighing in at two hundred fifty, strapped an additional carbon bank on the MBH and tied the input/output ports together to make the jump without interruptions. That's coming back in time, going forward will require much more matter."

"So, it's not a question of physically getting back, but just finding the best logical approach to execute the task?"

"That's correct."

"Where do we start?"

"I asked Larry to evaluate his forward jump sequence. I'll contact him and see if the analysis is finished. That will help us decide our first step. Kate was kind enough to volunteer cleaning up after we eat. She can assist me in the determination when finished."

"That sounds fine to me. I think I'll take a look around outside, maybe go for a short walk."

"Alright, but please ... be careful."

"You bet. I'll see you later. Oh ... John."

"Yes?"

"I'm just curious. Were you one of those who thought it'd be more expedient for me to have an accident instead of being conveyed forward?"

John blinked, then frowned. "Who told you that?"

Tom's eyes rolled towards Kate. "A futuristic little bird."

She pouted and looked away.

John leaned back. "Kate, what's this all about? You know the council member was joking when he spoke those words. It was just a humorous interlude to keep the discussion from stalling."

Kate grinned. "I told you Tom was stubborn. I needed all the leverage I could muster ... so," she shrugged, "I embellished a little."

They all laughed.

Tom walked out along the main corridor, trying to remember the rules to an old participation song in his collection. He could see the record jacket in his mind. It was blue against a white background with the performers picture in the upper right hand corner. Finally, he managed to plug in Kate's name, singing softly to himself.

"Kate, Kate, bo bate, banana fanna fo fate, fee fi mo mate, Kate."

He stopped, mumbling aloud while going through the words again. "Bate, as in bait ... fate, mate? You'd better watch yourself around this lady, Tom. Real close."

He was grinning widely nevertheless.

"We should never so entirely avoid danger as to appear irresolute and cowardly; but, at the same time, we should avoid unnecessarily exposing ourselves to danger, than which nothing can be more foolish."

- Cicero

Chapter 11
Beware The Local Fauna

Tom continued along the twisting maze that formed the main route through their stone castle. In a sense, the simple abode was actually pleasant. The natural skylights admitted adequate illumination for navigation and provided fresh circulating air, although the overhead openings did create inside puddles, and one had to be careful of their footfalls, unless they enjoyed wet shoes and socks. Out of curiosity, he revisited the newly acquired lavatory. It was interesting to note that the output of both the sink and toilet fed directly back into the recycling tank.

Tom turned the cold-water handle, cupped his hands under the faucet, and drank deeply. The refreshing liquid tasted surprisingly good. He looked for something to dry his hands, and after not seeing anything, shook them off and then wiped the remaining moisture on his pants. Upon exiting, he made a mental note to test John's sense of humor by complaining about the lack of paper towels and drinking cups.

The cave's opening loomed close ahead when a loud crunching sound caught his attention. A chuffing of air and the appearance of a massive, now familiar nose, brought him to a sudden halt. Their large, many-toothed friend had returned to pay a visit. Tom stepped around a large indent of water, pressed against the inner wall, and became perfectly still.

The slow grinding of huge toes on small stones resumed as the Rex moved along the exterior wall. Tom began to worry at the realization that the Rex's movements could be heard so easily through the wall. There had been no reason to consider how thick, or thin, the wall was before.

The movement outside stopped and the snuffling restarted. Tom's hearing had directed his vision along the wall. A small ray of light was cut off as the animal's nose found a scent that seemed to interest it. The area around the light source became hazy as a heavy snort of air blew in the dirt that had settled there. It became completely quiet. Tom's chest reverberated with his rapidly beating heart. His muscles felt like over-wound clock springs.

The wall burst inward without any warning. A heavy cloud of dust made seeing impossible. Tom coughed and his eyes started tearing. He waved his hands to clear the air. His fingers brushed against something unnervingly close.

Slowly, the ghostly outline of an enormous head struggling to press through the rock appeared less than a foot in front of Tom's face. The teeth were unbelievably large from his perspective. Its breath fouled the air with odors of a meat locker when its refrigeration unit had failed.

Fortunately, as the hole grew larger, the remaining wall became thicker, while the monster thrashed trying to gain entry. It was now a mere six inches away from Tom. With its head jammed in the hole, its jaws were unable to open, but the Rex's front teeth gnashed together like a horse cribbing on a fence rail.

The monstrous head settled for a moment, then started squirming again, but was unable to advance further. Tom was pressed to the wall so hard the rock was digging into his back, causing a sharp pain. He was so terrified that the thought of rolling one way or the other hadn't entered his mind. Finally, Tom alternately tried moving his legs, but both were held fast by rubble.

Just as suddenly as the traumatic event had started, it seemed to end. The giant muzzle stopped moving and appeared to give up.

As the air cleared, Tom could see the beast's left eye staring back at him. The ridge above it was torn and bleeding down into the eye. The Rex kept blinking, trying to clear its vision. There were several other lacerations around the lips, mouth, and jaw. The animal's breathing had slowed, becoming deep and throaty.

Going against all common sense, Tom reached out and touched the nose. It was warm, and the skin was surprisingly supple, not hard and scaly as he might have expected.

The beast's breathing changed cadence and it tensed, drawing back somewhat from the touch. Tom extended his reach and softly stroked its nose. The deep breaths returned and the great mass of flesh appeared to relax; the eye closed completely.

Tom bent over, clearing the rocks from around one leg, then the other. He shifted his weight and checked their status. They seemed uninjured. He eased out his shirttail, ripped off a large piece, turned, and then dipped it into a nearby puddle.

The tearing noise had caused the injured eye to reopen. Tom gently applied the wet rag to the animal's face as the eye followed its movements. The eyelid slid down, and the head just sat there as if in utter defeat and humiliation.

Tom spoke softly. "Hey, buddy, you're going to be pretty sore tomorrow. I bet this feels good though, huh. Let's see if you'll let me clean all those cuts. It looks like you just went fifteen rounds with some body basher."

The shirttail rag was rinsed and wrung out. Tom slowly approached the left side of the animal's skull, stepping carefully among the broken rocks. The eye remained closed through all of his movements. Tom clinched his teeth and gingerly dabbed the eye ridge with the damp cloth. Except for breathing, the animal remained motionless. His hand jerked back as a deep guttural growl emitted from the animal's throat. Only then did the eye reopen, and seemed to question the discontinuance of the soothing first aid.

Tom's heart was racing, but he reapplied the rag. "So, that's your way of saying you like this ... I hope."

His left hand stroked the nose as the right dabbed at the wound in an attempt to stanch the bleeding. The entire procedure of rinsing, dabbing, and stroking was repeated twice more; then the head began to withdraw. Tom backed against the wall again as the animal straightened and walked away.

Afterward, he cautiously leaned out the new side exit and called, "Take two tons of aspirin and call me in the morning, OK?"

The animal stopped at the sound of his voice. The huge head swung around, the low growl was issued once more, then the Rex left.

Tom was so engrossed in watching the Rex leave, and thinking about what had just transpired, he practically jumped through the hole when Kate's hand touched his shoulder.

She stared open mouthed, her face full of fear and concern. "What happened?"

"Our rather bulky friend made an unannounced social call. He didn't seem to care for our front entrance, so made his own. I have to admit, it's the first time I've heard of 'bring your own door'."

"Tom, this isn't some cute little squirrel you feed pieces of bread."

He laughed. "It's funny you should say that, because I was frightened into pretty much the same conclusion, even though he does remind me of an oversized Veronica with an attitude problem."

Tom looked away, and Kate knew there was more. "What are you not telling me?"

"Uh, I cleaned its wounds."

She grimaced.

Tom imagined her auditory signal etching the thought on some conscious level blackboard, while she mentally scanned the words over and over in disbelief. Then she would open her eyes wide and ...

"You what!"

Tom looked like a puppy that had just been caught peeing on its master's expensive new rug. "It was hurt ... just laying there as if it'd been defeated. I tried to comfort it. I have the feeling it doesn't want me specifically for a meal. The Rex senses its territory has been invaded and wants to protect it."

"Whether it eats or just kills you, you're still dead. How would you feel if I had taken the same risk?"

Their eyes traded movements. "I think I'd give you the benefit of the doubt and not interfere with something you thought was under control. It's not like I invited him. It just happened. The next thing I knew, there was this giant head in front of me, and it couldn't advance any further. I took a chance and the animal seemed to respond in a positive manner. It'll be back, I'm sure of that. We'll see what happens then."

The comments put her off guard. "I don't know whether to spank or kiss you."

Tom flicked his eyebrows. "Do I get a vote?"

Kate shook her head and half grinned. "I'll consider it."

John caught up with them as they stood there sizing up each other. He emitted a low whistle. "This certainly tends to erode my confidence about our safety within the cave."

Tom's gaze finally left Kate's face. "Yeah, for a minute I thought I was back in Detroit getting mugged. It was just like old times when I was a kid." He thought it was a good time to try and change the subject. "So, did the two of you come up with a plan to get us all home?" Tom knew Kate saw through the attempted diversion, but hoped it would work anyway.

She frowned. "Alright, we'll drop it for now." Her look softened. "Besides, I understand the point you're struggling to make.

John feels we can get back just like Larry did. We'll need to execute several alternate leads with someone supplying us recharged matter banks at our layovers. At this point, it's only a question of the TMT count.

The four that brought us here are being repaired. Their components have never been stressed to their limits before. They should be ready in about a week. Larry used the only two others currently available, and their condition is also being assessed. The main problem is John's. It's a special one of a kind creation. He left the plans and specifications with the designers in the tech labs. They're busy duplicating it."

She gave him a pensive look. "It may take two months."

John had been hanging back listening to their dialogue. "I'm sorry, Tom, it was my only option to get here."

"You realized you'd be stuck here for that long, and you came anyway?"

John shrugged. "After considering the circumstances, it seemed the least I could do was provide some sense of safety and minimal creature comforts." He hung his head, searching the ground with his eyes. "I've told Kate that the first thing I'll do when we get back is turn myself over to the authorities."

Tom glanced at her. "I'm glad to hear that, John. That'll keep me from having to do it."

Kate's eyes narrowed, then looked away.

Tom sighed. "Of course, we must reach an agreement on which parts to omit."

Both sets of eyes swung back to his.

John gave a tentative smile. "You'd be willing to do that?"

"Well, first of all, Kate would never forgive me if I didn't, and I couldn't live with those thoughts. Secondly, after all of the crazy stunts I've pulled, I'd be the world's biggest hypocrite to complain about someone just protecting his 'sister'. Just promise me one thing."

"What's that?"

"For God's sake, please don't leave me here alone!"

That brought a laugh from all. John vigorously shook Tom's hand. Kate hugged John, then kissed Tom lightly on the cheek, causing him to blush.

Tom began clearing the pathway.

John turned to exit the cave. "Follow me, Kate, and I'll show you my latest contribution in the advancement of TMTs."

Tom stared at one of the rocks, making it appear to be the subject of an intense examination. "John."

He stopped, half turned, and looked. "Yes?"

"What almost happened to us, especially Kate, really threw me. I'm sorry about this morning. I usually don't go off half-cocked like that. It was pretty dumb."

John's eyes closed and his head slowly bobbed. "That's all well and good, Tom, but I have no idea what you're talking about." He turned and left, conversing with Kate.

Tom interrupted his cleaning effort as Kate and John approached the new opening from outside. "Welcome to Burger Cave ... can I take your order?" Both just returned a blank stare. "Oh, that's right. No cars, no drive-through fast-food places."

John simply replied, “My TMT is in the corner … where the cave’s wall joins the mountain.”

Tom leaned out and saw the machine standing in shadow. “I’d feel a lot better if you brought that thing inside. You never know when my mischievous pet may return. He might just decide on adding both of you to his menu.”

“An excellent idea, but after this little incident, Kate and I already plan on taking it back into the large cavern where we’ll have plenty of space and yet won’t need to worry about being consumed.”

“Do you want some help?”

“No, thank you. Both carbon banks are almost empty and the entire mechanism currently only weighs between ten and fifteen pounds.”

Tom watched as John pressed the release, slipping the ring off the MBH. He smiled knowingly as John carefully checked the power status before sliding his arm through the ring and carrying it in the crux of an elbow. Kate easily managed the empty MBH.

Tom stood aside from his rock tossing and pressed against the wall to allow easy passage as Kate and John reentered the cave’s narrow opening.

“Are you planning to join us?”

“I want to finish clearing the passage, John. No sense in someone turning an ankle on a rock in the dark.”

John nodded. “Good thinking. Come look for us in the cavern when you’ve completed the task. At least I’m confident we’ll be safe back there.”

"A person who is too nice an observer of the business of the crowd, like one who is too curious in observing the labor of bees, will often be stung for his curiosity."

- Pope

Chapter 12
It's Not Fair

Tom rose, stretched his back, and tossed the last of the debris from the cave's primary front corridor.

Kate's insistent plea echoed down the hard rock walls a moment later.

"Tom!" She came racing up to him.

"What is it?"

"John's been bitten. Hurry ... please."

"Damn. Alright, let's go."

As he ran, Tom pictured John lying in the dirt, mangled and bleeding. He felt instant guilt for not having searched the cave more thoroughly, thinking there must be some larger entrance beyond where they had explored, or maybe even some animal's lair.

Tom came to a sudden, perplexed halt, upon entering the large cavern. John was sitting on a rock, apparently unhurt.

He looked up and gave Tom an embarrassed grin. "I told Kate not to bother you. It's probably nothing to be concerned about. I'm just a little lightheaded."

Kate stood silently, looking from one face to the other as the men talked.

"She said something bit you."

John extended the palm of his right hand. There was a small red welt in the web of skin between the thumb and first finger.

Tom knelt to examine the area and could see what appeared as nothing more than a couple of pinpricks.

"Kate and I were discussing my machine when I noticed movement on one of the rock shelves. Its beautiful coloration caught my attention."

Tom closed his eyes and hung his head. "Oh no."

John's brows pinched close together. "What?"

"Bright colors are nature's way of warning that something is either dangerous or highly poisonous. Is the animal still around?"

"No. It scurried off into the safety of some hole."

"Well, what did it look like?"

"It must have been a snake. I couldn't see the whole thing because it was coiled and fairly small. It was a vibrant red, yellow, and black."

An old saying from Tom's childhood came flooding back. 'Red touches black, friend to Jack. Red touches yellow, kill a fellow.'

"Do you remember how the colors were banded together?"

"Is it important?"

"Yes."

"I did get a good look at how it was marked. Let me think for a minute ... I'm sure the head was black. There were wide bands of red and black on the body ... and yes, they were definitely separated by thin bands of yellow."

Tom grimaced. "You're sure there was a yellow stripe between the black and red?"

"Yes. Positive."

"You're describing a coral snake."

"How dangerous are they?"

"Their toxin can be extremely lethal."

John was incredulous. "It's not fair. You practically go head to head with a dinosaur, twice no less, and I'm bitten by some tiny, seemingly insignificant creature, and you're stating I might die?"

"I'm not going to lie to you, John. It's a distinct possibility, mostly because we don't have any anti-venom and no way to treat you."

"Its mouth closed on my hand when I tried to pick it up. I saw the head pivoting from side to side, but I didn't even realize it was biting until I felt a stinging sensation."

"Coral snakes have small fangs, so it depends on how much venom was injected, if any at all. Defensive bites are sometimes dry, in which case we'd just have to watch for infection.

All we can do is keep an eye out for symptoms. For now, let's get you down and comfortable. We'll get some fluids in you and keep you warm."

Tom jumped up. "Kate ... try and contact Larry; maybe we can get some anti-venom shipped back. We'll also need an air-gun or needle, anything."

She ran to John's machine and starting pressing keys on the communication panel. "Tom, the machine went into standby, I need the password to reenter its system."

John had a spasm, then started to convulse.

Tom knelt down again. "Hold on, John's having a problem."

John's body stopped shaking. "I ... I can't ... breathe."

Tom slipped his arm under John's neck and elevated his head. "Is that any better?"

"A little."

"John, we need your machine's password. Please try."

His body shook violently. His tongue was swelling and beginning to protrude from his mouth. When John's teeth clenched, blood ran over his lips.

"Kate, I need help. Find something I can put between his teeth. He's biting his tongue off. There ... that small piece of driftwood, get it ... hurry!"

Kate ran, snatching up the stick. "Here."

"No. Hold it. I'll try and force his jaw open. Put it sideways as far back as you can ... okay, now ... good, that'll work."

"Tom, what are we going to do? We can't let him die."

"I'm really worried, Kate. This is happening too fast. Either the venom is super potent, or he's having a massive allergic reaction. He didn't show you his passwords?"

"He used his master, but it was typed and entered so fast I really didn't get a chance to see it all. It was an unusually long entry. 'Rump' something 'skin' ... I think."

"Rump ... skin ... rumpelstiltskin?"

"Yes! That's it!" Kate hurried back to the machine and typed, 'rumplestiltskin'. "No. It's indicating the password is invalid."

“Wait a second.” Tom laid John’s head down and ran over.

“Let’s see what you typed ... try reversing the L and E.”

Kate changed the spelling and hit the enter key again. “We’re in! Oh, that’s great. I’ll contact Larry immediately and inform him what’s happened.”

Tom put a hand on Kate’s shoulder and gently squeezed. “Hang in there ... John needs us.”

He walked back and checked John’s condition. There was no pain response to a pinch, weak and rapid pulse, skin showing signs of cyanosis, shallow breathing. “Try and hurry, Kate.”

“Okay, the message is on its way. Is he any better?”

“No. Much worse. God, I can’t believe how fast this is hitting him. We’re running out of time. Even if we do get the serum, it might be too late. There must be something else.”

Tom remembered how excited John was about some new update on the machine he could hardly wait to show Kate. “Bring up the screen where you set the direction of travel through time.”

Kate changed the display as Tom walked over. She pointed to a section of the screen. “Here ... two entries ... ‘Forward’ and ‘Back’. When one is selected, it’s highlighted, like this.” Her finger moved to an indicator in a corner of the screen. “If there were enough matter in the banks for transfers, this ‘ready’ would be green. But, as you can see, as I move it onto the various options, nothing happens.”

“Is this space between the selections normal?”

“No, but I don’t think that means anything. John may just have organized his screen differently. It can be programmed to display in any format the user chooses.”

“I thought I saw something flash when you switched. Try it again ... there, the ‘ready’ light glows green when it’s between the selections.”

Kate shook her head and frowned. “That can’t possibly be right. It must be an error.”

“I think it’s something John didn’t have time to tell you about. I’m willing to bet that’s a zero-spin tachyon setting. This machine is set up for a stasis field. He was probably too excited to worry about updating the display’s message text. If the serum can’t get here in time, or if it doesn’t work, this machine may save his life.”

“Tom, we don’t know that’s what this setting means, and even if it does, we don’t know if it’s been tested. That would be a big risk.”

“If push comes to shove, we’ll have no choice.”

Kate looked over at John and groaned. “If we just had a second TMT and sufficiently full carbon banks we could simply use ‘Expel’.”

“That’s the first mention I’ve heard of that. What does it do?”

“When you’re born in our time, part of the post-birth processing is to sample the baby’s DNA and catalog it into the MMT system. Then, any time someone doesn’t feel well they use the ‘Expel’ setting on a machine, and when they are transferred the system scans for any harmful virus or foreign material in the body and doesn’t reintegrate that substance. It’s an instant cure for anything from cancer to the common cold,” she looked up, “probably even snakebite.”

“Wow. So if John could be placed in a stasis field, even if he died, there’d be a chance to revive him later?”

“I don’t see why not. He would be reintegrated without the venom, and medical personnel would be available to handle other problems, such as restarting his heart.”

“Okay. That’s good to know. Let’s hope it doesn’t come to that, but if it does, we must work fast. I doubt if even your superior technology can reverse brain damage from lack of oxygen.”

“That’s true. Once a cell dies, it’s dead forever.”

They both jumped when John’s machine beeped, signaling an incoming message. Kate switched screens and scrolled through the note, while Tom looked over her shoulder.

> ‘Kate: I have something that might help, but there’s a problem. The only anti-venom available is synthetic. I did a remote scan of John’s machine and you don’t have any molecular banks on board, and the machine’s matter banks are too low to accept a direct transfer. We’re still working, but it doesn’t look good. – Larry’

She broke, turning to cry on his chest.

“Kate, are they talking about a synthetic molecular bank?”

Kate sniffed. “Yes, why?”

Tom glanced behind her. “Can we swap the cooker’s unit into the TMT?”

She wiped her face. “Oh, Tom! That just might work.”

After a quick peck on his cheek, she ran to the cooker, slid open a panel, and began searching inside.

Tom started toward the cooker, but before getting halfway there, she was on her way back.

Kate ran by. “Be thankful for quick disconnects and standardized parts.”

A TMT access door was removed, the molecular unit was installed in an empty bracket, and the I/O port delivery tube was swapped from one of the carbon matter banks, leaving the other intact.

Kate changed back to the message screen and typed, ‘Larry: rescan John’s machine and advise – Kate’.

A few minutes later, the answer returned. ‘Kate: Don’t know what you did, but it’ll work. Serum, needle, and field med kit on the way – Larry.’

Tom nodded. “Nice work, Kate, looks like you’ve got things under control. I’ll go check on John.”

“Stay clear of the scan lens on your way over.”

His gaze fell to the front of the TMT. “Check.”

He walked well around the space in front of the lens and knelt. John was laboring to take gasping breaths, and there was a heavy tic in one hand.

Tom was going to get some water and clean John’s face with a cloth, but decided upon waiting until after the serum was administered.

“Cover your eyes, here it comes,” Kate warned.

Light flashed ... and then the encouraging items lay on a transmit mat. Kate scooped them up and hurried over. "Did you ever administer an injection?"

"No, but I assume you know how to work the med kit, so I'll handle the needle."

Tom read the instructions written on the vial of serum, inserted the needle's tip through the rubber top, and drew up 4 CCs of the liquid lifesaver.

Kate attached some leads to John's arm and switched on a small monitor. "We may be too late; all of his vital signs are already in the red."

"Okay, here's what we'll do. Leave the monitor attached, and I'll give him the shot. You go prepare the TMT to use the unmarked setting we found. When that's done, bring me a transfer mat ... make that two if you can. If there's no improvement soon or ... well, then we'll use the machine and hope it does what we think it will."

Kate rushed off. Tom took an alcohol swab from the kit, wiped an arm, inserted the needle, and slowly pushed the plunger.

His eyes fell to the monitor.

Two transfer mats appeared next to his side. A hand draped over one shoulder while a hopeful face pressed against the other.

Tom softly breathed out, "C'mon, John."

An eternity of three or four minutes passed.

John's eyes opened, his head lifted, and he drew a deep breath. Then his body went completely limp and fell back. One by one, the readouts on the monitor went to zero. An alarm sounded. Kate covered her face and screamed.

Tom grabbed her by the shoulders. "Kate, we can't waste time, get to the machine ... KATE!"

She shook herself loose and ran to the device.

He placed the mats in front of the machine, then lifted John's legs and swung them over so his hips ended up next to the arrangement.

Tom placed his arms under John's and the big man was muscled into a sitting position.

He held the body balanced and looked up to Kate. "Ready?"

"Ready."

"Set the countdown for zero seconds and give me a signal. I'll release John, then you push the button."

Kate pressed a few spots and looked back up. "Go!"

Tom waited until her hand moved, then jumped away, turning his head en route. Bright light. John was gone. Kate stared at the panel. Tom rushed over. There were two messages.

> 'Subject: Picus, Jiaan – successfully stored.'
> 'Dump to disk? Y/N'

She was frozen in place. "What do we do?"

"Let's see if Larry knows."

Kate opened a dialogue. The slight lag between responses was maddening.

> 'Larry: do you know about the upgrades to John's machine?'
> 'Kate: yes, what's going on?'
> 'Larry: John died, we put him in what we hope is a stasis field.'

There was a long pause.

> 'Kate: did it ask whether you wanted a disk dump?'
> 'Larry: yes, should I?'
> 'Kate: reply yes, otherwise if the machine loses power John will be lost. There should be a pack of micro disks in the TMT. Just follow the prompts. Don't worry, you get him home. We'll get him back.'
> 'Larry: thanks, talk soon.'

Tom was already searching.

"Here, this must be it," handing a container to Kate.

She replied 'Y' to the request and followed the instructions, supplying blank disks as required. The process used them all, after which, she replaced the disks in their holder and sealed the cover. "What now?"

"I don't know. I'm too numb to think. It's been one of those days ... for all of us."

They stood and slowly rocked in each other's arms.

Tom caressed her cheek with his fingertips. "Let's knock off for today. You can contact Larry again tomorrow and ask for an update on the TMTs. Other than that, we won't touch anything that isn't in plain sight or go outside the cave, then hopefully, we can't collect any more troubles. We'll simply relax and wait.

What could possibly happen then?"

"You may be deceived if you trust too much, but you will live in torment if you do not trust enough."

- Dr. Frank Crane

Chapter 13
Crucible Of Trust

Kate woke first, gently wiggled from beneath the blanket, and headed for the inside bathroom. A minute later the toilet silently flushed and the sink was filling with water warmed by a small hydrogen-powered heater. She decided to bathe in the cavern's pool later, so for now would just wipe off the lightly accumulated dust and dirt. She checked the main corridor and saw no sign of Tom.

Kate unzipped her jumper and peeled to the waist, exposing an otherwise bare body. After washing, she patted dry with a towel and slipped her arms back into her apparel. The noise from the draining sink covered the sound of Tom's approach. Her elbows were pulled back on both sides stretching out a tense muscle as Tom turned the corner. "Oh, good morning."

She was startled by the voice and spun around, having forgotten about the open front.

"I didn't mean," his scan fell to her breasts, "oops," he shut his eyes and wheeled around.

There was a large irregular opening above them, and the sun brightly lighted the little alcove. The after image of her figure that formed on his retinas made him smile appreciatively. "Kate, I'm sorry. I had no idea you were, uh, undone."

She zipped up, and there was a minute of awkward silence while they both inspected imaginary items.

Tom was taken by surprise when Kate laughed. "Well, no harm done. I suppose, considering the circumstances, something like this was bound to happen sooner or later."

He faced back. "I mean it Kate. It was completely unintentional."

"I know."

She studied him for a moment and then giggled. "It's almost worth the embarrassment just to see your devastated expression." Kate started to pass and then stopped, searching his face. "I know there are times you've thought of me as an automaton, but out of feminine curiosity, what did you think?"

His brows arched. "You mean ... of what I just saw?"

She smiled and tenderly replied, "Yes."

He blushed deeply. "Well I ... that is ... "

Her hands rose and rested on his shoulders. Tom's gaze fell to the dirt floor, he swallowed hard, and a bead of moisture appeared on his forehead.

She raised his chin with a soft touch. Their eyes locked. "Tom, just tell me. Please."

"Okay. If ten were a perfect score, I'd give you a forty-two, which, going by 'The Hitchhikers Guide To The Galaxy', is the answer to life, the universe, and everything. That's not only a comment on what I just observed ... but on all I know about you to this moment."

Kate considered the reply, then kissed him lightly on the lips. "Thank you.

That's the nicest thing anyone ever said to me. Now, I'll go swap the molecule bank back into the cooker so I can make our breakfast." She winked. "The bathroom's all yours."

While Kate walked away, Tom thought that although fainting hadn't been on his original schedule, and he had never done so before, it might become a plausible outcome if he didn't manage to slow his thundering heart.

Kate was standing, tossing small stones into the pool as Tom approached.

"Making wishes?"

"Just contemplating."

"That's close enough for government work." He stood there with a smirk.

"What's so amusing?"

"I've decided to open a crisis center when we arrive in your time."

She was puzzled. "Why do that? We have excellent counselors already."

"Maybe, but this one will be exclusively for me."

Kate chuckled. "Oh, I see. What seems to be your major maladjustment?"

"Actually, there are several. It started with your description of my firing squad, being ripped out of my own time, then having my bodily atoms scattered hither and yon. These actions were closely followed by being thrown into the prehistoric and attacked by dinosaurs.

Now, there's a nice gentleman, whom I just recently met, who has been reduced to a string of binary ones and zeros, stored on a disk pack, and is sitting on a shelf in the same room in which I sleep." He took a deep breath and blew it out. "Finally, I'm faced with the fact that I'm falling in love with you."

Her smile twisted into a sly grin. "And of all these, is there one that's particularly frightening?"

"Definitely the last. But, it's a fear I intensely want to conquer."

"The fear, or the root of its cause?"

"Only the fear. Conquering the cause, if it could be done, would destroy the attraction."

"Hmm. Yes, I think you'll do nicely." She walked to the cooker.

He stared at her back. Now what were the implications of those words?

Kate indifferently examined the dust on the touch panel. "Good thing this is a sealed unit." Her eyes lifted to his, her voice carried an adroit trace of sexual innuendo. "What's your pleasure?"

Tom twitched. "Same thing as yesterday would be fine, except, would it be too much if I asked for sausage instead of bacon?"

Kate grinned and flicked a single brow once. "You're pushing the envelope, but I'll accept the additional encumbrance."

"You weave a powerful web of subtleties, Khattyba Bright. They fall like feathers in a breeze, but impact with hurricane force on an unsuspecting shore. It's most definite that you're going to drive me crazy. However, I have no doubt the process will be pleasantly magnificent."

Her eyes twinkled. "Here ... eat."

Tom watched with some amazement while inserting his plate and utensils into the cooker's recycler. "One thing I like about the future, nothing seems to be wasted."

Kate nodded. "That's correct. Almost everything is 100% recyclable in one method or another. It's because consumables are broken back down to the molecular level and stored as raw materials."

"Are you going to contact Larry and get a TMT update?"

"Already done. They should be ready day after tomorrow. Day after that at the latest."

"What about all the stuff John brought?"

"We'll top off the matter banks in John's TMT and transfer everything back, including his machine. Larry will send the necessary material. With all the low mass, it'll be easy. We wouldn't dare leave it here. There'd be too high a probability of something surviving until eventually being discovered in the future and create a real dilemma for someone attempting to explain its existence."

"So, we're going home?"

"Yes ... we're finally headed home."

"Are you worried about John?"

"No. First, worrying at this stage is obviously futile. Second, I agree with your intuitive assessment about the stasis field. I had no idea the labs were that far along in their work. No wonder John was so excited.

A stasis field is a perfect vehicle for suspended animation. There is zero decomposition because there is quite literally no body tissue to decompose. It also greatly reduces the need for all components of life support. They've had starships on the drawing boards for years, but have never been able to make it past that point. This may be the discovery that allows them to hurdle any last barriers towards producing a practical working model.

Since time is essentially nonexistent while in stasis, the speed of the ship isn't even all that important a factor, at least not to the personnel on board. The primary concern is the survival of whatever automated equipment is necessary to reconstruct the crew once it arrives at its destination. What a tragedy if something happened to it."

"A major bummer."

She grunted in amusement. "Yes, I guess that pretty well says it all."

"Huh, I wonder where that goes."

Kate followed the direction of his eyes. "What?"

"That rock ledge on the far side of the pool."

"I thought we weren't going to explore today."

"That's in plain sight." Tom walked to the narrow part of the stream feeding into the pool, hopped across on some rocks, and gazed upward. "It's a ramp leading up the side of the wall. I can see light up there." He followed the ramp, disappearing at the top amid a jumble of boulders.

Tom returned a few minutes later. "You should see it up here. A section of the original roof caved in, flipped over, and formed a kind of bowl. It's about seven feet across. A perfect place to lay and look at the sky.

There's a waist-high rim partway around the opening that's probably the result of wind and water erosion. I think I'll get some padding and take a nap. That should certainly be safe enough."

He started down the ramp, and then something caught his eye. "Hey, the rocks curve out and then back in again on this end of the pool. It forms a natural hollow. Looks like a great place for a bath, and afterwards, just sit and unwind."

Kate walked down near the front of the pool and stood on tiptoes trying to see where he was pointing. "Perfect. Just perfect. That's where I'm going to spend some quality time relaxing."

"All you need is some bath soap and shampoo."

Kate looked up and smiled.

Tom grinned back. "No. You're kidding."

She lifted a small bag. "I have it right here. Go get whatever's needed to make yourself comfortable up there for quite some time, because then I'm kicking you out."

He walked down the ramp, re-crossed the stream, and headed towards the front of the cave.

When Tom huffed back into the cavern, he noticed Kate's jumpsuit was wet from the waist down. Shifting his load of supplies, he looked over at the appointed bath area and saw several items lying on a natural shelf just above the water level. "Looks like you're all set."

"I was just waiting for you."

"Well, don't go over yet. Let me take this stuff up, and I'll be right back. I have a favor to ask."

"Okay. I'll wait." She sat on a nearby rock.

Kate looked up from her reading as Tom bounded across atop the stones. "What is it you want?"

Tom glanced over at the cooker. "Can that thing make snacks?"

"Tsk, tsk. Yes, of course. It has a complete menu and search facility. I'll show you how it operates, then you can find whatever you want while I read."

"It's so thin. What kind of book is that?"

"Electronic. The screen displays one page at a time. There's a sensor in the corner that follows your eye movement. When it senses bottom right flowing to top left, it displays the next page. Off to the left, it pages back. To the right, it skips one. It also follows voice commands for any other function you want it to perform, like 'go to' a certain page number or 'find' a specific passage."

"John just happened to bring you a book?"

"He knew I was an avid reader."

"You're making me jealous. Do you have another, or must I suffer?"

"I'm sure John brought a book or two. You can borrow them. There are many novels and articles stored in each one. I imagine he'd have something you'd enjoy."

"Great. The open sky, a snack, and a book, what else could I want?"

She gave him an intriguing grin. "Let me show you how to work the cooker. While you're playing, I'll locate John's reader."

Kate returned and stared at the mound of 'something' Tom had created. Moments later, she laughed so hard tears rolled down her cheeks. "I'm sorry, Tom, but what is that supposed to be?"

"It was the closest thing I came across that even resembled what I wanted."

"Let me try." She placed the weird looking conglomeration in the recycle bin and checked the settings Tom had made. "The parsing algorithms are extremely sophisticated, but somehow I think you managed to confuse the machine." She chuckled, "That seems to be one of your innate abilities. When you want chips, dip, and soda, you must let the cooker decide if they are meant to be mixed or separate items."

"Oh. I guess there's more to this than meets the eye." Maybe John was better at this than originally thought.

Kate pressed several spots on the panel. "Here, I think this will be more to your liking."

Tom laughed. "Yeah, just a tad. Thanks." He kissed her on the cheek.

She smiled. "I could get used to that."

"You'd better, because I could, too. You just have to give me some time." He glanced away, then back. "Well, thanks for the help. I'm off to my retreat while you're off to yours. I promise I'll give a yell if I need to come down the ramp. Join me when you're done. It really does offer a great view."

"Okay, I'll visit you later, but for now, I can't wait to soak in the water. There must be a hot spring flowing under the hollow. Did you notice how warm it is there?"

"No. The water was nice and cool where John and I had our little swim. I'll give it a try after you."

Kate waded over to the 'tub', soaped up with a cloth, and relaxed as she wiped away the grime of the last few days. It felt great to simply have clean hair again. Following a final rinse, she slipped down into the warm water, felt her tensions ebb away, and allowed Tom to become the singular topic of her thoughts.

Their relationship seemed stalemated. Kate was falling in love with him, but for some reason he appeared hesitant to let her. She felt Tom was a good man ... of that there was no doubt. He was painfully shy in one sense, yet wonderfully courageous in others ... a complete paradox. Well, she would figure him out eventually. Kate concluded that somehow ... they would discuss the situation tomorrow.

Tom positioned the foam padding in the bowl of rock, became comfortable, then proceeded to munch on his snack. He realized Kate was upset and knew he was holding back. Losing her was the last thing he wanted.

This woman made him feel happy to just be alive. He hadn't experienced so many positive thoughts since Shannon, and she had been part fantasy. Kate was entirely real. He had to open up, and became resolute ... tomorrow, for sure, they would talk.

The decision eased his mind. He would savor the book after a nap. Tom emptied the plate, drained the glass, arose, and set them aside. Upon resettling, he stared into the blue sea overhead, then shifted towards the center of the depression and was startled when it moved.

His arms flew outward to stabilize his balance, but found that the bowl quickly steadied. He slowly leaned one way, then the other, finding that the bowl rocked ever so slightly, in phase with his movements.

Tom's thoughts flashed back to his childhood, rocking himself into a dreamy slumber in front of the stereo whenever his parents argued. It had been one of the few things that gave him respite from their dreadful world.

He brought a knee up and swayed it from side to side. The bowl responded to each movement. Within minutes, his perception of reality passed from full awareness to a repose of total indifference.

Kate toweled off, dressed, slipped on her soft shoes and secured them with

Velcro straps. She crossed the stream without incident and started up the ramp. Tom's empty dish and glass were just outside an opening to the upper chamber.

Even though it was mid afternoon, it seemed oddly dark within, especially for allegedly having a seven-foot skylight. The reason became devastatingly clear as she turned the final corner. Kate backed against the wall nearest the stone crucible and covered her mouth to keep from screaming.

Tom was snoring away, completely oblivious to the menace that hung suspended mere feet above his body. The Rex's head filled at least half of the opening. It was fearfully obvious the creature had sufficient height and clearance to descend upon the sleeping human whenever it chose.

Tom was positioned on his back with his face turned toward her. Perhaps he could slide out of harm's way if she could awaken him without alarming the animal. She called to him in a loud whisper. "Pssssst, Tom! ... Tom!"

"Hmmmpfff." His eyes opened to narrow slits. Following a yawn, "What is it?"

Kate pointed.

Tom's drowsy consciousness tried to follow her meaning. His eyes opened wider when he noticed her alarmed expression. He smelled the foul odor, then gaped into Kate's eyes. "Tell me it's not the Rex." Her upward glance told him otherwise.

His gaze rolled slowly skyward, followed by a turn of his head. A shaky voice managed to speak. "Oh, hi buddy. I'm the one who comforted you, remember? Please ... remember." Nothing moved, and the only sound was the Rex's deep breaths. Clouds could be seen floating high above the unmoving behemoth.

Tom started to ease toward Kate. The Rex dipped its head; Tom flinched.

Kate looked away.

Giant teeth pressed upon Tom's stomach ... gently nudging. In a breathtaking moment, the Rex lowered its jaw down against the stone crucible and seemed to be offering Tom the torn left eye ridge.

"Oh God, buddy ... is that all you want? Kate, look at this!"

She turned back and squinted through closed fingers. Tom examined the Rex's wound. It was oozing a greenish bloody liquid and was obviously badly infected. "Was there any antibiotic in that med kit?"

Kate slowly shook her head. "You can't be serious."

"If it was going to kill me, it'd be all over by now. Check the kit, please. I'll need some water and bandage, too."

"Tom, you could easily escape now. If I come back and you're gone, I'll never forgive you."

Tom faced the Rex, patting its huge nose. The Rex issued its low throaty growl. "Kate, it trusts me."

"It trusting you is not my major concern."

Tom looked at her. She waved a hand. "Alright, I'm going, but don't be surprised if he wants a snack, too."

Kate stopped, took a deep breath, and slowly exhaled before reentering the chamber. Tom was sitting cross-legged, elbow on knee, and chin in hand, assessing the Rex. The animal simply stood there and seemed to be evaluating Tom.

She cautiously approached the altar bowl, her eyes adhered to the Rex. "Here ... water, cloth, antibiotic, and something better than bandage. It's a spray. The compound is moisture and dirt resistant, but allows oxygen to pass. Its wound will heal much faster. Tom ... you're not afraid?"

"As crazy as it may sound ... no. Although, I don't think I want to try and put a leash on it, or feed it Tyrannosaur chow." Tom stroked the massive face. It bobbed minutely with the application and release of hand pressure.

He cleaned the wound again, liberally covered it with medication, and finally applied the spray-on bandage. "I keep thinking I should name it, but all I can come up with is 'Butcher Shop Breath'. Here, give me your hand."

Her head jerked. "Why!"

"I want it to learn your smell as well."

She backed away, her eyes growing bigger with each step. "Oh no, Tom, please."

"Kate, look at him. He hasn't even presented a threat, let alone try and hurt me."

"Do you really believe you've tamed it?"

"Tamed ... no. The operative word here is trust, remember?"

As Kate warily approached, the Rex observed intently. "Tom, I am afraid."

"I promise you, any sign of aggression and we're both out of here."

Tom took her hand and slowly raised it to the Rex, his eyes searching for any change in the animal's body posturing.

It sniffed for what must have been an eternity to Kate, then chortled the low growl. The three of them had apparently formed the most prodigious association in the history of all time ... past or future.

Tom kept mumbling aloud, "Butcher Shop Breath, Butcher Shop Breath ... B-S-B, B-S-B," and then he had it. He extended his hand, placed it on the Rex's snout and decreed, "I dub thee ... Bisbee."

Kate stood in awe. "Amazing. Absolutely amazing."

Tom attends to the Rex's wounds

"Love is the purification of the heart from self; it strengthens and ennobles the character; gives higher motive and nobler aim to every action of life, and makes both man and woman strong, noble, and courageous.—The power to love truly and devotedly is the noblest gift with which a human being can be endowed; but it is a sacred fire that must not be burned to idols."

- Maria Jane Jewsbury

Chapter 14
Rainy Day Indoor Sports

Tom awoke to the strange patter of something falling. After a moment, he realized what he heard.

Kate stirred next to him. "Is that rain?"

"Uh huh."

"Looks like a wonderful day to stay in bed."

He laughed. "I don't know. I have a full morning planned at the pool, and of course later ... a dinosaur to train."

"Oh no. I've had enough dinosaur encounters recently to last for an eon. Today ... I was hoping we could talk."

He stared at the rock ceiling. "Okay. Let's talk."

"Do you still think about her?"

Tom's head spun towards Kate. "Who?"

"Shannon."

He sat up and leaned on an elbow. "That was ... eighteen years ago. What brought up this subject?"

"You seem to have a problem with our relationship, and I wondered if it stemmed from the fact you could never ask her for a date. Don't get me wrong, Tom. I think you're a great person, but you also have a closet full of skeletons."

"So, who doesn't?"

"I don't care about other people's closets, just ours."

"I assume you want to know why I didn't pursue her?"

"Yes ... please. It'd help me understand where we are."

"It should be obvious to someone with your background, training, and education."

"Humor me."

"Kate, look at the environment in which I grew up. My parents made sure I was fed, washed, clothed, and had a roof over my head, but that was the total extent of our relationship. They were divorced when I was four and remarried sometime after I turned five. Why, I'll never understand.

My drunken father's favorite pastime was putting me down. To him, I was stupid, lazy, no-good and worthless. You've heard of low self-esteem, I had none. His pet name for me was 'dreamer'.

He was a functioning alcoholic, constantly living in a case-of-beer induced stupor. Our entire father-son relationship consisted of one baseball game at

Tiger stadium. I spent most of my Saturdays tucked away in the dark corner of a bar with a soft drink and a bag of peanuts, while dear ol' dad sat for hours on end drinking with his friends.

Oh yeah, I mustn't forget the fishing rod he bought me. We went to a park, with a bar of course, and he stuck me outside by a mud hole in the rain so I could fish. The only thing I finally went home with was about a hundred mosquito bites.

One of my best memories was a summer night when my mom was working at the post office. Dad came home drunk, as usual. The problem with mom not being around was simply that dad didn't have anyone else to yell at but me.

But that evening I fooled him. I slept under my bed where he wouldn't think to look. He walked around the house ranting, raving, and calling me every name you can imagine. The drunken bum never did find me. I could have been laying out in the street dead for all he knew ... or cared.

He finally passed out in front of the TV, which was a typical late-night activity for him. Oh, did I forget to mention it was my birthday? I had just turned nine. Hiding under the bed was a present to myself of one night's peace.

I never knew my parents to sleep in the same room, let alone the same bed. They got their second divorce when I was fifteen. That left just my dad and I to fight it out, and physical confrontations were a real possibility. If you consider all this information, what kind of shape do you think my self-confidence was in by the time I reached high school?

Shannon was basically a nice girl I was lucky enough to talk with once in a while. She treated me like a human being, almost special, and I really got to like her. Why didn't I ask her out? My loving father had made me feel like I was the dregs of the planet. Living with thoughts like that, what on earth could I possibly have offered Shannon? Could I in good conscience take her home?

Even though you didn't have a legal family, you had tons of support compared to me." Tom studied her expression, then softly backhanded a tear from her cheek. "No, don't give me that look. I don't feel sorry for myself. In fact, I've been quite lucky in many ways. A high intelligence blossomed within me from someplace, and my career may have been short but highly productive.

Of course, I'm still young and literally have a new future in front of me. Above all, I've met you. I'm falling for you hook, line, and sinker, Khattyba Bright, and I love every second of the drop. If I go splat at the bottom, then so be it. That's a chance I'm perfectly willing to take. But, there's a problem. I don't know if I can ever accept the premise that I deserve you."

"You need to let me worry about that." She reached up and ran a finger down his nose. "What about the guilt?"

"Of her going to the prom alone?"

"Yes."

"I'll admit, that was a pretty crushing blow, although there's nothing I can do to rectify the situation. I guess that's just another bad memory I'll have to live with. She knew I liked her a lot, but the prom was an event I had never even considered. I figured she had at least a dozen boy friends and the last thing she needed was an unlucky number thirteen.

I didn't know when the prom was until a month later, at graduation. I found out from a friend after the ceremonies that Shannon had been turning down dates hoping I would ask her to attend the prom with me. I felt like a huge pile of dinosaur feces."

"I'm not trying to belittle your circumstances, but missing a prom date does seem like an unusual situation to become so obsessed about."

"That's the same thing at least a half dozen shrinks told me."

Kate took his hand and gave it a consoling squeeze. "Still, guilt can drive someone to the breaking point. It keeps a person going when everyone else would be smart enough to quit. That must be one of the reasons for pushing so much on all your projects." She watched his face break into a smile. "Okay, give. What's going on behind those deep-blue-sea eyes?"

His head shook slowly. "I can't tell you. It's too embarrassing."

She sat up and grabbed him by the shirt with both hands. "Remember all the words about trust you flaunted yesterday? I trusted enough that you practically fed me to a Tyrannosaurus Rex. Don't back out on me now."

He looked down. She reached out and cuffed him under the chin. "No. That's one of my rules I won't bend, even for you. Look in my eyes when you talk to me. I need to see you. I like looking into your eyes. I like what I see there." She softened. "I know it's hard now, but it'll get easier. Someday I hope you'll like looking into mine as much as I like looking into yours."

"I already do."

She leaned over and lightly kissed him. "Then prove it."

His smile returned. "You're a hard woman, Kate."

"Maybe. But I only want one man, Tom, and I've decided you're him." She leaned forward and softly brushed her cheek against his. "Now tell me what you found so amusing before. Please."

"Your comment about driving the projects so hard reminded me of an incident and my resulting current condition, and that made me think about tennis."

Kate's eyes closed and her head tilted slowly to one side. "Okay, I really want to hear this explanation. It sounds like you're going for a record."

"Well, one day we were looking for a new casing material to use in searching for a Tachyon type particle, and it kept blowing up. But, the cameras couldn't quite seem to catch the problem. So, I stood inside the test chamber, watching firsthand. I was wearing protective clothing and a face shield. Unfortunately, the vest didn't extend down far enough. When the cylinder exploded it caught me below the belt. The injury wasn't widespread, but there was enough. One of my testicles was damaged beyond repair. They had no problem sewing up the scrotal sack, but the gland itself was mutilated, so they implanted a prosthesis." Tom's face reddened. "Does slang still refer to a man's testicles as 'balls' in your time?"

"Yes, I've heard the expression."

"After the accident, my friends starting referring to me as the 'one ball man'."

"That's terrible."

"No. It was alright. I knew it was in jest. It actually helped me to adapt psychologically."

Kate frowned. "Okay. Where does tennis enter into the scheme of things?"

Tom extended his arms. "I have small hands for a man, so when I play tennis I can only hold one ball at a time. Most men, and a lot of women, can hold two. That way, if the first serve isn't 'in' they are ready to try the second. I always have to dig one out of my pocket or pick it up from the ground. Therefore, the 'one ball man' nomenclature also extends to my tennis game."

Kate chuckled. "You've done it again. You took something that sounded utterly ridiculous and made it make sense. Incidentally, I've always liked tennis." She nibbled his ear, then kissed his neck. "We'll have to 'play' together sometime."

Tom kissed her full on the lips, squeezing her so tight, Kate squeaked. His fingers smoothed her hair, then traced the curve of her cheeks. "How about now?"

She breathed out heavily, "Sounds agreeable to me."

They quickly slipped out of their clothes into game outfits.

The chair umpire pointed to one player, then the other. Each acknowledged they were ready. He started the match by signaling, 'Ready ... play.'

It had been wordlessly, but mutually agreed, that Tom would serve and Kate receive. Tom held the ball aloft signifying it was new. Kate nodded. Tom's first serve went wide of the box and was called 'out'. He was more careful with the next.

Kate adjusted her stance and signified the ball was in play. The point began slowly since neither was overly tutored, and any previous experience could be considered ancient history.

They gradually attuned to each other's motions and were soon moving comfortably on the court. An easy rally was underway, but over time their movements began to quicken.

The ball sailed around as if there were no net between them at all.

At length, Tom realized he had an opportunity to put the game away. Instead, in a gentlemanly gesture, he sent up a defensive lob effectively slowing the pace. Kate sensed the action and also checked her tempo, thereby extending the point.

Their performance became a slow, prolonged passion, calling endearments and encouragement to each other. Finally, when they were at the climax of the game, Tom arched his back and really let one soar. Kate moaned at the end of the point and acknowledged the shot by patting his buttocks with a hand.

Even though the game was over, the scoreboard still displayed the match at 'Love All'.

Tom lowered his face to hers, they kissed, then he shifted and lay on his back. He was sweaty; she was covered with a light patina of dampness. The air was heavy with a musky odor.

Kate turned, draped a naked leg half over him, and traced figures in his chest hair with a finger. Her hand slid softly up and kneaded the bread of his shoulder. The couple's breathing slowed, bodies relaxed, and their foggy minds allowed them to slip into a light, peaceful sleep.

They awoke sometime later. He softly stroked her hair, caressed her chin with his thumb, and fell into her eyes. "I love the rain."

"Umm, me too. With a little luck it'll rain all day."

Their bodies pressed together.

A particular admirer of Kate's, in Tom's south-of-the-belt club, started the rumor of a re-match.

The crowd went wild.

"The secret of a good memory is attention, and attention to a subject depends upon our interest in it. – We rarely forget that which has made a deep impression on our minds."

- Tryon Edwards

Chapter 15
Good News

Tom sat up. "I don't know about you, but I'm starved." He bent over and lightly kissed Kate. "It must have something to do with this new work out program I've started."

"First I exercise you, and now I have to feed you? Maybe I should just get an electronic pet. Then I wouldn't have to do either."

"Yeah, but it'd never be as much fun."

Kate smiled broadly. "Yes, I admit, that's true."

They pulled on some clothes. Kate stood and stretched. "Come along, Fido, and we'll put a little food in your bowl."

"Woof."

As Tom arose, his gaze brushed past a rocky shelf high on the wall. Something held his look. "How tall is Larry?"

"Maybe six-four or six-five ... I'd guess. Why?"

Tom pointed.

"What is it?"

"Would you leave a gun near an unconscious person?"

"Probably not."

"I wouldn't either. I'd take it from them and put it some place safe until they regained their senses. I think that's the belt I had my holster looped onto. I didn't notice it until just now. Considering recent events, however, I'm a little leery about putting my hand up there." Tom looked around and found a stick. "Let's try this." He slipped it through a loop of his belt and pulled slowly. "Ah ha." The belt dropped into his hands. He looked back up. "Hey, my calculator's there, too."

He tapped the front of the shelf with the stick, and when nothing happened, cautiously reached and took hold of the calculator with thumb and forefinger. "I figured both of these were lost when I was first introduced to Bisbee." Tom placed the belt and holster on a lower outcropping, the calculator in a shirt pocket. He grinned. "Amazing what you find just laying around, huh."

Kate squinted. "Don't look at me when you say that."

"Oh, I don't know. I'd say I did pretty well on both accounts."

"Hmm. Let's go eat."

Tom cleaned up the area while Kate checked the latest status of the TMTs. She let out an uncharacteristic whoop. "Good news! Everything seems to be ready for the beginning of our return trip. Larry has six jumps planned for us ... the same number he executed. We'll layover at each jump to allow synchronizing the difference in times so each jump will bring us out sometime between nine and eleven in the morning, wherever we are.

That will give us an opportunity to rest up, check our status, equipment, and hopefully plan for a smooth entry into the future. He said there were two scenarios and is working on both. Larry is still the only other person who knows about our little excursion and John's subsequent actions, although both plans will involve bringing in another member to act as Larry's relief ... probably Frank."

"The hologram guy?"

"Yes. He can be completely trusted, and I'm sure he'll be willing to help."

"Did he specify why there were two separate strategies?"

"No. He just stated that the details were being worked out and he'd most likely have you make a choice before our last jump."

"Why me?"

"He simply said you'd understand when the time came. I don't know what he means."

Tom shrugged. "Okay ... no problem."

Kate laughed. "He asked if we were managing to keep busy. I told him there were new developments almost every day. I left out the graphic details."

"Good thing. He might develop the opinion I'm a dirty old man."

"Well, I wouldn't say dirty ... and definitely not old."

"Do you think we should get busy?"

Kate walked over to Tom and sniffed. "You didn't use the tub yesterday, did you?"

"No. I guess it was forgotten about with all the excitement. Is it that noticeable?"

"Let's politely say you could do with a bath." She leaned against him. "There's room for two, so unless you object, today I'll keep you company. It's surprising the difference a day can make."

"Decisions, decisions. And I thought it'd be simpler living here."

Tom was rinsing off as Kate plodded over to the tub. She had a towel wrapped around her upper body and a few more in her hand. There was also a clipboard present. "Thought we could make up a list of things that get transported back and which to take with us."

"Sort of combining business with pleasure."

She handed him a towel. "Here, put this behind you."

"It's okay. The rock is smooth. I'm already quite comfortable."

"Maybe now, but I plan on resting against you."

"Ah."

Kate eased down between his legs and nestled back. "I'd like to take the toilet, but it only works in conjunction with the recycler. It would have to be filled and emptied with water each time. That would make it totally impractical, so that's out. Agreed?"

"I think all we need on that account is a shovel and brownie film."

"What's brownie film?"

"Toilet paper."

Kate laughed. "How euphemistic."

"I've done a lot of hiking and have read all about this kind of problem in a book called, 'How To Shit In The Woods'." Tom saw the disbelief etched on her face. "Seriously, that's the title."

"Fine. As of now, you're in charge of all latrine operations. Okay, what do you think about the cooker?"

"Unfortunately, it's in the same category as the toilet."

"Great to have, but again, impractical."

"Yep."

She sighed. "Then I guess we'll just have to survive on meal tablets for a few more days."

"As we move forward in time, there'll eventually be wild fruit trees."

Kate nodded. "That's true. I'll be looking forward to that."

"Really, when you think about it, all we need is bedding, water, food tablets, a shovel, and the TP. We'll be in contact with Larry or Frank and anything else can always be requested as needed."

"I suppose you're right. Maybe I was making this too hard. Let's just relax and think about it. Anything we come up with can be added to the list. Other than those items, everything else goes back."

They had just gotten comfortable when John's TMT beeped, startling them. "Probably just a warning signal that something is coming through," Kate commented.

Tom turned away from the flash, then studied the newly arrived canisters. "Matter banks?"

Kate visually examined the new arrivals. "Yes. Two carbon and one TE."

"If the TMT on the receiving end supplies the matter for reintegration, why do we need so much here?"

"Something has to supply the initial quarks for the tachyon generator."

"Why not pull the required matter out of the surrounding atmosphere like it does for oxygen, hydrogen, and nitrogen?"

She turned and intently studied his face for a moment. "That's exactly what John proposed. In fact, it's a side project he was attempting to perfect. Mostly, it's a problem of density. Density versus the time required obtaining the density, to be precise. Even though time stops for a subject undergoing an integration/transference/reintegration process, a real time event clock still ticks. The longer the entire procedure takes, the more an opportunity exists for a malfunction or some influence from outside the system to become a factor.

With current designs, the real time required inputting enough atmosphere for supplying the needed matter is considered to remain outside the definition of safe parameters."

"So, it's also a problem of quantity versus time."

Kate nodded. "Exactly."

"Well, I bet John eventually beats it."

"I do, too. He's a brilliant man."

"When does Larry have our first jump scheduled?"

"Tomorrow, anytime between two and four p.m."

Tom chuffed. "This may sound a little crazy, but I'm going to kind of miss it here. While I'm certainly sorry for what happened to John, there were several other recent occurrences that have been extremely positive." He hugged her. "I'll remember them always."

She turned and looked over her shoulder. "You're serious."

Tom nodded. Kate thought a moment. Then, as a smile slowly formed, "I can't believe I'm saying this, but I have to agree."

There were several successive flashes. Four TMTs stood gleaming in the light.

Tom rubbed his eyes. "Man, at this rate I'm going to need sun glasses. I take it you updated the coordinates to reflect the move inside the cavern?"

"To paraphrase your earlier statement, 'it seemed like a prudent action considering recent events'."

"Well, madam ... I'm getting antsy, so if you'll let me up, I'll dress and start gathering things together. Tomorrow's going to be a big day. Since the TMTs are here, we might as well use this same area for staging our exit."

"My thoughts exactly. I'll get dressed, too."

"I always say great minds run in the same gutter."

"Thanks," she turned and looked, "I think."

In under an hour, they collected a pile of articles and assembled them on transmit mats in front of John's TMT. Kate examined the heap. "I think John went a little overboard, don't you?"

"Probably, but I sure appreciated the effort. It was great to brush my teeth again. I forgot to pack my toothbrush after all. Following those first couple of days, it felt like something was growing on them, and my clothes had become nothing more than bloody rags. We're going to get John back, if for nothing else, so I can thank him."

"You're not upset this was actually all his doing?"

"I was at first, but it's turned out to be the greatest adventure of my life. I know he didn't mean for it to be like this. For God's sake, the man died. Imagine when he tries explaining that to his kids."

They looked at each other, their eyes saying unspoken words. He noticed hers were even more expressive than usual for some unknown reason.

Tom added a few last items to the pile. "Okay, I think that leaves just the bathroom equipment and the cooker. We'll use the cooker for breakfast and lunch, then I'll disassemble the toilet, sink, and water recycler, so we can return everything that remains." He grinned. "You know, if we shipped ourselves back in pieces, we could probably make it in one hop, too."

"Are you volunteering to go first?"

He laughed. "Uh ... no."

"I didn't think so."

Tom scanned the area. "That should be everything. I think we're ready."

"Not quite." Kate stood up and patted the rock she'd been seated on. "Sit here, please."

Tom sat. "Okay ... what?"

"This is something John was going to do. But, since he's not here, I'll perform the task. These are a couple of items John brought especially for you. They will greatly ease the effects of the teletransportation.

The possibility exists that you might still need the drug, but I rather tend to doubt it. I'll still give you an injection this time, and I can guarantee that between the two procedures, the jumps won't bother you any more than they affect me. Here, hold these diagrams where I can see them."

"It looks like the area behind a person's ear."

"That's correct." Kate held out two small disks for inspection. "I'm going to implant one of these behind each of yours."

"With what?"

She pulled a device resembling a pencil from her pocket. "This ... it's a micro-laser scalpel. When it's over, you'll never know anything happened."

"Uh huh, how about during?"

"I'll apply a local anesthetic, silly. This procedure wasn't perfected by the Marquis De Sade."

Tom looked her straight in the eyes. "I trust you Kate. Go ahead ... do it."

A numbing cream was applied to his left ear area, the disk inserted through a small incision, and then sealed. "Okay, now the right and we're finished." The procedure was repeated.

Tom looked up. "That didn't hurt a bit, and I don't even like going to a dentist. You're pretty good at this. How many does that make?"

"Counting your two?"

"Yes."

"Two."

Tom stared for a few moments, then shrugged. "Oh well, trust works." He touched around his ears. "They're not even tender."

Kate laughed. "These are smart instruments. All they really need from me is motion. They do all the work, but now I get to mark off another requirement towards my Senior Jump-Master certificate."

"Great. Now I'm a guinea pig."

"True ... but you're my guinea pig."

"Well, I'm certain that counts for something. I take it you have the same implants, or maybe better. The jumps don't seem to even phase you."

"Something better. It's called a DNA snippet. It was inserted into a few of my cells right after birth via an artificial retro-virus. Computer modeling predicted that a substitution of uracil for thymine in a single base pair on a particular gene would make all the difference. It modifies the codons that helps control balance ... primarily in the brain's vestibular apparatus. As I grew older, it transferred to more and more cells through the normal growth process. You've observed correctly. Jumps have almost no effect on me. Everyone gets a DNA snippet when they're born. Otherwise, there'd be no possibility of handling day to day movement on the planet."

Tom frowned in concentration. "Wait a minute. I don't remember the names, but I know the base pairs for DNA are A, T, G, and C. Uracil isn't one of those."

She nodded. "You're right. They stand for adenine, thymine, guanine, and cytosine. Uracil is actually an RNA nucleotide."

"What! Wouldn't that make the cell's nucleus completely unstable?"

"Not if you modify the correct restriction, ligase, and polymerase enzymes. Tom, the first rough draft of the complete human DNA molecule was completed in the year 2000. For now, I'm asking you to just believe me. After all, do you think we've been sitting on our hands all these years?"

"No ... but still."

When Kate stopped for a minute, Tom knew she was exploring a different thought pattern. "Remember when I said a TMT had to be in place before organic matter could be transferred?"

"I remember."

"The same is true of MMTs. When teletransportation tests were first started, that wasn't true. Even living things could be projected with total success. Then errors in transmission began taking place and no one could discover a reason. Fortunately, they began occurring before human trials commenced. The errors became more pronounced as time passed. Finally, all attempts at projecting any organic life failed. Nobody found the answer. So, MMTs or TMTs are sent first and that solved all the problems. There's never been a biological failure since."

"It sounds like a real challenge ... makes me wish I were a cellular engineer."

Kate watched Tom pull out his calculator. "What are you doing?"

"Time for some fun. First, I have to see if this thing is still working. If I punch in the sequence '1,2,3,4,5,6,7,9' and multiply by nine, the answer should be all ones. If that's true, then I know the arithmetic logic unit is functioning correctly." He showed her the display.

"I see, but why are you squinting?"

"I lost my glasses."

"You won't need them soon; I'll arrange for you to have some micro-surgery on your eyes and you'll have 20/20 vision, uncorrected."

"They've been performing a similar procedure since sometime in the 1980's, but I was always afraid once they started, it would never stop. Getting new glasses is much easier."

Kate nodded. "Additional surgery is a possibility, but any robotic optometrist can perform the procedure in perfect safety on an out patient basis."

"Maybe it's something I'll consider once I get used to the idea."

Tom returned to his calculator. "Now, I want to calculate the length of the day here. The earth is spinning faster than it does in our time, so the days are shorter and therefore the year is longer."

Kate reclaimed her rock. "Is this something important?"

"No. I'm just curious. I'll use a 24-hour day and the year 2000 as a baseline. I remember from some reading when I was a kid that in 280 million B.C. the year had 390 days.

If I set up a proportion between the three known facts, I can determine the length of a day at that time. Lastly, I'll use those numbers for interpolating the values for where we are now, say 150 million B.C., to find the span of a year and duration of a single day." Tom ran the numbers.

"Okay. In 150 million B.C., I get a year consisting of 377 days, and that corresponds to a day of 23 hours and 14 minutes." Tom frowned. "Of course, that's assuming the resultant products are linear, which they probably aren't, because I also remember that since 1900 the earth has lost approximately 1.7 seconds a year in its rotation time. If I multiply 150 million by 1.7, it generates an answer that has a lot more hours than there are in a day. Hmm."

Kate stood. "Well, I'm retiring for the evening. Are you going to crunch numbers all night, or are you coming with me?"

"Like I always say, 'you can lead a horse to water' ... "

Kate interrupted. "Oh, I know this one. But, 'you can't make him drink' ... right?"

"No. There is an old saying that goes like that, but that isn't what I say."

"Well, excuse me, good sir. And what do you say?"

"I say, 'you can lead a horse to water, but you can't make him float on his back'."

Kate frowned. "What's that supposed to mean?"

"It's another Morbius problem."

Her frown hardened into a grimace. "Wonderful. It'll probably drive me insane trying to figure it out."

Tom smiled and nodded. "Probably."

In the middle of the night, Kate sat bolt upright from a restless sleep. She shook Tom.

"Whazit?"

"I think I have it. There is no difference between what you said about the horse and the original saying. They both mean the same thing. You simply can't make the horse do something it doesn't want to do. Just like Morbius, I was too close to the problem. Is that right?"

"Mmmppphh."

"That's what I thought."

Kate laid back and almost instantly fell into a light sleep.

Tom turned away, shifted onto his side, and went back to his conversation with Sir Isaac Newton about massive bodies, the laws of momentum, and angular velocity. Sir Isaac was most impressed with Tom's application of physics in fooling the Rex. He applauded. Tom took a couple of imaginary bows, bumping his butt against Kate's hip.

She reached over, patted him, and mumbled. "Not now, Tom."

"History fades into fable; fact becomes clouded with doubt and controversy; the inscription moulders from the tablet; the statue falls from the pedestal. – Columns, arches, pyramids, what are they but heaps of sand, and their epitaphs but characters written in the dust?"

- Washington Irving

Chapter 16
Early Arizona

Kate moved from the cave's bathroom into the hallway, turning left out of Tom's way. He lifted the disconnected toilet and also turned left, which confused Kate. "Aren't you taking that back to the cavern with the rest of the equipment?"

"Yep. But I want to use it for a step-stool first."

Kate began backing toward the front of the cave as Tom followed. He turned into the alcove that had become their bedroom and placed the utilitarian toilet in front of a wall. Tom put a foot on top of the seat and peered onto a ledge. "Hey, what do you know. My glasses are up here, too. Good job, Larry." He inserted the hard case into his shirt. "Now, I'll take the toilet back and add it to the pile. Everything else is already gone except for that stuff and John's TMT. It's getting pretty close to post time."

"I'll be back there in a few minutes. I'm going to take one last look around and make sure we're not forgetting some item."

"Okay. Let's meet by the pool."

Kate walked into the cavern, looking for Tom. A minute later, he sauntered down the ramp on the far side of the pool.

He called across to her, "Just wanted to make sure I picked up my dishes and John's book. My memory keeps telling me I've done these things, but no harm in being absolutely certain."

She gave him a sidelong look. "You've already checked at least four times that I've counted. Personally, I think you're just looking for Bisbee."

A large grin grew across his face. "Well, yeah ... that, too."

"That, too, nothing. That 'only' is more like it."

He encircled her from behind. "Is that a complaint?"

"No, I just hope you would miss me as much as that dumb dinosaur."

He nuzzled her neck. "I don't know. That sure sounds like a complaint. What explanation are you going to concoct for the girls back home when they discover you're jealous of a T-rex?"

"Mmm. You have a point."

Tom grinned. "Besides, it'd be easy to tell if I misbehave around Bisbee. I'd come home missing an arm, or maybe a leg."

"That's also true. I guess there's nothing to worry about after all."

They walked around the last pile of paraphernalia and positioned themselves behind John's TMT. Kate updated a few settings and pressed a keypad. The pile disappeared. She altered the entries on John's machine one last time, then stepped aside. A button was pushed on Kate's wrist device, the numbers counted down, another bright light, and they were alone with the four pieces of machinery that had originally started their journey.

Kate opened and closed access doors on the TMTs and started handing transmit mats to Tom. "Place one under each TMT, please. The last two are for us."

Tom lined up the mats, then maneuvered a TMT onto each.

Kate pointed to where their mats should be positioned.

He looked up. "Aren't you forgetting something?"

Kate shook her head 'no' and pulled an air-syringe out of a pocket. "Pull up your sleeve." There was a hiss of air and the device was replaced in her jumper. "One final update and we can leave." She synchronized the programming of the four devices then walked onto the mat next to Tom's. "Ready?"

Tom saluted. "Ready, willing, able, roger-wilco, over and out."

Kate slowly rolled her eyes. "I take it that's a 'yes'."

"Yes, maam. How far is our first jump?"

She showed him the display.

"Whew. Okay, see you in ninety million years."

Another button was pressed. Moments later, the cave's mica encrusted rocks reflected a light show that resembled a large pack of fireworks going berserk.

* * * * *

Tom stumbled, but caught himself. He bent over and took some deep breaths. "That wasn't nearly as bad as the first time."

"Tom, wait until you see this."

He straightened and almost fell over again from the scene's visual impact.

"Wow. It's the most beautiful thing I've ever seen." He glanced at her and grinned. "Well, maybe the second."

She grinned back. "It's alright, I know what you mean."

They turned away from the glare as the second pair of TMTs caught up with them. Kate, Tom, and the machines were situated near the sandy shoreline of a large peninsula. An inland sea covered the area and formed a panorama that stretched to the horizon in three directions. A mountain close to the size of a modern day Everest commanded the view of the fourth.

Tom walked to the water's edge, bent down, wet a finger, and tasted.

"Ugh, salty and warm. This must extend all the way down to what will become the Gulf of Mexico."

"You're not thinking of going for a swim ... are you?"

"No way. I can't even imagine what's cruising around out there. Besides, I don't want some primordial shark bragging to his friends that he bagged the first human on record." Tom turned to face the mountain, put on his glasses, then pulled out the calculator.

Kate chuckled at the sight. "Tom the nature lover comes across one of the most fabulous views in history, and what does he do? Crunch numbers."

"For your information, Miss Bright, I'm just trying to figure a rough estimate of that mountain's height. My trig appears to be a little rusty."

"I can help."

"How?"

Kate aimed WD7 at the mountain's plateau and took a reading. "Let's walk a little higher on this rise ... about here." She sighted through a lens on the device, adjusted a few steps, and saved a setting. "We're now in the same plane as the base." Kate angled her device up towards the peak, took another reading, then held her position until a beep was heard.

"I could give you the answer, but I don't want to spoil your fun. Drop a perpendicular from the peak to the ground and you've got a right triangle. The two measurements you need are 29,847 feet for side 'C', and 62 degrees 15 minutes for angle 'A'. Okay, Newton, it's all yours."

Tom kissed her cheek and was all smiles. "Thanks. You're all right, no matter what John said." He stood there punching and mumbling, "29,847 divided by, left paren, 62.25 sin, one over 'X' to get the cosecant, right paren, equals. How does 26,414 feet for a height sound?"

Kate looked at her display, then raised her brows. "I'm impressed."

"Not as much as I am by that mountain. What's the relative time of year by our standards?"

"According to the date conversion routine, it's May 27."

"Does that allow for the shorter days?"

"Naturally."

"We have only traveled through time, right? No spatial distance."

"That's true. I don't think we've deviated more than 200 feet from where your Arizona house was originally situated on the hill."

"I realize the climate has drastically changed throughout the eons, but it's May 27 and this mountain is still three-quarters covered with snow. I'm sure it's sheer perspective, yet it looks ten times higher than the Bradshaws. I guess what's so deceiving is the fact that Prescott was at 5,300 feet and the Bradshaws topped out at around 8,000.

So, the relative difference was only 2,700 feet. Same in Flagstaff. Flag is at 7,000 feet and nearby Humphreys was almost 12,600. Again, the discernable difference was larger, but still only about 5,600.

When I went to California to visit a cousin and passed San Jacinto peak at 10,800 just west of Palm Springs, it was unreal. The altitude of I-10, the local interstate, was only about 500, making the difference 10,300, which was quite impressive. But this ... this is unbelievable." He entered another number then looked back up. "That peak is five miles in height." Tom put the calculator away. "The numbers don't do it justice. I'd rather just stand here and look."

Only minutes later, Tom turned, looked toward the sea, and then laughed. "Who would have believed I'd be purchasing ocean front property?"

Kate walked to his side and slipped an arm around him. "All of these changes are a little hard to conceive."

Tom returned the arm gesture. "I'm sorry. I hope I haven't been boring you."

"No ... not at all ... I've found everything you've said deeply interesting. I've never seen anything like this before except in pictures, and just like the numbers, they don't do it justice either. It makes me think about Olympus Mons."

"On Mars?"

"Um hmm."

"That used to be the tallest known mountain in the solar system."

"It still is ... fifteen miles high. That's three times higher than this one. Imagine that."

"I don't think I can."

"The best part is that there's a restaurant on top."

His eyes turned to hers. "You're kidding. I remember Mons being a volcano."

"It is, but it's extinct. The mountain is composed mostly of solidified silicas. Even so, they still managed to excavate a cavity its entire height. They used the central core for elevator shafts while building shops and guestrooms horizontally all through the mountain. Of course, everything is pressurized and the outer walls have special glass with metal shutters to withstand the sandstorms. It took three years just to clear the center corridor."

"Our years or theirs?"

"Theirs."

"That'd make it about, what ... five and a half earth years?"

"That sounds close."

They turned to face the mountain as Tom waved an arm outward. "It's too bad we don't have a grav-sled. I bet there are some amazing sights out there."

"In my time, there's a large visitors center with hundreds of permanent MMT installations near the Grand Canyon, although I've never visited it. The site would be interesting to see at this point before all the evolutionary changes and intrusion made by man."

"Sorry, that's a good idea, but you'll have to wait until we get back because the canyon hasn't even started forming yet. We're still about 65 million years too early. The entire rift was produced in only five million years. That's a long time to us, but geologically, it's practically overnight.

The whole United States from about the Rockies west was on a hinged plate. It kept rising and falling with the internal pressures of the earth, and this area was covered with inland seas several times.

It wasn't until the area stabilized and the Colorado Plateau rose, that the Colorado River started cutting the canyon. In fact, the river originally flowed into the Rio Grande, which finally emptied into the Gulf of Mexico.

As the Pacific plate shifted northwest, Baja broke away from mainland Mexico and created the Gulf of California. A headwater opened at the north end of it. When the headwater and the Colorado River eventually met, combined with the uplifted Colorado Plateau, the canyon started to form.

Since rivers cut mostly only downward, the wide gorges and steps along the canyon system are from the actions of erosion caused by wind and rain."

Kate blinked. "I thought you were a physicist. Where did you learn all this information?"

"Physics was always my first love, but all of science is my mistress."

"Is it time for me to be jealous again?"

Tom laughed. "Only if it makes you happy."

She gave him a tight squeeze.

"Oof. Okay, muscle lady, when's our next jump?"

"I haven't checked yet. The view was too overwhelming."

Kate walked to the first pair of TMTs. "Larry must be downloading the programming now. The display is changing as we speak. There's also a message, 'Do not leave until receiving further information updates'."

"I wonder what that's supposed to mean?"

Kate shrugged. "Only exactly what it says, I imagine. Ah, here's the time ... 7:30 a.m. tomorrow."

"Kind of early."

"Why, do you have a late date?"

He whispered into her hair, "I'm working on it, but I'll tell you, these time changes are going to be murder."

"Shall we do a little window shopping while we're here?"

"Might as well, but it looks like all the shops are closed. However, before we go, let me do one thing. You'll thank me for it later."

Tom removed the small narrow-bladed shovel from a pack, built a knee-high mound of sand, then dug a hole in the middle down to below ground level. With a flourish he stabbed the shovel into the soil and slid a roll of toilet paper onto the handle. "Madam, the latrine is ready."

Kate clapped as Tom bowed. "Now, how do you feel about that stroll with such an enterprising gentleman?"

She curtsied. "Charmed, I'm sure."

As they walked, the remainder of the morning and early afternoon was filled with side-trip investigations and light conversation about the surrounding area. Lunch at 1:30 consisted of meal tablets and water from a canteen. Their water supply was replenished from a crystal clear stream near the mountain's base. At 4:00 they headed back to their landing site, gathering driftwood as it was encountered. Tom stooped and sifted a white powder-like material with traces of yellow through his fingers. "Have you noticed anything unusual during our time here?"

"I don't remember seeing a single animal ... there's hardly any plant life either."

Tom nodded. "Yeah. That's really strange. I've been thinking about where we might be, in the scheme of time periods. Our ninety million year jump probably put us just over the line into the Cenozoic.

That's right after the disappearance of the dinosaurs. It was one big extinction level event. Are you familiar with the Alvarez comet theory?"

"The one predicted to have impacted in the Gulf of Mexico at Chicxulub?"

"Good memory, I would never have gotten the city. But yes, that's the one. Has it ever been proven correct?"

"Proven, no. Widely accepted, yes. Why?"

"Do you recall discussions about the iridium layer?"

"Yes, I do." Kate looked at the whitish grains spread over the area. "Do you think that's what this substance could be?"

"It would make sense. The timing is certainly right. What's the chance of getting an ounce or two of hydrochloric acid sent back?"

"I don't think that's a problem. What do you intend to do with it?"

"If this material is iridium, it'll become iridescent in the acid. That's how the element got its name."

"Why not send a sample back and let a lab test it?"

"If the Alvarez theory hasn't been proven yet, then we don't know when, or if, it ever will be. I'm afraid of what it might do to the future's timeline if all of a sudden we provide irrefutable proof.

Ask for a small empty vial, too. I'll take a little with me and keep it under wraps until we can get some help on what to do with it. Here's something else to think about. If we test it here and it proves to be other than iridium, then this all becomes a null point and we'll have one less problem to deal with."

Kate nodded. "Your idea definitely has merit. I'll contact Larry when we return to our base."

Upon reentering their 'camp', they stood staring at the small pile of equipment that had arrived during their absence. Tom started picking through the collection. "I don't like the looks of this. See if there are any new messages, and I'll get a fire started for the night." He scooped out a bowl in the sand and began snapping pieces of wood for kindling. "Man, what I wouldn't give for some hot dogs and a bottle of soda."

Kate smiled at his last comment, then displayed the message screen. "There is a lengthy communication. I'll read it and give you the highlights."

Tom was sitting cross-legged in front of the fire when Kate walked over, arms laden with packages, and sat next to him. "So what did you find out?"

"Our next jump takes us into the Oligocene. Larry is concerned there will be an abundance of predatory mammals and sent an electric fence to help keep them away while we're sleeping. It consists of a solar-powered charger and short posts running a single wire between them. We'll use it as a protective perimeter. It should serve our purpose. Oh, here's your acid and vial."

"What's the other stuff?"

"A little surprise ... open them."

Tom examined the first package. "This one reminds me of butcher's paper. Oh, wow ... hot dogs!" The remaining parcels produced small amounts of relish, mustard, minced onion, ketchup, potato chips, buns, and marshmallows. He leaned over and they lightly kissed. "This is great, Kate, thanks."

She laughed. "Just remember ... half of it's mine. Ah, one other thing." A tall plastic container was presented.

Tom examined the outside, then opened the top and sniffed. "A carbonated beverage. If you keep this up, I may want to just stay here." He searched through the driftwood for just the right length sticks, loaded two with dogs, and gave one to Kate. "Here, welcome to civilization."

Kate smiled sheepishly. "Well, almost. I'm afraid there's nothing to use for spreading the condiments. You'll have to use your fingers."

Tom gave an exaggerated sigh. "Okay, so it's back to the Dark Ages."

They leaned together, bunned their dogs, crunched chips, and when the need arose, blew out their flaming marshmallows.

Tom added some wood to the fire and spread their sleeping bags, while Kate gathered up the debris from the impromptu picnic dinner. After bedding down for the night, they stared at the mountain, which had become a dark and ominous companion.

He felt her shiver. "Are you cold?"

"No. I just had a strange feeling, perhaps one of those premonitions we discussed the other day. It seemed to tell me something really terrible is lurking in the near future."

"Maybe it's the view of the mountain at night. It gives me the creeps, too. Just imagine though, it'll probably be gone when we come out of our next jump, but we'll still be going strong."

She propped up on an elbow, looking down at him. "Do you think we would have gotten together if all this hadn't happened?"

Tom studied her face in the firelight. "I think something had already started between us before we made the first jump." He laughed. "Recent occurrences have no doubt accelerated our relationship, but I have no complaints concerning that regard. How about you?"

Kate snuggled into his arms and yawned out her answer. "I feel the same. I was just taking a reality check." She yawned deeply again. "All that walking really made me tired."

"Me, too," Tom chuckled, "But it was great not having something chase us for a whole day. I think you can safely put that menacing intuition behind you. If the remainder of the trip is this uneventful, then our worries may be over."

Kate was already breathing slow and deep. Tom quickly slipped under the same shroud of fatigue.

A short time later, Tom's eyes popped open. "Oh no ... Kate, wake up, we've got to go back."

She came awake slowly. "Huh ... what are you talking about?"

"John ... we forgot John! He's still sitting on that ledge in front of the cave where we slept."

She moaned and rolled over. "I replaced John's disks in his TMT while you were off looking for Bisbee. John was returned to our time along with his machine."

"Oh, that's right ... I remember now, you told me. I guess it was just a dream. Your ominous suspicions must be haunting me."

"Umm, go back to sleep."

Tom draped an arm over Kate and closed his eyes, but some insightful little maw persisted in nibbling at the extreme fringes of his conscious awareness.

"Mishaps are like knives, that either serve us or cut us, as we grasp them by the blade or the handle."

- Herman Melville

Chapter 17
Unintentional Overnighter

Kate pressed a button to silence the alarm on WD7. Tom stirred next to her. "Is it time already? It seems like I just dozed off."

"Come on, sleepy head. The day is waiting, and we have work to do."

She handed him a meal tablet. "Here's breakfast."

"Yummy."

"On second thought, lay there and face the mountain for a minute. That'll give me a chance to use the sand cone."

Tom blinked. "Oh, that. Interesting choice of terminology."

"It's not any more obscure than brownie film."

His head returned to the pillow. "Don't pick on me. It's too early."

"I make my points whenever I'm able. By the way, I made an improvement to the latrine last night. I expect the upgrade to be carried forward as others are built."

Tom pulled the blanket over him. A muted, "Yes, maam," filtered through the fabric.

"Okay, I'm finished."

Tom rose and strolled over to the modified sand hill. A sheet of cloth had been placed over the 'seat' with a hole cut in the middle. "I take it that's to keep the sand off your bare bottom?"

"Yes. I think you'll appreciate it when you have to sit down."

Tom snickered. "I have to admit, that's a good idea. I imagine I would have done the same thing the first time the need arose."

Kate smiled. "Well, don't let it happen again. You've been warned."

"A little testy this morning I see."

"Actually, I'm in a great mood. A couple more jumps and we'll be home. We'll have clean clothes, hot baths, auto-cooked food, and indoor plumbing. I can't wait."

"Alright, if you'll be so kind as to look the other way, I'll do my thing, and we'll get busy."

"Roger, Dodger, over and ... whatever else you say."

Kate became a model of industry. In the time it took Tom to expunge his watery waste, she had both sleeping bags and half the 'camp' positioned for the next jump. She impatiently waited for him. "What are you doing now?"

Tom managed to get the words out between laughs. "Brushing my teeth. How about downshifting a couple of gears. The future will wait a few more minutes. Besides, I still have my little experiment to perform."

She ran over and hugged him from behind. "Okay, this time you play and I'll work, but just wait until I get you home."

"I don't know. Staying here is looking better and better."

That earned him a swat on the butt. "Ouch. You little monster."

She twirled away, taunting him.

Tom retrieved his bottle of acid and added a large pinch of the whitish grains. Kate stopped long enough to watch. He swirled the mixture and held it up to the light. "Wow. Look at those colors. I can't guarantee it, but it sure looks like iridium to me." He filled the small dry vial with a sample of the grainy powder, added the cap, and placed it in a shirt pocket. "That question seems to have found an answer." Tom surveyed the surrounding area. "We may have a problem getting out of here."

Kate noted his search. "Why's that?"

"Think about what special material is contained in the transmit mats that allows the scan system to delineate us from the background."

"I thought about that yesterday when you theorized this material may be iridium. But, I reasoned that if the system could bring us in, it'd take us out."

"Logical, except for one drawback. It's like comparing our current situation to pouring a glass of water into a pool. Until the water is mixed, there's no challenge telling them apart. However, once that happens, it's a whole different set of circumstances. I'm not saying we're going to have difficulty, but if we do, it won't be a surprise."

Tom watched her emotions crash. "Whoa, Kate, I'm sorry. I didn't mean to ruin your mood. If something happens, we'll work around it. Let's give it a shot and see."

Kate nodded. "You're right."

They stood on transmit mats surrounded by their equipment as the timer counted down. A bright flash ... then nothing.

Kate moaned, "Oh no." She checked for an error message. "It reads: 'Foreground indistinguishable from background – transmission aborted'. You were right to be worried."

"Trust me, I'm not gloating."

"What if we try clearing an area of the iridium?"

"That's my girl. It's worth a try."

Kate sighed. "You don't sound convinced."

"I think it's too well mixed into the soil. But, I've been wrong before. I hope this is one of those times. Otherwise, maybe all we need to do is find a big rock and clean it off."

"I vote to try that first."

"Okay. Lead on McDuff."

Kate wandered around and found a large, flat outcropping. "How about this one?"

"It's your call."

"Tom, I need your help."

Tom opened his arms and issued the most comforting smile he could. "Kate, come here." She was cemented in place. "Please."

Kate approached slowly, stopping in front of him. "What is it?"

He enfolded her into his arms. "I take it you're frightened."

"Petrified is more the word. If this doesn't work, we're stranded for the rest of our lives." She searched his eyes. "You know the answer, don't you?"

"I think I do."

"Tell me."

Tom shook his head. "Kate, somehow you've done more for my self-confidence in the short time since I met you than anyone and everyone else throughout my entire life. For some oddball reason, you believe in me. I've never felt so alive and it's absolutely wonderful, so I'm going to try and return the kind support. I want you to relax, think about the problem, and come up with a solution. I'm going for a walk, but before I go, I want you to kiss me."

She gave him a quick kiss. "Why were you so adamant about it?"

"If you have to ask, it didn't work. Do it again."

This time Kate kissed a little longer and pressed somewhat harder. "Ah, I think I'm getting the idea. Go on, get out of here. Come back in about an hour."

Tom laughed. "I don't have a watch, but I can guess when it's about time."

He walked away.

When Tom returned, Kate was busily moving their equipment and TMTs onto the cleared rock outcropping.

He ran over. "Kate, I didn't mean for you to do all the work. Just come up with an idea, and I'll be glad to help."

She smiled. "I know, but being busy is good therapy. I'm almost ready to try your first suggestion. I guess it all depends on how wide an area the scan lens envelops. If plan 'A' doesn't work, I already have a plan 'B' on the drawing board. If you'll be so gallant as to hop onto your mat, we'll find out."

They positioned themselves and she started the countdown.

Another flash ... another dud.

Kate rechecked the error log. "Same problem. There's just too much iridium in the area, it's confusing the lens system. I really had hopes this would work."

"Hmm, I did too."

Kate experienced a moment of panic. "Was this the plan you would have used?"

"Yes, but it was only my plan 'A', too."

She seemed visibly relieved. "Okay, for my next trick, we'll need some logs and something to hold them together."

Tom's smile covered his face. "A raft. That's, what I was thinking."

Kate smirked. "It reasonably follows that the only way to escape the effects of the iridium interference is by moving away from the land."

"You got it skipper. This is probably going to take the rest of the day. You'd better inform Larry what's happened."

"Already done. But, since this attempt didn't work either, I'll contact him again and reschedule a time for tomorrow. Meanwhile, both of us will get busy."

Tom chuckled. "What a tyrannical taskmaster."

They remembered seeing assorted sized logs on the previous day's trek, so the route was retraced. Four to six footers would suffice. The missing link was something to hold the logs together. Larry couldn't just send them something because it would get left behind with the raft.

Tom got an idea. "Let's see if we can find a cave with vegetation on top. The roots will probably grow down into the roof, which we can cut off and use as ropes. The roots will eventually rot, freeing the logs, making them effectively nothing more than driftwood again. No one will ever be the wiser."

Kate laughed. "Maybe I should start calling you Tom Sawyer."

"Okay ... Huck."

By early evening, a small raft had been assembled and positioned at the shoreline near camp. Tom examined their handiwork. "We'll launch it tomorrow about an hour before jump time and give it a good wash. We want to make sure it's as free of iridium as possible. It looks clean now, but as they say, 'better safe than sorry'. Besides, it'll be nice to cool off after the work."

Kate had been listening while checking incoming message traffic. "Larry has rescheduled us for 11 a.m. If nothing else, you get to sleep late. You didn't plan all of this, did you?"

"Nothing doing. Even I wouldn't go to all this trouble for just a couple hours of added sleep. I'm going to start a fire; it feels like it might get pretty cool this evening. We have plenty of wood left over from the deck ... might as well put it to good use."

Kate frowned. "Are meal tablets okay for tonight?"

"Fine with me. I'm too tired to even cook marshmallows again."

It was completely dark by the time the fire was going, and they had settled for the night. Fifteen minutes after bedding down, the world no longer seemed to exist.

Somewhere around two, Kate began thrashing beneath the blanket. Shortly afterward, she sat up wide-awake, screaming. Tom came alert, grabbed his gun, and stood by the dying light of the fire searching for trouble while wiping the sleep from his eyes. "Kate, what is it? I don't see anything."

She regained control. "I'm sorry, Tom. It was just a nightmare. There was noise, things flying through the air, and general confusion. I really don't know what it was. Come back to bed."

Tom stoked the fire and settled next to Kate. "Hey, you're shaking. Come here, let me hold you."

She snuggled closer. "Thanks, that's much better. I'm okay now. I'm sure it was nothing."

They slowly drifted back to sleep.

*   *   *   *   *

Tom extended a hand and patted around the area next to him without meeting any resistance. He knew he was alone in the 'bed', even before opening his eyes.

Tom sat up, stretched, and looked toward the water's edge, noticing that Kate had tugged the raft into the water and was washing it down. She had a rough night, so it seemed important to be extra nice around her today.

He crawled from under the blanket, stripped off his pants, pulled on some shoes, and went to join her. "Hi ya, kiddo. Aren't you up kind of early?"

She placed one fist on the raft, the other fist upon her first, and set her chin atop both. "I was almost afraid of going back to sleep last night. I don't understand what's happening to me."

"I think everything is catching up with you. Once we get under way, things will probably settle down again."

"I hope so. I can't take many more nights like that. I was in such a good mood yesterday and now I feel," she looked to Tom, "empty, or maybe lost. I just don't know. Whatever it is, I can't shake it."

"Is there anything I can do to help?"

"Will you hold me for awhile?"

"Sure, you delegate all the tough jobs to me, but I think I can handle that one." He waded over and slipped his arms around her. "What time is it?"

Kate tilted her wrist. "Almost nine."

"I'll hold you for two hours, but no more, because then, it'll be time to leave. Oh, I meant to ask, are you wearing shoes?" Her shoe-covered foot broke the surface. "Good thing ... I was really going to be upset if you were out here barefoot."

"That would almost be inviting trouble. Believe me, another dilemma is the last thing I want. I have seen some fish, but they've all been small. Nothing scary."

"I was more worried about some kind of sea urchin."

They stood in the sun with the waves lapping around them. Tom gently rubbed her back and arms. After perhaps ten minutes, she leaned back and looked up to him. "Thanks, Tom. That was more therapeutic than you can imagine."

"Oh, I don't know about that. I'm human ... well, at least once in a while."

"I'm feeling much better, maybe even a little foolish."

Tom pursed his lips. "Nonsense. With all we've been through lately, you have every right to feel apprehensive." He laughed. "Maybe you're afraid once we get back to the real world you'll be bored."

"Oh, only you would dream up something like that. Come on Sawyer, let's get to work."

"One second. We don't have any champagne, but for luck, even this contraption should be properly launched. Trouble is, I have no idea which end to call the bow. Well, no matter." He splashed some seawater on the deck. "I christen thee ... the interstellar galactic transport, 'Run-A-Ground'."

She grinned tightly. "How could a name like that not inspire confidence? Interstellar transport?" Kate shook her head. "Talk about delusions of grandeur. Even John would be impressed." She started walking up the beach. "Now ... Sawyer."

"Let me make sure our ship is secure, then I'll be right behind you, Huck."

Everything that could tolerate moisture got a dunking in the water to wash away the sand and stray iridium before being set on the raft. Tom started loading the TMTs aboard, placing them on the required transmit mats.

They were ready to jump ahead of schedule, so Kate informed Larry of their plans for leaving early. Larry acknowledged in the affirmative and remarked that no problem was foreseen. He reminded them to set up the electric fence upon arrival and wished them luck.

Tom had buckled on his gun and chambered a round. The raft was freed and poled away from the iridium-contaminated land. Wind was light and waves were gentle. An unusually fidgety Kate counted down the numbers. Successive flashes sent them on the way.

"But not long; for in the tedious minutes' exquisite interval – I'm on the rack; for sure the greatest evil man can know bears no proportion to this dread suspense."

- Froude

Chapter 18
Those Darn Cats

Tom started straightening, but was knocked to the ground as something massive smacked into his back and tore away his pack. A large furry blur flew past. There was a lot of noise. Metal was being rendered into scrap, piece by piece. Kate was screaming for help. He struggled to his feet and heard heavy footfalls approaching from behind again.

Tom dove to his side and rolled, coming up in a crouched position. The gun came out and he thumbed off the safety. The hairy demon skidded to a stop and whirled toward him. He brought the weapon up and fired. The animal lay still.

He searched for Kate and saw that her left wrist was in the mouth of a huge cat. One of its front paws was raking her abdomen. There was blood on her jumper. Tom aimed and fired at the animal's body. It went down with its legs kicking at the air. The others ran off to regroup. The area became still and quiet.

He holstered the gun and raced to Kate's side. Her wrist was mangled, splintered bones showed through the wound and surrounding tissue. What was left of WD7 was imbedded into her flesh. She rocked from side to side, half in shock, half hysterical. "Kate, I've got you. It's going to be all right."

He ripped off part of his shirt, wrapped it around her wrist, then quickly scanned the area looking for the cats. They were still keeping their distance.

The shredded jumper was lifted from her stomach. He froze, not believing the damage. Her skin was laid open, the liver was visible. Worst of all ... there was a fecal odor. The cat had torn her intestines. Tom realized peritonitis would soon follow. He tore off the rest of his shirt and packed it against her abdominal wound.

"Tom, how b-ba bad is it?"

"It's bad, Kate, but you're going to make it. You hear me. You're going to be okay. I promise."

She passed out.

Tom looked around at all the ruined equipment, remembering Larry's report that the last two TMTs were still not repaired and John's single machine couldn't be used to alternate lead. They were stuck here with no communication, and apparently, without hope of getting out.

Tom reexamined Kate's wounds. His heart sank, because at that instant, he felt she was dying, and there was nothing he could do to prevent it.

He placed a hand on the butt of the gun as two of the great cats slinked toward one of their fallen comrades. Tom let them drag the body away thinking it would buy him some time. There wasn't a lot more he could do for Kate at the moment, so he started checking over the broken equipment. One of the TMTs looked semi-intact, but the other three were questionable at best.

The fence charger unit and its solar collector were undamaged, but the battery that would power the device at night had been bitten. One of the cats must have gotten quite a rotten taste in its mouth from that experience. All the electrolyte solution had leaked away.

There was a large tree similar to an African Acacia about forty feet from their current location. Other than the single tree, the nearby landscape was almost completely barren except for a rock escarpment that the cats apparently made their home. Tom decided he would set the fence up around the tree as a first line of defense. Positioning themselves in the tree's branches would provide a secondary barrier. He planned to hang the broken metal pieces from the tree limbs hoping they would act as a deterrent, or at least give a warning when the animals approached.

Prior to the move, he grabbed the second dead cat by the hind legs and tugged it away from their proximity, figuring they would come for it next.

Tom grabbed up his pack, then lifted Kate and carried her to the base of the tree. One towel was folded and placed under her head; a second replaced the shirt as a bandage over her belly.

He noted with some relief that the bleeding had slowed considerably. Kate had proven to be one tough lady, but considering the wounds, he couldn't help wondering if she had any chance for survival at all. Tom pressed his balled fists hard against his forehead, desperately trying to hold back the tears. He knew Kate was completely dependent on him, so he shook off his mood and got to work.

About an hour later, Tom had the electric fence installed and charged. He made the perimeter much smaller than originally planned, but it had allowed him to string four wires instead of one. Strips of cloth had been tied along the fence wires, which hopefully would keep the cats from charging blindly through them. The equipment had been gathered into a pile near the base of the tree. Both canteens were undamaged and full of water. The bag of food tablets was likewise intact.

Tom had emptied their backpacks and used them to fashion a makeshift hammock strung between two strong branches. Kate was safely enclosed within. His gun belt held the towel firmly against her stomach. He had covered her with a clean shirt and tied the empty sleeves around the tree limbs, holding her confined in case she became conscious and tried to move. The remains of a shredded blanket had been doubled and covered her for warmth.

Kate's previous words about 'standardized parts' and 'quick disconnects' sifted through his memory, triggering the search for a power supply in one of the TMTs' rings. Tom surmised it might be used to keep the fence charger working during the night. The search proved productive because even though the power supply was set at 24 volts DC, it also had an outlet for 12, matching the input requirements of the charger. He'd have to be especially careful around the ring since the passwords and other safety features were bypassed to keep the ring's power supply 'hot'. It was a small reserve. He hoped it'd last all night.

Tom doubled a second torn blanket and tied the corners to tree limbs adjoining Kate's. It became his sleeping quarters and lookout tower.

The cats had left the area for now, presumably to escape the heat of the day, or find water. Either way, they were gone.

After checking on Kate, he made a decision to try and sleep.

A snapping, hissing, and growling brought him awake. There were at least a dozen cats attacking the fence. So far, the fence was winning. Tom decided that if he picked off a few more, maybe they'd learn to stay away. He pulled his gun and sighted at the closest animals. It took seven shots to put three of them down. Then the unforeseen happened.

One of the larger cats charged the wires and ripped them off their insulators. The fence shorted out. The cat that had charged was stunned and became disoriented, but the others drew closer. He fired six shots in quick succession before the hammer fell on an empty chamber. Three more cats were down. The others had finally fled. He pushed the release, dropped the empty clip onto his blanket and slapped his second, and only other, fifteen-round magazine into the butt of the gun.

Tom thought for a minute, and then looked at Kate. He might be able to hold the cats off once, possibly twice more. After that they would be completely vulnerable. Being eaten alive didn't sound like the best way to die, and Kate would be utterly defenseless. The full magazine was released and two bullets were removed. These were loaded into the empty magazine to be saved for just such a contingency.

Tom felt the heat coming off the gun's barrel after the extended firing, so he hung the weapon by the trigger guard on a broken branch stem within easy reach from the ground. He jumped down, switched off the power, dragged the dead cats outside the perimeter, and repaired the fence. The sun was nearing the horizon when everything was finished. Tom noticed the charger had already switched to its alternate power source, which was being supplied by the TMT's ring.

Some of the metal pieces were rearranged so they hung closer to the ground. After a look around, Tom climbed into the tree and checked on Kate. She appeared to be resting as comfortably as possible. Finally, he reclaimed his previous position, opened a canteen, and gulped down a food tablet.

Now, there was nothing to do but wait.

Tom's head jerked as a ray of morning sunlight caught him square in the eye ... just before he heard the tinkling of metal. He sat up with a start. The ring's power supply must have become depleted, because another group of cats were beginning to slink around the tree, pawing the obstacles hanging in front of their faces. His gun came out. One of them saw him move and crouched, ears back, hissing. It prepared to scale the tree; skin bulged as massive muscles tensed.

Tom fired a bullet into its back before the leap. The injured cat attacked another animal, mistaking it for the cause of its pain. General mayhem broke loose. As Tom fired, the cats charged the tree, the hanging metal, and just as often, themselves. They had no idea what was 'biting' them. One leaped into the tree, almost knocking Tom from his precarious hold. The cat was about to attack Kate when Tom shot it in the only target it presented, the butt. The cat roared with pain and jumped from the tree doing a crazy spinning dance upon hitting the ground.

When the cats left, there were seven more dead and injured. Tom watched as the remainder all cowered past a particularly large cat. It looked like the same one that had charged through the fence, presumably the alpha male. If he could kill it, maybe he'd cut off the serpent's head for awhile.

The gun's magazine was ejected, and the remaining shots were counted. There was a grand total of four, including the one still in the chamber. All the cats had left the immediate area except for the leader. It lay there watching.

Tom reasoned that if the fence could be mended again, it should protect them the rest of the day. The solar collector would be receiving enough light by now to power the charging unit. Tom hung the hot gun on the branch stub again and scrambled down from the relative safety of the tree.

The charger had faithfully switched back to the solar panel, but as expected, was indicating a ground fault. Tom turned off the power, cleared away the dead cats, and started twisting the fence wires back together.

The leader cat's eyes never left Tom, and his left the cat only when absolutely necessary.

Tom stood staring at the devilish carnivore as the fence became operational once more. The animal was laying about sixty or seventy feet away.

Since yesterday was the first time he had fired this gun, he had no idea how accurate the sights were at that distance. It would probably take two or three shots just to get close. But, if he could move nearer, taking out the alpha male would give him a day, maybe two, before a new leader would rise through the ranks. That would be worth a couple bullets. After the ammunition was gone, it was over anyway.

So far, the cats had not attacked from the rear of the perimeter. Tom disabled the power long enough to remove only the top wire between two backside posts, restored the power, stepped over, and began circling around towards the front. The cat's head lifted higher as if it were extremely interested in this new development.

Tom made sure his weapon's safety was already off while gradually closing the distance between him and the tabby from hell. The cat allowed Tom to approach within approximately forty feet, then arose, retreated, and resettled again. When he got within about the same distance, the cat repeated its earlier maneuver. Tom noticed how close to the escarpment he was getting and realized this might be a trap.

As he started to back away, the lead cat issued a signal and a horde of its companions leaped over the top of the rocks and ran towards Tom.

It was over.

He would use his four remaining shots and go down. He considered using one on himself, but having failed Kate, he felt he didn't deserve an easy death.

The thought of them tearing into her froze him in place.

Instinct overrode fear as a flash and movement to his left brought the weapon up and prepared for firing. He quickly checked his action as John's TMT appeared. The bright light had temporarily halted the cats' charge, but soon they started forward again.

Tom literally jumped as a loud siren began blaring. The cats stopped, then lowered to the ground hissing and growling with their ears madly twitching. Suddenly, they all bolted away over the far side of the escarpment. Tom ran to the machine, picked it up, and headed back toward the tree with the siren still wailing.

Upon arrival at the backside of the fence, he set the TMT down and covered his ears while looking for some way to shut off the noise. He saw a touch pad marked 'RESET', but something stayed his hand. It might reset the entire machine and clear any messages that might have also transferred.

Searching the outside of the device, he found a handwritten note taped to an access door. 'To stop alarm touch SILENT on inside of TMT.'

The door was opened and the keypad pressed. A comparative peace and tranquility returned. Tom whirled as he heard something, waving the gun from side to side.

Nothing there.

Again a noise. This time he realized it came from high in the tree. Tom climbed up and found Kate awake, but had to listen closely since her words were mostly clicks and hisses. "What was all the racket?"

"John's TMT is here. We can reestablish communications. I promised you would be okay, and I always keep my word. I know this may be a dumb question, but can I do anything to make you more comfortable?"

"Can I have a drink of water?"

Tom knew that gut wounds and liquids didn't mix. "Alright, but just a sip." He allowed her to wet her lips and not much more.

"Can you take the blanket off, too? I'm hot."

He removed the blanket and felt her forehead with the back of his hand. She was burning up. An infection must be spreading rapidly. He gave her hand a squeeze. "I'm going to check the machine for messages."

Tom slipped down and hurried to the TMT. It was already positioned at the comm panel. The cursor blinked, patiently waiting at the end of the transmission.

> 'Tom/Kate: lost contact with all four machines – assume you are in trouble and need help – sorry so long in contacting you – had to search and find position of last known signal. Kate: you know what to do. Tom: enter message and press SEND - machine will remain powered up and in standby mode. All password checking has been removed. - Frank.'

Tom thought about what had happened, what was relevant, and composed the shortest note he could.

> 'Frank: Kate seriously injured. Laceration to lower body area – internal organs visible – intestines torn – fecal matter leaking into abdominal cavity. Left wrist has multiple compound fractures. Feels like she's running a high fever. Need antibiotics and pain meds ASAP. I don't think any of our TMTs

are functional. Solar battery damaged – need replacement. Also, desperately need 9mm cartridges. – Tom.'

Tom pressed the SEND key and tried to take his mind off matters by aimlessly wandering and picking up the brass casings from his spent bullets. He was pocketing the last two when the TMT beeped.

> 'Tom: terribly sorry to hear about Kate. We'll do everything we can to help. All meds and med kit will arrive soon. Ran a quick check to find out 9mm cartridges were for a handgun. May be hard to get. Will send handheld TASER – stuns but doesn't kill. Also needs minimum one minute to recharge between firings. Hope it is of some use. – Frank.'

Tom leaned on the TMT, wondering what possible good such a weapon would be in this predicament. His eyes were closed, body frozen in place, fingers tightly gripping the ring ... frantically trying to hold onto whatever nerve he had left.

The flash was visible through Tom's eyelids. He quickly circled the TMT and inspected the newly arrived items. There was a note from a Dr. Tang about using and dispensing the drugs. One was a powdery substance that was to be sprinkled directly into the open wounds. Dr. Tang expressed grave concern about the fecal emission into the body.

A monitor like the one used on John was present with several sticky notes attached. One of them was a diagram depicting how to plug the monitor into an auxiliary port inside the TMT so Dr. Tang could remotely retrieve the information it would provide. Tang indicated the next move would be determined by Kate's condition.

Everything had arrived in a small tote bag. Tom replaced the items, put the tote's strap around his neck, and scrambled into the tree with the remote connection trailing behind.

He attached the monitor to Kate's arm as she had previously done for John, and switched on the power. The transmit and receive indicators alternately blinked as the device gathered and sent its vital data.

A few minutes passed, and the TMT beeped again. The battery and another small tote bag appeared on the transmit mat. Upon investigation, the bag was discovered to contain several plastic pouches. Two were marked 'Whole Blood – Type O, Rh+', and two were plain saline solution. There were also ampoules of antibiotics and an infusion device with a label stating: 'Place against inside of wrist – this side out'. A separate diagram illustrated how everything attached in sequence. Tom positioned the device according to instructions and added a pouch of blood, saline, and one of the ampoules.

Kate's eyes fluttered open and she commented as he worked, "Looks like the designation 'doctor' has taken on a new connotation for you."

"I was ordered to get all this paraphernalia functioning and then read a message waiting for me on the TMT. I'll do my job and you do yours. Just lay back and rest."

She managed a smile and weakly stated, "Yes, sir."

He scanned the area and then attended to the beeping TMT. "Alright, alright, I'm here, shut up." Tom rubbed his forehead thinking next time there was a chance, he'd ask for some aspirin. He brought up the message and started to read. The machine became quiet.

> 'Tom: There's no way, or time, to break this gently.
> It should be obvious that Kate's abdominal wound is life threatening. Her circulatory system is dangerously close to collapse. Our initial idea was to employ the same procedure used with John. Put Kate in stasis and send her home. Unfortunately, according to the data, this is not an option. Your first comment will probably be that John was already dead when placed in stasis, so why won't it work for her. The difference is that John simply had a poison needing to be extracted from his system. Kate has massive tissue and organ damage, is suffering extreme blood loss, and is in shock. The disintegration phase at this point would kill her as surely as a bullet to the brain. My estimate is only a five to ten percent chance of successful recovery if stasis is attempted. I'm sure this is difficult to believe, but her best chance for survival is staying with you.
> Frank and Larry have been working, under John's direction, in conjunction with the medical labs on a project that is well into the animal experimentation stage. They were prepared to begin human trials on small-scale injuries soon. Having this procedure available now may well prove to be the difference between Kate living or dying.
>
> There are two important factors. One – we MUST have access to the TMT's memory that last transported her. Two – Once the process begins, it cannot be interrupted. There is no restart; it's a one-time exchange. Instructions and equipment are forthcoming. – Dr. Tang.'

Tom stood staring at the message. His stomach was doing cartwheels. He climbed back into the tree and tried to reassure Kate ... as well as himself.

"Hey, kiddo. It looks like you get to be my guinea pig now. The guys are cooking up something special just for you." He checked the monitor. "You're running a fever, but the color in your face is better. Let's see how the juice is doing." Tom inspected the pouches. "Looks like it's time for another can of tomato." The empty blood pouch was replaced. "The antibiotic and saline are still okay."

Kate managed to nod. Her eyes were barely open. "Did they say what they were going to do?"

Tom shrugged. "I'm not sure. Instructions and equipment are being prepared. Whatever they're doing requires the TMT memory record of your last jump. When it all gets here, I'll read through it and bring you up to date.

For now, close those beautiful green peepers and toddle off to dreamland."

"The heart bowed down by weight of woe to weakest hope will cling."
- Alfred Bunn

Chapter 19
Here Kitty, Kitty

Tom had just suspended a fresh saline pouch when the familiar pattern of beep, flash, package arrival had transpired. Kate had fallen asleep, so he hung by a branch and dropped quietly to the ground.

He inspected the two ends of a cable. One end was marked 'John's', while the other was labeled 'Kate's TMT memory'. Both ends appeared to be normal comm plugs. It was the tangle of wires and circuit boards in-between that alarmed him. Some of the loose wires went to a destination, some didn't. There was one section held together with nothing more than common black electrical tape. A printed sequence of instructions accompanied the cable, but there were portions crossed out, with corrections written in the margins.

The entire setup would have been extremely upsetting except for the remembrance of many experiments he had performed that employed similar looking collections of confusing parts.

He muttered aloud, "As long as it works, who cares what it looks like."

The TASER weapon and strange looking cable were the only pieces of equipment, so he gathered up the printed sheets and reclaimed his vigil point.

Tom read, but wasn't sure he believed. He had to continually remind himself that this design was three hundred years in his time's future. It was only an extension of technology they utilized every day. Still, after the last page was finished, he stared off into nothing, wondering if it would work.

Kate had awakened and watched him reading. She gave him a minute to collect his thoughts and then asked, "What's the bottom line, doctor?"

Tom scooted closer and checked the infusion device, deciding to change the antibiotic ampoule. "Are you familiar with a Dr. Tang?"

"Yes, Peter and I are good friends. Brilliant doctor. He's right at the forefront of medical technology. Is he the one who sent the supplies?"

"Yes. That's not all he sent. There's some sort of interface cable that'll hook John's machine into the TMT's memory that last transported you. From what I can gather reading the instructions, they first need you strong enough to withstand a disintegration. Then they're going use the EXPEL process, which you've mentioned, to remove any existing infection. The problem remains that fecal matter doesn't manifest as being foreign. To purge it from your body cavities, Frank added some of his holographic code for reconstructing and replacing the injured areas by exploiting an image from your TMT.

I guess you could call it a human match-merge process using your current body as input one, and the image from your machine as input two. You're nodding. Have you heard of this before?"

"Peter and John's team have been working on it for a few years now. It's referred to as the Tang-Picus project ... sometimes abbreviated TP. Kind of apropos, don't you think?"

Tom grinned. "I think the pain meds must be doing their job because your sense of humor has returned. You're obviously feeling a little stronger and if we're going to do this, now is probably the time. The bad thing about pain relievers is that injured people think they're better and try to move around. That's when they do even more damage. So don't move. I'll prep the machines and get the transmit mats in place for you to lie on. You just stay still, got it?"

"Aye, aye, sir."

Tom kissed her cheek, checked the area, and slipped down from the tree with the packet of papers.

He positioned John's TMT and laid the transmit mats end to end. The most important thing he needed to find was the primary TMT, which had transmitted Kate. Checking the first resulted in an 'UNKNOWN' designation. He assumed 'unknown' meant him, since his DNA was not cataloged into the system. The second didn't respond, and the third was also 'UNKNOWN'.

Tom hesitantly tried the last. It was Kate's, but it was the secondary. That meant the only TMT not to respond at all was the one they needed. His hopes tumbled. Tom walked to John's TMT and sent the bad news. It only took a minute to get a reply.

> 'Tom: As long as the main body housing is intact, the memory is probably still viable. It uses EPROM strings to retain data even if the power has failed. We won't know until you actually make the connection. Good luck. – Frank.'

Tom's spirits rode up the other side of an emotional roller coaster. He routed the cable between the two machines and thought he'd float away when the message 'Data Access Successful' displayed. The first hurdle had been cleared.

He repositioned in the tree hoping that getting Kate down would be easier than putting her up. "Are you ready?" She simply nodded.

He hooked the tops of his shoes over some limbs, then eased her down into the crotch of the main branches, letting his chest slide against the trunk. Afterwards, he dropped to the ground, reached up, and managed lowering her the rest of the way. "That wasn't as hard as I thought it was going to be. I trust the service was acceptable?"

She whispered, "Remind me to tip you when we get home."

"I bet you say that to all the hired help."

He gently placed her on the mats. "Okay, my job is done. According to the instructions, all the programming is downloaded and ready for execution. It's up to technology and some computer code now. I hope these guys are as good as you think."

"They are, Tom. I'll be back to annoy you in no time."

"I'll be counting the minutes, about thirty from what Frank said." Tom knelt close and held her hand. They locked eyes.

She squeezed his fingers. "Tom ... I love you."

He swallowed hard. "I love you, too, Kiddo. Make sure you come back to me."

She smiled and closed her eyes.

Tom removed the infuser and blood soaked towel, rose, and pressed the 'RUN PROGRAM' keypad. There was the expected blinding light and Kate disappeared.

The scan processing code recognized that metal parts don't normally belong in a human body, so what remained of WD7 dropped to the ground. Tom stared at it for a minute, then enclosed it in an empty saline pouch; the bag was added to the broken parts pile.

Tom was astonished as he watched the 'Time To Reintegration' clock. The seconds were a blur and the minutes flew by like seconds. It took him a moment to understand that the processor was alive in its own world, and this was just another example of time being only a relative concept.

The clock appeared to stop with 2:32 left. Then the seconds ticked away at a snail's pace. He realized the program had probably come across one of the injured areas. It was busily trying to reconstruct the three-dimensional image of the damaged tissues using a map depicting the region before the wound occurred. The whole idea made him shiver.

Tom decided to busy himself inserting the new battery into the fence charging circuit. While switching off the power, he noticed the solar collector had replenished the energy supply in the TMT's ring. At present, he didn't think anything about it.

The battery had been inserted into the circuit and the power restored. Tom walked the fence line visibly checking the connections. John's TMT beeped. He closed his eyes and waited for the flash. Nothing happened. He ran to the TMT expecting a message. It was there, flashing in large red letters.

'Double Bit Error During Memory Access At Address: 41FB-30D3-1C0D'.

There were three seconds left on the countdown clock. He stopped breathing and held onto the ring as more messages unfolded: 'Interpolation Started' ... 'Subroutine Downloaded' ... 'Interpolation Canceled' ... 'Subroutine Started' ... 'Data Bits Recovered' ... 'Memory Access Successfully Completed'.

The last three seconds ticked away and the area was brightly lit once more. Tom squeezed his eyes closed and gasped, leaning against the tree because his relaxing muscles couldn't quite manage to support him.

Kate's voice endearingly called to him. "Hey, Sawyer, do you plan on standing there all day, or are you going to help me up?"

They stood rocking together in each other's arms. Then he caught movement on the escarpment. "Uh oh, I think we're going to have company."

She turned and they watched as over thirty cats came prowling towards them. Tom hustled over to John's TMT. "If I push the SILENT key again, will the alarm come back on?" She nodded. "Good, but I'll wait until they're a little closer, maybe it'll have more effect."

He picked up the TASER weapon. "Meanwhile, you get up into the tree; here, take this with you. Get out on one of the larger branches. That way only a single cat can come at you from one direction." She hesitated. "Kate, I can fight better if I know you're reasonably safe."

"Okay, but be careful. Don't take any of your crazy chances. I didn't go through all of this just to watch you get killed." She turned away, but then looked back. "How many shots do you have left?"

His gaze lowered. "Four."

"Do you think you should save two for us ... just in case?"

He couldn't help but laugh. "Ah, counting those I have six."

She smiled back. "I see what you mean by 'Great minds – same gutter'," and hurried into the tree.

Tom opened the access door and placed a finger on the alarm keypad, paused, then pressed at a point when he thought the cats were close enough. The ear-shattering wail drove the cats into a frenzy, but they stayed their ground because the alpha male was following and growled at any who started to run. Tom silenced the alarm and looked up at Kate. "If it's not doing any good, then we might as well be able to hear each other."

He pulled out his gun and waited, trying to keep the leader in sight. They all milled around, feigning charges at the fence, then changing direction. The leader was quickly lost in the milieu.

Kate screamed. Tom whirled. The lead animal had circled around, jumped the fence from behind, leapt into the tree, and was now stalking Kate.

Tom darted around the tree's base, but Kate remained in the line of fire.

Kate discharged the TASER. The huge animal dropped onto the branch, but didn't fall from the tree. The weapon was designed to stun a large man, not a 500-pound Saber Tooth cat.

The cat began to recover quickly and regained its footing. There wasn't enough time for her weapon to recharge, so Tom did the only thing that flashed within his mind. He jumped up and grabbed onto the cat's tail.

The cat dug its claws into the bark while turning and adjusting its stance. A giant paw swung back, slashing against Tom's chest, knocking him to the ground. His helpless form seemed to change the cat's mind. Tom became the preferred target. The cat prepared to pounce.

Tom searched the ground for a weapon. The TMT ring lay within reach. He snatched it up, pulling the wires loose attached to the charger. The loss of external power triggered the ring's circuit; it became active.

Tom held it at arm's length and snarled, "Here kitty, kitty."

The animal leaped. Its right front paw hit the ring just above Tom's left hand. The combined weight and momentum snapped his wrist like a proverbial dry twig. He howled in pain as the ring swung out; the cat's paw slipped inward. There was a loud sizzling sound, as of bacon on a hot griddle ... and the cat was gone.

Tom grabs the Saber-Tooth cat's tail to save Kate

Tom becomes the Saber-Tooth's preferred target

Tom dropped the ring, held his wrist, and turned away as the stench of singed hair and burned flesh made him gag. The loss of their leader stopped the remaining cats in their tracks. When the odor reached their noses, they turned and ran as one. Kate hurried down from the tree and held Tom.

There were four trails of blood down his front and what dangled from his arm's end looked like an alien's interpretation of a human hand.

"Looks like you get to try the procedure next." She popped up, and then had to lean against the tree trunk for support.

Tom struggled to his feet. "Kate, are you alright?"

"Just a little dizzy. I'm sure my blood level is still low, and my electrolytes are surely out of balance. I'll just have to take it slow, but I'm okay. I'll contact Larry and set you up for a trip through the nether world."

"It appears that Frank is taking calls for now."

"Good. It's about time Larry took a break."

While Kate prepared John's TMT to do its magic once more, Tom picked out the two TMTs that had indicated an 'UNKNOWN' subject. He handed them to her. "It's one of these."

Kate promptly displayed the information. "It's this one with the '-P' for a suffix." Tom nodded understanding. "The list is complete. Go lay on the mats and try to relax. The procedure is totally painless, and the next thing you know you'll be ready for more action."

He looked around. She reassured him. "I doubt if the cats will come back. There was nothing but the look of raw fear in their eyes when they got a whiff of what was left of their leader. Besides, your wounds aren't nearly as bad as mine were. I'd be surprised if the process will require more than ten or fifteen minutes."

Tom reclined on the mats. "Okay, don't forget to turn and baste me half way through."

A grin spread across her face. She was about to push the keypad when his voice stopped her. "Kate, I want you to know something. I may still joke around, but when I thought I might lose you, part of me grew up incredibly rapidly. It's important to me that you know you can depend on me."

"I've never doubted that for a moment, Tom. Not once. Now go to sleep, rest, and be well my sweet prince."

"In that case, fire when ready."

Kate initiated the process.

* * * * *

Tom's eyelids fluttered, and he blinked away the fog. She was kneeling next to him. "Kate, I'm ready. Go ahead, push the button."

"You're done. Fourteen minutes and 12 seconds to be exact."

"I'm done?" He lifted his head and checked his wrist and hand. "Wow. It works!"

Tom jumped up, maybe a little too fast. "Whoa. I'm dizzy ... and this time I'm not trying to fake it."

There was a double flash of light and two TMTs materialized. One was beeping. Kate pressed a spot, and the machine became silent as the comm screen came into view.

> 'Kate/Tom: Have been monitoring your progress remotely. Hope everything is well. We found the problem with one TMT. It was an intermittent short in the Tesla coil. The second TMT proved to have the same problem. It's going around that the two of you are rough on equipment. Send back what's left of the gear. We're preparing another package for you including a change of clothes. There's a jump sequence window open in 45 minutes so you won't have to spend the night. - Frank.'

They hugged and danced around, then started gathering all the apparatus in front of John's machine. Kate sent everything back, finally shipping John's TMT last.

A tiny flash, and three, small, cardboard boxes sat on a transmit mat in front of one of the newly arrived TMTs. Tom picked a box up and read the cover: '50 Cartridges, CAL. 9mm, 115 GR. BALL'. Under the print was a stenciled label: 'Property of Smithsonian Institute, Washington, D.C.'.

He chuckled at the source. "It's a little late, but now, I'm ready for anything, or anyplace."

Kate shivered. "Well, if it can be anyplace, I hope it's warm because of my thin blood."

She no sooner finished her thought when there was another flash of light. A large pile of heavy artic wear appeared before them, including boots, gloves, parkas, hydrogen powered heater, and a tent. The irony was great comic relief.

They stared at each other and then doubled over with laughter.

"For myself I am an optimist – it does not seem to be much use being anything else."

- Winston Churchill

Chapter 20
Anonymous Anomalies

Tom squinted at the TMTs. Kate walked up from behind, encircled his torso with her arms, leaned around, and studied his face. "Judging by the wrinkles in your forehead, I'm going to assume that either you've lost your glasses again, or you're deep in thought."

He tenderly rubbed her arms. "Correct on both counts. My glasses ended up in the trash pile with the other equipment. The iridium sample is gone, too. What has my attention, though, are the TMTs. How do we handle the jump with only two?"

Kate opened her mouth to speak, but a beeping TMT captured her attention. "Do you want to bet that's Frank sending an answer to your question?"

She brought up the comm screen. Tom rested his chin on her shoulder. Their eyes floated over the message.

> 'Kate/Tom: you have the last functioning pair of TMTs available. The programming is set for a simultaneous tandem jump. But, if you travel separately, I can take you twice as far and eliminate additional jumps. However, that would obviously mean you'd have to fend for yourselves at each location while I transmit matter to recharge the banks. Together, you'll integrate at the end of the Pleistocene. Temperatures will be rising, but the weather is expected to be highly unpredictable with a lot of precipitation. I'm moving your integration site to Montana because the southwest will be covered by an inland sea created by melting glaciers. I'll leave the final decision concerning the jump to you. – Frank.'

Tom squeezed Kate's hand. "There's no way I'm leaving you alone. I'll listen to anything you say, but after what we just went through, my vote is for staying together."

"You're not going to get any argument from me."

Tom breathed a sigh of relief. "I thought you might put up a token resistance in favor of keeping the jump number to a minimum."

"Heh, heh. After being shishkebabbed by a cat. Not a chance."

Tom blinked in surprise. "Uh, great. So, how's this going to work?"

"Essentially, there's no difference. We'll just be traveling together."

"Won't our atoms intermingle?"

"No, silly. Our bodies will have separate tachyon maps. MMT installations are a luxury on Mars and in the asteroid belt. They sometimes transfer up to fifty people in one cycle. Some of the public facilities on earth function in the same manner. We just can't be touching, or a safety interlock will prevent the disintegration phase from occurring."

"Okay. Well, that jump window is getting close. We'd better suit up so we'll be ready."

She nodded. "Fine. We can't leave here soon enough to satisfy me."

Tom pulled on the heavy clothing while Kate entered some minor changes. She turned to check his preparations and burst out laughing at the strange, bulky vision standing in the warm sunshine.

"C'mon, Kate. I'm beginning to parboil."

She wiped a tear from her cheek, but continued to giggle. "Sorry, Tom. I'll hurry."

Soon, one of her glove-encased fingers was poised over a keypad. "Okay, Montana. Here we come."

A biting, bitter-cold wind blasted them. Heavy snowfall restricted visibility to about twenty feet. Kate grabbed the equipment so it wouldn't topple over. "I've got this TMT. Be prepared to grab the other one when it arrives."

Tom leaned close so he could hear, then gave a thumbs-up signal. "Understood. I'll get the transfer mats, too." He finally managed to stuff the pads inside his suit. A minute later he followed Kate's example and was packing snow around the second TMT's legs for support.

Tom swung Kate around so they faced out of the gale. "I don't see shelter anywhere, and there's no way I'm going to try and put the tent up in this wind. I'll build a wall out of snow for some protection."

Kate nodded. "How can I help?"

"I'll use the shovel to pile up the snow. You pat it down with your gloves. Try and form a lip over us. Hopefully, that'll keep us a little warmer."

"Right. Let's get started. I'm freezing."

The finished enclosure was small, but effective. Kate had managed to send a message informing Frank about the storm and that they'd attempt contact again when the weather stabilized.

Their hydrogen-powered heater was only set on medium to prevent melting their shelter, but combined with the thick clothes and heavy sleeping bags it provided adequate comfort.

There was nothing left to do but ride out the tempest.

They had zipped their two bags together and were facing each other. Kate reached up and softly stroked Tom's face. A minute later she pushed back from him and grinned. "Is that what I think it is?"

"Sorry, I can't help it."

She wiggled back against him. "I wasn't asking for an apology. I was thinking more along the lines of your exercise program."

Tom matched her grin. "You realize, tennis will never be the same for us. Most couples have 'our song'. We have 'our game'."

"How are we going to do this?"

"We can put our clothes at the bottom of the bags. That way they should stay warm."

“Mmm, let the games begin. Oh, Tom ... that was a beautiful serve.”
“Just let me get my ground game started. Wimbledon, eat you heart out.”

While Tom’s breathing was returning to normal, he noticed Kate reach out. “What are you doing?”

“Turning the heater down. The storm is letting up.” She rubbed her hand over his chest. “Right now, I’m plenty warm enough. You have a great bedside manner, Dr. Hughes.”

Tom felt down into the bag. “We’re probably going to nod off. We’d better put our clothes back on before we do. They feel like they’re getting cooler.”

They somehow managed dressing without elbowing each other to death. Sleep soon overtook them.

They awakened together at the sound of heavy crunching on the snow. Tom looked up at the overhang, then studied Kate’s face. “Now what?”

She shrugged. “At least the storm is over.”

He worked the gun out from under his parka. A moment later, a pair of long twisted tusks loomed into view over their heads.

Kate pressed her face against Tom’s chest. “Oh no, not again.”

“Wait a minute. We might be all right. I think it’s a wooly mammoth. According to research literature based on fossil remains, they were strictly vegetarians just like the modern elephant.”

“I hope they read the same material.”

Tom smiled down at her. “I guess we’re about to find out.”

The animal issued a low throaty growl. Kate hunkered down again. “Are you sure it’s not a Rex or something?”

“No. Not in this era. The dinosaur king is long gone. It’s probably just curious about our TMTs and this big mound of snow in the middle of nowhere. Look, the sun’s coming out. We can get a good look at this guy.”

“Do we really need to do that?”

“After what we’ve been through, this should prove to be uneventful.”

“Why am I not convinced?”

The decision was taken out of their hands as the crunching restarted and moved around the mound until a giant orb of hair stood facing them. Its trunk came snaking forward, sniffing their clothes and finally their faces. Kate flinched and turned away. Tom removed a glove and offered his hand. The tip of the beast’s nose inspected his fingers. He softly stroked the prickly wormlike appendage.

The mammoth concluded the interview with another guttural noise and then seemed to lose interest, becoming more intent on finding food somewhere under the snow cover.

Tom scrambled out to meet their visitor. Kate poked her head out, and sensing no immediate danger, overcame her fear and joined him. She pointed at some anomaly. “What’s wrong with its belly?”

Tom cautiously approached the animal’s midsection. “I don’t know. Its skin is different colors ... and appears to be moving. Maybe it’s really sick.”

Watching for a reaction, he nudged it in the side. Tom was so startled he fell over as dozens of large creatures flew away, back toward the mammoth’s direction of origin.

Kate hastily retreated. "What are they?"

Tom arose and began a closer inspection of the remaining unknown organisms. "They appear to be some sort of insect. Oh my God ... I don't believe it. They're butterflies."

"In this climate? Where would they have come from?"

"My question exactly. There must be some sort of warm-weather pocket near here for them to survive. We should follow this thing's tracks and see where they lead."

"Oh, Tom, I don't know about this."

"C'mon, where's your newly remanufactured sense of adventure?"

"In one piece again, and I'd like to keep it that way."

Tom followed the fleeing insects with his eyes. "I'll bet it's a cave. No, scratch that idea. If the mammoths can enter, it must be a large cavern. That would be a plausible explanation."

"Great. Another cave."

"Hey, it'd be safer than out here in the land of zilch ... not to mention warmer."

"What about those huge cats? Are they still around?"

"Yeah, that's certainly possible, but these guys are probably part of their diet, so they're not going to live in the same place. If it is a cavern, we should be pretty safe with a bunch of mammoths around. It must be nearby, too. Those butterflies would instinctively stay close to their life-sustaining habitat."

The mammoth started turning, and to Kate's surprise, Tom jumped in front of it. "Tom! What are you doing?"

"It's headed back. Quick, bring your bag of food tablets."

Kate hurried as best she could in the deep snow. "What now?"

"We want to know where it's going. Right?"

"Yes ... I guess so."

"Then stall it while I tie our equipment onto its back. Just feed it. That should delay its retreat for awhile."

"It's not going to be interested in these tiny morsels."

"Give it a handful. I only need a couple of minutes."

"What are we going to eat?"

"We can get more from Frank."

Kate sighed. "Alright, I'll try."

She fed the animal half a dozen tablets, and soon, the tentacle like proboscis prompted for more. "It's working."

"Good. Lead it over here."

Tom climbed on top of their snow wall with the sleeping bags. "It's too tall to load from down there."

Kate moved and stood by the wall. The mammoth followed like a well-trained dog. She offered it another course, which it gladly accepted.

Tom unrolled the sleeping bags, tied their straps together, then slipped one on either side of the animal's back, with the openings toward the top. The TMTs were quickly disassembled and placed in the improvised carriers, followed by the other few pieces of equipment. He took a final look around and jumped down. "Okay, that's it. Now for us."

"Where are we supposed to sit?"

"On the built-in seats, where else?" He gently stroked the animal's face, sat on a tusk, and then leaned back against the huge nose. "Hop on the other one. Hold on, and remember to pick up your feet."

Kate approached slowly, sat on the opposite incisor, then gasped when the animal lurched into motion. "Well, it certainly seems docile enough."

Tom stretched out and locked his fingers behind his head. "Nothing like traveling first class."

After a short ride, they crested a rise. In the near distance was a low mountain with a large opening at the base. The animal continued to lumber in that general direction. Tom pointed. "There's our cave."

Kate absently nodded. "Tom."

"Uh huh."

"You do realize our only way home is strapped on this uncontrollable beast's back."

"Yep."

"What if there's nothing we can stand on when we want to retrieve our equipment?"

"Already have it covered. I stored the MBH tubes vertically to give the bags rigidity. To get them off, you'll stand on one side and I the other. We'll push up on the bottom of each respective bag, and the animal will walk right out from under our improvised luggage rack."

"You thought of all this on the spur of the moment back there?"

"Yes. Why?"

"Never mind. I just wondered."

"No, really. What is it?"

"I guess I'm still adjusting to the way you think. Fast assessments just seem to come naturally for you. I need to sit and ponder something before reaching a decision."

"There's nothing wrong with that, Kate. But, you obviously haven't had to think under pressure very often. Thinking quickly on your feet often comes from necessity, not by design. The downside is that abrupt decisions sometimes lead to frustrating mistakes."

"Then wouldn't it be better to postpone?"

"You don't always have that option. Besides, there are times when a bad decision is better than being locked in a stalemate about what to do next. There are situations when doing something wrong is better than doing nothing, because then, there's no progress. You do your best to weigh the different outcomes, make a choice, and live with it."

"I wish I were more like you."

"No. Bad idea. I hope you take this as an observation and not a criticism, since that's the way it's meant. I have the ability to make instant decisions in action situations because of my experience. You're more adapted to people problems that require a reasonably quick, yet thoughtful, resolution.

You're also the better decision maker when circumstances are passive and there's enough time to wade through several choices. But, give me a structured scientific problem and I can work on it forever, striving for the best solution and never give up. We complement each other. I don't want you to change ... at least not in that respect."

"So, you're admitting there is some way in which you want me to change."

"Yes, but I'd be the first to agree, I must change in that regard, too."

"In what way?"

"You'll have to wait and see."

"Grrrrrrr."

"Careful, you're liable to scare our friend here. He might think a nasty cat is around."

"You're the one who'll think a vicious kitty is around if you neglect completing this train of thought."

Tom teasingly tittered, "I'm sure you'll remind me."

Their conversation abruptly ended as the wooly beast entered the cavern. The walls just inside the opening were thinly covered with a species of lichen. As they traveled further, the lichen gradually thickened and finally gave way to a heavy growth of variegated mosses. It was also becoming warmer. Looking up, they saw a multitude of small slits and cracks in the overhead rock that produced a dazzling aural display, formed by crisscrossing shafts of light.

Their animal taxi was apparently headed for a pool at the base of a wall, which appeared to be fed by melting snow streaming down from high above. Surprisingly, instead of stopping at the edge, the indifferent beast continued to slowly wallow into the water. Tom motioned for Kate to dismount, then called out as their ride sloshed past, "Push up on the bag as it passes, then we'll carry the equipment back to the shoreline."

With the weight supported by their effort, the baggage slid off the mammoth and down into their waiting arms. A flurry of residual butterflies rose in the air as the animal's splashing feet sprayed its belly hair. They watched in amazement as the beautifully colored insects gradually disappeared deeper into the spacious interior. Then, aided by Kate, Tom carried the gear and stowed it safely amid a jumble of dry rocks.

They decided to check outside before removing their cold weather clothing.

Tom and Kate hitch a ride on their prehistoric taxi

"Variety of mere nothings gives more pleasure than uniformity of something."
- Richter

Chapter 21
Fun In Montana

Tom and Kate stepped out into the frigid air of late afternoon. Both scrutinized the area for any other signs of life. He bent to examine a partial indentation interspersed within the mammoth's trail. "I could swear there's an impression here besides our wooly friend's, but the area has been so obliterated by the animals and the wind I can't be certain. We should keep our eyes open just in case. I'll keep my gun handy, too." Tom snickered under his breath and stepped away.

"Where are you going?"

"Just over here."

When Kate turned, something struck her in the back. She spun around to find Tom grinning, packing another snowball. "What do you think you're doing?"

"Oh, c'mon, don't tell me you've never had a snowball fight."

"For your information, Mr. know-it-all, I've never been outside in the snow before today."

"Then it's about time you had some fun." He let fly with another projectile.

"That does it!" Kate scooped up a fistful of snow and enjoined the battle.

Tom laughed riotously at Kate's poor inability to even hit a standing target.

Sensing her shortcoming, she ran and tackled his legs, forcing him down on the ground, where he allowed himself to become completely defenseless.

They rolled in the snow until bumping into something hard. Both looked up. A giant hairy head lowered and stared at them. It was a sobering view.

Tom snapped out of the reverie. "I guess we should move unless being squished is a good thing."

"I'd find that highly suspect."

"It must think we're completely nuts."

Kate laughed. "Are you actually assuming there's any possible room for error?"

They rolled away and scrambled to their feet. The walking fur ball trudged into the cavern.

Tom hugged her tightly. "Now, wasn't that fun?"

Kate replied breathlessly, "Yes, and we even managed to live through it."

"Hey, here's something that's easy." Tom fell stiffly back into the snow.

Kate giggled. "Now that I can do."

"Wait. You haven't seen the best part. Move your arms up and down, legs in and out ... like this ... then get up." Tom carefully rose and pointed at his masterpiece. "It's called a snow angel. That's about the limit of my artistic ability."

Kate flopped into the snow and followed his example. A minute later they stood together, smiling at each other and their creations. Tom scooped up some more snow and began packing it.

Kate ducked away, "No, Tom, please. I've had enough."

"This isn't for throwing. There's one last thing we should do." He replaced the ball in the snow and started rolling it. "We have to build some snow ... people. Place a large sphere on the bottom, medium size in the middle, and a small one on top for the head. Watch what I do, then make one of your own. I'll make a man, you make a woman."

He watched Kate struggle as he finished his bottom. "Here, let me help you with the first two. Then you're on your own."

They worked quietly, each paying attention to their own figurine.

Tom blocked the view of his design while watching Kate complete hers. "That's pretty good for a beginner. The illusion of arms, legs, and facial features are a real imaginative touch."

"Let me see yours." He moved away. "Oh, Tom. That's obscene!"

"I was just trying to be anatomically correct."

"Does it have to be in that ... condition?"

"It's not his fault. Your snowwoman affects my snowman the same way you affect me."

Kate leered. "I'm back to not knowing whether I should spank or kiss you."

"Can I have both?"

"You are definitely impossible to predict. Let's go back inside."

She hooked her arm around his. After a few steps, Tom stopped and held her at arms length. "Remember that comment I made about us changing?"

"Of course."

"I'm not sure how to say this. In fact, I'm not thoroughly convinced anything need be said at all. But, since I've started, I may as well finish.

In order to survive the pressures of my job, I got in the habit of clowning around a lot, probably to excess. I need to tighten up a little so I can become more centered. You, however, need to lighten up. Give life a chance to let you laugh more. What we just did is a great example. You actually let your hair down a little. Being around each other may bring this about automatically, but I decided to just spit it out so we could chew on it together. Food for thought, as they say."

Kate contemplated for a few moments. "Okay, I'll take it under consideration."

"Okay? You're not upset?"

She smiled and poked him in the ribs. "Nope. Like I said, it's something to think about." She started off again. "Come along, Fido."

"Woof." Tom hurried to catch up.

Kate unzipped one of the bags. "I'm going to set up a TMT and contact Frank. I'll let him know we're okay, transmit our new coordinates, and ask about our next jump."

"Sounds like a plan. I'll give you a hand."

She was entering the message when Tom tapped her shoulder. "What?"

"Ask for a bale of hay."

She just stared.

He jerked his head toward the pool. "You know, for our friend in the bathtub over there."

Kate blinked. "Where in the world is Frank supposed to get a bale of hay?"

"Well, he probably knows someone, who knows someone else, that somewhere has a horse who needs hay." Tom moved his hand in a small circle. "Ya da ya da ya da."

Kate chuckled and skewed her head. "Alright, I'll add the inquiry, but don't be surprised if he writes back wondering if you've had a relapse from that bump on the head."

"It's not like he has to go get it. Someone can just beam it over to him, right?"

Kate nodded. "Yes, that's true," then laughed out, "I can just imagine the look on their faces when the request is received." She pressed the send key and looked at Tom. He was gazing toward the interior of the cavern, his eyes sparkling. "Okay. Let's go."

His brows furrowed. "Where?"

"Exploring, where else. It's written all over your face in capital letters. Let's just wait long enough for a reply from Frank."

"You're the best."

"Hmm, I'll try and remember that next time I'm being attacked by something."

Tom was somewhat stunned. "Kate, that wasn't my fault."

She leaned against him, mooning up into his eyes. "I know that. I'm just teasing."

The carefree banter caught him off guard. "Oh."

Frank's reply arrived and Kate casually scrolled through the text. She softly cackled at Frank's response about the hay and then her face lit up. "Oh, Tom. There's another window open in less than three hours. If the cats hadn't destroyed our TMTs, we'd be home in one more jump. As it is, we have three to go. According to the note, our next will take us deep into the Holocene." She looked at Tom. "You're the ancient history expert. Isn't that when humankind first developed?"

"The first modern man, yes, but early man existed long before that. I believe it was Homo erectus that became established in the period we're in now. Neanderthals, and then later Cro-Magnons flourished in the Holocene. They were our direct forerunners."

A warning beep startled them, then a TE canister, two carbon banks, a wrist device (model-16), and finally, six large bales of hay materialized out of the light. Kate studied the comm screen, laughing softly.

"Enough suspense, Kate. What's it say?"

"Don't ask."

"Why?"

"No, you don't understand. That's what it says. 'Don't ask'."

Kate strapped the new multi-purpose apparatus onto her wrist and checked it against the TMT. She noted it had already been set to local time. Tom pulled the hay into the middle of an area away from their equipment cache, then stood there rubbing his hands together. "Well, are you ready? I'm dying to see the rest of this place."

She teasingly rolled her eyes. "I would have never guessed."

The further they walked, the more amazing the locale became. Mosses faded into a myriad of flowers bursting with spectacular colors, some with fruit. A few plants looked more like trees, with thick stems that resembled branches. There were even birds flitting excitedly through the air, and small animals scurrying within the underbrush. Finally, they arrived at the heat source. It was a huge, bubbling, steaming pool. Tom squatted on a dry mud flat and waved his hand over the turbid water. "Man, that almost burns. This region must be situated near a geological hot spot, maybe directly over a magma dome." He pulled his shirt away from his body and fluffed it in the air. "Whew, I think I've had enough. Let's head back."

Kate nodded. "That's okay by me. I'm practically drenched. The humidity must be one hundred percent ... more, if that's possible."

"There is a phenomenon known as super-saturation, but I've never heard of it being applied to the concept of relative humidity."

"Me either. This place would be an ecologist's paradise if they could tolerate the environment."

"Think I'll stick to physics. That way I can only be blown up, but at least its quick instead of a slow meltdown."

On the return trip, Tom deviated from the center pathway and skirted close to an outside wall. He paused, reaching for a particular blossom that had caught his eye. His hand froze in mid air. Something else captured his attention and he spread the vegetation apart for a better view. "Kate, come look at this!"

She hurried over. "Oh my, that's unbelievable." She scanned the area, becoming edgy. "Do you think they're still around?"

"I doubt it. Whoever drew these has probably been gone, or dead, a long time. The pictures are completely concealed by the foliage." He cleared a larger area. "Look at the detail in this one. The artist was quite talented. I couldn't draw something like that if my life depended on it."

"It certainly proves the cats were here at one time or another." Her hand panned across the image. "That plainly depicts a pack of saber tooth cats attacking a wooly mammoth."

"Technically, I think it'd be referred to as a pride, but since they're not actually lions, I'm not sure. So, I'll let you slide on that one."

She stuck out her tongue.

"Why, Kate, you're just one surprise after another."

Kate waited while Tom took a deep breath, mentally preparing for their departure. A shocked expression exploded on her face. "Tom, I just realized ... you didn't have an injection before our last jump."

"I know, but things were pretty hectic at the time. Besides, you said I probably wouldn't need the drug once I had my implants. It was fine. I think I can do without the shot from now on."

"Okay, but if you have a problem, don't hesitate to inform me."

"Will do." Tom made a sour face and snapped his fingers as he stepped onto the transfer mat next to Kate's.

She worriedly halted the countdown. "What's the matter?"

"I forgot to pick you a flower. That's why I stopped next to that wall in the first place. When I saw those drawings it completely slipped my mind. I'm sorry."

"Thank you for the thought. That is what counts." Her eyes flicked over his for a moment. "I really do think you're a romantic at heart."

"Is that another play on words?"

"No. Just a factual observation."

"Well, don't spread it around. I get more mileage out of being a grump."

He leaned down and they lightly kissed. When he straightened, Tom touched a fingertip to her nose. "I love you, kiddo. Push the button. Let's see what's next."

Five wooly mammoths grunted and jostled for position around the hay bales. Only one was curious enough to interrupt its meal while watching the unfamiliar intruders in their preparations. After the flash of light and soft pop of rushing air, it slowly lowered its head and resumed the banquet, acting as if this had been just another ordinary day in the eons-old ice age.

A single hominid head rose up out of the dense undergrowth. When he was convinced the strange creatures were gone, he forced his squat, powerfully built body through the tangle of leaves.

A short time later, several others of his kind followed. They gathered around and watched as their life-long friends munched on the oddly shaped plants, then settled for the night as the sun slipped below the horizon.

In the morning, the group of heavily animal-skin clad people would mumble and marvel at the beautiful impressions in the snow outside their home. Afterward, the men would gawk open mouthed, and the women would stare wide-eyed at the huge comical projection on one of the snow idols.

"Wonder is involuntary praise."
- Young

Chapter 22
Hi, Honey - I'm Home

Tom raised his face and hands to the sun and stood for a minute, basking in its kind, gentle warmth. Afterwards, he turned a slow complete circle, observing his new surroundings. "Now this is more like it. It feels like about 70 degrees ... perfect weather, complete with a blue sky, white fluffy clouds, and thousands of trees as a bonus. I could comfortably live here."

Kate cocked an eyebrow. "Hmm. Think of the paradox that would create. Humankind getting about a twelve thousand year head start over its previous beginning."

"That's true. In which case, it makes me wonder if you and I would ever exist. Of course, if we didn't, how could we be here contemplating it? A paradoxical thought indeed."

"Well, let's keep it theoretical."

He sighed, "Okay, we won't stay. We'll pass quietly through ... no problems ... no troubles ... no muss, no fuss. Are you going to contact Frank?"

She answered warily following his somewhat surprising soliloquy. "Yes. I was just preparing to do that."

"Why didn't Frank and Larry simply compile a schedule for all of our jumps?"

Kate softly laughed. "They tried, but gave up when we kept going off on tangents during our extracurricular activities. You know, little things, like dinosaur chases, iridium problems, and battles with saber-toothed cats."

Tom nodded sympathetically. "Oh, yeah. How quickly one forgets the boring stuff."

She became busy with the TMT; he scanned the area. They were situated within a copse of young deciduous saplings surrounded by a dense growth of taller, well-established pine and spruce. One direction gave way to open sky, indicating a break in the trees that tantalized Tom's curiosity. "Kate."

She looked up from the touch panel. "Yes?"

"I'm going to scout the area. I'll be back in a few minutes and help you set up camp."

She replied somewhat sternly, "Please, be careful," and returned to the message. He was nowhere in sight when she finished.

The TMTs' matter banks were replenished and Kate had just returned the empty canisters when Tom pushed through the trees into the small clearing.

"Hi ya, kiddo. Everything okay?"

"You seem to be in a jovial mood."

"Why not? Things are going smoothly, we only have two jumps left, and so far, this time and area are peaceful."

"That would certainly be a welcome change. Anyway, we're set for our penultimate jump tomorrow afternoon ... about four. Frank expressed concern about our being in the open, so he sent the electric fence again and promised this one would be even more effective. He even included some insulated handles so the top two wires could be detached and stepped over without turning off the power. Did you find anything?"

Tom bent and pawed through the equipment. "There's a small lake only about two hundred feet from here. The water's a little chilly, but not bad. Nice place for a swim. Think I saw some fish, too," then added with a chuckle, "just plain fish ... no man-eaters."

"Fish sounds better than food tablets. Too bad we don't have a way to catch them."

"Au contraire, my sweet. Do not despair. I think fish may be on the menu yet."

Kate blinked. "How?"

He flicked his brows twice. "I have an idea. Let's set up camp, then I'll show you."

Tom cleared an area, scooped out a hollow, and lined it with stones to contain a fire. The electric fence and its associated equipment were erected next. It enclosed the entire stand of young trees, hopefully creating a small island of safety.

When all else was ready, Tom collected a long sturdy stick, a length of tough vine, a thick flexible twig, and removed the mosquito netting from one sleeping bag.

He stripped the twig of bark, formed it into a circle, and secured the ends with vine. Mosquito netting was snapped onto the circular twig, and the resulting product was attached to a tip of the stick with more vine. Tom proudly displayed the contrivance to Kate. "Voila, let's go catch some fish."

She grinned widely. "You really think it's going to work?"

He shrugged. "Only one way to find out."

They walked along the alternating rocky/sandy shoreline until they came to a cluster of large boulders forming a three-sided pool in shallow water. A leafy branch was spread out over the area providing shade from the hot sun. A small group of speckled lake trout was floating casually near the bottom of the pool.

Tom put a finger to his lips, then pointed. "Look at those beauties. They must be at least two or three pounds apiece. One of them would probably feed us both."

Kate whispered back, "I still think cooking them will be the easy part."

Tom displayed his mock indignity. "Have some faith," then eased into the water toward the open side of the pool, and deftly lowered the 'net' into position. He stationed it under a fish and started to lift when his foot slipped off a mossy stone and he fell into the water. The net flew into the air and landed on the shore as his hands reflexively dropped to break his fall.

Kate shrieked a laugh. "Now is a pretty poor time for that swim!"

Tom splashed into a sitting position. "Damn ... I would have had it."

Their heads jerked in unison at the sound of something flopping on the sand. "Kate! We've got it. Step on the stick, I'll be right there."

She chortled in admiration. "I'll be. Mr. Physics slash historian becomes Mr. Fisherman. Why does that not surprise me?"

Tom the fisherman slips up (down?)

Tom stood there grinning ... and dripping. "I'd better clean this here. There's nothing in which to keep it alive, and once it dies, the gills and guts will rapidly deteriorate."

Kate grimaced. "Charming."

He hunted around and found some sharp shells to use as tools. Once the fish was cleaned, he simply wrapped it in vegetation. "Okay, let's head back to camp. I'm getting hungry."

"Do you need any water for cooking?"

"No. The flesh will get mushy. We'll start a fire and bake it in these green leaves. It'll be fine."

Tom placed the plant-wrapped fish on the hot rocks in the center of the fire. After about twenty minutes, he turned it using a piece of bark. Kate gathered some large flat stones, wiped them clean, and then used more leaves as bedding for the food. She also found a thicket of bushes, bearing fruit that Tom identified as blackberries. They were added to the meal.

Tom patted his gut. "That wasn't half bad, even if I do say so myself."

"Where did you learn to perform this little miracle?"

"I think I mentioned before I've done a lot of hiking. Believe me, you get tired real quick of boxed and freeze-dried meals. So, I read some books by fellow hikers and learned a lot about preparing food on the trail. This is just a sample. You'd be surprised what those people can cook up with just one pan."

"Do you have any more surprises up your sleeve?"

"I saw some trails ... want to take a walk?"

Kate's gaze floated over the camp. "Alright, but maybe we should hide the TMTs and equipment before we leave."

"Good idea." Tom pointed. "That stand of spruce over there will probably work."

It only took a few minutes to stash the equipment within the entanglement of tree boughs. Kate stood close to a TMT and was apparently making some adjustments.

Tom watched inquisitively. "What are you doing, Kiddo?"

"I had time to examine some new features on this wrist device while you were exploring. One function is a homing signal in case we get lost. I just synced my WD with the TMT. It's all set."

"Great. Let's see the sights."

They followed a grassy trail until it ended at a tee. The new trail was mostly fresh dirt. Tom stopped so abruptly, Kate bumped into him. "What is it?"

He knelt on the ground and examined a print. "We're not alone in our little paradise."

Kate peered over his shoulder. "Should we go back?"

Tom searched in both directions. "No, I think we're okay for now. If they're still around, our existence will soon be known. Perhaps it is already."

Their heads snapped up at the sound of something rapidly slapping the dirt. An extremely hairy and bearded male humanoid was bearing down on them. He was madly waving them out of the way and shouting, "Ahyah! Ahyah!"

Tom sprang up, jumped off the path into the brush, practically dragging Kate after him. "I think he's warning us."

The man sprinted past ... closely followed by a huge wild pig with tusks that were impossible to miss. The path was quickly checked for more animals, then Tom pulled his gun with one hand, and tugged Kate's hand with the other. "C'mon, let's try and help this poor guy."

Only about a minute passed before they caught up. The man was standing in a large cul-de-sac surrounded by a natural rock wall. There was a huge, gnarled old tree on one side. Oddly enough, instead of seeking an escape, the man appeared to be urging the agitated swine onward.

Kate grabbed Tom's arm. "What's he doing? Is he suicidal?"

"I've no idea," Tom lowered the gun, "but I'll hit him for sure if I miss the animal, so we'll just have to watch and see."

The man harassed the confused creature with stones and several feigned assaults, finally provoking the pig to attack. It pawed the earth and charged while the human calmly stood his ground.

Movement from above caught Tom's eye. Another man dropped from a low hanging, leaf-covered branch ... falling directly on the pig's back. It slid to a stop on its belly as its overloaded stubby legs collapsed from the additional weight. Before the pig could move again, the second man grabbed it by the snout and viciously pulled back and around. Sounds of snapping vertebrae echoed around the enclosure. The animal's body twitched with postmortem muscle spasms, and then lay motionless.

The man on the pig arose and his companion joined him. Tom moved cautiously forward, stopping a few feet from the men and slowly extended his hands palms up. Tom's strange attire obviously troubled the men at first, but his unkempt beard and hair seemed to help set them at ease. Kate stood statue still and observed.

The shorter of the two men moved a hand to his chest, "Orm."

The taller mimicked the action, "Wern."

Tom waved Kate forward. When she joined him, he pointed to himself, "Tom," and then at her, "Kate."

Both men looked first to Tom, then Kate, echoing disjointedly, "Tum ... Kaat".

Tom smiled and nodded. "Close enough."

Orm hefted the pig by the front hooves while Wern picked up the back and they started their journey. When Tom and Kate didn't move, Orm stopped, released a hoof, and motioned them to follow, "Sim ... sim."

Tom looked down at Kate. "That pig is big and heavy, so I assume we're fairly close to their home turf, but I'm letting you make the call on this trip."

Kate jiggled her head. "It's a heady thought, but you must be rubbing off on me. Let's go."

Tom snorted a laugh. "Then we're off to see the wizard."

Orm and Wern occasionally jabbered in their terse language en route. Tom and Kate overheard several words, but were unsure when they referred to people or things. Orm halted a few times saying 'orta' to Wern first. Then he whispered 'ess', and both listened before continuing the trek.

The meaning of other words such as 'r-rack', 'sool', and 'nosh' were a complete mystery. For certain, the pig was called an 'oomba'.

Orm called out, "Orta," and the procession came to a halt near two, thick, upright forked pieces of wood that had been driven into the ground. A wide, dark stain covered the area between the posts.

Wern and Orm placed a heavy straight stick on the pig's belly and proceeded to secure its legs with twists of dry grasses carried at their sides. The dead animal's posterior end was hoisted onto one of the forks.

Wern pulled a sheathed shard of rock from inside his clothing, reached down, slit the pig's throat, then rose and continued along the path as if it were all in a day's work ... which was probably true.

Orm appealed to Tom, "Sim," and walked away.

Kate was staring at the draining blood. Tom faced her away, "I know it's gory, but I'm sure it's necessary. C'mon, let's follow them."

Just ahead, around a bend in the trail, was a small settlement. Orm and Wern were addressing an increasingly large knot of people while gesturing toward Kate and Tom. A level of heightened awareness and excitement quickly spread throughout the people.

Several young women carrying small hand tools made from shells and flaked minerals broke apart from the group and walked toward the slain pig. They stared and gave a wide berth to their oddly dressed visitors.

Kate and Tom greeted them as they passed, then stopped at the outer perimeter of the camp when Orm came running toward them, "Orta ... orta."

He halted next to them holding a hand near his mouth, "Ess," then stood silently and waited.

Wern emerged from a thatched lean-to on the far side of the village, followed by another man and a woman. Both were stocky and overly rotund. Tom had to almost bite his lip to keep from laughing as the couple walking toward them looked like waddling ducks. The people throughout the camp stopped wherever they were as the couple approached, bowing their heads in respect.

Tom leaned closer to Kate. "This must be the head honcho and his mate. When they get here, we should politely acknowledge their presence and let them take the lead."

Kate's head bobbed in agreement.

Tom and Kate lowered their gaze and deeply nodded once as the royal pair arrived. This action apparently appeased them since both showed their teeth, nodding in return. The male gestured towards himself, "R-rack," then indicated his companion, "Vige."

Orm introduced Tom and Kate, addressing each in turn. A crowd was forming around them and the chief stretched his neck, ostensibly looking for someone in particular. That someone emerged as the tallest person in camp except for Tom. He strode forward, parting the people as Moses had parted the Red Sea.

There were thick, dark-blue lines on his forehead, red dots on the backs of his hands, a collection of long ebony feathers hanging from his waist, and a string of either teeth or claws around his neck.

His fingernails were curled and the small, deeply penetrating eyes were as black and shiny as lumps of glassy volcanic rock. The softly flowing, gray-streaked beard and hair, couldn't disguise the sneer on his lips.

He slowly, almost menacingly, raised a tight-fisted hand to his chest while a deep, raspy, booming voice rang out, "Sool." The man stared directly at Tom for a moment, squinted his eyes, then turned and silently walked away.

The chief and his companion gauged Tom's reaction, then grinned once more and also turned away, apparently leaving Orm in charge of the visitors.

The crowd broke up, chatting softly amongst themselves.

Kate slipped her trembling hand into Tom's.

He patted it. "We're still alive, so I guess that went well."

"That man will give me nightmares."

"Yeah, I'm afraid he's the prototype of all future bullies. They rule by fear, intimidation, and harassment while trying to convince you they are good, wise, and know what's best for everyone. They lie to your face as easily as water flows through a sieve, then swear they don't have a clue why you won't trust them. I hate his kind. Self-righteous ... self-important ... self-justifying ... self-serving hypocrites. I guarantee ... he sees both of us as a threat to his domination of these people. Mark my words ... this guy is trouble."

A startled Kate uttered slowly, "What triggered all of this?"

Tom grimly responded, "Please, just tell me again that it's better in the future than in my time."

She slowly nodded. "I'm confident you'll find that's true."

"Thank you. You've made my day." He stared at the ground for a minute and then shook his head. "I'm sorry, Kate. This is certainly not the time or place for expounding on my personal beliefs or demonstrating my peevish idiosyncrasies. I guess I'm becoming a neurotic paranoid. Forget it, let's just try and enjoy the time we're here."

Orm had been shifting his weight, standing in nervous, silent puzzlement during their conversation. In response to its end, he offered a tentative smirk and waved an arm towards the remainder of the camp.

Kate poked Tom in the side, finally reversing his frown. She leaned over and looked up into his eyes. "I think our friend is offering to show us around. It'd be pretty rude of us not to accept. How about it?"

Tom sighed deeply. "Actually, that sounds like a fine idea. Maybe it'll help me abandon this tempestuous mood."

Clearly, one of the most fascinating things about the settlement, aside from its surprising cleanliness, was a communal cooking pot. It had somehow been chiseled out of a large, single piece of rock and then supported over a fire pit by smaller stones below its base. The clan's younger women cleaned the vessel, half filled it with water, and then kept a fire stoked underneath.

Elder ladies cleaned potato, carrot, and beet like roots, adding them along with some other unknown herbs and greens. The root vegetables were not uniform in size or shape as modern crossed breeds, but looked tasty nonetheless. Lastly, the earlier group of women returned with many platters of chopped oomba, completing what evidently was a stew like meal.

Tom closely scrutinized one of the empty platters, then showed it to Kate. "This is clay. Not only that, it's been fired." He turned, looking back at a previously inspected object. “I’ll bet that hollow rock pile is a kiln. This place is amazing. I would have never anticipated this level of sophistication. They’ve combined hunting with rudimentary tool making and a basic form of agriculture. Did you notice the women preparing the roots? They were saving seeds and cuttings to replant.”

A moment later he laughed softly to himself. Her eyes left the platter. “What’s so amusing?”

“It’s so different from what I always envisioned. I half expected the men to be clubbing each other and dragging the women around by their hair. So much for movies’ views of things.”

Kate scoffed, “Just don’t get any wild ideas.”

Sool the scary dominator

"I cannot tell how the truth may be; I say the tale as it was said to me."
- Walter Scott

Chapter 23
Dinner For Forty-Seven

Tom and Kate were allowed to investigate by themselves for several hours. They came across a shallow pit where fecal matter was dumped, allowed to dry, and then mixed with the soil when the people planted. Tom commented that the FDA would probably frown on that practice.

The bulb of a certain lily plant was used for soap, and clothing was made, naturally, from tanned animal skins, of two shades no less. Lighter skins were created using the gallnuts growing on oak trees, while using the oak bark itself produced darker colored skins.

They were walking alongside a stream flowing just outside an open area when Orm found them. He stood atop the embankment coaxing, "Tum, Kaat ... sim." Then he repeatedly jabbed his fingers towards his mouth. "Nosh. Sim ... nosh."

Kate grabbed Tom's hand and lightly tugged. "I think he's indicating we should come and eat dinner."

"Ah. Another fine idea."

Tom and Kate sat cross-legged on a woven grass mat next to Orm. Wern was sitting a few spaces down with a woman. Apparently, Orm's current status was that of a bachelor. Two of the young women were passing out bowls of the stew. The methodology was to sip off most of the broth, then eat the solids with your fingers. The cuisine was delicious. Kate and Tom had no problem complying with the local eating custom.

Dinner was obviously the festive culmination of a long, hard, busy day. The entire population was present. Tom smiled to himself as he saw Kate's head gently bobbing as her gaze swung slowly around the circle, visibly counting noses. He was doing the same. "I get forty-four; how about you?"

Kate looked back, "Forty-five."

Tom scowled. "Wonder who I missed?"

One of the servers turned. Kate extended a finger in her direction, "Did you count the child on her back?"

"Nope. Ah hah, that makes forty-five. Forty-seven, counting us. Should make for an interesting evening."

Tom had no sooner finished expressing the thought when the chief arose and walked to the approximate center of the gathering. A hush fell over the assemblage. Silence ruled, except for the crackling fire and spitting sparks.

The chief moved quite gracefully, considering his size. His body language and serendipitous grunts began to spin an engrossing tale. It was evidently of past hunts and daring do. When he finished and returned to his place, the crowd murmured and nodded vigorously in appreciation of his story.

Orm and Wern went next, telling of today's pig capture. Certain parts were quite humorous. It was short, but skillfully presented, and well received.

Somewhat unexpectedly, a woman followed. The account was apparently of a lost love that died valiantly protecting others during a bear attack. Her arms and body flowed with grace and purpose. The lover's pain and agony was depicted in her facial expressions, moans, whimpers, and heartfelt screams. There were several sniffles and wet eyes before she ended.

No one else arose. Outwardly, the show was over.

Kate leaned against Tom, shivered, and wiped a tear from her cheek. "That was absolutely beautiful. No wonder it was saved until last."

One by one, all heads turned in Tom's direction. Orm nudged him, gesturing that he should take the circle. Tom laughed and slowly shook his head, waving a hand 'no', desperately, but respectfully trying to refuse.

The people would have none of it. Orm stood and his powerful muscles buoyed Tom to his feet. A push started him towards the center of attention. He looked at Kate and shrugged. She rose and hurried over to whisper in his ear, "Think of all we've been through in the last several days. You're the quick thinker. Pick a beginning and go with it," and returned to her seat.

He started slowly, clumsily, envisioning their first jump. His mind raced trying to recall the body movements that the preceding performers associated with particular events. Tom assured himself the people couldn't possibly understand all his animal interpretations, but rapidly became aware that he had certainly captured their imaginations.

The story accelerated as he encountered Bisbee, then the snakebite, but slowed again at the iridium problem. When the tigers took the stage, two of the children were so badly frightened they began to cry and were whisked away. Tom's flying shadows and exaggerated efforts only strengthened the captivating atmosphere. Even some of the grown women left following that depiction. The remaining crowd was totally mesmerized by the wooly mammoth. In the end, he stood there exhausted, sweating profusely.

Kate ran over and hugged him tightly. "Oh Tom, if we were staying you'd probably have a new career."

The people grunted, whistled, and cawed. Several patted him on the back, openly in awe. When the chief arose, the din gradually faded. He walked across to Tom, placed a hand on his shoulder, and gave one sharp nod. Then he turned and retired for the night. Evidently, a high honor had been bestowed on Tom.

Sool walked alone in the dark. The muscles in his neck were stretched taut; fingernails were biting into his palms. His grinding teeth were audible above the background murmuring of the departing throng. He stealthily, hatefully, made his way home to formulate secret plans.

Tom wiped the sweat from his face. "God, that was too much like work, but they sure seemed to like it."

Kate looked around worriedly. "Yes, maybe too much. I don't know, Tom. We may have a problem."

"Why?"

"Sool left just as you finished and passed right behind me. He was making some kind of horrible sound." She activated the homing signal of her wrist device. "I think we'd be much safer spending the night at our own camp."

His gaze slowly panned the area. "You're probably right. Let's not take any chances with that maniac. Orm's waiting. I'll try and communicate our intentions."

Tom started by vigorously rubbing and patting his belly, then extending a hand and gesturing toward the village, hopefully thanking Orm and his people for the meal. Orm's face exchanged several expressions, including joy, puzzlement, and even fear.

Tom whispered to Kate. "Well, either he finally got the idea we're showing our gratitude for the food and hospitality ... or he thinks we want to cook and eat the entire village."

Several pantomimes later, Tom believed he had conveyed the general impression that he and Kate must leave, and that Orm shouldn't follow. Even by the dying firelight, Orm's facial features confirmed his obvious disappointment. Tom smiled broadly, then gently took hold of Orm's shoulder and gradually squeezed. "Thank you, friend."

Orm beamed and emulated the action, "Tan ... ku ... fend."

Tom chuckled, "Like Kate says, it's the thought that counts."

A half moon was rising over the tree line as Tom and Kate walked away. It was a significant mental struggle for the couple not to look behind, thinking ... Orm might interpret the action as a signal to follow. The moonlight barely provided sufficient illumination to stay on the path, but Kate's wrist device kept them heading in the proper direction.

Nevertheless, they doubled back several times to find the cutoff for their camp. Finally, they saw the charger's red 'power on' light along with the white cloth strips he had tied to the fence wires. Tom manipulated the top insulated handle. "Can you make it?"

Kate stumbled. "Not quite. I'm so tired, and I really can't see that well."

"Okay, hold it." He released the pressure on the second handle. Kate stepped over, followed by Tom. The wires were replaced with no mishaps, but by that time Kate was out of earshot, so Tom mumbled to himself, "Thanks, Frank. Nice touch."

Kate unrolled the sleeping bags onto the ground, completely ignoring the tent. Tom rekindled the fire. Twenty minutes later an owl began to hoot, but they didn't hear it. The lone individual that had followed them back to camp remained hidden deep in the shadows.

A crouched figure eased silently forward until he stood at the fence line ... staring. The moon was now high in the sky. Its soft radiance glinted off the shiny metal wires, destroying the illusion that the cloth strips appeared to be floating in midair.

The tall grass was heavy with dew. He pushed down on the top wire, intending to cross over. Instead, his hand sizzled and smoked. An agonizing pain shot through his entire body. His howl carried through the night.

Tom awoke and sat up. He swore he heard something stealing away through

the trees. Kate stirred next to him. "What's wrong? Why are you awake?"
"I think an animal may have come in contact with the fence. It's gone now ... go back to sleep." He lay back down, but remained alert for awhile and listened.

* * * * *

Sool arose at first light. He immediately went to the chief with his story. The strangers were harboring and commanding powerful evil spirits. The proof was etched bloodily across the palm of his hand. These outsiders had been in their village, therefore, they knew their weaknesses. For the safety of the people, they must be punished. R-rack was easy to convince since Sool's tale terrified him. The chief appointed five men for Sool to lead. They gathered weapons and raced away down the path. The sun had yet to clear the trees.

Tom was gathering wood for the fire and contemplating catching another fish for breakfast. Kate was bathing at the lake.

A rock whined past his head and cracked off a tree. Several men were running his way twirling slings over their heads. He reached for his gun but realized it was still lying next to his sleeping bag. Tom raced for his weapon yelling as he went, "Kate! Look out! We're under attack!"

A second later, a large stone glanced off his temple. He staggered and went down.

Kate was just exiting the water when Tom's warning caught her attention. She grabbed a towel and ran into a dense group of trees. Luckily, it was a gravely area and she left no tracks.

Sool's men searched, but found no trace of her location. Kate quietly worked her way back until she was close to their camp. She tearfully watched as a long heavy stick was placed behind Tom's neck and his wrists were bound to the ends.

The fence was still intact, so when Sool and his men reached it, they picked Tom up and dumped him on the other side. Sool had warned them about the evil barrier. He picked up some still damp wood and tossed it against the wires. The men backed away at the sight and sound of the crackling electric current sparking into the ground. Then they obediently ran and jumped over the fence again, as Sool had previously instructed.

Tom was drug to his feet and led away.

Kate was relatively confident the area was clear, but remained cautious. She crept into the trees around the TMTs and began preparing a mental checklist. She knew she was incapable of wielding Tom's weapon, so she'd have to obtain one of her own. A few minutes later, her fingers danced frantically over the keypads.

Tom half walked, half lurched into the village. Sool had placed a twisted grass rope around his neck and commanded him like a tethered animal. When R-rack saw Tom's condition, he started doubting Sool's story, but a couple of the men confirmed the demon's existence. It protected Tom and Kate, allowing them to pass unharmed.

According to rule, the medicine man was in charge of the clan's spiritual security. R-rack had no choice in deferring to Sool's judgment.

The people expected Tom to be punished, but then released. There were many verbal and visual protestations when Sool led Tom to the wall of long sleeping. It was a cliff leading to a three hundred foot drop. Sool had only sacrificed animals to the spirits before.

The sky had been getting cloudier all morning. That fact had not escaped Sool's notice. He repeatedly slapped a hand against his chest calling out his name, then stood with his fingers stretching towards the firmament.

Almost on cue, a lightning bolt and deafening peal of thunder responded to his demands. The people became silent, sensing that perhaps, this was meant to be. As Sool prepared to push Tom over the edge, he opened the ceremony with a chant.

Orm could stand no more. He rushed the medicine man, but Sool had been expecting the action. He withdrew a long sharpened stick from inside his clothing and watched Orm's approach from the side of his eye.

Orm's own momentum proved to be his worst enemy. Sool swung the weapon up and across. The shaft entered Orm's chest at a sharp angle, glanced off a rib, pierced a lung, and then ripped into his heart. His legs crumpled and he died, literally before hitting the ground.

Tom was essentially defenseless, but after witnessing the slaughter of his friend, attacked Sool anyway. Sool spun, catching Tom below the sternum with an elbow, knocking out his wind. He collapsed, falling to his knees and resting on his forehead.

Sool yanked Tom up and drug him toward the abyss.

With all eyes fixed on Sool, nobody noticed Kate enter the setting. She was dressed in a plain, full length, white hooded robe with deep baggy sleeves.

She screamed, "ORTA," and was rewarded with instant silence and a cessation of all movement.

Sool felt invincible. Defeat was never even considered. He dropped Tom and stomped towards Kate. She held up the flat of a hand and said "Orta," again. Sool didn't even slow down.

Kate threw her arms to the sky and cried out a blood-curdling wail. That caused Sool to pause, but he quickly recovered and resumed his march.

Kate had no choice. She leveled her left arm directly at Sool's approach, crossed her right hand over and rested it on top of her left wrist. She waited for Sool to get closer.

When he was about ten feet away, she pressed down on her left wrist. A switch closed. The TASER weapon fired from within her sleeve. A bright blue electric halo enveloped Sool, instantly causing him to loose all voluntary muscle control, yet remain totally conscious. He crashed to the ground.

Kate's emotions were churning, but she walked calmly and untied Tom. He shook his head and expelled a great sigh of relief. "Thanks, Kiddo. That was one hell of a show. For a while, I thought I was going to fly like a wingless bird. I'd hug you, but I don't think I can move my arms yet."

He kissed her on the cheek, then arose and gingerly limped in Orm's direction. Death's cruel gray mask covered his face. Tom checked for a pulse anyway, closed Orm's eyes, then stood and made his way toward Sool.

He gritted his teeth and placed a shoe tip by Sool's head, then pulled it back, preparing to deliver a vicious kick. Sool stared helplessly.

Tom held his foot suspended for a moment, lowering it to the ground as Kate approached.

She was shaking. "I don't think I've ever experienced your depth of rage, Tom. Hopefully, I never will. I can easily understand why you think he should die. Considering the circumstances, I'm sure I could find it somewhere in my heart to eventually forgive you for killing him.

Even so ... knowing you as I do, I'm certain you'd never be able to forgive yourself. It'd destroy you as surely as Sool had pushed you over that cliff. In destroying you, it'd also destroy us. He'd win doubly by proxy. I love you. If you love me ... walk away."

Everything caught up with him at once. Tom covered his head with his hands and screamed out all the frustration, pain, and senseless loss.

She pulled him close. He melted into her arms.

A few minutes later he sniffled and asked her, "Why?"

"I don't know my love. Let's get out of here. Let the people deal with him."

Sool began to recover shortly after Tom and Kate left. The people formed a large circle with their backs to him. The ritual meant that as far as they were concerned, he no longer existed.

The circle had a single opening leading in one direction ... away from the village. A lone person wouldn't survive long.

Banishment was a slow, cruel death.

Kate sponged Tom's temple with a wet rag. The wound was thankfully superficial. It had mostly just stunned him. She checked the time. "We're late for our jump, but we're still well within the window. Are you ready, or would you like to rest first? I'm sure Frank can reschedule." She added with a smile, "He's getting used to it."

"Absolutely no way. Let's get the stuff together and go."

She cooed, "Yes, my wonderful love."

Just before the countdown reached zero, Sool charged from the surrounding bushes. His stone hatchet flew directly at Tom's chest. From this distance, he couldn't miss.

Less than an instant later, it passed harmlessly through the empty space where Tom had been standing. Sool roared in anger. He saw the remaining TMT and stormed towards it. He hoisted a club and smashed downward with all the force his body could summon.

The odds were a million to one. Sool's club contacted the TMT exactly as the machine reached its final disintegration stage ... causing it to malfunction. The scan lens flashed after the safety interlocks had expired. His body disappeared, but there was no tachyon map to direct its destiny.

Sool became what Kate had described once as ... galactic flotsam.

"Disguise yourself as you may to your fellow-men, if you are honest with yourself conscience will make known your real character, and the heart-searching one always knows it."

- Payson

Chapter 24
A Sheep In Wolf's Clothing

Tom impulsively ducked as soon as he reintegrated and looked behind ... expecting to see whatever Sool had thrown lying on the ground. "Where the hell did it go?"

Kate found his reaction amusing. "You were never in any danger. If you tried to move before and couldn't, it's because you existed in TMT controlled space. As long as you're under its constraint, the machine is your protection. Until the disintegration or reintegration phase is complete, it'll repel any object from its realm of influence. In this case, the object must have passed through just after you disintegrated. You were completely safe either way."

She thought for a minute ... then continued. "A time window does exist when an entity can make contact with the machine during final D/R processing, but that window is phenomenally small. A successful invasion of that gateway could only be performed during the purposeful execution of a malicious act, and anyone with the misfortune to accomplish the task would be getting what they justifiably deserved."

Tom visually investigated the area while considering her words. Their delayed arrival would still put them here in the late morning. He shaded his eyes and found the sun. It should be in the southeastern sky. Tom oriented himself accordingly. There were majestic, snow clad mountain ranges, close in the west, and distant to the north. The eastern and southern vistas ran over low hills to their respective horizons. The local land was flatter than it had been in many jumps. There were groups of trees scattered randomly in all directions. He guessed the closer ones to be a mixture of scrub oak and cottonwood. For the most part, it was open prairie, covered by waving green grasses and a multitude of brilliantly colored wild flowers. Obviously, the great expansion leading to Kate's future hadn't happened yet. At least not here.

He noticed her continually checking the time. Then he reasoned why. "Looking for the second machine?"

"Yes. It's definitely overdue." Kate punched up a recovery panel on the primary TMT. A fail-safe code was waiting. "Oh no."

Tom hurried over. "What is it?"

Kate frowned in concentration. "Sool. He must have somehow damaged the second TMT beyond its ability to function. It was only able to send a warning, then self-destruct."

"We got this close and now we're stuck?"

"No. I think we're fine. Let me do some research. Remember, the receiving TMT supplies the necessary matter for integration, which for our last jump will be a fixed-installation at the final destination. Ours only needs enough to build the tachyon map. This model was designed for securely sending a 200-pound person from 500 years in the past to my present time."

"I can follow you better if I know our current and target dates."

"Frank brought us as far forward as safely possible on this jump." Kate checked her wrist device. "We made it to 2162. Our target is 2341."

Tom ran the data in his head. "Okay, follow me on this. Mass and time traveled are inversely proportional. But, even if we double the mass from 200 to 400 pounds, the time is only halved from 500 to 250 years. We only require 179, and our combined weight is only about 280 pounds. We're home free."

"Almost."

"Alright, tell me what I missed."

"Recall the problem you had when calculating the length of a day back in the Jurassic, and what John said about energy requirements approaching baseline time."

Tom laughed. "I don't know if I can. My memory has never been the greatest, and relatively speaking, that was 150 million years ago, but I'll try. Let's see. John said energy requirements rose at an ever increasing rate as you approach your original timeline. One of my computations involved the reduction in earth's spin rate. Ah, I see where you're going with this. Both problems involve non-linear mathematics. So, we can't assume a doubling of mass will effectively allow only a halving of time. In reality, the reduction may be much greater. Correct?"

"Impressive."

Tom hung his head. "No, not really. Actually, I'm embarrassed. I should have deduced that from the beginning."

Kate pressed against him. "I'll still give you high marks."

He kissed the tip of her nose. "You're benignly prejudiced."

"Guilty as charged."

"Hmm, I'll have to think of an appropriate punishment."

"I can hardly wait."

They lightly kissed and held each other, then Kate gently pushed away. "Okay, my research is finished. I can state for certain that we'll make it to my time on our next jump."

Tom pointed an accusing finger. "You've known all along."

"Of course. Frank said this one would bring us home."

"Why didn't you just say so?"

"I like watching you squirm."

"So, like I said, we're home free."

Kate giggled, "Almost."

He stared. "Kate, you know I enjoy it when you tease, but this is getting a bit silly."

"I'm sorry, Tom." She beat her fists gently against his chest. "I'm just so tired I've become giddy. Let's walk over to the nearest trees, find some shade, throw down our sleeping bags, and get some rest."

"Sold. You certainly won't have to twist my arm for that one."

Tom began gathering up the bags.

Kate typed on the TMT. "I told Frank we had to get some sleep. The incoming message alarm is forwarded to my WD. I asked that we not be disturbed for at least four hours unless necessary. I'm ready if you are."

"What about the TMT?"

Kate turned a slow circle, looking in all directions. "If there's anything out here to worry about, I sure don't see it. The machine should be fine right here. Let's go." She started off. Tom fell in behind. A minute later they approached one end of a large stand of trees, surrounded by a heavy patch of low-lying brush.

The sound of people talking woke Jake from a light sleep. He listened, but heard nothing. Maybe it was just imagination. No, there it was again. He stretched all six and a half feet of his tired, tanned, wrinkled body and ran a hand through his heavy shock of hair. "Damn it. If there's someone around, they're on my property."

Jake muttered quite often, and his left cheek had a tendency to spasm when he became stressed. His animals were loosely tied to some low branches. He walked the few feet to where they stood and eased the ancient 30-30 from its scabbard. A round was levered into the trusty family heirloom, then he peered through the foliage. Jake slipped off his thick glasses, blew off the dust, and wiped them on his shirt ... thinking he must be seeing things. When the glasses were back in place, he looked again. The strange looking contraption was still there. "Must be some more of that damn government spy equipment."

The rifle butt was brought up and nestled against a shoulder. Jake drew a bead and slowly squeezed the trigger. The gun bucked. One side of the TMT's ring disappeared. Inside the MBH, a micro-relay clicked ... directing the machine to self-destruct.

Kate and Tom dropped to the ground. He pulled her close and piled the bags in front of their heads. She looked back, tapped Tom's shoulder, and pointed. "Evidently our entire conversation was for naught. Now we're stranded."

Tom peeked over the bags. "What kind of idiots blast away at anything they see?"

Kate laid her head against him. "I just want to sleep."

"C'mon, Kate, stay with me a little longer. Whoever made that shot must have a rifle. A handgun is no match at this distance. We'll have to hope we get an opportunity if they come closer." He unbuckled his belt, slid off the green nylon holster, and hid it under the bags. The gun was tucked into the waistband behind his back.

Jake watched as the strange machine melted towards the ground. A few minutes later, a powdery substance blew away with the wind. "What the hell was that thing?" Tic. He pushed through the bushes for a closer look. His eye caught movement off to one side. The rifle came up and swung around in the same direction. A new target had been found.

Tom watched as the grizzly old man drew near. "I think we're about to meet our discourteous host." He slid a hand slowly towards his back.

Kate's head popped up. The approaching menace was angrily assessed. She jumped up and stormed toward their threat before Tom had any chance to stop her. "Kate! What are you doing? You have no idea ... oh crap."

He jumped up, trying to catch her.

Jake stopped in his tracks. His eyebrows shot up, pulling his eyes wide open.

Some crazy woman had bounded up from nowhere and was quick-marching directly at him. Tic. Tic.

Kate began lecturing like an overindulgent parent who'd finally taken enough from their precocious child. "What are you? Some kind of homicidal maniac! We're lost ... and I'm terribly sorry if we're on your precious property, but that's no reason for you to start shooting at anything you come across. All we wanted to do was escape the heat of the sun and get some sleep. If you want to kill us for that ... go ahead, blast away."

Tic. Tic. Jake kept his rifle leveled on Kate, but backed away as she continued to inch forward. Tic.

Tom caught up and edged between them.

"I'm sorry, sir ... it's not turning out to be a good day. We're both extremely tired. She's telling the truth about us just wanting to rest."

Tom scanned the man from head to foot. Gray cowboy hat, gray hair and mustache, narrow face – approaching cadaverous ... steel gray eyes, red bandana around his neck, light blue shirt, embroidery on the pockets, pearl covered snaps instead of buttons, wide leather belt with a wider silver buckle, blue jeans, and cowboy boots.

The man presented every aspect of a western gentleman cowboy.

Tom took a protective stance. Kate continued to fume. Jake wondered if some of his meds were beginning to affect his mind. He eyeballed the strangers, mentally cataloging their physical traits.

The female had reddish-brown hair, sizzling green eyes, and was dressed in a dusty, full-length white robe. The male had disheveled blondish hair, blue eyes, sported a beard and mustache, large bruise on one side of the forehead, scabbed over wound on the other, a torn, dirty, and bloody brown shirt, khaki pants and some kind of outdoor shoes. He gave the impression of having just been through some private war. Overall, they appeared harmless, but he thought it best to use his standard ruse anyway.

"I don't take kindly to trespassers on my ranch." Jake lowered the gun, slapped a knee, and laughed. "But, ya'll sure don't look like no gov'ment people."

"Government people?" Tom and Kate chimed together.

Tom reasoned he could get to his weapon easier if the old man were distracted, and Kate seemingly had the situation under control, so he backed out and let her do the talking.

"Why would the government be on your ranch?"

"Spyin' on me, why else?"

She took another quick look around, thinking maybe she missed something. "Why would they take the trouble to spy on you?"

"Don't think they take to my politics none."

Now Kate had the picture. The man's chipset had a few bent pins. "Well, I see Mr. ... uh."

"Jake ... people 'round these parts just calls me Jake."

"It's nice to meet you ... Jake."

She offered her hand. "I'm Dr. Khattyba Bright ... please, call me Kate. I'm ... a weather researcher. The machine you shot away was nothing more than an advanced tracking station. This gentleman with me is my assistant, Mr. Thomas Hughes. As I've already stated, obviously we don't know our exact position, although we thought we did." She lightly brushed against Tom. "I told you ... pay more attention to the map."

"I'm sorry, Dr. Bright. She's right sir; I'm afraid this is my fault. We certainly had no intention of trespassing. If you'll kindly direct us off your property, we'll be more than happy to oblige."

Jake considered the situation. "Lookit here, missy. I don't recollect seein' any vehicles or other animals. How you plan on leavin' ... walk?"

"Yes sir. We walked in ... I'm sure we're capable of walking out, but we've gotten turned around. As Mr. Hughes indicated, if you'll just point the way, we'll leave immediately. We really don't want to cause any trouble."

"What'll happen then? You got someone ta meet ya?"

"Yes sir. There's a built-in homing device in my wrist ... watch. The other part of my team will locate us using its signal."

Jake rubbed the stubble on his chin and thought, 'Something's not right. These people are almost too polite, and if that was a weather station ... then I'm a two-headed calf ... and where did they walk in from? Carrying supplies no less. It's almost two miles to the fence line in any direction. The closest town is nearly twenty-five. Maybe I should investigate a little further. Keep them close until something definitive can be found.'

"I'll tell ya what. Ya'll come back ta the ranch house. Be there in fifteen minutes. Shor' don't want the 'sponsibility of somethin' happenin' ta ya on my land. Ya'll can rest, get washed up, and call from there." He casually bounced the rifle on his arm. "I insist. It's just proper manners like."

Kate's eyes slowly widened while watching the weapon's movement. "Fine, Jake. I'm sure Tom agrees. We'll be happy to accept your ... invitation. Just give us a minute to gather our equipment."

"I'll wait right here."

Tom and Kate walked toward their bags.

Jake had noticed Tom standing with one hand behind his back. When Tom turned, he knew why. The bulge from the gun was obvious. He also realized once his own gun had been pointed away, the younger man could easily have gotten the drop on him, yet Tom had never made a move.

Tom waited until they had distanced themselves from Jake, then talked in a low tone. "What do you make of this guy? He talks southern, but has a western drawl, and there's a sly intelligence behind those eyes that doesn't match his limited vocabulary." He chuckled. "I think he bought the weather station bit about as much as I did."

"I have to agree. More than anything, he's curious. Maybe he still thinks we're gov-ment people. Tom, I don't want someone to get needlessly hurt. Let's just go along and see what develops."

"Okay. I have a feeling he might be telling the truth. After all, I know we're not." Tom slid his gun back into its holster within the sleeping bag.

Jake held the bushes spread open with his rifle barrel as Kate and Tom passed through with their gear. He noticed Tom's gun was no longer present. "I've got two horses and a mule. I'll split the one horse's load 'tween the other two. Ya'll ride Lady Sue together. Ain't no saddle, but in fact, ya might be more comfortable without it since ya'll be riding double."

Jake made sure they were watching when he put his rifle away, then placed two saddle blankets on Lady Sue.

Kate rode behind Tom, her arms around his waist with her head against his back.

Jake mounted his horse and eased away, leading Lady Sue and the mule by their reins.

Jake the gentleman cowboy

"I like to believe that people, in the long run, are going to do more to promote peace than our governments. Indeed, I think that people want peace so much that one of these days governments had better get out of the way and let them have it."

- Dwight D. Eisenhower

Chapter 25
Musical Faces

True to Jake's word, about fifteen minutes later they rode under a wooden arch with 'Bar Triple J Ranch' burned into it. Both ends of the arch had a short unbroken line with what looked like three fish hooks, minus the barbs, hanging from it. Kate was asleep. Jake slid off his horse and tied the animals' reins to a hitching rail. He steadied Kate while Tom dismounted, then eased her down into Tom's arms. "Whooee, your doctor friend is really out. Follow me son, I'll show ya where ya'll can let her rest."

"Thank you, sir. It's deeply appreciated."

Jake stopped. "Look son. If we're to git along, start callin' me Jake. Knock off that sir stuff."

"Okay ... Jake."

He led Tom into a cedar ranch house, through a great room with an open-beam ceiling, and up a curved wooden balustraded stairway to a loft. "There are two bedrooms up here with a bath 'tween them." Jake pointed to the second. "That one'll be a little quieter. Why doncha put her in there."

"Great. I don't want to be rude, but would you mind if I just collapse in the other?"

"Not a' tall, son. Go right ahead. We can talk when your mind's feelin' better. I'll git your gear and stow it just inside the front door."

"Thanks, Jake. Thanks a lot."

Tom laid Kate on her bed and passed through the bathroom into his room, leaving the door slightly ajar.

The wiry old man went downstairs to his study.

Jake hit a button on his wireless keyboard, waking up his computer link. He highlighted a search program and tapped a mouse key, bringing up a data entry panel. The names Thomas Hughes and Khattyba Bright were typed and entered, along with their descriptions and approximate ages.

Jake sat back and waited.

There were no hits for Kate within the specified parameters. The only match coming close to Tom was labeled as deceased 149 years earlier. "This is most curious. Who are these people ... and what do they want?"

The computer caught Jake's voice. "Why do you bother with that silly antiquated keyboard?"

"Sometimes I think better if I start with my fingers."

"Shall I run a more in-depth search, Jake?"

"Yes, Gidg. Tie in ... check all historical and governmental files. Look specifically for photographic and biographical data. Use the visual scans you've done since their arrival as benchmarks. Allow for aging ... younger or older."

"Message understood. Beginning search."

Jake left to retrieve a cup of coffee, then reentered the room and settled into a form-fitting easy chair. He picked up a book and thumbed it open to a page marker. A short while later the computer announced it had completed the search. He sat up, his attention riveted by the results.

Eleven identities for Hughes, and seven for Bright had been located, but only one hit for each was highlighted. They were based on an exact name and/or photographic match.

Dr. Thomas Einstein Hughes, a.k.a. Thomas Edward Baker, disappeared on or about October 17, 2013. According to the photo ID, there was a 99.6% probability it was the identity of the gentleman upstairs.

Jake read the biographical data. When finished, he stared blankly into space ... contemplating. "Interesting. Extraordinarily interesting." Tic.

What became more intriguing was the dossier on Kate. According to the computer, Khattyba Bright was really Janet Cork ... or vice versa. She had been enrolled in a Birmingham, Michigan high school in the year 1996 at age 17 ... 166 years ago.

"Gidg, what is the probability correlation for Bright?"

"Sole evidence is photographic image of subject at age seventeen, but there is a 95.3% correspondence, Jake. This includes eye and hair color, bone structure, skin texture, facial features, and a small scar on lower left chin.

If you can possibly obtain DNA, fingerprints, or even a hand writing sample, I can improve identification to a 100% level for both subjects."

"Good ... but I don't think that's necessary at this time, Gidg."

He inspected the early picture of Janet/Kate on the display screen. Yes, there it was. A faint scar about one quarter of an inch long. Almost undetectable, unless you were purposely looking for it.

"Print images of both subjects ... enhance Kate's to allow for aging."

"Message understood. Printing and enhancing."

Jake examined the results, after which, he decided his guests had some explaining to do.

"Gidg, maintain a class C security alert. Keep the subjects immobile."

"Should I use a sedation aerosol, Jake?"

"Only if necessary, and then just enough to make them drowsy, not unconscious. We wouldn't want to create embarrassment or invite suspicion by having them wet the bed. Allow them a little latitude for normal functions. Just keep them from snooping around. I have a meeting to attend and will return later tonight."

"Message understood. Security class C enabled. Have a nice day, Jake."

Jake decided to check his haymow before leaving the ranch. He entered the barn's side door and looked into an old medicine chest's broken mirror mounted on a wall. The hidden retina scanner confirmed his identity and a pneumatic lift descended from the upper loft. He rode it up into an area crowded with electronic equipment. "You guys have any idea how these people got onto the property?"

"Absolutely none, Jake. We had you on long-range scan, taking your nap. These two literally appeared out of nowhere. Damndest thing I've ever seen. Were you able to come up with anything?"

"Yes. But you're not going to believe it. I have an appointment with the publisher. I'll be back later, and maybe we can have a chat. Ask the computer for current information. I'm sure you'll find it enormously entertaining."

* * * * *

Upon returning from his trip into town, Jake revisited the hayloft. "Hi, Dale. Anything new?"

"Naw, pretty much ident, ident."

"Where's Charlie?"

"Getting some sandwiches and drinks. Gidg said the coast was clear. Your two house guests are taking a shower."

"Together?"

"Uh huh."

"I thought they seemed overly friendly towards each other. So, what did you guys think of the data?"

"We've discussed something like this happening someday. We think these two are time travelers. That's the only thing that makes sense. Either that or they're government moles and it's all a deception to throw us off guard. I'd be careful until we know one way or the other."

"Okay. You guys maintain a low profile. I'm going to confront them with my evidence and we'll see what shakes out." Jake leaned on a tabletop, looking at a display screen. "Gidg, anything interesting happen while I was gone?"

"Not unless you'd consider watching someone urinate interesting."

Jake chuckled. "You've been tinkering with your humor generating subroutines again."

"I'm just trying to adapt my dialogue capability so people feel more comfortable communicating with me."

"Good girl. You're doing fine. Personally, I think the whole world is going to fall in love with you ... except for the rats of course." Jake headed for his study to organize his thoughts and have Gidg politely summon his guests.

Tom and Kate had toweled off and were beginning to dress when a disembodied voice floated through their rooms. "Good afternoon. My name is Gidget Gadget. I'm a computer interface. Most people call me, Gidg.

Please don't be alarmed. Jake doesn't allow me to be used for anything perverse. I automatically distort any human guests appearing on a viewing screen that are not fully dressed. I have informed Jake that you are awake and seem rested enough to join him downstairs. He took the liberty of purchasing new clothing items for each of you. They are just outside your respective doors. Please descend to the lower level at your earliest convenience."

Tom's gaze caught Kate's eye then flowed over the room. "Thank you."

"You're welcome ... Dr. Hughes."

Tom and Kate immediately caught the inflection. Their eyes locked.

After retrieving the boxes, both were found to contain one piece, short-sleeve pullovers with matching solid colored pants. Tom's was tan with dark brown markings and belted with Velcro. Kate's was light blue with subtle multi-hued flower prints. Blue and brown pairs of slippers accompanied the outfits.

Gidg's voice returned as Tom and Kate reached the bottom of the stairs. "Please go through the great room, make a right into the dining area, and continue into the kitchen. Jake is preparing food and liquid refreshments."

They walked along trying to spot any speakers or cameras, but none were obviously visible. As they entered the kitchen, Tom noticed a simple wedge of rubber holding the door open. "Hi, Jake." He smiled and pointed at the rubber piece, "You seem to run the full gambit of technology."

Jake looked up from his work. "Sometimes it's the simple things that work best. Hey, you two look good in those outfits. I hope you don't mind. Just figured you'd be a lot more comfortable in clean clothes."

Kate and Tom exchanged glances at the improvement in Jake's English and proper speech in general. "We really appreciate the effort, but again, the last thing we wanted was to create a problem," Tom replied.

Jake's eyes twinkled. "Yes. I'll bet remaining as inconspicuous as possible is a priority for you." He gestured to some chairs. "Sit. Please. There's melon, bread, meat, fruits ... help yourself. I was hoping we could talk while we eat."

All three took a seat.

Tom noticed a small pile of paperwork laying facedown that Jake was ominously tapping with his fingers. He tried opening the conversation with indolent chitchat. "Your computer has an interesting moniker."

"Gidget was my late wife's name. Gadget just struck my fancy one day and it stuck. Some people think it's a little obtuse designating my computer interface Gidget, but it makes me feel like I'm still talking with her. I loved my wife very much, and I miss her terribly. She was my lifelong friend as well as companion."

Kate was busily munching on food, so Tom carried on alone. "I'm sorry for your loss. How long has it been?"

"It'll be two years next month. I handle her death better as more time passes, but it's still difficult." Jake decided to ease into his investigation. "What exactly ... was that machine I ruined?"

Kate quickly swallowed. "It's termed a Tabulating Monitoring Transceiver, or TMT. All types of weather information is collected and transmitted to a central site for integration with other data. As you probably realize ... the global weather patterns have changed remarkably over the years.

We collate the data in hopes of discovering ways that will dampen those changes so as to have a moderated impact on the environment."

Jake slowly nodded as he wrote the letters 'TMT' on a piece of paper, then casually drew lazy circles around them. Transceiver was the only word that really seemed to fit. He check-marked the second 'T', gazed into each of their eyes, and chose to play his ace. "I'd like the two of you to look over this bit of information Gidg gathered for me. Maybe you can help a tired old man make some sense of it."

Tom and Kate took the sheets of paper as they slid across the table. His file was much thicker, so Kate completed first, then rested her chin in a hand watching him read. When he finished they looked at Jake ... not knowing what to expect next. "Unless Gidg is wrong, which is highly doubtful, both of you are anachronisms. Tom seems fascinated by the computer. Kate just takes it in stride. So, judging from my information and your reactions to the present, Tom is from my past, while Kate is from the future. I have no idea how you met; in fact, it'd probably be unwise for me to know, so I won't ask." He leaned forward. "But, I'd love to hear about anything you feel it'd be safe mentioning. For instance ... does the first 'T' in TMT, in reality, stand for time?"

Kate embarrassingly whispered, "That's a possibility."

Jake drew a line completely through the letters. "I won't ask anymore about the machine. That also might prove to be precarious."

For some reason, Tom thought about the Bar Triple J logo he saw that morning. He picked up a pencil, doodled it on a paper, and responded to Jake. Kate watched and listened. "You definitely appear to have the advantage, Jake. You certainly don't seem to be the country bumpkin we first encountered."

Before Jake could comment, Kate grabbed Tom's wrist and excitedly moved it aside. "Why did you draw that?"

Tom was partially stunned. "Uh, it was on the sign hanging over the ranch's entrance. You were asleep and didn't see it. Why is it so important?"

Kate stared at Jake and began ticking off bits of information on her fingers. "Montana ... the year 2162 ... wife's name Gidget, died in 2160. That design you doodled is the brand for the Bar Triple J ranch owned by Dr. Jackson Julius Johnson, dual PhD ... nickname Jake. One doctorate is in Political Science, the other's in Computer Science and Technology. You're working on a monumental book that describes how the world's population would be better equipped for change and equanimity if guided by computers instead of politicians. It's titled," she stopped, "no, that might be dangerous. Maybe you should tell me."

Jake softly replied, "Years Of Change."

It became so quiet, you could almost imagine hearing Gidg breathe.

Tom spoke first. "Well, will the real ... whoever we are ... please stand up. Apparently, it's fairly safe when Jake and I talk, while Kate, my dear, may have to remain mostly mute. If you do speak, you'll obviously have to choose your words carefully. So, Jake, what makes you think a computer can run the world better than humankind?"

"Isn't it self-evident? A computer has no possible ulterior motive. Have you ever read Asimov?"

"Isaac Asimov?"

"Yes."

"Hey, I'm a sci-fi buff. Anyone who reads sci-fi that's worth their salt has read Asimov."

"Do you remember the three laws of robotics?"

"I can't quote them verbatim, but yeah, I remember. I assume you've basically incorporated that philosophy into your computer system?"

"Exactly. But, as it's explained in my book, the computer doesn't run the world. It's a guide ... a tool. It examines situations and conditions, then considers all relevant data and suggests the best solution to a problem. It may even list several ideas for action in order of preference.

Humankind always has the last word. However, no one person or even one same specific group makes the final decisions. That group is always randomly selected from among a field of qualified people, the qualification based solely on knowledge of the subject and psychological profile of the individual.

There's no infighting, no lobbyists, no professional politicians, no political parties, and no secrets where public domain is concerned. Private individual information remains just that – private, while public information is available to any person on the planet."

"Are we talking about some kind of utopia?"

Jake shook his head. "Oh no. A utopian society encompasses much more than this. In fact, because of the basic flaws in all people, myself included, a utopia is probably a quixotic destination. I'm thoroughly convinced we can do much better than we're doing now, but it'll take an impartial advocate to get us there." Jake laughed and continued. "We've tried just about everything else and none of them have worked. Everyone except the ruling class is suppressed under communism. An oligarchy or dictatorship imprisons its dissenters. Capitalism, with its supposedly inherent democracy, taxes people to death, then wastes the money on whatever the government chooses.

When you think about it, they're all essentially the same. They really only differ in degree of implementation and the camouflaging of their actions. Under each, the rich get the best education, the poor are forgotten and starve, while the middle class supports everything. My solution won't be perfect either, but I certainly believe it's a large step in the right direction. I've found a company who's agreed to go out on a limb and publish the book, even though they'll take a lot of censure from the government."

Tom nodded. "Let's say I agree with you in principal. How are you going to convince the populous at large they might be better off being led by a computer than their fellow kind?"

"I'm not." A sly grin crawled slowly across Jake's face. "I'm not much of a public speaker, so I wouldn't try even if the opportunity presented itself."

Tom blinked. "Then ... who will?"

"Assume you have a problem. Several different salespeople tell you they have a product that will solve your problem. Would you simply take them at their word, or would you rather see the products in action so you can determine their effectiveness?"

"I'd much rather judge for myself."

"Precisely. In the computer versus human scenario, I'd just be another salesperson. That's where Gidg would shine. After the book is published, Gidg will be accessible through the net by anyone with a computer link. They can ask her questions on how she would handle a given situation and compare it with the one being proposed by her human counterparts. She'll list her reasons and give comparisons on cost, effectiveness, and most importantly ... fairness. Let the people pick the winner. Gidg has nothing to hide.

You say you're a sci-fi buff. Here's something else about my research. In all my efforts, I could never find a simple, straightforward way to explain the problem with politics, as it exists ... until I came across an extraordinary piece of literature by Arthur C. Clarke during my inquiries. May I presume you've also read works by him?"

"Yes. Quite a few."

"I discovered a particular passage in his book 'Imperial Earth', I believe on the first page of chapter nineteen, published way back in 1976. It describes how the people in it solved their political problem by having random candidates selected from pools of people with the desired qualifications. It also mentions how the human race finally realized that some jobs should never be allocated to volunteers. Instead, those who were selected by computer, should be carried 'kicking and screaming' into their positions so they'd do a great job in order to be released from their post early. Of course, it was strictly a fictional work, but still, that pretty well sums up my whole philosophy, simply and eloquently, don't you think?"

Kate and Tom nodded in unison.

"Besides, Gidg can be a lot of fun. I prefer the machine answering in a woman's voice, which just so happens to mimic my wife's when she was healthy, but Gidg can converse in any manner the recipient wishes, in either gender, or any language. This is for you, Tom. Gidg, be a twentieth-century man."

There was a slight pause, then a deep, husky voice answered back, "Yo! Adrian."

"Do another."

Gidg slurred, exaggerated, and extended, "I'll be back."

"One more," Jake prompted.

A tightly controlled voice rang out through an audibly perceived image of clenched teeth. "Are you feeling lucky, punk? Are you? Go ahead ... make my day."

"Okay. You can go back to your normal, lovable self."

A soft, sexy, feminine voice replied, "Thank you, sweetie."

"Gidg, we have company ... not quite that lovable."

"Yes, Jake."

Jake looked from one guest to the other. "Versatility, total honesty, complete fairness, 100% accuracy, and the ability to do more research in five minutes than a million people could accomplish in a day. What more could anyone ask?

But, if you want people to be responsible, you must give them responsibility. The system would provide all individuals a facility to read, discuss, and evaluate group decisions ... before and after implementation. Gidg would be the perfect tool to bring about that end." Jake plucked up a strawberry and popped it into his mouth. "And that, dear friends, concludes my meager attempt at persuasion."

Tom's head was slowly bobbing. "I know people in my day were sure fed up with the ranting and raving of politicians' promises to get elected. Once they were in office and an official member of the good ol' boys club, they pretty much did whatever they wanted."

"If my book does well, and people become enthralled with its political philosophy, there'll be no regressing. After a time, the eyes of history will look back and think the computer has always been there as an aid in the governing of the world. Kind of like a ... I'm not sure how to put it."

Tom moaned, "A one-sided door."

"Yes, exactly. Only one direction seems reasonably viable. I like that. Would you mind if I decided to use it somewhere in my book?"

"No. Not at all. Just don't dwell on it too much. It's guaranteed to drive you nuts."

Kate gave Jake a knowing smile. He stared into her eyes for a moment, then placed a hand over hers. "I don't suppose you could give me a hint as to whether my efforts are all in vain?"

She covered his hand with hers. "I think it's safe to say you'd be extremely pleased, Jake ... and proud."

Jake withdrew his hand and looked away. "Fortunately, the book is nearly finished. Just some proverbial 'i's and 't's to dot and cross." His gaze returned to her. "You're probably aware of the urgency."

Kate nodded.

Tom's forehead wrinkled as he searched for meaning in the exchange.

Each sat quietly for a short while ... munching on food and mentally chewing on their own thoughts.

Kate jerked as her wrist device began beeping. She elatedly looked to Tom. "It must be John's TMT."

"Has to be. It's the only one left. Question is ... where is it?"

"Probably out on the prairie. Those are the last coordinates they'd have for the transmission. Jake, will you take us back?"

"Be my pleasure, missy," then laughed, "I even promise not to shoot this one!"

"Of all sad words of tongue or pen, the saddest are these: 'It might have been'."

- Whittier

Chapter 26
Awkward Goodbyes

Jake led Lady Sue over to Tom and started mounting his own horse, but Kate interrupted. "Jake, can we take the mule, too?"

"Sure, Kate. May I inquire as to why?"

"With your permission, I'd like to bring the TMT back and leave from here. I also have a favor to ask."

"Ask away."

"I know this may sound crazy, but I don't know what it is yet. My companions have mentioned a question that Tom needs to answer before we depart for my era. You and/or Gidg may play a part in the decision."

Jake shrugged. "No problem, missy. No problem at all. Anything that Gidg or I can do will be an honor."

"Thanks, Jake."

They returned to the ranch about 45 minutes later. Kate and Tom set the TMT up behind the house. She read a message stating that Frank and Larry were frantic about having lost contact. Obviously, the TMT Jake shot had been damaged beyond its ability to even send an emergency communication.

The long-awaited question was there, too. Kate sent a short note indicating all was well and that she would explain in detail when they arrived. "I need that favor now, Jake. Let's all go into your study."

Jake poured a cup of coffee for Tom and one for himself. Kate decided to have milk. He sat in his easy chair and offered a sofa to the guests. "Okay, Kate, what's this big mystery question?"

"Actually, I should describe it more as a situation than a question. A welcome party was planned for Tom's scheduled entrance into the future. However, we got sidetracked and ended up in the past instead. As time travelers, we could still enter my epoch at the proper moment, and be on hand for the reception. We would be alright.

During our travel forward, relative time has passed in the future, and events have occurred involving others. Without allowing for this time transit, it would be impossible for them to explain the causality of these specific events.

At separate points, two of my co-workers existed in the past with us. Returning at the originally expected entry point would make everything easy on us, but creates a highly plausible condition in which one or more of my friends may be caught in an irreversible time-loop. If we return to my future's 'now', which would allow time for these particular actions to unfold, my friends would be okay, but Tom and I would have a lot of explaining to do. So, the question posed to Tom is: what route do we take?"

Tom's jaw dropped. "I'm supposed to decide this?"

"Well, as John once stated, you're the guest of honor. Since we caused your involvement, everyone is willing to let you determine the outcome."

"Oh, thanks."

Jake raised a finger to get their attention. "This is the most fun I've had in a long time, but may I make a suggestion?"

"By all means", Tom and Kate breathed out together.

"I think both of you are overlooking our resident expert on evaluation and resolution. Gidg, have you been listening?"

"Yes, Jake. A logistically fascinating set of circumstances."

"Would you be willing to help our wayward tourists?"

"It will be an absolute pleasure to assist in any way I can."

Jake gestured toward the ceiling with the palm of a hand. "She's all yours, Kate."

"What is your view on this matter, Gidg?"

"It is my considered, but humble opinion, that there is no decision to be made. As I understand the situation, the probability of one or more future-time participants becoming entwined in a world-line temporal circular displacement is so high as to be considered a certainty. Therefore, in a purely rational sense, your return must allow for the occurrence of future events that have already transpired."

Kate's gaze swung around. "Tom?"

"I think she said it all. There's no way I want to endanger people just to avoid some possible unpleasantness. If this is all they want to know, then I fully agree with Gidg ... the decision is essentially self-defining. Let's return to your 'now' versus the originally planned entry."

"Okay. I'll prepare a message and see if they have any suggestions on precisely 'when' to bring us home. I'll be back in a few minutes."

"Can't you relay the request to the TMT from here on your wrist device?"

"Yes, but I'd have to pick out each letter with a tiny stylus. It's much easier and faster if I use the machine's keyboard." She rose and left the room.

"Well, Jake, it looks like you'll be rid of us soon."

"Actually, I'll be sorry to see you go. Your visit has been most remarkable." Jake chuckled. "It must be tough on Kate though. She must be frantically editing every word she speaks, terrified of disclosing some fact that could be detrimental to the future timeline. How much has she told you?"

"She's mentioned some things ... but not a lot. I'm trying to mentally prepare myself for a real eye opener."

"I envy you. I don't want to steal her thunder, but there's already a mining operation on the moon and a settlement on Mars. Who knows what another hundred plus years has wrought. The whole idea is kind of mind boggling."

"I don't really have any authority to say this, however, maybe you could come into the future once your book is published and its impact on society has been resolved."

Jake smiled and laughed softly. "No, although extremely tempting, I'm afraid that's not possible."

"Why not? They took me."

"Thank you for the thought ... but, you'll understand in a short time. Would you join an old geezer in a farewell cocktail?"

"I'm not much of a drinker, yet if there's ever been a time to make an exception ... it's certainly now. What do you have?"

"How about trying some Martian ale? I'll warn you though, it's potent."

"After what Kate and I have been through in the last week, I'm confident I can at least handle a stiff drink."

Jake opened a cabinet, revealing a bar. "Do you think Kate will want something?"

"I don't know. She hadn't even had coffee when I first met her. You'll have to wait and ask."

"Agreed." Two clear, plastic bottles of dark liquid were retrieved from the bar's interior. "For now, we'll start on these."

Jake had been perfectly correct about the ale. Tom was feeling its effect when Kate returned. She walked into a room ringing with laughter. "It seems like the two of you are having a good time."

Tom looked up. "I was telling Jake about some of our exploits in the past. He thought the ride on the wooly mammoth was a riot. Would you like to join the celebration and have a brew?"

"You were only talking about things that happened in the past?"

"Of course. Hell, I don't know anything about the future."

She turned to Jake. "I'm sorry, but I'm also worried about any records that would depict the actions that have taken place here."

Jake gave Tom a wink. "You called that one right on the nose."

Tom nodded. "I told you she was sharp."

"Gidg."

"Yes, Jake?"

"Inform Kate of the regimen you've designed."

"It's designated Bitter-Root. Phase one will build an in-core index consisting of file pointers to any references containing information regarding your visit. Immediately after your departure, a program will execute following this chain and delete all files and format-1 DSCB's, over-writing them with binary zeros so they can never be recovered or traced by any means.

When phase one completes, phase two will fence the memory area where the index and program just executed reside. It will be automatically reinitialized, so that it also will contain nothing more than zero-values."

Gidg paused. The hair on the back of Tom's neck became erect. He could swear he heard a sob in the background before Gidg continued. "At this point, no record, or memory, whatsoever, will exist of your visit ... or you."

Kate frowned, thinking she had heard something during the pause, too. "Okay. I'm satisfied that the timeline is fully protected. In that case, I'll have one of whatever you two are drinking."

She glanced at her wrist device. "We don't have long. Part of our return strategy is to arrive at 2 a.m., my time. That's when the fewest people will be around to involve. Most of them now know the story and are anxious to help."

Jake looked sad. "How much time do we have?"

"An hour and fifteen minutes."

Jake handed her an ale. "Then we better start guzzling."

Three bottles clinked together.

Kate giggled as she set down her third empty container. "Wow. This stuff is dangerous. I feel really weird," she brushed her fingers over her mouth, "and my lips are numb." She stood and stretched. Their elderly host was almost asleep in his chair. "I'm sorry, Jake, but it's time for us to leave. We'll prep the machine and then wait for you."

He observed her from under heavy eyelids. "Thank you, Kate. There's a short update for my book I'll dictate to Gidg. I promise not to be long."

Tom playfully bumped against Kate while she attempted to double-check the downloaded instructions. "Tom, please. I'm already having enough trouble focusing. Make yourself useful; take the canisters and top off the matter banks."

He kissed her neck and did as she asked. Afterwards, the empty cylinders were placed in front of the TMT for return.

When Kate finished her task, she found him standing silently. "Tom, you have a strange look on your face. What's bothering you?"

"Just that earlier exchange between you and Jake about the urgency in finishing the book. It's been bugging me ever since. Is Jake in some sort of trouble," his expression hardened, "or danger?"

Kate sighed. Her gaze dropped, then returned to engage his. "Jake is dying. He won't live to see the actual publication of his book."

Tom turned away just as Jake rounded a back corner of the house. "Are you two trouble makers about ready for takeoff?"

Jake offered an outstretched hand. For a moment Tom just stared, then something deep inside managed to unravel one of the old tough knots in his hardened heart. "Sorry, Jake. That's not going to get it done."

Without even thinking, Tom reached out and hugged the old man tightly.

A startled Jake responded, "What's all this?"

Tom quickly wiped his face with the palm of a hand. "I guess I'm just going to miss being around a crotchety old timer like you." Another knot loosened. "I'd give almost anything if you could have been my father."

Kate gasped.

Jake froze, then slowly recovered, finally slapping Tom on the shoulder. "Are you kidding? With a son as wild and crazy as you, I probably would've forgotten all about the book and simply skipped the planet looking for some stability and mental self-preservation."

Kate punched Tom's other shoulder. "See. Once people get to know you ... they want to get away ... fast."

He grinned. "So what happened to you?"

"Maybe I should apply to be Jake's daughter, because I'm probably becoming just as outrageous, especially after all we've been through lately. The two of you are definitely my kind of people now."

She turned to Jake and slipped her arms around him, giving him a kiss on the cheek before pulling away. "Goodbye, Jake. Thanks for everything."

"Be seeing you, Kate. Drop by any ... time. I'll be here." A silly smile spread from beneath his mustache. "Maybe I'll find a way to slip you a note."

"Can Gidg hear us?"

"Yes." Jake twisted, gesturing up and behind. "She can see you, too."

Kate blew a kiss in the indicated direction. "Goodbye, Gidg. Thanks for your help. We love you, too."

"Goodbye, friends. Soon, I won't have the capacity to remember you. Please ... remember me."

Kate pointed to the scan lens. "We need a little room, Jake, and you might want to shade your eyes."

He retreated a few steps.

She was about to energize the system when Tom's hand stopped her. "Hey, Jake. If I ever pass through this way again, I'll bring my pet. We'll have to keep him away from your horses though. He could probably eat one with three bites!"

Kate pushed the button.

Jake stood alone with Tom's last words rattling through his thoughts.

Tic. Tic.

Tic.

"Gidg?"

"Yes, Jake?"

"Please load and execute Bitter-Root."

There were a few moments of crushing silence. Then, in the saddest voice Jake ever heard Gidg emulate, she replied, "Message ... understood."

Jake turned and looked directly up into the micro camera lens. "I know, Gidg ... I know."

"We should live for the future, and yet should find our life in the fidelities of the present; the last is the only method of the first."

- H.W. Beecher

Chapter 27
Homecoming

Kate and Tom popped back into reality. They were standing on a raised platform under a single lamp, emitting a dim, diffused light.

John's machine flashed into view, appearing about ten feet away and below. The area was eerily quiet. Even after their eyes adjusted to the dark, the limits of their vision still fell away into feathery shadows.

"Uh, Kate, you were a little bombed when you messed with those settings. It looks like we came out in somebody's closet. Does any of this look familiar?"

She shrugged. "I checked the settings ... but no changes were required. This appears to be the main TMT portal, although ... it should be situated in a huge, brightly-lit room."

"Oh, God. Do you think John's playing around again?"

Kate vigorously shook her head. "No. Not after what we've been through. He'd never do this to us. I don't understand what could've gone wrong. Let me check..."

The holographic walls disappeared and the area became flooded with illumination. It seemed like dozens of people came charging and shouting towards them. In reality, there were only seven.

Kate went airborne; her entire body was whisked off the ground and flung in huge circles. She released a joyful shriek. Tom looked up into the hazel eyes of a red-haired giant that was currently pumping his hand up and down like the translated motion of an old-fashioned mechanical windmill in a storm.

A breathless Kate landed next to Tom. She reached up, patted the shoulder of the man who was trying to take Tom's arm off, and managed to grab a breath. "Tom, this is Lanfrance Angstrom ... better known as Frank."

She gave the tall man a soft, playful poke in the side. "He's probably the one responsible for our confusion at entry."

Frank became concerned. "Oh, Kate. I'm sorry. I wanted you to have a minute of peace and quiet before we descended on you. Really. Great galaxies; I apologize if I've upset you."

"Forget it, Frank. We're too happy about being home to let it bother us. I just had to taunt you, proving I haven't changed all that much."

She turned and introduced her body pilot. "This other wild guy is Lropold Faust ... Larry. These are the boys that have been our guardian angels."

Tom looked from one smiling face to the other. "They've been a lot more than that. I have to tell you guys, there was more than once when I didn't think we were going to make it. What you did for Kate after the cats attacked was utterly astonishing. If I hadn't been there, I still wouldn't believe it.

It'll take a while, but I have to find a way to do more than just say 'thank you'. I'll never feel right until I do."

Kate was searching the faces. Larry gave her a tight smile. "If you're looking for John, he's in his office. I think it was mentioned a couple of messages back that we were about to bring him out of zero-spin stasis. The decoding was performed only two days ago. It took a little time figuring everything out because we had to rely entirely on his procedure log. Fortunately, John makes copious notes. Something may have gone wrong during the process. He's doing well, but as I've also tried to imply in my messages ... there are complications. Rose has been working with him."

Kate nodded in sad understanding.

Frank butted in, trying to change the subject. He pulled his shirt outward. "Hey, what do you think of these fancy, high-tech, custom-made name tags? We thought they'd help Tom get to know us quicker."

Tom scanned the variously designed, hand-printed sticky-notes, then exclaimed, "Where's ours?"

The small crowd chortled an appreciative chorus of laughter.

Tom leaned close to Kate. "Who's Rose?"

"Our senior Psych Tech. She'll help you get oriented. You'll love her." She grabbed him by the shirt, stared into his eyes, and snickered. "Of course, you won't take that literally."

He grinned. "Hey, she's your friend."

"He's pretty interesting, Khatty. I hope he doesn't come between our friendship."

Kate turned to face the voice. A short, slim, attractive lady with dark hair and eyes stood with her arms open. Kate's arms flew open, too. "Rose! Oh, it's so good to be back. Have we got some things to talk about!"

Rose hugged, then released and stepped back. "Yes, and as Larry just indicated ... I'm afraid John is one of them."

Kate's smile waned. "How bad, Rose?"

The others gathered closer to listen.

"The boys put him through an 'expel' process during decoding, which removed whatever poisoned his system. Physically, he's perfectly healthy. His heart was a textbook restart. Cognitive powers are as strong as ever.

Long-term recall is the only known problem ... although the memories themselves are still viable. That's been verified with a psych probe. Every one I touched was vocalized immediately, but he reports it's like listening to a recording of someone else. He's unable to connect, indicating they're all disassociated."

"Will he remember us?" Tom asked.

Rose tilted her head. "That's the question of the hour. We're hoping the two of you may be the trigger that fixes whatever's broken. The computers have run every test known to medical science, including some from other disciplines. Zero abnormal results.

Therefore, it's our combined opinion that a block was induced before he died in the Jurassic. Since the block was caused by trauma, the only suggestion the pool of people and computers have offered ... is introducing a mental shock in an attempt to re-associate the memory/neuron pathways.

Khatty, why don't you finish the introductions, and we'll move the reception to John's office. He's expecting us."

"Fine. Tom, just to make it official ... this is Dr. Rosalba Petals ... Rose."
"Hi, Rose. I understand we may be seeing a lot of each other soon."
"Probably several short meetings to get your orientation started. Then I'll probably be handing you off to the computer so you can advance at your own pace."

Kate led another lady forward. "Hello, Tom. I'm Ysabel Lebasy. It's wonderful to meet you at last. My specialty is superluminal applications. Mostly neutrinos and tachyon class particles. I'm sure there are many stimulating conversations in our future."
"That's a nice thought, Ysabel, but I'm suddenly so far behind the times ... I can't see how I could possibly offer anything new."
She smiled sympathetically. "You must keep something in mind, Tom. Although knowledge may become outdated ... intellect is always fresh."
A hand thrust forward. "Hi, Tom. I'm Xarles Moody ... one of the non-technocrats. I oversee projects and act as liaison between TheTwenty and the world at large. You've fallen into a select group. Welcome aboard."
A lady about three inches taller than Tom, with blond hair and blue eyes, stepped forward giving him a hug and a light kiss on the cheek. "Pleasure to meet you, Tom. My name is Mrena Damask. I work in particle beam waveguide design. You needn't worry about being obsolete. Many of your theories, with only minor changes, still apply to our technology. Two of your books are required reading for some classes.
As you may have noticed, considering the bulk of information, our special interests are decidedly narrow. Someone like you, with a wide knowledge of many disciplines, may be singularly effective assisting us in melding our cognitive base. Welcome to our century. I look forward to working with you."
Next, a petite hand took hold of his. "Hello, Tom. I'm Breeanya Aurora. My specialty was just burgeoning in your time. I work almost exclusively with nanotechnology."
Tom nodded. "In my day, that was defined as machines at the microscopic level."
"Yes, actually macro-molecular. We operate in the atomic region and soon hope to reach sub-atomic. We routinely transform and reconfigure matter using only nanobots instead of huge, clumsy cyclotrons. Nanotechnology opened an entire new world of manufacturing and research. Many of the TMTs'/MMTs' improvements and newer functions are heavily dependent on our designs. Well, I guess I'm the last of TheTwenty you'll meet for a while. The rest are off-planet. A few are on our moon but most are on Mars. I think there might be one or two doing consulting in TheBelt." She checked with the others. "Is that still true?" They gave affirmative nods.
"Kate ... so this is part of your extended family?"
"Yes, Tom. They're all members of TheTwenty, and as John once mentioned, we think of each other as brothers and sisters. They turned out just to meet you. Come on, let's find out what happens when John sees us again." She pointed. "His office is through that door and down the hallway."

The small tangle of people came to a halt. Kate began explaining for Tom's benefit. "Lesson one. As you just noticed, our labs have real doors for security and safety reasons. This wall looks solid, but it also has many doorways. That's because most of our offices, workspaces, and even apartments have a holographic door, or holodoor. They're outlined in a fine line of light. Can you see it?"

He looked, then squinted. "Oh yeah, I can just make it out. This one's green."

"Correct. That means anyone has free access to enter or exit. When it's yellow, that indicates caution since someone is about to walk through the doorway from the opposite side. A red line is the same as a lock. Nanobots rearrange matter and the holograph will not permit passage either way.

We'll let the others enter first. They'll inform John we've arrived. I'll have them lock the door, so when it turns green again, we'll know to follow."

Tom gave a short shake of his head, as Rose and her companions appeared to pass right through the wall. "So how long do you think the acclimation process will take?"

Kate chuckled. "Trust me. You'll be a wall-walker in no time. Just remember to look for the red line. Otherwise, you'll end up with a flat nose."

"Good thing I'm not colorblind."

"That's a genetic disorder we routinely repair at the pre-fetal stage, so the condition doesn't exist in our time. I'm sure we could work something out for anyone else if the need arose."

The line turned green. "Follow me. Let's see if we have any luck reconnecting John's memories." Kate strode through the wall. Tom trailed behind, but was uncomfortable without feeling his way with a hand first.

"Hello, Kate. Yes, I do seem to have a vague remembrance of you." John hesitated, "But, unfortunately, nothing specific comes to mind. Good evening, Dr. Hughes. I'm told we've also met before," John's facial expressions slowly ran through a kaleidoscope of changes, "but if we have, I'm sorry to say I can't place where or when."

"Give it time, John. I'm sure it'll come back eventually."

"Perhaps. Meanwhile, if there's ever an occasion I can assist either of you, please don't hesitate to ask. I'm out of my office quite often trying to re-familiarize myself with things I apparently knew before my lapse of memory.

Kate ... do you know my personal assistant, Alyce Cramdin?"

"Yes, John. We're old friends."

"Ah, good. Then you can leave a message with her if you need to contact me when I'm out. I check with her on a regular basis."

John sighed. "I have to admit, Kate, I'm somewhat disappointed our meeting didn't re-establish some contact with my past. I think we all had our hopes pinned in that direction."

"I'm sorry, too, John, although, I agree with Tom, we all need to keep a positive attitude."

John's gaze slowly swung around the room. "Well, people, I'm rather tired. I stayed just long enough to welcome our guests and state that I'm glad they're safe. There's good reason for celebration, so my office is yours for the remainder of the night. Good evening, everyone."

Kate started to object but caught Rose's quick shake of her head, so remained mute. After John's departure, she asked Rose, "Why didn't you want me to interfere with John's leaving?"

"He's at a great disadvantage with the loss of his ability for recall. It's as if we're playing a game where we know all the rules and he doesn't. John actually feels uncomfortable around us at present. It'll change, but he needs time to work things out."

Kate gave Rose a heartfelt hug. "I'm sorry. Obviously, everyone's expectations were set on our being able to jog John's memory. I almost feel like we let you down."

Rose pursed her lips. "Don't be ridiculous, Khatty. They were hopes, not expectations. We'll just have to think of something else.

Come on everybody, I'll order drinks and we'll all toast the long-awaited arrival of our errant, adventurous travelers."

Frank moved between the two females and jiggled their shoulders, "Now we're talking."

The festivity was conducted in a subdued, but friendly and open atmosphere. Nonetheless, as with all true professionals, the conversations soon drifted to work-related projects. Tom sat in awe at the advancements and levels of sophistication that science had achieved in 300-plus years. He was pleased about being able to follow the theories, but became quickly and effectively lost when current techniques entered into discussions.

As the hour neared 5 a.m., the party started to break up and, one by one, people began excusing themselves.

By 5:15, the travel weary, but elated couple, was alone.

"We listen'd and look'd sideways up! Fear at my heart, as at a cup, My life-blood seem'd to sip."

- Samuel Taylor Coleridge

Chapter 28
First Night Jitters

Tom and Kate sat side by side on a settee in John's office. She leaned against him; his arm was draped over her shoulders. "It's funny, Tom. I was just thinking about my apartment and the labs. They have pretty much been my world. They were my anchors to reality."

"Umm. Sounds familiar."

"And yet, after only being away for two weeks ... the first planning for your trip forward, the second fighting for our lives ... I can't really remember all that much about them. I can picture the layouts ... but I fail to recall any detail. Now it all seems so transient and unimportant. Maybe you were right about my being bored when we returned. I'm glad we're back ... and yet I know I'm going to miss all the excitement." He simply chuckled in response. "What is it?"

Tom stroked her cheek with the back of his fingers. "You have a tendency to wax philosophical when you're tired. We should probably call it a night before you start rewriting the collected works of Plato, Socrates, Kant, Nietzsche ... et al." He sat up. "By the way ... where are we?"

"This is our main research complex just outside the town of Imuris, in the middle northern part of what used to be Mexico."

"Used to be? What is it now?"

"Just a part of the world. A lot has changed from your time. There are no countries or associated borders ... at least not officially. The social structure of humanity has evolved into one homogenous mass of culture.

Oh, the computers will still display the old boundaries if you request, but cities have become nothing more than huge connections of buildings and are officially simply denoted by numbers on a matrix of longitude and latitude."

"So I take it you live somewhere close in old Mexico?"

"No, I just work here. I reside in what the locals refer to as Perth."

"Not ... Australia?"

"Yes, that's the one."

"This is a twice daily commute?"

"Tom, why are you so surprised? I told you almost everyone on the planet uses MMTs for transportation."

"Yeah, but I thought you meant from one building to another, or between towns ... not globe hopping on a whim."

"With our technology, what's the difference?"

"At least ten or twelve thousand miles."

"Just another fraction of a second."

He noticed her big smile. "You're enjoying this ... aren't you?"

She yawned. "I can finally understand, and appreciate, the amusement my friends felt that were stationed in your time when I first arrived."

"I don't know, Kate. Even after three hundred years, I can't believe all the countries steeped in traditions and customs are gone."

"I'm sorry, Tom. I didn't mean to mislead you. The borders have disappeared, but not the traditions. People still proudly cling to their heritage. It's just that certain events have caused the global population to rethink their relationship with each other in the overall scheme of things. The population has not only learned to tolerate each other's differences ... but actually enjoy and embrace them.

The one event that foremost comes to mind was the pandemic of 2218. A new stretch of land was being cleared near the Mutaba River in East Africa. The area was known to be a source of Ebola. On happenstance, many of the workers had colds. All it took was a joining of Ebola's cytoplasm with the common ailment. The viruses swapped certain plasmids and an airborne version of Ebola was born. Once it appeared, the carnage was already predisposed because of our instantaneous mode of travel and the new virus's extended ten-day incubation period.

Almost four billion people died that year. The only thing that kept the mutated virus from wiping out the entire human race was the fact that, in exchange for its new mode of dispersal, it had lost part of its virulence. The newly-formed strain of Ebola became 50% lethal instead of 90."

Tom pressed back against the cushions and gave her a blank stare. He slowly mumbled, "four ... billion ... people."

She slowly nodded. "It could have been worse, but almost two billion had already relocated off-planet. If you caught it, and everyone did, you had a 50/50 chance of survival. It forced the world to cooperate on a scale never attempted before. Unfortunately, the 'expel' process wasn't available yet.

By this time, Jake's political philosophy was gradually beginning to gain wide acceptance in theory, but not implementation. Once the threat of global extinction was past, his ideology caught fire since massive cooperation had been the single most prominent factor in the survival of Homo sapiens.

The key to cooperative effort had been the unemotional, neutral, suggested directive of computers. While the world in general was panicking, they quickly and accurately determined all the logistics of distributing food, water, medical aid ... and the disposal of all those decaying, disease-ridden bodies."

"How was that gruesome task accomplished?"

"The corpses were loaded onto huge grav-sleds, taken into orbit, and then transferred to space ferries. Finally, they were ejected in bulk quantities from large pressurized tubes on computer-generated trajectories that caused them to eventually spiral into the sun."

"That must have taken quite a long time."

"Months of coordinated effort."

Kate yawned again and stretched. "I'm sure Rose will cover some of this information. Then she'll turn you over to the computers and you can search indexes and ask for details on anything interesting. I think I've about had it. Ready for beaming over to my apartment?"

"More than ready. Look ... the sun's coming up."

She checked her wrist device and chuckled. "Sorry, Tom. It's about the right time, but that's just another hologram. We're ten levels below ground. One nice thing about living halfway around the world is the difference in local time. I can work here to 6 a.m. and still be home in time for dinner, catch up on paperwork, mail, and get a full night's sleep. Come along, Fido. John's MMT station is over here in the corner."

He grinned. "You haven't called me that for a while."

"Well, we have been busy."

Tom followed Kate towards the transport. His gaze ran along a bookshelf in passing. A particular title halted his progress. He slowly ran a reverent finger over the title's letters. "Do you have a copy of Jake's book at your apartment?"

"Not a hard copy, but it's certainly available online. Why?"

"When reading for enjoyment, I still like holding a book in my hands. I savor the turning of pages." Tom opened the cover. "Do you think John would mind if I borrow this?"

"That's a first edition. It's actually printed on recycled paper. Still, I'm sure it's okay. Computer."

"Yes, Dr. Bright?"

"Please leave a verbal note for Dr. Picus stating that we've borrowed his book, 'Years Of Change'."

"Message understood."

"Ready, Tom?"

He remained frozen in place. "Kate, we could be in big trouble."

"Why? What did you find?"

She returned to his side. Tom looked up ... his eyes fixed on hers. "Jake changed history."

"How?"

"Look for yourself."

Kate read beneath Tom's finger:

> 'This book is dedicated to the memory of
> my loving wife, Gidget. She was my
> life-long friend and companion.
> In addition, I'd also like to honor
> my quasi-adopted son and daughter,
> Tom and Kate.'

"You're right. The second part certainly wasn't there before." Kate tittered, "That crafty old rogue. He talked of finding a way to leave us a message. And yet, I don't see a problem. No last names are mentioned. And as far as anyone knows, these people could've been friends.

The only ones that would have recognized it back then ... are dead now. Anyone who understands it now, isn't going to say anything. It'll just be another puzzle for historians to quibble over. Don't worry about it. Let's go."

"It's nice to have you back, Dr. Bright. I've followed your exploits on the private research web. I'm relieved that you're safe. Welcome."

Kate stepped off the transmit mat. "Thank you, computer. It's great to be home again."

Tom was so surprised, he appeared to be stuck in place. "You live in a warehouse?"

Kate laughed. "What makes you think that?"

"That far wall must be at least 200 feet away."

"Nope, just another holographic image. My apartment is a square ... 40 feet on a side ... and ten feet high. Walk toward the far wall and see what happens."

Tom started for the other side. "This is amazing. As you walk, the perception is altered. It just seems like you've traversed all that distance."

"Just a second. You'll really like this. Computer."

"Yes, Dr. Bright?"

"Generate a summer's night celestial sphere. Use the information in Tom's file to fill in the rest."

Moments later, the room dimmed and the ceiling dissolved into a starry night sky. The scene was complete with chirping crickets and animal images padding quietly along forest trails through the fallacious dark.

"Maybe now you'll understand, Tom. This is why everyone lives in cities. You have all the convenience ... yet can easily be anywhere you really want. All the real physical walls are insulated with white noise. A bomb could go off next door and you probably wouldn't hear it." They examined the computer's creation for a minute, then she walked towards him and semi-collapsed into his arms. "Bed."

He hugged her. "It has been one hell of a week."

They took turns visiting the bath for the usual end-of-day activities, where Tom learned about the waterless electrostatic toilet and oral cleansing facilities, then retired to her bedroom. She manually adjusted the mattress tension to accommodate the weight of an additional body and they crawled under the covers. Kate snuggled next to Tom and quickly fell asleep.

The mind is an amazing thing. It'll allow you to sleep through all sorts of normal night sounds. A small shift in a building; the start and stop of a ventilation fan; functioning of automated equipment; even the tossing and turning of someone next to you. It's the unusual ... out of the ordinary occurrence that instantly snaps you awake from a deep slumber.

Kate's eyes popped open. She sat up and listened ... wondering what had awoken her. She felt Tom next to her and peered down at him in the darkness. Kate shivered. Intuition told her something was wrong. She whispered, "Computer."

The computer examined the situation and faintly replied, "Yes, Dr. Bright?"

"Night lights, please."

The ceiling slowly changed to a soft glow. She stared. Tom's eyes were agape and seemed to be fixated on nothing. His breathing was shallow. "Tom?" She gently nudged him. "Tom." Kate waved a hand over his face, then flicked it towards his eyes. No blink response. She shook his arm, and finally pinched his skin ... hard. Nothing. Her thoughts began to unravel, and then abruptly ... Tom was back.

"Ouch!" He rubbed his arm. "It feels like something bit me. Hey, what's going on?"

She sat there ... not knowing what to say next.

Kate pulled two marshmallow covered hot chocolates from the auto-cooker and slid onto the chair next to Tom's at the kitchen table. They quietly sipped for a moment. Without looking at him, she reached and softly covered his hand with hers. "Okay, do you want to tell me what that was all about?"

"My anxiety attacks must be back. I haven't had one for a long time. All the recent events and stress of a new environment must have caught up with me."

Kate's eyes darted around. "I don't remember reading anything about anxiety attacks in any of your information profiles."

"There was nothing to read. I never said anything, so they were never recorded. Most of them occurred in high school ... like I said ... years ago. In fact, I didn't even realize I was having them at the time. It wasn't until I inadvertently came across a magazine article about them sometime in my twenties that I finally figured it out. At first, I assumed everyone had the same problem now and then.

I still remember my first day of high school. All the hustle and bustle was disorienting. I became stressed and confused. I ended up sitting in the same study hall for three class periods in a row. Then things came back and I went to the next class on the list. Everything was easier after that.

Every once in a while I'd forget where my locker was, or once there, I couldn't remember the combination. Sometimes I took erroneous books to class, or ended up in the wrong room. Eventually I outgrew it, or so I thought.

The episodes returned in college, but only a few. When I started working, I had a couple, too. It's been at least four years since my last incident." He turned to face her. "But I never blanked out like this."

Kate sat quietly ... mentally digesting the information. "I think this was more than just an anxiety attack, Tom. I pinched you hard enough to make my fingers cramp, and there was absolutely no reaction. You'll see Rose soon. I want her to examine you."

They returned to bed and the rest of the night passed peaceably, but the tinge of fear that had been visible in Tom's eyes ... was now beating in Kate's heart.

"Where there is much light, the shadow is deep."
- Goethe

Chapter 29
Ill At Ease

Tom watched as Kate placed the dirty breakfast plates in the kitchen's recycler. "Don't you ever wash anything?"

"Sure, but it's more ecologically prudent to recycle than use water. Recycling just uses energy, and we have many sources of cleanly produced power. Solar, fusion, and geothermal generating plants are the ones most common. I take it you haven't gotten that far with the computers?"

"No. I decided on starting with the year after I disappeared and follow only the major news items leading to the present. Otherwise, every time I begin with a topic, it explodes in so many directions, and with so much detail, that my thought processes become totally overwhelmed. Then ... I must keep taking breaks just trying to absorb what I've read.

So far, I've only made it to the year 2018. Of course, it hasn't helped my concentration when I keep thinking of all those tests three days ago."

"The results should be collated, analyzed, and available this morning. We'll beam over to the med-plex when Rose announces she's ready. It may be nothing, Tom, and if it is something unexpected ... our doctors can fix it."

She encircled him with her arms. "Believe me, at this point I couldn't stand the thought of losing you for any reason. You'll just have to trust me on this one."

He smiled. "Okay ... just so long as you're not running for some political office."

She giggled. "Oh, you're terrible. You really are."

"I know. But then again, that's probably one of the reasons you love me."

"Dr. Bright."

"Yes, computer."

"Dr. Rosalba Petals requested that I inform you she is prepared to receive Dr. Hughes. If he will step onto the MMT platform when he's ready, I will transport him directly to Dr. Petals' office."

"Thank you, computer. Well, Tom, it looks like the show's all yours."

"You're not coming?"

"It doesn't sound like I was invited. I had a feeling she'd rather do this one-on-one. Don't let it worry you. That's the way Rose likes to work. I'm sure she thinks I'd just be a distraction."

He pulled her close. "I like the way you distract me."

"That's good, because I'm sure we'll have reason to celebrate when you get the news. Now, Fido, the sooner you depart, the sooner you can return."

"Woof."

She kissed his cheek. "Good boy."

Rose stood behind her desk. "Good morning, Tom, have a seat."

He faked a smile. "What, no couch?"

"The chair will recline if you wish. It'll rock, swivel, vibrate ... just about anything it takes to make you feel more at ease."

"A simple seat will do."

"Fine."

Tom jumped up. "It moved. I think it tried to grab me!"

She laughed. "Sorry, I should have warned you. It adjusts to your body size and posture."

"Oh. Somehow, this doesn't seem like a good start. Is there some way you can tell it to just stay a chair?"

She chuckled. "Computer."

"Yes, Dr. Petals."

"Please suspend all physical functions on the enviro-chair."

"Message understood. Command accepted."

"Okay, Tom, try it now."

"Thanks. I'm nervous enough."

Rose eased back in her chair, placed a thumb on her upper lip, and simply observed for a few moments. "Tom ... am I the problem? Would you rather talk with a man? We certainly have a multitude of other medical specialists if you'd like to choose someone else. Perhaps I was wrong assuming you'd feel comfortable with me."

"No, Rose. Your assumption is perfectly valid. It's just that I've been exceptionally fortunate concerning my health. I guess I've just come to take it for granted that I'd always be healthy. Since my arrival, I've become edgy ... jumpy. Did Kate tell you I had another episode last night?"

"Yes, she mentioned it earlier this morning. Was it as bad as before? Did you lose total contact?"

Tom rubbed his hands together as his eyes explored the room. "Yes. I have no memory of what happened during my blackout." His eyes found hers. "Do you have any idea what's wrong with me?"

"Shall we start with the short answer?"

"Sure. Anything."

"Computer. Would you please indicate whether our initial findings are good news or bad?"

"My pleasure, Dr. Petals. Good slash bad, good, good, bad."

A smile slowly spread across Tom's face, finally ending with a soft laugh. "Well, I admit. That's certainly concise."

Rose lightly applauded. "Good job, computer. He reacted exactly as you predicted."

"Thank you, Dr. Petals. It was my pleasure to try and break the tension."

"That was the computer's idea?"

Rose nodded. "Yes. Unfortunately, I have the harder job of explaining it all. Let's start with the first bit of good news. All the tests confirmed that your blackouts are not caused by anything physical. There are no blood-related problems, lesions, or other abnormal growths of any kind. The slash bad was added simply because a physical problem would probably have been easier and definitely much faster to cure."

"What if it had been an inoperable brain tumor?"

"Ah, there's no such thing in our time, Tom. We'd simply flash freeze you, melt a small area surrounding your brain a few cells wide, and make the repair. After a short convalescence you'd be better than new."

"What would become of my memories, thought processes ... not to mention personality? Wouldn't just the trauma of the surgery cause irreparable brain damage resulting in a change to all those properties?"

"No. Before the procedure begins, we use a psych probe and literally record the affected regions while mapping your brain. I know that's a lot to accept, but the procedure is performed flawlessly every day. It's only one of the many processes performed anytime someone uses an MMT.

If the repair replaces or removes damaged tissues, the corresponding neuron-synapse map is restructured when your memory and other functions are restored ... automatically. So, even though your brain may have been physically altered, mentally you'd be exactly the same.

All of this brings us to the second bit of good news. The problem has been defined ... but before I get into that, I'm going to jump to the last of the good news and that is ... I'm completely confident the problem can be stabilized."

Tom lowered his gaze. "But not cured?"

"In a condition like this ... I believe we're only speaking of a difference in semantics."

"Alright, even if I accept that premise ... it still seems the last indicator was more bad news."

"Yes, that's true, but only because we have a lot of hard work ahead of us."

"I've never been afraid of hard work. Generally speaking, I thrive on it."

"Good. Then essentially, you can consider the bulk of the problem all but behind you. For the most part, all that's required is time and many in-depth conversations. I'll be using a psychoanalysis discipline called Time Displacement Hypnotherapy. We might need to wade through all the unpleasantness in your childhood years. Do you think you can be comfortable with me directing your passage?"

"Well, except for Kate, you're the one person I've come to know best in the short time I've been here. I did find ample information about you on the net. From what I've read, it would plainly seem I'm in capable hands. No ... I don't foresee any problem."

"Great. I'm glad you mentioned Kate. She's asked me to keep her in the loop. However, doctor-patient confidentiality is every bit as sacred in our time as it was yours. Therefore, if keeping Kate informed is acceptable ... I'll need your permission."

"I don't have any objections to that, either. I'll sign whatever papers are necessary."

Rose checked her display. "No need. The computer has just recorded and filed your agreement."

Tom's surprise registered on his face. "That's something I need to ask about. Is the computer always listening? Is it part of every conversation? What happened to this time's highly touted privacy?"

"Kate said you borrowed John's copy of Dr. Johnson's book."

"Yes, I did, but I've been so busy reading articles on the net I haven't gotten far with it. What's that have to do with anything?"

"The answer to your question is actually a large part of the basis for Johnson's philosophy. When Dr. Johnson first conceived of his computer-led society, he realized the first and most important aspect of the programming would be protecting the software and hardware from tampering. The bulk of the initial design went towards satisfying that dilemma.

Johnson and his followers didn't believe in governments or world leaders hiding secrets from the public, but they certainly advocated individual privacy.

Therefore, their thinking was quite simple. Anyone has the right to view public data, but only the owner can access information that is labeled private.

Private data is encrypted a minimum of three levels deep, with the decryption keys being constantly rotated through memory. There are so many safety mechanisms we could spend days discussing them."

"Okay, Rose. I don't want to flog a dead horse, and there's obviously more about this concept of privacy than meets the eye. So, let's move on. Maybe I've been trying to avoid the idea that there's apparently something wrong with me psychologically."

Rose studied the reports that were running across her screen. Although she had terminated the chair's physical operations, the passive sensory gathering functions were still collecting statistics on Tom's condition. The data showed that he was currently experiencing a high level of anxiety. "I can tell you're upset. Would you like to talk about something else first?"

"This may sound crazy ... uh, hmm ... maybe considering the situation that was a poor choice of words, but I've been wondering how a person with a first name of Rose ends up with a last name of Petals."

The lady grinned. "That's simple. I picked it."

"Are you implying that the people of this time get to choose their own names?"

"No, but we of TheTwenty did. Let me run a quick check on what Kate has told you about us. I don't want to keep covering the same ground."

Tom slowly arose from the chair. "Wait a minute. Those were private conversations. How are you able to scan them?"

Rose waved her hands in a placating gesture. "Easy, Tom. Give me a second to explain. Kate assigned me as co-owner of the records during her time in the past. That's a normal procedure for anyone returning from a mission. However, I can only access her side of the conversations since I don't have an assignment from you."

Rose's finger tapped on her screen. "Ah, the first incident occurred while spending your last night at home. Listen, I'll demonstrate a privacy example.

Computer ... please replay Dr. Hughes' response to the conversation in question regarding TheTwenty."

"One moment, Dr. Petals ... I'm sorry ... I am unable to find a consent from Dr. Hughes for that purpose. Therefore, the data in question remains inaccessible by you."

Tom eased back down into the chair. "I'm beginning to get the picture. This whole privacy issue is starting to make a little more sense. Sorry, Rose. I didn't mean to alarm you."

Rose was paging through Kate's recorded data. "Humph. There isn't a lot here about TheTwenty. Just a little information about the origin of the project and that there were twenty of us conceived in vitro ... and it appears later dialogues didn't add any meaningful data."

She shifted position. "Alright, let's talk about names. All of us were given first names by the director of the project. For the first twelve years of our lives, we were simply known as Rose, or Khatty, or John of TheTwenty, which, as you know, was the designation for the project itself.

When we turned twelve, the venture was terminated, and we were placed in standard educational facilities. At that point, our surnames needed to be addressed. So, we were given two years to find a last name we liked. At fourteen, it would become our own.

As for me, I have always been interested in the workings of the mind. At twelve, I was already fairly competent at self-hypnosis. One day I wrote my first name on a card, placed it in front of me, and went into a self-induced trance. When a timer brought me out, I saw the writing and immediately chose the first word I associated with it for my last name. Evidently, even at that age, I was into continuity and closure. I've been Rose Petals ever since."

Tom chuckled. "And the others?"

Rose smiled and nodded. "Ah, yes ... the others. Some of them have much more interesting stories."

"Hey, I like yours. I think it's pretty neat."

"Well, I admit, there are also those that are pretty tame. John's always been fascinated by the idea of time travel. He was especially captivated with the possibility of moving forward. One day while doing some research, he happened to come across the name Picus, which is the Roman god of the future. It was a natural choice for him. At the same time, he found Aurora ... Roman goddess of the dawn. Breeanya's favorite time of day is sunrise. So, when John told her about his find, she happily adopted it for her name.

Frank has been into holograms, lasers, and theories of light ever since anyone can remember. Some people tease him that he's nothing more than the result of a collision between two photons. Anyway, as I'm sure you're aware, light waves are measured in angstroms ... hence his last name.

Ysabel is a different story. It was only a week before her fourteenth birthday, and she still hadn't found a suitable name. She was working in the lab, setting up a special electrostatic lens to see if a tachyon class particle could be deflected by it when she caught a glimpse of her nametag in a common collimating mirror. She reports staring for a few moments, smiling to herself, and then instantly recognizing that she had become Ysabel Lebasy."

Rose locked her fingers and leaned forward on her elbows. "Do you remember meeting Mrena?"

"Sure. My first night here."

"Was there anything that you found particularly striking about her?"

Tom closed his eyes, trying to create an image in his mind. Almost a full minute passed before his eyes reopened. "I don't know, Rose. She was a tall, attractive lady. The only thing that really seems to stand out ... were her rosy cheeks."

Rose lightly slapped the desktop. "That's it. Everyone remembers that about Mrena. We girls would sometimes tease her when we were young. In the end we confessed it was just a tinge of jealousy. She happily accepted the explanation, but she decided to take it a step further.

She had the computer research 'rosy cheeks', and an obscure find ended up giving her a last name. Not the obvious rationale about blood vessels being close to the surface of the skin, but having to do with an origin of the word 'Damask'. Most references mention cloths from the ancient city of Damascus, but one ... romanticized the pink petals of the Damask Rose, referring to any comparison as being 'soft as a rose'.

With her six-foot height, an IQ of 210, and an angular body, she hoped the meaning would make her feel more feminine. Therefore, when she turned fourteen, Mrena of TheTwenty was updated to Mrena Damask in the role of planetary citizenship.

Larry has always loved the early literary classics. He has often jokingly stated he'd sell his soul for the sake of knowledge. When he found Faust ... it was a marriage in nomenclature just waiting to happen.

Xarles was probably the easiest and most self-evident. He's always been somewhat argumentative and temperamental, so Moody fit him to the proverbial tee.

I believe that brings us to the last of TheTwenty you've met ... your lady fair, Khattyba. Any guesses?"

"Kate is an extremely intelligent lady, but I'd want to believe she picked her name for a reason other than simply being incredibly obvious.

There was a thought I had on the first night we met, but at the time we were doing some fairly heavy mental sparing. I admit she had the element of surprise, so consequently she was definitely winning.

I never mentioned it at the time, but upon her saying I could address her as Miss Bright, I remembered an old limerick written just after Einstein formulated his special theory of relativity around 1905. It was about a lady named Bright that traveled faster than light. I don't suppose that would have anything to do with it?"

Rose frowned and tapped a fingertip on the desktop. "Hmm. I'm afraid you just deflated my balloon, because you're absolutely correct. I'd have never thought for all the universe you'd guess the right answer."

Quiet fell over the room while Tom studied the ceiling. Rose studied her display. She noticed Tom's anxiety level had dropped considerably, so decided to loosen the reins and let the horse run free a little longer. "Kate tells me you're trying to catch up on the events between your disappearance and the present. It sounds like you're being overwhelmed. Maybe I can show you a few tricks on manipulating search indexes that may be of some assistance paring down the data."

Tom nodded. "I think anything would help about now." He glanced away. "Kate's tried to support my research, but I keep finding myself inadvertently shunning her aside."

"She's mentioned that. It's something we need to discuss. Let's do the mini index-tutorial first, then take a break. I always schedule two sequential sessions for a new client. We'll get into your problem when we return." Rose pulled a rigid, letter-sized transparent piece of plastic from a drawer and handed it to Tom. "This will exhibit the same images I display on my screen so you can follow my commentary. I'll request only level-1 indexes with a historical impact ranked 8 or higher, excluding all lower indexes for now. That should keep the list short. Do you want to start over with 2014?"

"Yes ... fine."

"Okay, here we go."

"The multitude which does not reduce itself to unity is confusion; the unity which does not depend upon the multitude, is tyranny."

- Pascal

Chapter 30
Impromptu Orientation

Tom watched in amazement as the information Rose typed emerged on his sheet as if by magic. There were no controls, wires, or other connections ... and if he turned it over, the letters appeared in reverse.

He followed along as she explained her parameter choices and their associated value ranges. When she was satisfied with her regimen of arguments, the computer was instructed to commence its search.

After a short interval, the tablet blanked, and the following list scrolled into view:

World History Chronology
(2014 To 2341)

2014 Linked solar arrays transmit power via satellites - supply 20% of global requirements.
First large multinational permanent space station established.
2016 Anti-gravity sleds begin displacing planes and automobiles.
2018 Gold, silver, other common metals found in Tycho crater on moon.
First tachyon class particle re-discovered.
2019 Underwater explosion of methane hydrate deposits accelerate global warming.
2021 Laser drilling makes geothermal energy feasible.
2024 Mining leads to first permanent moon base.
2025 Geothermal power generators supply 25% of global energy.
First manned Mars expedition.
2027 First successful test of fusion reactor – uses optically coupled lasers.
2031 First fusion reactor goes online.
2034 Fusion power becomes common.
2037 World's oil production curtailed.
2038 Energy wars – exchange of nuclear weapons – 900 million die.
2040 First permanent Mars base established.
2041 World's natural gas supply is exhausted.
2043 Last internal combustion engine manufactured.
2050 Global air/water/land reclamation begins.
2065 Manned mission orbits Venus.
2080 L4 is built.
2096 L5 is built.
2110 Global warming stabilizes.
Ozone layer reestablished.
2140 Moon established as retirement community.
2164 Dr. Johnson's book is published.
2172 First computer-led society advocates elected.

2188 First MMT test.
2192 Moon recognized as sovereign governing body.
2218 Global pandemic – 4 billion die.
2226 First global council established.
2231 Global peace established under computer-led society.
2245 First TMT test.
2254 Global Life-Credit established.
2278 Mars recognized as sovereign governing body.
2300 Solar System Standard (SSS) for time/date established.
2308 TheTwenty are born.
2312 Asteroid Belt recognized as sovereign governing body.
2341 Dr. Thomas Hughes arrives.

Tom began scanning the list. His eyes quickly stopped at 2018. "I'm surprised it took an additional three years to find a tachyon particle when they had all of my research notes guiding them."

Rose's forehead wrinkled. "What makes you think it was three years?"

"Well, I assumed I originally made the discovery in 2014."

"No. It wasn't until 2017."

"Then ... why did Kate pull me out so early?"

"She concluded from her simulations that the impact on the timeline would be more aptly tolerated."

He considered the remark. "She's good at her work, isn't she?"

"Second only to John ... and when subtlety is imperative, I think she might be even better. John is more prone to use brute mental force sometimes. By the way, your friend Dr. Judson, who rediscovered the first tachyon class particle, wasn't as modest as you. He named the particle after himself. If I remember ... you named it Tempus ... is that correct?"

"Yes ... from the Latin for time."

Tom resumed his scan. "What are optically coupled lasers?"

"The ignition circuit for a fusion reactor. Hundreds of small lasers are placed in a spherical arrangement around a much smaller globular container. The container is highly polished on the inside to trap the laser light.

Special microprocessors compute even the small time for electrical signals to flow between the lasers so they will all fire simultaneously into the central container where a tube introduces cooled hydrogen. When the lasers fire, the hydrogen is instantly heated to 30 million degrees and starts the hydrogen-to-helium transmutation. The entire apparatus is enclosed in a graviton generator, keeping the hydrogen under tremendous pressure. Unless the hydrogen supply is terminated, the reaction becomes self-sustaining."

"How safe are they?"

"There are no dangerous or polluting byproducts. The only accident to date occurred when a single bank of the igniter lasers received power and blew apart the opposite side of the hydrogen containment sphere. That problem was rectified when a pre-ignition recognition circuit was added. Nothing dangerous has happened since."

Tom nodded, and his eyes returned to the list. "I see we finally had an exchange of nuclear weapons. What countries were involved?"

"Mostly, the Middle-Eastern oil-producing nations. Only 7 warheads, ranging from 10 to 50 kilotons were released, but as you can see, 900 million perished in the conflagration. It was an unprecedented grudge war, and only heavily populated areas were purposely targeted. At least they used clean neutron bombs that didn't leave any residual radiation. The superpowers managed to stay out of the confrontation. In fact, it was the threat of launching their weapons that quickly ended the conflict."

Tom shook his head. "Have we finally learned?"

"When we became a computer-led society, the first thing machine logic recommended was to ban all weapons of war. It seems intensely ironic a mechanism we built endorsed a course of action that should have been patently obvious from the beginning."

"What are L4 and L5?"

"They're gigantic cities built in space at the same-named positions, called Lagrangian points. Just a second, I'll bring up the data.

Ah, here it is. I'll read it since I requested that the computer maintain your display in static mode.

> 'In a two-body system, such as the earth and moon, 5 points exist where a relatively small object can maintain a fixed position with respect to the two main masses, indicating that these points are gravitationally balanced.
>
> Three lie on a line between the earth and moon. One is behind the moon, one in front, and the third behind the earth. However, any entity placed at one of these three points and then subsequently struck, will simply drift away into open space, indicating that these sites are unstable.
>
> The other two points, known as L4 and L5, are located at the outer vertices of equilateral triangles formed with the earth and moon and also lying in their orbital plane. These points are gravitationally stable and objects placed here will only oscillate if perturbed.'

Although their masses are insignificant compared to the earth or moon, they are worlds within themselves and will probably be the next populated zones requesting autonomy."

"I'd like to visit at least one of them someday. Have you ever been to either?"

Rose shook her head. "No. Never a real desire I guess. I don't harbor any urge to go off-planet. At present, I'm perfectly content on earth."

"Kate said the first incidence of computers actually beginning to lead society didn't occur until after that horrible pandemic in 2218. It shows here that the first advocates were elected in 2172. I take it that was just the start of their movement?"

"Yes. As you can see further down, the first global council wasn't established until 2226."

"Is that the main governing body of the planet?"

"Not in a political sense. It's more an expediter of the population's generally accepted consensus on plans put forth by the computer systems. There's also an ethics committee, which helps verify that the computer's ideas can be realistically integrated into human society. Together, they review the actions required and decide which local councils should be selected to actually implement those actions. There's always a little fine-tuning all the way down the line. In the end, everything is reviewed one last time before implementation. If everyone is in agreement, the actions are performed and the next issue is opened for discussion. It's extremely effective and efficient."

Tom frowned. "There must be dissenters sometime."

"It occasionally happens. I never meant to imply the process is perfect, but the computer keeps tabs whenever concessions or further adjustments are performed. During the next cycle, when that same section of the population is involved, it will probably receive some slight preferential treatment, thus keeping the process as fair and balanced as possible.

The people realize this and complaints are seldom filed. If it occurs, the computers arbitrate until all sides are satisfied. Under this system, everyone's individuality is secure, yet we are able to maintain unity among the mass population. Clearly, this is a gross oversimplification of the process, but seen strictly as an overview, it should still give you an idea of how it works."

"I'm impressed, but doesn't it leave opportunities for abuse by these people?"

"The members are all chosen at random by computer. Their tenure, by local time, is always 13 months ... twelve months active, and one month of overlap with the previous board. This allows time for new members to become procedurally acclimated and promotes an effective exchange of information and status on active projects."

"Is there a chance the computers could actually assume control?"

"Their primary design is still to sift and store data, not for ruling civilizations. That was never Johnson's intention."

"Kate tried her best to assure me this time was better than mine. So far, I haven't seen, heard, or found anything that would dispute her claim. I think I'm going to like it here." He laughed. "Good thing, too. I don't know if there's a lot I could do about it. Okay, what's this solar system standard?"

"The world had enough problems keeping track of time and dates in your era. Think what it's like with space stations, L4, L5, the moon, Mars, and settlements in the asteroid belt. Everyone needed the ability of pointing to one timepiece. Enter the solar system standard.

The standard year has 360 days, but doesn't bother with months. Each year simply starts at day 1 and counts from there. It's a lot like the old Julian calendar, except there are no leap years, daylight savings, or any other adjustments.

These dates apply to the entire solar system no matter where you are. Each day has exactly 24 hours and is tracked in 24-hour format. Hours, minutes, and seconds have never changed. Using standard time, 15:00 - day 150 on earth is the same as 15:00 - day 150 on Mars, or anywhere else. The locals, no matter where they live, have their own time and date, and the computers convert back and forth whenever needed. What is it? You look puzzled."

"I was just wondering what happens when humankind eventually travels to the stars."

She chuckled. "I guess we'll have to cross that bridge when it comes."

Tom sat up and laughed. "This last item has to be a joke."

Rose smiled and nodded. "Kate said you have a good sense of humor, so I had the computer throw that in just for fun. You're well known, but your arrival is not that historically significant. I'm afraid only your discovery of the graviton would show up if we went back a few more years."

Tom shrugged. "Well, at least I made the list."

Rose stretched. "It's about time we took that break. I didn't get around to having breakfast and I'm starved. Now that you're rich, I'll let you buy."

"Rich? I haven't the slightest idea how I'm even going to pay for these sessions. I don't understand."

"Oh. Then may I assume no one has told you about life-credit yet?"

Tom's eyes returned to the plastic plate. "I noticed something here about it ... I thought it was life insurance or something."

"No, nothing like that. Any person born into our world, or that migrates to earth from somewhere else in the system, is given 1 million credits in an account for getting started. It covers all the fundamental requirements such as education, housing, food, and other essentials for an extended time. That way, people have an equal chance for success in their endeavors.

Once they're established and working, then they can start repaying society as they can. You qualify as an immigrant, so as of your arrival, you have 1 million credits in an open account."

"Is that the same as dollars?"

She shrugged. "We only use credits. No actual physical currency ever changes hands, so I honestly have no idea. Come on, let's go."

"Wait. Did you say you haven't eaten yet?"

"Yes ... why?"

Tom grinned. "This could be a real problem. You're probably going to want at least two doughnuts and a drink, if not more. With three hundred years of inflation behind me, doughnuts are probably a hundred-thousand credits each ... so, there goes my fortune."

Rose laughed, then led the way.

"All that lies between the cradle and the grave is uncertain."
- Seneca

Chapter 31
Rude Awakening

The grav-lift slid silently down a shaft, slowed, sped horizontally for a few seconds, continued its descent, and then finally came to an almost imperceptible halt. The doors parted, allowing Rose and Tom to exit into the hallway. He turned right, towards Rose's office ... she to the left.

Rose jerked to a stop when she realized their separation. "This way, Tom. Sorry, I was thinking ahead and automatically headed for an assessment lab. I want to copy your memory and develop some baseline models before divulging my diagnosis."

"All of my memory?"

"Yes, just like the MMTs do, except this process will cross-reference each memory according to type, duration, intensity, mood, etc. The procedure's exceptionally involved and can often be quite lengthy ... sometimes taking as long as fifteen or twenty minutes. The lab is at the end of this hallway."

Tom stared at the floor, watching it slide beneath his feet as they walked. "It's nice that you can order from your table and the food is delivered by those little robots. I'll bet at least half of the back wall contains nothing but auto-cookers."

Rose nodded. "It saves a lot of time and frustration and, of course, there's no standing in line."

"I noticed something else interesting about the cafeteria. With all the people coming and going, no one used the MMT I saw stationed in a corner."

"It's there strictly for an emergency. People don't abuse its presence out of respect for the privacy and relaxation of others. All the flashing would be distractive and considered quite rude."

"You don't have the occasional jerk who thinks they're special and doesn't play by the rules?"

She smiled. "First of all, it's not a rule, just a socially-accepted refinement. Second, I think you'll find most of the jerks, per your reference, weed themselves out of our society because they're not tolerated. They find a home in TheBelt where rules are practically nonexistent. Once there though, people experience the repugnance of living among only the blatantly inconsiderate, change their attitude, and desire a return to one of the more civilized worlds." Rose halted before a doorway outlined in green light. "This is it. I reserved the lab for thirty minutes, which should prove more than adequate for our purposes."

She flowed through the wall. Tom followed with an outstretched hand, stopping immediately once inside. His eyes slowly scanned the interior of a room seemingly composed of nothing more than white tiles. Rose walked to a long, narrow, padded table in the middle of the otherwise empty expanse and patted its surface. "Hop up, please. Then lie down and relax."

Tom complied, but his eyes widened when she secured his arms and legs. Rose caught his reaction and chuckled. "Don't worry. I'm going to administer a mild sedative, then place you in a holograph. The straps are in place solely to keep you from rolling off the table in case you fall asleep."

She pressed a flush panel in a nearby wall, which released a small door. A multitude of soft sticky tabs with short projecting wires were retrieved. Several carefully selected styles in varying colors were positioned around his head. "These are sensors that'll transmit all the required data to the computers for recording. There ... we're all set. Where would you like to go today?"

A short interval transpired while he pondered the question. "How about a deserted beach on a tropical island, doing nothing more strenuous than watching the clouds play tag on a beautiful day. Other than that, tell the computer to use its imagination."

"Sounds like a good choice. I'm almost jealous."

A hiss of air injected the drug. "You'll become more relaxed as this takes effect. After the recording is complete, I'll give you something that will counteract the sedative and we'll return to my office. The computer will have processed and organized the data for my perusal by the time we arrive. We'll go from there."

Rose initiated the hologram ... instructing the machine to embellish as it saw fit. The table became a hammock swinging in a cool salty breeze situated beneath a blue sky dotted with variously shaped puffs of cotton. The sun trickled through a canopy of swaying palm-tree branches populated by colorful singing birds. Hermit crabs scampered across the sand looking for food in the foamy hiss of gently retreating waves.

Minutes later, Tom's eyes slowly closed and he floated out to sea.

Rose and Tom entered her office ... each reclaiming their former seats. "I'll be with you in a minute, Tom. I want to do a preliminary scan of the results." Rose became completely engrossed in her work. A couple 'oo's, 'ah's, and one 'oh my' slipped out. She blushed when she looked up and saw his stare. "My apologies, Tom. That was certainly unprofessional of me. I'm so accustomed to reviewing this type of data in private ... I guess I just forgot you were present."

He shrugged. "That's okay ... I've been there, too. So what's the verdict?"

She thought for a moment. "Let me show you the data. That way we'll have a common basis for discussions." Rose returned the plastic view-plate he had used earlier. "I'm going to split the screen, showing a model on top, followed by your graphs on the bottom. There are literally hundreds of different waveforms available, but I'll display only those of greatest importance in helping us solve your problem. In particular, pay attention to waveforms one through three.

Wave one is a depiction of self-image. The farther it falls below zero, the more a feeling of rejection is perceived. Two is the P/R ratio ... perception to reality. The broader it varies above or below zero, the more conflict exists at that point in time. Wave three is guilt. It only extends upward from a base line. Higher peaks indicate correspondingly greater guilt levels being experienced at that moment.

We'll watch the model first. I'll replay the graph relatively slowly so you can get an idea of what to expect. It consists of one person's memories for a year and will take approximately four minutes at this playback speed. The computer automatically condenses long periods when the waves remain within narrowly confined margins."

Tom watched, fascinated, as some stranger's memories oscillated across his viewing plate. At first, there didn't seem to be any connection between the different wave patterns, but the longer he observed, the more he became aware of some underlying, intertwined relationship. "That's amazing. They were just wavering lines to begin with, but after a while I could almost sense the mood swings and thought-pattern changes. It's a little eerie."

Rose nodded. "I understand. Even after all the cases I've studied, I still feel that way sometimes. Before we watch your graphs, Tom, let me warn you about something. People of your time were a lot more stressed than in mine. Your patterns are going to exhibit a great deal more variability compared with the ones you just witnessed. Expect it. Don't let it upset you.

I've asked the computer to scan through about ten minutes of data at a greatly increased rate. From my experience, this will probably cover your first twenty years of life. The first few are purposely bypassed since they are excessively unfocused. An infant's brain obviously hasn't learned to accurately transfer sensory input into memories. Are you ready?"

He nodded.

"I'm instigating replay ... now."

He shook his head and looked up at Rose when the display finished. "It looked like a nightmare compared to the model. What were the gaps I noticed?"

"They weren't really gaps. Those points were of a greater variance than could be displayed without rescaling the screen." Rose came around her desk and knelt next to Tom, placing a hand on his arm. "It's a given that you won't understand contemporary psychological jargon, so I had the computer convert my findings into terms with which you'll at least be familiar. How does latent hebephrenic schizophrenia leading to an induced catatonic state sound?"

"Terminal."

Rose laughed. "It's not as bad as it seems and ... as I've indicated ... not completely accurate either.

The schizoid tendency isn't between personalities, but between your conscious and sub-conscious mind. Hebephrenia is the stage when your intellectual deterioration begins. Catatonia is the catch phrase for your muscle rigidity and general mental stupor.

Some of the definitions are even overlapping, but in layman's terms, that's the best I can do. Bottom line ... your blackouts, currently a level-2 catatonia, are caused by conflict and rejection ... and just to make it more interesting, we'll throw in some self-perceived guilt.

Rejection by your parents, especially your father, should be painfully clear. The conflict is mostly between your interpretations of self. I don't know the source of the guilt at this point, although the graphs clearly indicate it exists.

Tom ... I'm going to ask you two questions. From my experience and the data, I'm already confident of the answers, but ... well, I'd simply like to note your reactions. About how many times during your life have you wished you'd never been born?"

"I'm not sure. Several at least."

"How many times have you contemplated suicide?"

His eyes flicked away. "More than I'd care to admit."

"Thank you ... I know that must have been unpleasant."

She studied his face, squeezed his arm, and returned to her seat, acting as if nothing had been revealed. "Those spikes are the only things that cause me serious concern. We'll need to look at a lot of the data, but those particular memories should be reexamined in detail."

Tom squirmed in his chair. "If bad memories and guilt are causing my attacks, won't bringing up the past make them worse?"

"No. That's the beauty of Time Displacement versus regular hypnotherapy. Let me try to explain the difference.

Under normal hypnosis, you follow the guidance of a hypnotist and report what you see in your mind. The key problem is that you are still witnessing events from your own perspective. This almost always leads to a heightened state of apprehension.

TDH uses your computer-stored conscious powers to create an impartial entity. Your memories are also retrieved from the computer and displayed in a three-dimensional holograph where your compiled character exists, while you observe in total detachment, allowing your conscious mind to be completely bypassed. You are lightly sedated throughout the process, acting as just another independent observer ... therefore, no anxiety whatsoever.

The entire scenario gives us two inherently powerful tools. Since the memory unfolds before us, it presents another common basis for discussion ... and allows you to date the memories occurrence so we can develop a timeline."

Rose glanced at her wrist device. "Speaking of time ... there's a few more things I want to cover before we close out this session.

Kate has helped me research your past. Your disappearance created quite a bit of notoriety and several articles were written in worldwide publications discussing your childhood, education, and early discoveries. They've aided me tremendously in preparing for your therapy.

Onion peeling may sound trite, but it's the best example of explaining our future sessions. Your problems are deep, and we'll need to proceed cautiously ... one layer at a time. When we get near the core, you will have been stripped of any remaining ego defense mechanisms. Your emotional state will be extremely vulnerable. Before arriving at that point, I'm going to request an action you probably won't like, but hope you'll accept anyway for your own safety.

Whenever a patient may be placed in what I would term 'mental danger', I reserve an apartment here at the med-plex. I'm urging you to take my advice and live there ... alone ... for the short time when you'll be most exposed. Will you agree to my request?"

Tom stared silently for a minute. "I realize this is a subjective question, but can you tell me what kind of timeframe we're talking about?"

"We have a Discovery-Day meeting coming up in five weeks. They're held quarterly. Everyone gets a chance to discuss the progress of current projects and any breakthroughs that have occurred. Unfortunately, your peak period of susceptibility will fall one week before through one week after the meeting date. I've asked John to assign you some work, which will hopefully help keep your mind busy. I think it'd be best if you move to the med-plex three weeks from now and stay for at least one month."

"I'll agree if you really think it's best."

"I do."

"Does Kate know?"

"No, the determining data wasn't available until today, but she's well acquainted with the disciplines of TDH."

He shook his head. "It's too bad. Kate had been looking forward to celebrating when we found out my problem."

Rose leaned forward and made direct eye contact. "Tom ... you should. We know the enemy, and we understand what it'll take to win. By all measures, a celebration is in order."

A flashing dot in the corner of Rose's screen announced the arrival of her next patient. "Our time is up, Tom. One last piece of advice for now ... lean on Kate. She wants to help as much as possible ... and remember ... you should feel good about this. I'll wager that in the end you'll feel better than you ever have before. Be here at 2 p.m. tomorrow. We'll do our first TDH and schedule future appointments afterward. I'll see you then."

* * * * *

"Hi, Tom. I've already inhibited the chair's functions, so you can sit and relax. How do you feel today?"

"Kate and I had a long talk last night. She explained a lot of things to me, and even mentioned my growing animosity towards her. After that, we just held each other. I'm primed, Rose. Kate and I want to be happy together. If this is what it takes, then I'm all for it."

Rose beamed. "That's great news. Just stay with me, Tom. Kate is probably my closest friend and I'm learning that you're a good person. Your happiness is important to me, too. I'll do my best not to disappoint either of you. By the way ... I came across the fact that you play chess."

"I did for a period, but not lately."

"Well, maybe you can think of our sessions as an ongoing chess match. In this case though, there are teams. Our team consists of you, the computer, and myself ... with Kate as a bonus player. The other side consists of resentment, rejection, deep sadness, missed opportunities, and many bad memories.

Together ... they constitute a formidable opponent, but we're the light-colored pieces, so the first move belongs to us. We'll need to choose it wisely and play conservatively, planning our strategy well in advance. Are you ready?"

Tom's fingers mimicked a motion across an imaginary game board. "King's pawn to king four."

Rose smiled. "Exactly. Let's begin."

"That which is not allotted the hand cannot reach; and what is allotted you will find wherever you may be."

- Saadi

Chapter 32
Opening Moves

Kate stopped at Rose's office, and after not finding her present, headed for the closest cafeteria. Ten feet within the entrance, she spotted Rose reading in a quiet back corner, waved, and then worked her way through a maze of tables. "Hi, sis. Are you going to the discovery meeting?"

"Definitely. It's good to catch up on what others are doing now and then. Besides, Tom's giving his first presentation, and I want to be there so I can keep an eye on him."

"You've been working with him for about a month, and I know we've talked, but what's your current assessment of his progress?"

Rose tapped her folder. "Your timing is impeccable. This is his latest evolvement report. I'm amply impressed with his improvement. If he can get through the next couple weeks without a traumatic incident, I'm confident of a successful and safe conclusion to his treatment. Nevertheless, Tom's reached the most treacherous position in his therapy. His entire ego defense mechanism has been stripped away ... as a result ... even the slightest turmoil could quickly escalate and dangle him over a dangerous psychological precipice. I've taught him some rational exercises to perform when he becomes stressed. They'll help him remain focused and resist emotional involvement.

There's also a tranquilizer infuser attached to his arm the computer will activate anytime it recognizes danger. Unfortunately, he's refused to wear it during the meeting. I've tried convincing him there's no stigma involved, but he refuses to listen.

Actually, I made an effort in persuading him not to attend in the first place, but when he became quite morose, I finally relented ... hoping it would ultimately be the lesser of two evils. However, having said all of that, we're ahead of schedule and are about to begin transforming his shattered psyche. I don't suppose you'd be interested in having him home a week or two early?"

Kate wiggled in her chair. "That'd be great. It's absolutely amazing how abruptly the apartment became empty without him around. You'd think we'd been together for several years."

"He really misses being with you, too. I guess all it takes is finding the right person." Rose smiled and returned to her reading.

Kate sat quietly, keeping her thoughts to herself ... or at least making the attempt. "Speaking of the right person ... what about Jorge?"

Rose's eyes flicked up to Kate, then back to her page. "What about Jorge?"

"I never hear from him. Do you two ever have any contact?"

Rose continued scanning her report. "I've offered him my assistance anytime he wants, but apparently he's not concerned about his problem. Recognition is the first step to recovery, and he lives in constant denial. Until he at least acknowledges he needs help ... he'll remain unreachable. At this point, I'm afraid there's nothing that can be done." Rose looked back up. "Hmm, maybe I'll introduce him to Tom someday. Perhaps a real-life before and after comparison would open Jorge's eyes."

Kate giggled. "You're probably right. Tom's personality is enough to open anyone's eyes."

Rose teased, "Honestly, Khatty. I was speaking psychologically."

"So was I," Kate smirked. She checked the time. "Shouldn't we be leaving?"

"I thought the meeting was at 10 a.m. our time." Rose pressed some buttons on her wrist device. "Let's see. The meeting is at nine sol-standard. That's sixteen hundred in Mexico and, uh oh, 9 a.m. here. It's 8:50, we'd better hurry."

The pair left the cafeteria and used a public MMT station located in a hallway alcove for transportation to their main complex.

Kate started singing nonchalantly as they walked towards the meeting room. "Tom, Tom, bo bom, banana fanna fo fom, fee fi mo mom ... Tom."

Rose lightly grabbed Kate's upper arm. "What in planetary orbits was that nonsense?"

"Tom sings that verse every now and then with my name, so I had him teach it to me. It's from a song back around his time." Kate winked. "He really misses his music."

"Speaking of his music ... how's your little project coming along?"

"We ran into a few problems, but it'll be finished in another couple of weeks ... just about the time Tom should be ready to come home. Here's the room ... want to bet Xarles will be the last to arrive with some feeble excuse?"

"It wouldn't be vintage Xarles without one," Rose scoffed.

The ladies sat at a long conference table opposite Tom and John. The two men seemed to be deep in discussion. Larry flanked John's other side and was listening intently. Xarles swept into the room. "Sorry, everyone ... I was detained by pressing business."

Most of the ongoing conversations continued unabated. Kate and Rose traded smiles. Xarles gaveled the meeting to order. It worked the second time. "I'll take this opportunity and welcome everyone to the quarterly discovery meeting. As usual, those residing within the perimeter of our moon's orbit will join our proceedings live. The remainder of the audience will be able to correspond with the attendees through standard interspatial web connections on a delayed basis. There are two new faces in our midst today, both sponsored by Dr. Jiaan Picus. John, would you do the honors?"

John pushed back his chair and stood. "Thank you, Xarles. It'll be my pleasure. It's an interesting note that both guests traveled quite long distances to be here, but via radically different modes of transportation."

John signaled for the man on Tom's far side to arise. "First, let me introduce Dr. Zacarias Wytt, professor emeritus of exobiology, who has just arrived from the Mars Polytechnic Institute. Zack trekked from Mars to our moon, exploiting the space-based innermost MMT ring, then onward toward L4 via a shuttle ... where he delivered an impromptu lecture.

He finally reached earth by hitching a ride with returning engineers who were testing modifications they installed on a new model of ex-atmosphere grav-sled. Personally, I consider the entire voyage quite a feat for anyone, let alone a man who has just celebrated his 100th birthday."

Tom stared open-mouthed at the gentleman. He was about five-ten, slim, and had a salt-and-pepper beard with a little gray in his hair. There were also some telltale wrinkles, but he looked absolutely nothing like his stated age.

He would have guessed the man to be in his late forties, or possibly early fifties at the oldest. Perhaps the MMTs' 'expel' process really did work miracles.

John continued. "Zack's team, myself, and many others have been collaborating on a new type of propulsion system utilizing the Casimir-effect. Of course, as many of you know, my memory loss has caused me to severely curtail the number of my current projects owing to my inability for recalling their previous status and sometimes, absurdly enough, even understanding their function. Professor Wytt made the trip in order to keep the Casimir-drive project on schedule. I have gratefully accepted his generous offer to direct the venture and consider myself deeply in his debt.

In case you're wondering why a retired exobiology professor is directing a project dedicated to applying research in the province of cavity quantum electrodynamics, the answer is quite simple. Zack's first three careers, which total sixty years, were all in different fields of physics. Thank you, Zack." The men shook hands and Zack sat down.

John's eyes fell on Tom. "Our next guest probably doesn't need much introduction because news about him has been on the net quite frequently ever since his arrival. I'm sure you've heard something about him unless you've been hiding in TheBelt. Please stand, Tom.

Among his many notable developments, Dr. Thomas Hughes was the first to discover the type of particle required for moving through the fourth dimension, collectively known as tachyons. Therefore, he is considered the father of time travel.

Appropriately, he started his trip forward from 2013, but subsequently retreated 150 million years into the past, along with my co-worker, Dr. Khattyba Bright, before they began advancing again. Apparently, this may have been due to a miscalculation on my part. The error is currently under investigation by the time council and any decisions will be forthcoming, and subsequently, publicly accessible. Xarles ... I reciprocate ... replacing the regulation of the meeting back into your capable hands."

Tom hadn't known about the investigation and sat down heavily. He remembered the agreement that John, Kate, and he had made when they were still in the Jurassic, but unfortunately, that was just another memory John had evidently lost the ability to recall. The inquiry must have been started before he and Kate had been able to return.

Yet, John said he had panicked and overrode the system. That meant there shouldn't be any record of the actions that followed. The council would probably just conclude that indeed a mistake had been made, John would possibly get a reprimand, and the incident would be closed.

Fine. Let it be.

Xarles began calling on people to give their reports. There were many, but most were concise and the first two hours passed quickly. At 18:07, he took note of the residual speakers ... there were three ... and one was John.

He decided to recess the meeting for an hour, knowing that when they reconvened, the remaining presentations could possibly run late into the evening.

"It is the province of knowledge to speak, and it is the privilege of wisdom to listen."

- Oliver Wendell Holmes

Chapter 33
Middle Game

Xarles called the meeting to order once more. "Please take your seats, ladies and gentlemen ... thank you. Dr. Picus will be our next speaker. John ... you have the floor."

John arose, leaned forward, and methodically spread his fingertips on the tabletop. "Thanks, Xarles. As I mentioned previously, Tom and Kate ended up traveling far back into time ... much farther than anyone has ever ventured before. Some exciting and extraordinarily interesting statistics were compiled from that trip, and our engineers have developed a plan for updating TMTs and MMTs utilizing the information obtained.

It was a complete surprise when we discovered the vast amount of energy required to travel forward from the distant past. Evidently, as tachyon class particles re-approach a time traveler's point of origin, they tend to behave like mass particles nearing light speed ... the closer the approach, the more power required. These disparagements prompted us to rethink the manner in which tachyon and neutrino maps are encoded. We decided that if the process could be enhanced, then the requisite energy levels would be reduced by an equivalent proportion.

Each quantum particle has a characteristic known in physics as spin. The neutrino has a single spin denoted as 1/2. Since the neutrino is used for traveling only in real-time, its spin has no effect and suits our purposes completely. For time travel, however, the spin of a tachyon class particle determines its direction of motion in the fourth dimension; that is, forward or backward through time, with a corresponding spin-state of +1 and -1.

A discovery only a few months ago uncovered zero as a third existing spin-state for a tachyon. If +1 propels you forward ... and -1 hurls you back ... then you can well envision that zero could be the ultimate suspended animation vehicle. It could virtually make a person immortal."

John paused, allowing his audience time to absorb this information before resuming. It was obvious he had captured their rapt attention. The off-handed explanation of the new spin-state had served his purpose. "My apologies, however ... for I digress. After an object has been prepared for teletransportation, its map is superimposed on either a neutrino or tachyon stream. Obviously, this indicates that enormous quantities of particles are required along with an associated amount of energy.

We've recently discovered that we can create a reference feature by using polarization. This indexing ability would provide an almost infinite number of directions in which to orient a particle based on the tri-dimensional coordinate system of a sphere. Using this method, each orientation can be manipulated so as to combine several map positions together, thus allowing the disintegration/reintegration process to operate at a molecular, or even more likely, the cellular level. In turn, this would reduce the total number of necessary particles by several orders of magnitude, with a commensurate decline in energy requirements. Are there any questions before our idea for a second upgrade is addressed?"

Question lights blinked on in front of almost everyone seated around the table, and soon, the outside communication channels were inundated. Xarles was overwhelmed as he attempted to handle the influx of responses. "John, you can't throw out something like immortality then pass it off as a mere digression. I imagine all of these inquiries express the same sentiment. Can you enlighten us a little more?"

"Sorry, everyone. At present, my hands are tied. My backers and fellow workers were concerned with how the general populous would react to the announcement. They're watching now ... and I told them I'd mention it in passing and let them observe the interest it might attract. I believe they're firmly convinced about the depth of its impact.

The zero-spin tachyon project is just part of a much larger, more ambitious endeavor. I'll probably be in a better position to disclose additional information in a few months. You'll have to wait until then."

The stunned listeners accepted John at his word. The question lights began to individually darken and eventually the comm-ports were cleared. Xarles managed to collect himself and restart. "Evidently, everyone knows to avoid further questions when you've stated additional information isn't forthcoming. You may as well continue with your second report, John."

"Actually, Ysabel is going to speak from another section of this complex concerning an upgrade for the MMTs' scan mechanism and also elaborate on the enhancement I just discussed. Computer, tie in to TheTwenty's lab and see if she's ready."

"Message understood ... checking status ... Dr. Lebasy indicates all is prepared. Establishing link ... transferring control."

Ysabel's image appeared on a large, holographic circum-linear screen above the conference table. "Good evening, ladies and gentlemen. Welcome to our primary optics workshop.

The MMT has been in inexistence for almost 100 years, and like most technology, it's evolved through many enhancements and upgrades. The newly announced improvements will lack a reference-frame without some background, and perhaps throwing out a few numbers. But, even with that in mind, I've tried keeping the details to a minimum.

Everyone knows the first successful test involved nothing more than a single grain of sand. Yet, that tiny matter speck required being cooled to almost absolute-zero temperature, and utilized over ten full seconds of disintegration/reintegration time using a fixed-beam rated at 100 billion nanobots per nanosecond.

It would require another five years of experimentation until the first animate matter would be successfully transmitted. The initial beam still consisted of 100 billion nanobots and fired in a nanosecond ... but more importantly ... it also doubled in quantity every five nanoseconds thereafter.

This doubling of quantity per unit-of-time was the breakthrough process that eventually made teletransportation a plausible reality." Ysabel chuckled. "It's already been a long evening, and I can't help but notice that some people are becoming restless. Let me split the display and provide some visual cueing alongside my image. Hopefully, that'll perk up your interest."

Sections of the screen began scrolling experimental results, short-term objectives, achievement dates, and other various data as Ysabel resumed her commentary. "Another three years passed before researchers celebrated what they thought was the first successful transmission of an entire plant. Upon further investigation, however, it was discovered that after a short time the plants tended to lean, sag, or droop in one or more directions.

It was ultimately determined that the offending posture was caused by the plants' cells randomly collapsing or compressing. The term 'induced cellular hyper-elasticity' was contrived to describe the phenomenon. Its causative factor was the still comparatively long reintegration time, which created some cell walls that were elongated ... making them weaker than normal.

Upgrading the disintegration/reintegration beam to double every nanosecond solved that particular problem. Eventually, animal testing began once the capability of the D/R beam reached more optimal performance levels. The apparatus continued firing a preliminary 100 billion nanobots, but its doubling rate dropped to three pico seconds.

Our current configuration still fires the same initial beam, but the doubling rate has been lowered to only 1 pico second for each burst thereafter. This works out to a total D/R round trip of 112 pico seconds. But, even at that rate we still suffer cell loss in the neighborhood of 112 cells per D/R cycle, although this is far less than the body loses every day through normal attrition.

The problem remains that the induced loss still randomly affects healthy tissue, whereas attrition loss is due to natural cell death."

Ysabel drew a deep breath and slowly released it. "Well, now that everyone knows where we are, let me tell you where we're going.

John's upgrade to the mapping process will reduce the number of required particles from roughly 7.0×10^{27}, at the atomic level, to 1.0×10^{13}, at the cellular level. Obviously, this represents a tremendous decrease in requisite particle transformation, and subsequently, a substantial savings in energy requirements, not to mention a greatly increased safety factor.

This information covers the bulk of the upgrade, but we decided to add one more twist. The beam design itself has been untouched for almost all of these 100 years. We've tried multiple beams before, but couldn't maintain collimation around a common central axis. In non-technical terms, whatever we sent ended up as an unrecognizable blob of protoplasmic techno-goop.

With the addition of John's indexing scheme, multiple-segment beams have become feasible. The implementation of a three-segment beam, which is the most stable, is made possible by applying the Zeeman effect. This essentially encloses the indexed particle beam in an intense magnetic envelope, causing it to split into several additional usable wavelengths. The result of this development will decrease the D/R time by an additional one-third.

Okay ... bottom line statistics. Here's what these enhancements mean to everyone. Perhaps you earlier caught the implied association between cellular loss and D/R sequencing. That is, a person loses roughly 1 body cell for each pico second spent in the matter-teleportation cycle. Hence, a round trip of 112 pico seconds equals, on average, a loss of 112 cells.

The round-trip processing time will fall to an average of 12 pico seconds with the application of both enhancements. Comparatively speaking, I think everyone will agree these are extremely worthwhile upgrades and should be implemented as soon as development and testing will allow.

That ends my presentation. Are there any questions?"

People looked around with some whispering amongst themselves, but there was no outright verbal response.

"Ysabel."

"Yes, John."

"Perhaps you might mention when these changes are scheduled for distribution and how they will be installed."

Her head nodded on the screen. "Yes, you're right. Sorry."

"That's okay ... please continue."

"Testing should be completed in 45-60 days. The software portion will be downloaded into all existing MMTs soon afterward. The required hardware will be beamed to all units and installed by any compatible household dom-bot whenever convenient for the occupant."

Xarles broke in. "Thank you, Ysabel. Speaking of domestic robots, I just requested some make their way here and bring a portable auto-cooker. We've only two speakers left, and I'd like to continue without breaking, but I'm sure some refreshments would be appreciated."

Heads bobbed in agreement.

"Xarles."

"Yes, Ysabel."

"Frank Angstrom has tied into the link and would like a word with you."

"Fine. Put him through."

"Hi, Xarles. Sorry to interrupt, but I have an urgent request."

"Go ahead."

"I have a holograph arranged for Professor Wytt's presentation. There's another holograph I promised to prepare for a group of friends, but I didn't realize we'd be running this late. According to the agenda, Dr. Hughes is our next scheduled speaker. Is it possible to switch his presentation with Zack's, so I'll have time for setting up the other holograph before my guests arrive?"

Xarles looked over. "Gentlemen, is that satisfactory to you?"

Tom and Zack exchanged glances, shrugged, then both indicated their acceptance. Xarles nodded. "Then it's agreed ... Professor Wytt will be our next presenter."

Xarles was about to give Zack permission to proceed when the dom-bots rolled through the doorway. "Serve Professor Wytt first so he may begin. You may wait on the remainder while he speaks."

Zack ordered an icy glass of water with a lemon slice and took several sips. "Ah, I didn't realize how dry I was. Thank you, my mechanical friend."

"You're most welcome, Professor Wytt. It's an honor to assist."

Afterwards, Zack hoisted his glass towards their moderator in a toast. "Excellent idea, Xarles. I probably wouldn't make it through my presentation without it. May I proceed?"

"Whenever you're ready, Zack."

"Thank you. As John previously mentioned, the main purpose for my trip to earth is the Casimir project. Therefore, I'm sure it's no surprise that your itinerary lists this item as my topic for tonight.

I must embarrassingly admit that this is the first discovery meeting I've attended, live or otherwise, so I came prepared to thoroughly discuss the basis for the drive, which is the Casimir-effect itself.

It would require covering general relativity field equations, standard cosmological models, finite temperature, and constant-curvature hyper-spheres ... at a minimum. Then, having worked through the mathematics, we'd have to renormalize any solutions to eliminate the resulting infinities.

However, after witnessing all of your fine 'overview' presentations, I realize none of that is necessary. So, you can all relax." There were many appreciative smiles and a smattering of applause in jest. "Instead, I'll present some background on the Casimir-effect and just exhibit a holograph of the drive's working model."

Zack glanced at Tom. "I don't mean to make my co-guest uncomfortable, but the Casimir-effect was first proposed by Hendrik Casimir, the effect's namesake, about 30 years before Dr. Hughes was even born. Basically, Casimir predicted a small attractive force should exist between two parallel, uncharged conductive plates if they were brought close enough to each other.

His anticipation was based on the belief that the vacuum of space was filled with virtual particles that winked into and out of existence in accordance with conventions mandated by quantum theory and the Heisenberg uncertainty principle, which dictates that it's impossible for any universal point to exist in an absolutely zero-energy condition.

The attractive force exists because these virtual particles emit different wavelengths of energy. As the distance between the plates decreases, more and more wavelengths are excluded from entering the gap, although all waves continuously apply pressure to the outside. Eventually, pressure outside the plates exceeds inside pressure, thus pushing them together.

This collective vacuum power source is termed Zero Point Energy, or ZPE, and its first detection was purported to be as early as 1958, although the results were admittedly 100% uncertain because of the comparatively crude measuring devices in that time.

Four decades later, it was re-ascertained twice. Once by Lamoreaux to within 5% of the predicted value, closely followed by Mohideen and Roy, to within 1% utilizing an atomic-force microscope.

The Casimir-effect and ZPE became ardent investigative subjects during the early 21st century. Quite a few unexpected little quirks came to light throughout the research. I'm sure Tom could attest to that.

Boson type particles, such as photons, created an attractive force, while fermions produced an opposite result. The amount of energy available in a prescribed area of vacuum could be altered by the mere presence of matter within it. Even geometry played a part. Whatever force was normally produced would become reversed if the flat plates were replaced with hemispherical shells.

At one point, ZPE was thought to be a possible cause of cold fusion, sonoluminescence, and even inertia. Unfortunately, as time passed, no one could derive a working conception of how to effectively tap into the vacuum as a free energy source, so interest gradually waned and funding disappeared.

Even its most stalwart supporters became disillusioned, allowing the Casimir-effect, along with ZPE, to slip into a long and undeserved obscurity.

That was pretty much the status quo until just a few years ago when a colleague of mine, Galt Pio at Mars Polytechnic, ventured to earth for the first time. When he returned he couldn't stop talking about two things. One was the fact that you could walk around outside anywhere on earth without even a skin suit. The other was what he witnessed in an electronics museum.

Apparently, Galt came across the display of an old-fashioned variable tuning capacitor. It consisted of two sets of parallel metal plates in close proximity. When a knob was turned, one set of plates would slide between the other, but not touch. The moving plates reminded him of an article he had read about ZPE at some point, and its associated disappointments.

My friend stood there turning the knob ... watching the plates ... knowing he was seeing something important, but not recognizing what it could be. That's when the obvious hit him. Only one set of plates was moving. The device consisted of a stator, stationary part, and rotor, the moving part. Galt conjectured about experimental problems concerning the Casimir-effect and ZPE in general, and started wondering what would happen if only one plate, or set of plates, was allowed to move when applied within that technology.

Now, if our holograph expert is still awake, I'll show you what developed from Galt's early speculative thoughts. Frank, please run the Casimir-drive presentation."

"Initializing image, Zack."

A long, thin cylinder materialized at head-height and centered along the length of the conference table. What appeared to be the front was fitted with a large dish, while the rear flared into exhaust nozzles. There were also several differently configured antennae sticking out from the sides at various angles.

"Looks like a typical interplanetary ore carrier," Xarles commented.

"Precisely," Zack confirmed. "Completely automated and operated only by robots. The dish is an ordinary space-scoop that funnels free-floating hydrogen-gas into compressors, storing it for later use. Hence, most ships of this design use common fusion reactors for propulsion.

This one, however, is equipped with two superlative differences. Allow me to illustrate the first. Enlarge the forward detail, Frank ... thanks. Note the mechanism just behind the scoop. Can you zoom in on the Casimir-drive?"

"Just the drive by itself?"

"Yes, please ... ah, that's great. You can clearly see the two thin plates that form the basic drive unit. Each is constructed from a single layer of dipole nanobots. They are designed and built to exist in only one of two possible patterns that can be rearranged in pico seconds. The lone input required is a minuscule clock signal to toggle them between configurations.

Frank ... would you please run the simulation at one image per second so we can see the drive as it cycles ... thank you. Notice that when the plates are flat, they are drawn together by the Casimir-effect. Once they approach to within .6 nanometers, the plates are automatically reconfigured into hemispherical shells, which is the all-important key.

Remember, when in that position, the attractive forces reverse and push the plates back apart. This type of maneuver wasn't possible without the advancement of nanobot technology. Twenty-first century science required an external input of energy to push the plates apart, so the device could never become self-sustaining.

The front plate is firmly attached to its support rod only at the center. The rear plate is connected to a cushioning mechanism that acts as a shock absorber and allows for the trivial amount of required movement. Since the rear plate moves and the front plate is stationary, it creates a slight difference in energy absorption, which provides as a net result ... forward thrust. That's the entire heart of the Casimir-drive."

The attendees watched in silent awe as the model began inching slowly through space. Zack beamed with pride for a few moments, then continued. "Since we've established a solid background, let me show you the second little marvel aboard ship.

Pan back to the Casimir-generator, Frank. There ... that's it. This display's a cross-sectional view of another application developed for extracting power directly from ZPE. Essentially, it utilizes the same concept as the basic drive, except for three important differences.

One, neither plate is anchored. They both move freely, thereby generating no thrust. Two, both sets of dipole nanobots are metallic in nature ... and three, the unit is surrounded by a magnetic field. I imagine we all learned in Science-101 what happens when a moving conductor cuts through lines of magnetic force ... it produces an induced electrical current. In this case, the current is alternating, or AC, because the plates oscillate within the field.

The current is converted to DC by rectifier circuits, which then powers all the onboard micro-electronic equipment ... and in this case ... it's all for free. Thank you for your patience. That concludes my presentation."

Zack waved towards the camera. "Thanks for the help, Frank," then he turned towards Xarles. "I'll return you-," but Xarles was mouthing something.

Zack watched in puzzlement for a moment, afterward, he caught the meaning. "Oh, that's right. Sorry, I guess I should ask for questions."

A light came on near one end of the table.

Zack pointed, "Yes, sir."

"The generator inside the ship is not enclosed. Wouldn't the mere presence of an atmosphere overpower the extremely weak force of ZPE and completely negate the machine's output?"

Zack nodded. "Yes, absolutely. Good point. But remember, this is a totally automated deep-space vessel, operated and maintained only by robots. Therefore, it has no need for any life support whatsoever, including air.

Conversely, any Casimir-generator operating aboard a passenger vehicle would need complete shielding and vented directly to the outside vacuum."

Another light. "Zack, you stated yourself that most ships of this type, be they freight or passenger, are normally powered by fusion reactors, which are highly efficient and practically maintenance free. Once underway, their fuel is readily obtained en route through space. I can easily understand the importance and immediate applicability of the Casimir-generator, but do you think the Casimir-drive is really necessary, or even practical?"

Zack quickly glanced at John, then back at the questioner. "For now, let's just say that the further a ship is from a massive gravitational source, the scarcer the free-hydrogen may become. We believe this will become more significant as civilization moves deeper into, uh ... the solar system."

Zack scanned the room. "Any others? Guess not, back to you, Xarles."

Their administrator checked his wrist device and smiled. "It appears that Dr. Hughes has the somewhat dubious honor of extending us into the longest discovery meeting to date ... and we all know what that means."

Xarles flicked a quick glance towards Rose. She shot back an anxious look, changing his mind. He pursed his lips and nodded an understanding, allowing Rose to visibly relax. "Ah, well, being that Tom is a first-time guest, I suggest we forego the usual friendly razing as mock punishment and instead just give him our courteous and undivided attention. I see from the schedule you're also going to talk about MMTs. Is this related to the other reports?"

"No, not exactly, Xarles. They covered the new upgrades. Mine describes some unusual historical events concerning the development of matter-projection versus common everyday transmittal and reception, known simply as T/R. After delving into the records, I believe I've developed a theory explaining why projection doesn't work when applied to animate objects.

In preparation for which material should be included, I instructed the computer to randomly select 1,000 people, both on and off-planet, and send them a questionnaire about MMTs. I was surprised to find that fully a third of the people responding weren't even aware that MMT was the acronym for Matter Modulated Transceiver. So, I'm hopeful my findings will prove interesting."

"Okay, Tom ... they're all yours."

"Through every rift of discovery some seeming anomaly drops out of the darkness, and falls, as a golden link, into the great chain of order."

- E.H. Chapin

Chapter 34
End Game

Tom stood. "Good evening, everyone. I'm confident you'll all agree that the first detail to report is good news ... my discourse will be short. That's because, as mentioned, I don't have a product or invention to present ... only my theory. Since my conjecture concerns MMTs, their previous background, especially as presented by Ysabel, is coincidentally well timed and greatly welcomed.

We're told MMTs can't project animate matter, which of course includes human beings. As previously stated, it requires two stations acting in concert, the first transmitting ... the other receiving," Tom glanced at Kate and smiled, "well, for the most part anyway.

However, as anyone would quickly discover, any complete history of the machine will clearly show this was not always true ... and that is exactly the premise my presentation revolves around.

Since I'm currently undergoing treatment with Dr. Petals, my therapy requires isolation. Because of that, my investigation began partly as curiosity, but mostly for something to keep me mentally occupied. As my research intensified, the reason why projection initially worked, then failed, became deeply cloaked in mystery, taunting my scientific intrigue until it completely absorbed me.

I pored through all lab reports and experiment logs concerning MMT development that were available. The standard transmit/receive methodology progressed from inanimate to animate matter, finally culminating with people. At that point, human trials were temporarily halted because early results plainly exhibited that the effects of teletransportation were so mentally and physically traumatizing that some form of circumvention was required.

During this period of respite, as drug trials and biofeedback mechanisms were being initiated for use with T/R, the concept of projecting matter without a receiver was proposed. Otherwise, the researchers reasoned, the maneuver would require traveling to a destination via common transportation methods toting an MMT along before anyone could ever teletransport there.

By the time T/R trials had resumed on a limited basis, a plan for MMTs to use projection had been formulated. It was based on the matter-matrix, a discussion of which would be wholly out of context here. The most noteworthy point, is that as projection reached its first human trials, T/R was already realizing total success because a retrovirus was being used for delivering DNA alterations into the body, enabling it to withstand the rigors of teletransportation.

In contrast, projection's negative side effects proved to be even more pronounced than the standard T/R method, so further projection trials were delayed while T/R was scheduled for production. In retrospect, this proved to be a fortunate turn of events. If advancement of both transfer methods had continued on a parallel basis, the results could have been disastrous because shortly after adapting projection to utilize the DNA altering virus, a total failure occurred during a mouse transfer.

Almost all of its cells were completely destroyed. The animal reintegrated as nothing more than a blob of hair-encrusted gel. The experimenters were horrified. All work on the projection method was halted, and what followed became the most confusing period during the entire MMT development cycle. I've posted a complete listing of my research on the net, so I won't bore you with details.

But at this point, all the early T/R trials were rerun without any failures or problems. The technicians concluded that the danger only lay in using projection, so the manufacture of T/R machines continued. There were a few sporadic mechanical failures, but, as Kate once pointed out, no others have occurred during the past forty years because of all the safety improvements.

Although I'm certainly not an expert in the field, I've nevertheless come to the conclusion that projection should be totally feasible based on the preceding experimental evidence. Once something is proven as workable, it subsequently fails for only one of two reasons. Either a part malfunctions or ... something is altered from the original design. Since the logs indicated the machinery always checked out ... then the answer lay in finding what had changed."

Tom took a breath and was about to resume when a question light came on, so he waited. A tall, dark-complexioned young man with coal black hair stood. His lank form seemed to ripple with sinuous, almost threatening muscle. He appeared to be no older than his middle twenties, somehow seeming out of place amid the current gathering of more experienced, mostly elderly people.

"Dr. Hughes, my name is Baud Ullric, and I manage the programming department supporting MMT development. I have a deep vested interest in your subject matter and have been looking forward to your findings ever since the forum for this meeting was posted. However absorbing your presentation has been, there is nothing so far we couldn't have gleaned from simply reading your report on the net at a more convenient time. It's late and we are obviously tired. So, even at the risk of seeming rude, I must inquire if you are just laying a foundation for some future resolution, or do you believe, as you stated, that you currently have an explanation to this quandary?"

Tom flushed. A perceptible darkness of unwarranted guilt began to crowd around his peripheral vision. He took a sip of water to cover his reaction while performing some of Rose's mental gymnastics.

Dr. Petals hastily retrieved a small monitor from a pocket, placed it in front of her, and cupped her hands around it. She intently studied its display, paying particular attention to a certain indicator. If it wavered below a corresponding green line, even for an instant, she would halt the proceedings and give Tom an injection. But he seemed to be so deeply involved with the academic position of his delivery that his emotions were at least temporarily being kept at bay. She waited for him to continue.

Finally, after delaying to recover, Tom smiled and responded, "I believe the answer is a qualified 'yes'. Be patient for just a few more minutes."

Baud regarded Dr. Hughes curiously for a moment, grunted, then sat down. "In that case, I offer my sincere apologies for the interruption. Please proceed."

Tom consulted his notes. "Ah yes, so the problem was reduced to finding what had been altered during the course of projection development. The obvious starting point was the DNA retrovirus, since before its introduction projection appeared to also work perfectly for animate matter.

But after backtracking, forward tracking, and even side tracking, I couldn't find any reason for the retrovirus not to function the same as it did for the T/R method of teletransportation. Frankly, I was baffled. The only questionable entry I could find was about a grav-sled mishap while delivering some data disks containing software changes. Evidently, two disks were expected at the MMT labs and one of them had reportedly lost its label.

At first, I dismissed it, but considering that I had nothing else to go on, I decided upon following up this one clue and see where it led.

I followed a chain of data links and found an entry from the company that delivered the disks. According to the report, the grav-sled was involved in an accident when it bumped into another sled. Obviously, the driver had manually disabled the auto-evade mechanism for expediency in heavy traffic.

One of the other items being carried was a box containing several bottles of common cleaning solvent. A single bottle broke on impact and spilled part of its contents over the protective metal cans containing the data disks. The grav-sled operator inspected the cans, wiped them off, and discovered the errant label. He reattached it to the respective container.

On the surface, when the delivery arrived, it appeared there was no foul ... and therefore no harm. But, due to a previous computer lesson from Dr. Petals, and a lot of practice, that benign perception changed when I performed a multi-index cross-reference search. It confirmed that both disks had to be reentered into the system manually because their labels were misaligned.

Since machines originally labeled the containers, I can understand why one would have required human intervention. But why two ... unless ... both labels came off and one inadvertently re-stuck due to the jostling received following the accident."

Tom paused and slowly circled the table with his gaze, attempting to draw his listeners closer. "Worse yet, what if that label had coincidentally reattached to the wrong container?"

Baud interrupted. "Dr. Hughes, don't you think all this stretches the imagination beyond comprehension. It seems just as likely that the one label reattached to the correct container, or simply became loose and slipped. Even if you're somehow correct, why wouldn't the attending personnel have investigated the incident?"

"Let me cover your second point first. I firmly believe that under normal conditions, a switch in labels would have been identified, but consider the working environment at the time. The roads were clogged with electric vehicles and the sky was overcrowded with anti-gravity sleds. Billions of people were constantly in motion, yet travel was essentially at an impasse, so the worlds' governments were pressing hard on the scientific community to perfect the T/R method of teletransportation.

Accordingly, untrained personnel were being shuffled in and out of clerical support positions, and forced to work with people with whom they shared no common experience or knowledge. I'm amazed anything was accomplished, but somehow the technicians persevered and managed to continue producing positive results.

Once T/R was perfected, the governments had all they wanted, or needed, from the teletransportation technology. As populations began using T/R, the roads became free, and the skies cleared. Projection also worked perfectly for inanimate matter, so an MMT could be sent ahead to receive transfers via standard T/R protocol. As a result, scarce resources and trained personnel were being turned over to other, more urgent ventures.

As to the probability of the labels getting switched, I freely admit it was merely a remote chance, but because of their contents, I think it's the only explanation that makes sense."

Baud's eyes narrowed and he challenged Tom once more. "What could possibly be on the disks that would foster such a belief?"

Rose checked her display again, but Tom's readings were okay. His emotions were in check, his mind definitely in control. She became amused realizing Tom was now baiting Baud, drawing him in, making him an unwitting accomplice to his story.

Tom kept Baud waiting a few seconds before responding. "One disk contained some backup code for the T/R system, the other contained updates to the projection method for the retrovirus, matching its capabilities with T/R."

"So?"

"Think about it ... if the T/R backup code was reapplied to the same system, it would do no harm. But applying it instead of the retrovirus update to the projection system would result in failure."

Baud was livid. "No! That's impossible. One set of updates couldn't be applied against both systems. The verification algorithms wouldn't allow it to be implemented."

"It may not work now, but back then, the original projection code was cloned from the T/R system. As a consequence, both had the same function-module and subsystem-IDs, so any update at least one number above the last level of code would be accepted. It was also a complete module replacement, thereby nullifying the VERIFY statement."

Baud persisted. "It's still not possible. The first projection trials following the update worked perfectly. Check the records for yourself."

"I did ... dozens of times. That's what I couldn't understand either, at first. But remember, I wasn't under any time constraints when I attempted to solve the mystery of why projecting animate matter failed. I had the luxury of reading all the experimental results and data at my leisure. I also had a highly advanced computer system with powerful new search engines at my disposal ... and that made all the difference. That's how I found, what I believe, is the key to the entire problem. In an obscure paper, there was a single passage indicating the prime culprit, and from that I deduced the following.

As the cells divide, the altered DNA replicates, too. More and more cells would contain the ability to handle teletransportation. However, without the code update, cells containing the altered DNA would be destroyed upon reintegration because it would be identified as foreign material to the body.

The first test subjects, after the update was supposedly applied, were recently injected plants and mice. Only a few cells were altered and thus destroyed upon reintegration, but without any visible effect.

The mouse they sent later was much older and many of its cells had the new DNA. Accordingly, the reintegration process destroyed them, making it a completely unstable, unviable organism."

"What makes you think the subject's age was a factor?" Baud spit out.

"The only known clue to the catastrophic failure was written in the closing notes on the project. One of the team members felt confident the breakdown had something to do with the subjects as they aged. That's the culprit I was referring to before. There wasn't any signature. Only the initials RJU were found at the end of the entry. After that, all projection research was canceled, and no one has ever seen the need for it to be reopened."

Tom was surprised at the revelation's transformation-effect on his intellectual adversary. A wide, satisfied smile slowly crept across Baud's face. "Dr. Hughes, is there any chance you'd consider allowing me the honor of working with you towards a final solution?"

"I'll go you one better, Baud. Even if my hypothesis is correct, and that's all it is at this juncture, I don't have the expertise to take it any further." Tom chuckled. "Not to mention the funding or authority. If you're interested, I'd be happy to turn over all my notes and let you and your team take it from here."

"Thank you, I'd be absolutely delighted ... and most grateful."

Tom looked around. "Are there any questions?"

The room remained silent.

Xarles rested an elbow on his podium, allowing his chin to settle into the 'V' formed by his thumb and forefinger. "Ladies and gentlemen ... it appears that we can finally bring our meeting to a conclusion. Thank you for everyone's fine presentation. Let me remind you to check your message queues at your earliest convenience. I've pre-scanned the list and found none that were marked urgent, so you may delay until you've had a good night's sleep." He chortled. "I just hope that's still possible after Tom's somewhat shocking disclosure. His words will probably be echoing in each of our minds as we step onto transfer mats for the trip home. Nevertheless, I bid you all a good evening and anticipate everyone's return next quarter."

"How frighteningly few are the persons whose death would spoil our appetite and make the world seem empty."

- Eric Hoffer

Chapter 35
Checkmate

The meeting room had cleared. John, Larry, Rose, Kate, Tom, and Zack remained seated at the table. Xarles had joined them. They were casually conversing about the presentations of the evening. Tom was commenting, "I understand why Baud was defensive about his department, but why the technicians of 100 years ago? That doesn't reflect on him or his team."

"At first, he probably thought you were looking for a source of blame concerning projection's failure," John offered.

"Finding blame was never my intention. I was always just searching for a logical explanation."

"It was obvious Baud realized that towards the end. Maybe that's why his attitude changed," John added.

Xarles shook his head. "That wasn't it. It was when Tom gave RJU credit for the key to his solution."

Tom leaned forward. "Do you know who RJU is, Xarles?"

He nodded. "Raymond Jacob Ullric ... Baud's grandfather."

Tom's eyes widened. "Are you sure?"

Xarles laughed, "I'm a people-person. It's my job to know trivial, but nonetheless important little things like that."

The group sank into a quiet interlude, each with their own thoughts. Tom looked over at Rose. "I suppose you want me back in my cell soon."

Rose smiled at the reference. "Yes. I didn't want you here in the first place ... remember? It worried me when Baud retorted against you so strongly, but you handled it well. You've obviously been practicing those mental exercises regularly. I'm proud of you. It won't be long before I'll be turning you loose on society again." She laughed. "Maybe I should advise them to use the time wisely."

John stretched. "Well people, if we're still going to meet with Frank, we should either be on our way or inform him of a postponement."

"It's not that late, and I think it'd be awfully rude to cancel now," Kate scolded.

Everyone's head nodded in agreement.

"Can I go?" Tom inquired.

"No," Rose answered instantly. "You can talk with Kate for a few minutes, then I want you headed back to your apartment. We'll wait outside."

"Yes, maam."

The group assembled in the hallway and waited for Kate. Zack motioned Dr. Petals aside. "Rose, I'd like to ask you a favor. Before Tom returns to his apartment, could I have a few words with him? I promise it's strictly business, and I won't keep him long."

She squinted while considering the request. "Alright, I think it'll be okay, and I'm sure Tom won't object. Maybe a little longer outside his 'cell' will do him some good. I've been extremely strict about rationing his external exposure. As long as you remember why it's necessary."

"I do. John filled me in on Tom's condition. By the way, don't wait for me. I'll catch up with you at Frank's lab."

Kate exited the meeting room a short time later. "Everybody ready?"

"Just a second." Rose poked her head in through the doorway. "Tom, sit tight, Zack wants to talk with you. I said it'd be okay as long as you keep it within a reasonable time limit ... and get that infuser back on."

Tom saluted.

Zack entered the room. The others ambled towards the holography lab.

Everyone watched as Frank donned the equipment onto Kate. She wanted to go first so she could be sure and surprise Tom the next time they met. This would help her understand Tom's viewpoint, and add to their common ground for discussions; besides ... it should be fun. Xarles shuffled from one vantage point to another. "Would you mind telling me again exactly what it is we're supposed to witness? I'm still not sure I understand."

Frank smiled at him. "It's called a one-sided door holograph. Tom asked me to design it so he could visually encounter an ending point of finite space. He says the concept has been his nemesis ever since he can remember.

We were working on it together until he went into isolation. He keeps sending suggestions through e-mail after watching models execute via computer simulation. He says he can't wait to experience the actual version again. This session will include all of the updates. I've never tried it myself ... it seems I'm always too busy." Frank stopped and stared at Xarles. "In all honesty, the way Tom describes the scene, it sounds extremely unnerving and disorienting." Then he shrugged indifferently, returning his attention to Kate's equipment and his previous oration.

"The holo executes in two parts. First, it'll hold the door in a fixed position, relative to Kate. The door will visually pivot in three dimensions, thereby remaining parallel to her point of view. There's a camera," he pointed, "mounted here on top of her headgear. It'll display exactly what she sees on a screen while attempting to observe the door from different locations.

But remember, the door is fixed relative to her position, so she'll always see the same presentation ... ergo, we get to view the door from different angles as she shifts her local. It gets really interesting when she's on the opposite side of the chamber looking front-on towards the door."

"Why's that?" Xarles mused.

"The door is generated as having only one side, hence the holograph's name. Consequently, if Kate is facing towards us, looking at the door's front, then by default, we'll be looking from the backside, which logically doesn't exist. So, we'll have the ability for observing her, but she won't be able to see us. In addition, we'll be able to see the door, as seen from her perspective, displayed on the screen simultaneously."

Xarles blinked. "It all sounds impossible."

"It's based on a special interference pattern that's generated when certain wavelengths of light intersect at oblique angles. In truth, it's an optical illusion, but it looks blatantly real. During the second phase, the door will remain fixed relative to the room. Kate will then be able to move toward the door's backside. But as she approaches an edge, the door will seem to get thinner. It will then become nothing more than a barely visible vertical line when viewed directly from anywhere on the perimeter, and as she passes through its plane, the door will disappear altogether."

Xarles slowly shook his head. "Now it just sounds crazy."

Frank chuckled. "Wait ... it gets even better. My last update reduces gravity within the chamber to 5% of earth normal. Kate will be essentially weightless, using only these compressed-air jets that we commandeered from a space suit, for maneuvering. That reduces the reliance on, and intrusion of, external stimuli."

Frank finished his explanation to Xarles, and hooking up Kate's equipment at about the same time. "Okay, you're all set." He handed her one last, small, cylindrical item. "Here's a remote emergency switch. If you reach a point where you can't speak, or simply think you're going to lose it, press this button. It'll instigate an immediate shutdown. Don't worry if you're in the air, the gravity will increase slowly and you'll float gently to the floor.

We won't be able to assist you until approximately five minutes after the holo terminates. In order to build one this dense, I must use high intensity lasers that generate a heavy concentration of electrostatic charge in the chamber's air. You'll be at the same potential voltage difference as your surroundings, thus you're completely safe, but anyone entering the chamber before the charge dissipates would be at a much lower ground state and electrocuted instantly. So, good luck, you're on your own for awhile."

Frank waved his arms in small circles. "Everyone else into the control room, please."

Xarles stopped by the exit. "As I understand it, anyone remaining inside will also be at the same electrical potential, so they, too, should be safe. Can I stay and get a closer view?"

Frank shook his head. "Not unless you want the lasers to slice you into easy-to-carry little pieces."

"Then how do you know Kate will be safe?"

"This holo was designed for a single participant."

Frank pointed at the projectors scattered around the walls and ceiling. "The laser beams always enter at a 90-degree offset from that person's current position. Wherever the subject moves, the target's profile coordinates are automatically updated to protect them. In this instance, the computer would consider the safety of anything else as secondary. Still want to stay?"

"No, I think I'll come with you."

Frank laughed. "A wise choice."

Larry took a seat in front of the main operator's console and initiated the holograph's loading sequence. It took a few minutes while the holo image stabilized and the gravity within the chamber dropped. Frank applied his talented touch to some specially calibrated equipment for fine-tuning.

"It's amazing. I swear I could reach out and touch the door," Kate commented. "I'm going to try moving around it."

She stopped for a rest following several attempts to circumvent the door. "It's so frustrating. No matter how I maneuver ... around, over, or even under, it always appears to be in the same position in front of me. Are you recording everything?"

Larry chuckled. "Absolutely. I wouldn't miss any of this for the world. You look like a kitten I saw in an animal documentary ... chasing its own tail."

Rose flipped on a nearby microphone. "How are you feeling?"

"The lack of gravity and sensory feedback made me nauseous a couple times, but I fought it. I'm also having trouble using the jets. It seems I don't fire them enough, or too much. Either way, I end up spinning a little, but I think I'm okay. Even though this is getting somewhat boring, I can't wait to watch the playbacks together on separate screens. Tell Frank I'd like to proceed with the second phase."

Frank cut in. "I was wondering how long it would take for you to tire of the game. Still, it creates a good base of experience in eliciting an understanding for the principles Tom was trying to demonstrate when he described the holograph's parameters. I think you'll find the second phase a lot more interesting. Try and hold your position ... it's loading now."

Kate stared at the re-imaged door. "It looks exactly the same."

"Move around, you'll see the difference," Frank suggested.

Now as Kate moved, the door stayed in the same place instead of repositioning with her. As she stood in front and leaned outward trying to peek past the edge, the door stretched, as if curving away, foiling her attempt. "I thought you said I'd be able to see behind it."

"You have to walk around, not just lean," Frank coached.

Her second try caused the door to appear visually thinner, just like Frank predicted, then vanish altogether. "Where did it go?"

Frank chuckled. "It's still there; you're looking at the side that doesn't exist."

Kate moaned, "This is becoming positively annoying," then used her jets, encircling the door from various directions, causing her to become dizzy. She tried stopping, but hit the wrong jet, making her spin even faster and start to tumble.

By the time she regained stability, her stomach content was threatening to erupt up her esophagus. Kate was afraid to speak, fearing what might exit her mouth besides words, so she closed her eyes, crossed her arms against her chest, curled into a fetal position ... and pressed the switch.

The computer sensed the emergency deactivation, and as part of its standard protocol ... broadcast a cautionary alert throughout the complex.

* * * * *

Zack took a seat while Tom fumbled with his tranquilizer infuser. The Velcro ends weren't quite connecting properly. Zack reached over and held one end. "There ... how's that."

"Thanks, I've got it," Tom answered as he made some final adjustments.

His finger was still poised over a button that would convert the device from manual to automatic mode when Zack excitedly blurted out his news. "Tom ... we want you to work on the Casimir-drive project with us ... as soon as you're able. It's something we hope you'll give serious consideration."

Tom's eyes flashed to Zack's; his body froze as his mind began digesting the input. His arms dropped to the tabletop ... the button forgotten. "What makes you think I could offer anything compared to the brainpower already on the project? Most of them are highly-trained specialists."

"That's just it. Everyone knows a lot about his or her own specific little world. What we need in pulling everything together, is a generalist with enough knowledge across all fields to see the big picture. You're a perfect fit. Well, it'll give you something to think about."

"I doubt if I'll need to do much of that. I'll want something to work on now that I've given Baud the projection problem. Will you send me some preliminary data so I can get a broad idea of the project's status?"

"Absolutely, Tom, that's not a problem whatsoever."

Tom stood. "C'mon, we'll celebrate. Let's go to the cafeteria ... I'll buy. How about coffee and a piece of pie?"

"I don't know. Rose said you should be getting back."

"It's okay. My infuser's in place ... the computer will keep tabs on me."

"Alright, maybe for awhile, but I'd like milk instead of coffee."

Tom laughed. "You guys are always driving a soft bargain, but, okay ... it's a deal."

The men had finished their conversation and snacks, and were just rising from the table when the alarm sounded. "Attention all personnel ... there is a level-4 precautionary alert in the main holography laboratory. Please refrain from entering this area until the problem has been cleared. Thank you."

Tom looked at Zack. "That's where our friends went."

"Yes, I know. They were going to try one of Frank's holographs. Something to do with doors, if I remember."

Tom steadied himself on the table. "Not the one-sided door holo?"

"Yes, I think that's it. Why?"

"It was my idea, hoping it'd help me deal with this crazy notion about space not being able to end. It can be extremely distressing ... maybe even dangerous ... especially if Frank has added all our proposed changes. Was Kate going to attempt it?"

"She wanted to be the first."

Darkness began to crowd in around Tom. He started some of Rose's exercises, but he couldn't concentrate. All he could think about was Kate. "If she gets hurt, it'll be my fault."

"Tom, it's only a level-4 cautionary. They issue those if someone breaks a fingernail. I'm sure everyone's alright."

The darkness around Tom deepened. He was developing tunnel vision, his emotions spiraling out of control ... a formless guilt beast was threatening to charge. Tom stumbled towards the cafeteria's emergency MMT and stepped onto the transmit pad.

Zack followed. "Tom, come back and sit down, please. The alert will almost certainly clear in a minute or two."

"I've got to find Kate. Computer ... take me to the main holography lab."

"I'm sorry, Dr. Hughes. That area is on alert status. Without an over-ride password, I'm unable to fulfill your request."

Tom forced his muscles into action. He jumped off the platform and bolted for the door. Zack was bordering on panic. "Stop him! Please, help me."

Arms reached out as Tom sped by, but none were a match for Tom's adrenalin charged body. He entered the hallway and dashed towards an open grav-lift.

"Rose, talk to me."

Dr. Petals scanned the screen displaying Kate's transmitted vital signs. "She's okay, Frank. Her heart and respiration rates are a little high, but nothing to worry about. She just needs a few minutes to recuperate."

"Larry, do me a favor and turn off that alarm."

"Sorry, John. I'm so used to them I hardly notice anymore."

As soon as the alarm was silenced, a softer beeping began issuing from a countertop. Larry rolled his chair over. "Rose ... it's your med-alert."

Rose hurried over, snatching up the device as she arrived. "Oh no, it's Tom. Most of his signals are in the red. I don't understand how that's possible. His infuser should have activated long before this. Computer, give me the location of Dr. Thomas Hughes."

"Dr. Hughes just tried beaming to your current location moments ago. He is now in a gravity lift, presumably still heading for the same destination."

"Get an e-med tech here, computer ... and make sure they bring a grav-stretcher."

"Message understood, Dr. Petals."

Rose leaned against the counter. "There's a high probability Tom's going to be delusional by the time he arrives. I'm going to need everyone's help restraining him." They all nodded. "Frank, Larry, why don't you wait on either side of the entrance. John, Xarles, be ready with me."

A profound hush fell over the room and outside area. They easily heard the whoosh of opening grav-lift doors ... followed by quick, heavy footfalls approaching on the carpeted hallway.

Surprisingly, Dr. Hughes didn't stop at the doorway. Instead, he sprinted past ... down to the holograph chamber's observation window where he saw Kate lying curled on the floor ... unmoving. "Oh God, I've killed her. I've KILLED her. I ... I ..."

His hands squeaked against the glass as he started to tumble towards the floor. Frank and Larry arrived just in time to catch him. Tom saw the guilt beast take form as it towered over him. Its claws were slashing through the air; froth slavered over its many sharp and pointed teeth. Even though Tom's eyes closed, his mind was conjuring up a vision of escape. His arms and legs began flailing in a pathetic effort to obey. Ahead was a rock wall with just a slit of an opening. Tom ran ... dove through ... spun his head around to confirm if the beast was following ... but the portal was gone. It was Tom's personal one-sided door leading nowhere. All feelings and sensations were gone. There was only inky darkness and utter silence.

Dr. Petals pulled up one of Tom's eyelids, then checked his pulse. "He's alive, but either comatose or catatonic ... I'm not sure which at this point."

She examined the status of Tom's infuser, looked up at her companions and sighed. "It received the activation signal but couldn't comply. He forgot about changing the setting to automatic mode. Help me get him back to the lab. The med-tech should arrive any second."

Frank and Larry each grabbed one of Tom's arms. Xarles and John supported his legs.

The med-tech was stepping off the transmit mat as they reentered the control room doorway. He laid the grav-stretcher down and opened it. "Put him on here."

The men complied with his direction while the tech kneeled and immediately hooked up a portable diagnostic monitor. After viewing several screens, he arose and addressed the group. "My best estimate at this early stage is somewhere between a 3.5 and 4.5 catatonia. He needs to be in a med-plex ... immediately."

The tech strapped Tom in place, then adjusted a hand-held control ... raising the stretcher to a vertical position hovering several inches above the floor. He guided the downward pointed end to the MMT and thumbed a wheel on the control, letting it settle onto the transmit mat. "Computer, please transfer this gentleman to emer-7 west. Preliminary arrangements have already been completed and doctors are standing by."

"Message understood. Transferring ... now."

The med-tech stepped onto the MMT. "Sorry citizens, I must leave without delay ... I have another call. Your colleague has already been processed into the system. The on-line Information Administrator will direct you to the closest station serving his section whenever you request. Computer, next destination, please."

There was a flash and the group of friends was left standing in quiet disbelief.

A breathless Zack came scuttling into the control room. "I've been looking all over for you. I mistakenly got off on the floor above and was searching through the wrong labs. Is Tom here?"

Rose explained what had occurred. Zack fell into a chair, simply shaking his head, "Oh no. That's terrible."

Everyone jumped at a knock on the holograph chamber's window. Kate stood with her forehead pressed against the glass. She was crying.

John hurried over, unlocked the door, and she fell into his arms. "We're all sorry about Tom, Kate. Did you see what happened?"

"I saw enough."

Rose ran her fingers through her hair, then clasped them behind the back of her neck. "I need to take care of a few things, but then, in view of our situation, I'd like it if we all met together before going home. How about my workplace in approximately 45 minutes?"

Rose walked into her office, followed by a woman who remained in the background. Rose's eyes flowed over the group, mentally taking roll. "I'm glad everyone stayed. This is one of those times when we all feel some blame ... and yet ... none of us can logically be held accountable for what happened to Tom.

Zack feels bad about delaying Tom's departure. Larry stated he could have overridden the alert since there wasn't any real danger, but didn't think to do so since that's not normal procedure. Maybe I should have refused Zack's request to talk with Tom. One of us should have told Zack not to mention the holograph

... the list goes on and on. As a result, we're all experiencing the 'what if' syndrome, so we must allow time for tears ... yet also help each other be strong through this crisis. Then, regardless of the outcome ... we must move along.

I'm not going to mince words. I've been informed there's a distinct possibility Tom will slip into level-5, and no one has ever returned from there. The computer is constantly monitoring his condition. If he somehow manages rising to level-3, the neuron stimulators will activate automatically and then there'd be a good chance he'd pull out of his catatonic state altogether."

Everyone's expression became grim. They were all medically knowledgeable enough to understand Tom's level of danger.

Rose continued. "Since I'm personally involved in the situation, and therefore too close to the problem, I've asked Jaen Kozakura if she'd act as grief therapist for the group. She'll be available anytime one of us needs counseling, or just when someone to talk with is needed."

John moved closer, placing a hand on Rose's shoulder. "Where's Kate?"

"She didn't want to be alone tonight, so she's staying at my apartment. I sedated her before returning. Kate is sleeping soundly now. I've decided a short emergency leave is in order for both of us ... to help her get through these first few difficult days."

Rose's head drooped. "The events of the day have certainly caught up with me, and I feel exceptionally tired." She waved the woman that had entered with her forward. "I think you all know Jaen ... I'm going to leave you in her good hands. I'll be in contact with everyone on our private net. Good night."

There were many hugs and tight smiles as Rose walked amid her small circle of companions.

Finally, she turned and slipped through the doorway.

The computer held the dom-bots parked at their storage stations, per Rose's request, while she wandered aimlessly around her apartment. She checked on Kate, then mindlessly cleaned places that were spotlessly hygienic and aligned items that were already perfectly positioned.

An emotionally crushing shock was delivered when she spotted her antique Staunton authentic-wood chess set. The stinging memory that a chess match had been the symbol of her and Tom's ongoing sessions was almost a physical blow. Her skilled estimation told her that Tom had essentially zero chance for recovery. Rose stared for a minute, then opened the display-case door ... reached in ... and gently laid the light-colored king on its side.

She softly breathed, "Game over."

Rose clung to the case for support, as her petite body grew unusually heavy and slowly slid towards the floor. Her previously held private despair began running in tiny raised rivulets over her cheeks.

"He gives not best who gives most; but he gives most who gives best. – If I cannot give bountifully, yet I will give freely, and what I want in my hand, I will supply by my heart."

- Warwick

Chapter 36
Future Past

Two weeks had passed since Tom's mishap. Although his rate of deterioration had slowed, he was nonetheless still sliding deeper into a mental abyss. Medical specialists and the computers had exhausted all possibilities of breaking whatever psychological vise-grip into which he had fallen.

With all hope gone, Dr. Petals had begun to professionally distance herself from Tom. Kate was determined to keep searching ... until the day Tom took his last breath. If there was nothing in the present ... maybe, with Rose's help, she'd be able to find some valuable piece of data in the past.

Rose decided to scrutinize the data again. She was glad to have someone looking over her shoulder making sure nothing would be missed. "I keep hoping to find something new, Kate, but so far ... it doesn't look like there's anything we can use.

This downward spike in his self-image when he had the chance to ask that girl out ... and couldn't ... broke the back of what little ego he had. Then this huge barb of guilt when he found out she didn't have a date for the prom was the final blow. I had to rescale the screen display twice to fit the peaks. His waveforms slide slowly, but continually down from that point onward.

The computers have sifted through the data forwards, backwards, and probably even upside down. All the other medical techs agree with our findings, too. Tom appears to have crawled so far out on a psychological limb, there's just no way of reaching him.

As long as he holds somewhere in the level-4 area, we're in the game. The neuron-stimulators are still standing by and ready to engage if he spontaneously rises anywhere near level-3. At that point, the probability is higher that he'll come out of it." She sighed. "If only we could've somehow prevented him from getting that far out on the limb in the first place."

Kate glanced away. "Maybe that would work."

"I'm not following."

"What you just said. You just gave me an idea. I'll call you later."

Kate hustled towards the MMT station.

The computer realized Dr. Rosalba Petals was busy. A few nanoseconds passed as it considered whether the incoming call would qualify as an emergency. It decided not, so patiently waited while quietly signaling for her attention. Rose finished dictating her latest update, leaned back, and stretched. "Yes, computer?"

"Dr. Khattyba Bright is anxiously awaiting permission to beam directly into your office. Is clearance authorized?"

"Please. By all means, proceed."

Kate appeared almost instantly. Rose noticed the strain on her face as she tried moving forward, even before her body completely stabilized. A small folder of printouts on recyclable vellum began waving madly through the air. "Rose! I've got it!"

"I assume this concerns helping Tom?"

"Yes. There are inherent risks, but I believe they are absolutely minimal." Kate laid the info pack on Rose's workspace and immediately began pacing. "I'll need the time council's permission before implementing ... and to get theirs ... I need your endorsement first."

"Computer, is there anything remaining that requires my personal attention today?"

"Checking appointment list, Dr. Petals. All have left notice they are willing to reschedule, if necessary, except for Darlyne Rosenberg. She's already been waiting for two days."

"Contact Ms. Rosenberg. Inform her she's next. When she's ready, give me a minute to prepare, then beam her directly here. Defer the others."

Rose picked up the packet. "This will have to wait a short time, Khatty. Sorry. Of course, with a patient here, you'll need to leave."

"No problem, Rose. I was going to disappear anyway." She gestured towards the packet. "Otherwise, I'd be trying to point out all the pluses, minuses, and possible pitfalls of this rather unorthodox scenario.

Besides, that'll give me time to run a retrograde psych profile, compare it against the standardized forward looking model, and look for divergence in either direction starting at the center."

"Excellent idea. That will confirm or refute whether the congruency algorithms are resonant and properly aligned. What are the early indications?"

"Less than .1 percent skew at situation of initial impact, then 99.8 percent congruence to present time."

"Does that include cyclics and identities?"

"Yes. On all levels."

"That's impressive work, Khatty. Maybe you should consider Psych Tech for your next career."

"The only interest I have now ... is getting Tom back. Until then, I'm not going to be worth much for anything else."

"Well, we certainly don't want to lose you, too. Let me take care of Ms. Rosenberg and I'll attack your proposal."

"Thanks, Rose."

"You bet. Remember, Tom's important to all of us ... so are you. I'll call as soon as I develop an opinion. You understand, it'll have to be wholly unbiased and purely objective?"

"That's as close to a guarantee for safety and success as possible." Kate added coyly, "In my opinion, you're the only person qualified to do the critique."

Rose chuckled. "Take your buttering-up brush and get out of here, I've got work to do."

Kate stepped onto the transport mat. "See you ... sis."

Rose concluded her session with Darlyne, recording her impressions and opening recommendations afterward. Darlyne was still a relatively new contact, and Rose wanted at least one additional in-person encounter before deciding whether her case could be competently handled by the addition of yet another holographic Dr. Petals. It would be number 27, and was the only way Rose could keep up with her 50-hour work week, when she treated an average 520 clients daily. "Computer."

"Yes, Dr. Petals?"

"Please assign a 'do not disturb' to my station. Route through only emergency or Dr. Bright's calls."

"Message understood."

Rose picked up Kate's submission and moved from her chair to the one reserved for patients. It was designed to help them relax. As she maneuvered to become comfortable, the semi-solid fabric became more elastic. Once she settled, the covering compensated for her body weight and became firmer again. She smiled at the remembrance of Tom's first session in it.

Rose flipped the cover over and began to read. As each page was turned, she became more excited ... and allowed herself to become somewhat optimistic. The chair tried to compensate by increasing its subtle massage until the intensity finally increased above the subliminal level.

"Computer, I'm alright. You can return the chair to its normal settings."

"Very well, Dr. Petals. I was becoming concerned."

When Rose finished, she closed the report and stared at the changing, soothing patterns flowing across the ceiling. "My stars, this just might work."

"Were you addressing me, Dr. Petals?"

"No, computer. Just mumbling. In my line of work, you find yourself doing that a lot."

"I understand."

"Computer, please see if you can reach Xarles Moody." Rose checked the time. "Aw, powdered moon dust ... he's probably at home." She sighed. "Oh well, his residence number is in my private comm list."

"Mr. Xarles Moody, as in president pro tempore of the time council?"

"Yes, that's the one."

A few heartbeats passed. "Link is established, Dr. Petals. Mr. Moody requested voice only. He is relaxing in his hot tub."

"Understood."

"Hello ... Rose?"

"Yes, Xarles. I deeply apologize for disturbing you at home, but I have a situation where time may be of the essence."

"How can I help?"

"It concerns a time-change proposal submitted by Khatty Bright."

"Why the urgency? Can't it go through proper channels?"

"I haven't told Khatty yet, but Tom Hughes has just slipped into a level-5 catatonia."

"I know that's bad. What's the prognosis?"

"In about two weeks his brain stem will begin deteriorating and the autonomic nervous system will begin to fail. We can keep him alive for a while longer, but his vegetative condition will quickly intensify to a point where all life functions will eventually be completely dependent on machine support.

Even that support will fail as his vital systems begin to shut down. Once that happens, he'll have approximately five to seven days before his cells start dying of hyper-toxicity. Death will follow shortly thereafter."

Xarles sat up in his tub. "I'm terribly sorry to hear this, Rose. And yet, I fail to make a connection with Kate's proposal."

"It's all explained in Khatty's documents. I'll have her ship me a complete set describing the project, attach my E-sig, then send copies to everyone on the council. The connection and urgency will become clear once you read it. I grant you, it's a decidedly unconventional method of treatment, but if Khatty succeeds in proving its validity, then I'm hoping you can give it top priority."

"If it warrants the condition ... I'll make it happen."

"Thank you. Again, I'm sorry for the after-hours call."

"No problem, Rose. I know you wouldn't exercise the option if you didn't consider it vitally important."

"Goodnight, Xarles."

"Computer, see if Khatty is handy."

"Checking, Dr. Petals. Yes. Dr. Bright is available. Shall I establish visual and/or vocal communication?"

"That won't be necessary if she can beam to my office."

"I will relay the message, Dr. Petals."

Seconds later, Kate appeared and stepped off the platform. "Rose, please tell me you have good news."

"That all depends. How much of this were you able to verify?"

"I ran 443 simulations and found a miniscule 5,769 minor variations."

"That's all? Wonderful. What about the timeline divergence accumulation factors?"

"A total of 1,957 deviations, with a maximum discrepancy of 1.414 units from primary, occurring approximately 9 years, 2 months after introduction of the designated change at target date."

"You've found no other negative factors?"

"Absolutely none."

"What about the risks?"

"Nothing more obvious than on any other mission."

"Not quite true, Khatty. Although the variations are minuscule, they exist. One of them may affect Tom's performance, or yours, during that wild trip forward through time. Judging from the story you told me, the risk to you is probably ten times greater than Tom's. It's possible the change could cost you your life. That's quite a gift. Are you sure?"

"Ten times minuscule, is still minuscule."

"What about the present? Even if you manage to dodge all those bullets of deviation, because of the change you introduce in the past, he may not love you upon arrival here."

Kate lowered her eyes. "I'll live. If we don't do something, Tom won't."

Rose raised an eyebrow. Did Kate already know about Tom?

Kate didn't know how much longer she could keep it together. Her eyes started to glisten. "Tom wouldn't think twice about doing the same for me." A tear rolled down her cheek.

Rose grimaced. "You understand, it's my job to play the devil's advocate in these situations?"

"Completely. We've been through this before."

"True. But this time it's personal, so I suppose I'm being ultraconservative and overly sensitive." Rose sighed with relief. "Okay, Khatty. I'm convinced you've done your homework ... again. You've got your endorsement."

"Rose ... I just found out about Tom."

They hugged and sobbed in each other's arms while their professional masks dissolved in a trickle of salty water. Rose grabbed a tissue, blew her nose, then offered the dispenser to Kate. "I want you to send me a complete copy of the project ... include all the details, not just overviews. The red tape has already been cut, so we're halfway there. Have you thought about who to send back?"

Kate sniffled and dried her eyes. "Altair Byrngelson. She's the correct age, has a thorough knowledge of the target period, and has performed over a hundred simulations. It'll be her first real-world outing, but in my opinion, she's ready, and certainly enthusiastic.

When I broached the subject and she realized whom she'd be helping, she reached over and cleared the screen, stating that all the other candidates had just become ineffectual and unacceptable."

Rose nodded. "The danger to Altair is almost nil, but her performance will be crucial. It's the cornerstone of success for the entire mission. Are you comfortable entrusting that kind of responsibility to a rookie?"

Kate smiled. "Seems like I recall someone asking that question about me once, but I ended up going anyway."

"John's always been easier on people than me. I'll be relieved when he can resume handling the time computation checks again. This double duty is killing me. The stakes are a lot higher now, too."

"I fully understand the gamble. Altair's still my choice."

"Psych profiles only tell us so much, but since she's your protégé, I'll skip the detail and run a standard background personality test cross-indexed against the mission profile. If there are no red flags, I'll defer to your judgment. Let's get things started."

Two days later, Kate and her team completed the project's checklists. Altair was given a final briefing. She was surprised at the subtle simplicity of the objective, yet appreciated the tremendous consequence of its impact.

Rose walked off an MMT platform, over to Kate, and placed a hand on her shoulder. "I'm going to prep Tom. He'll need to be restrained and sedated. I've also asked the team to keep an eye on you, too. Obviously, I'm hoping for the best, but it's only prudent to prepare for the worst. When were you planning to join me?"

"As soon as Altair beams out. She'll spend approximately two weeks in the past, but to us, the project will evolve almost instantaneously, and her return will only be seconds later. I've asked her to join us upon her arrival. She deserves to be present when Tom awakens."

"If he awakens."

"No, Rose. I won't accept that premise. When he awakens. Maybe he won't love me anymore ... I guess it's possible he may not even like me. But if this works, he'll live. At this point, that's the only issue of importance."

"Okay, I'll see you in Tom's room."

"How are you doing, Altair?"

"I'm sorry, Kate. I'm really on edge."

"No need to apologize. In fact, if you weren't nervous, I'd be worried. Try humming. That always seems to work for me. As the countdown nears zero, close your eyes. The next thing you know, someone in the past will be tapping your shoulder saying you've arrived. After that, you'll probably be so excited you won't have time to be nervous anymore."

Altair threw her arms around Kate. "Thanks for your belief in me. I promise I won't let you down ... or Tom. I'll get the job done even if I have to punch her in the nose."

Kate laughed. "After seeing your propensity to convince, I doubt if that'll be necessary." A team member signaled Kate. She nodded. "They're ready, Altair. Up you go."

Altair stepped upon the transmit mat, smiled ... and started humming. Immediately after the flash, Kate ran for the MMT platform ... then stopped. She remembered that, to her, it would only be seconds before Altair returned.

Altair beamed back. The first things Kate noticed were the schoolbooks and a change in clothing. It took Altair a moment to get reoriented. When she noticed Kate, she shouted, "Kate! It worked." She jumped off the platform and hugged her mentor tightly. "Oh, I'm so glad you're still here. I thought you'd be with Rose."

"I decided to wait so we could beam over together."

Kate and Altair stepped off the public MMT's mat in the med-plex's waiting room. "It's this way, Altair."

Medi-bots floated overhead on magnetic ceiling tracks as the pair made their way down the hallway. After passing through the holodoor, they found Rose sitting on the other side. Kate looked to Tom, then Rose. "Any change?"

"No. Not yet. We'll have to wait while the sedation wears off."

Altair's gaze drifted from one lady to the other. "Why the sedation? I thought he was comatose."

Rose answered, "Not comatose ... catatonic. He could come out of it at any time. The possibility exists he might be a raving maniac. That's the reason for the sedative and restraints. This way we'll be able to observe him waking gradually. The brainwave monitor will give us advance warning if he's going to be dangerous. Were you able to convince the girl?"

Altair nodded. "Yes. It was actually easy. She already liked him. He just kept shying away."

Tom moaned. His eyelids fluttered.

Rose pushed up from her chair. "He's coming around. We'll know soon." She began intently studying an angled, overhead bank of display panels.

Kate stood next to his bed. Tom's eyes rolled slowly towards her. "Ka ... Ka", he cleared his throat, "Kate. What happened?"

"Easy, Tom. You've had a close call, but you're going to be okay now."

He choked on a short laugh. "Another one? I thought ... we ... were ... past all that ... when we finally arrived ... in your time." His hand moved towards her, but was stopped short. He raised his head just enough to check the impediment. "Why am I ... tied down?"

Rose walked over and began releasing the straps. "These were just a precaution, Tom. Your scans are normal. I'm extremely happy to say these aren't needed. Welcome back."

"Scans? Rose..."

She put a finger to his lips. "I want you to rest for at least a few more minutes. Those are doctor's orders. Then I'll reveal everything that's happened."

Rose ordered medications through the room's computer interface and then inquired of Tom, "Does your head hurt? Any pressure?"

"There's a little pain."

Rose updated the list and asked the machine to execute her instructions. "Okay, Tom, it's important that you close your eyes, relax, and remain quiet."

A multi-armed apparatus swung out from the wall while several colored liquids ran into a small bottle that began agitating. The resulting mixture was pressurized in an air gun. Finally, with a hiss of air, it shot into Tom's arm.

Rose requested the computer to give her a ten-minute silent count.

"The allotted time period has elapsed, Dr. Petals."

"Thank you, computer. Tom, how do you feel now?"

He opened his eyes, rolled his head on the pillow, and sat up. "Wow. I don't know what that stuff was, but can I have some more?"

Rose chuckled. "Sorry, only one medical cocktail to a customer. I don't think you want us peeling you off the ceiling. Okay, Tom, I need to ask you a few questions. Feel up to it?"

"Sure."

"Do you remember a girl named Shannon when you were in high school?"

Tom was stunned. "What in the world does she have to do with anything?"

"Please, it's important."

"We dated our senior year and most of the following summer."

"How did you meet?"

"In physics class."

"No ... how did you start dating?"

"That's kind of embarrassing. I always wanted to ask her out, but my dad had pretty much beat my self-confidence into the ground. Shannon asked me to a Sadie Hawkins dance."

"That's a tradition where the girl asks the boy?"

"Yes."

"What happened after that?"

"We had a good time and got to like each other. Pretty soon we were dating steadily. Rose, please, this is really starting to worry me. Why all these questions about a girl from my past who has been dead and buried for three hundred years?"

"It'll become clear in a minute. One more question, Tom. How do you feel about Kate?"

"I'm not sure what you mean."

"Do you hate ... like ... love her? What?"

Tom stared. "Why would I love Kate?"

Kate's eyes closed as her hands clenched around the bed rail. Rose turned away. The room became utterly quiet except for the beeping and clicking of medical hardware.

Tom broke the silence. "Hey ... just because she's the prettiest, smartest, sexiest, and most wonderful lady I've ever met. We've been through things other people couldn't even imagine ... saved each other's lives ... and she's made me happy ... which isn't an easy task. I ask you ... is that enough reason to love her?" He smiled and took Kate's hand. "That part of my memory is fine. Yes. I love her ... with all my heart."

Tom found himself in a room with three laughing females ... crying their eyes out at the same time.

Tom pleaded, "Now, will someone please tell me what's going on?"

Kate squeezed his hand. "We changed your past."

"Why?"

Rose answered. "I'll explain. What's the last thing you remember?"

"Kate was inside the one-sided door hologram. Something went wrong, and I couldn't get to her."

"Do you recall our conversation about how mentally defenseless you'd be in a stressful situation?"

Tom nodded. "I think so."

"When you thought something had happened to Kate, you felt responsible. Everything crashed down on you. Since you were obviously an introverted child, most of your ego defense mechanisms basically self-destructed long ago because of your father's constant badgering and belittling. We stripped away whatever was left during our sessions.

You've always seen yourself as deeply flawed. This perspective would have made it almost impossible for you to ask your apparent dream girl for a date. Your conscious mind was terrified of her rejection while your subconscious was horrified at the thought of her accepting. In that case, your imperfections would have been projected onto her signifying that she was inadequate, and that was totally unacceptable. This theory also explains your growing angst around Kate.

All of these previously combined incidents prevented you from ever dating Shannon in your original timeline. That stage in your life proved to be the biggest single downward spike of your self-image. You never recovered. It was the beginning of a long constant slide toward mental oblivion.

It led to one failed relationship after another, which, over time, culminated in a total withdrawal from any social life.

As your loneliness and frustrations grew, you turned all your energies towards your career, which was probably the single greatest factor saving you from suicide. Your fight to stay alive and protect Kate, during your forward travel through time, was actually a temporary boost for your ego.

Once you arrived here, however, the dangerous challenges disappeared and your career position became threatened. Your single, long-time bastion of support crumbled. Couple that with your underlying doubt that you deserved Kate, which you expressed even as you were falling in love with her, and your mental conflicts eventually assumed undefeatable proportions."

"You're saying ... I went nuts."

"Fundamentally, your perception of reality formed a ball and rolled into a dark, unreachable corner of your mind, never to be heard from again. You would have died. The only way to save you was modify that dreadful negative spike. So, we sent Altair back and had her talk Shannon into asking you to that dance. The rest, as they say, is history."

"You just indicated I would have rejected the girl. What would have been different this time?"

"Ah. That was Kate's stroke of genius. The key is the fact that the girl approached you. It nudged your concept of self up a notch, opening a small time-based window of opportunity which allowed for your acceptance."

"Is that all you changed?"

"Kate's simulations projected other trivial associated differences that always exist with a time alteration. Nevertheless, the substantial answer to your question is 'yes'. There was an outside possibility one of those small variations may have distended through the years, causing some major upheaval in your life ... even madness ... hence the precautions. That danger always exists, too, but particularly in this case, the end more than justified the means."

"So I'm different?"

"Only in your interpretation of self ... your inward view. You'll probably externalize almost exactly the same as before."

"But I'm cured?"

Rose gave him a strained smile. "Yes and no. Yes, I'm confident you're out of danger. No, this isn't over yet. It's a three-part ... adventure. The first ... hardest part is over. Next, I'm expecting a normal reaction from our sessions of Time Displacement Hypnotherapy. It would eventually have happened anyway. You just took a rather unusual shortcut. That's one problem ... and there's no predicting when the response will occur. It's different for everyone."

"What symptoms do I look for?"

"That's another problem. I can't tell you. Being a physicist, you're obviously familiar with the old Heisenberg uncertainty principle. In certain instances, subatomic particles for example, the very act of observation can change or influence an object. The same basis exists here. If I try and explain what to anticipate, the attendant expectation may alter the future outcome of the actual experience. We'll all just have to wait and see."

"That's not at all comforting."

"Sorry ... but for now, it's the best I can do."

"When can I leave?"

"Soon as you agree to my prescription."

"For drugs?"

"No, your routine for the next couple of weeks. No exertion. You are to stay home ... relax and rest. Do some reading ... listen to music ... whatever. I want you to recover some physical strength before returning to work. Oh, there's one other thing." Rose waved Altair over. "I'd better introduce this young lady so you can express an appreciation for her effort."

"Many are always praising the by-gone time, for it is natural that the old should extol the days of their youth; the weak, the time of their strength; the sick, the season of their vigor; and the disappointed, the spring-tide of their hopes."

- C. Bingham

Chapter 37
Shock Value

Tom was relaxing a few days later, attempting to enjoy some sort of modern syncopated music, when Kate beamed into the apartment. A box was positioned on either side of the mat by her feet. He arose and walked her way. "Want some help with the packages?"

"No. They're on grav pads. Thanks anyway." Kate removed a small patch of encoded material affixed to the top of each box. Afterwards, she quickly scanned the latest arrangement of her apartment. "I guess I'll put them in the atrium."

She crossed the floor and placed one patch on either end of a table, then pressed a button on her wrist device. Each box rose from the transmit pad, floated over, and landed softly on its respective patch. "These are for you. It's part of a surprise Larry, Frank, myself, and many others have been working."

Tom inspected the outside of the boxes. "What's in them?"

"If I told you, that would ruin the surprise, silly. Go ahead ... open them."

Tom grinned, sat on the sofa, and began work on one of the packages. As he began removing the contents, his hands froze ... because he wasn't sure what he was seeing. "Kate ... is this for real? It looks like part of my CD and video collection." He excitedly opened the second box. "Wow. More of them ... this is great. How'd you do it?"

"At first, I thought it'd be easy. I figured I'd contact my friends in the past, have them gather your recordings, then transmit the entire package forward, but ... things got complicated.

Unfortunately, because of our jaunt into the Jurassic and then the delay before our arrival here, I didn't get the message to them in time. The authorities padlocked your home after it was discovered you were missing.

To make things more difficult, the local mayor thought it'd be good economics for the area having your home added to the community tours. Following that, a day guard was posted, and a security system installed.

In the end, my friends took turns sneaking your belongings out a few at a time and making duplicates before having them returned. Of course, while they were at it, they used more contemporary media for compatibility. They did their best to make them look the same."

Tom reexamined his treasures. "They look identical to me."

"Anyway, it took a lot longer than originally planned, but these boxes constitute the last shipment. The rest are hidden in a holoroom I had the computer construct. That's one of the reasons I kept changing the look of the apartment, so you wouldn't get suspicious. It's in a back corner. Come on ... it's time for the grand unveiling."

They walked to what looked like the corner of two walls. "Computer."

"Yes, Dr. Bright?"

"Remove the holoroom, please." A few moments later a real corner of the apartment was revealed. Several boxes were stacked on the carpeting. "That's all of it, Tom. Your complete video and music collection."

He enfolded her into his arms and they slowly rocked together to some common, unheard, natural rhythm. "Kate, I don't know what to say, except thank you."

"You're more than welcome, Tom. Everyone was glad to help. We're all happy and relieved that you're getting well." She grinned. "By the way, your Pez dispensers are here, too."

"It's quite a mental jolt seeing all this stuff again. There are a lot of memories attached."

Tom froze.

Kate's cheerful expression changed to one of alarm. "Tom ... what's wrong?"

"Huh? Oh, sorry, Kate. I didn't mean to frighten you, but the shock of seeing all these familiar things just gave me an idea how we might help John get his memory back. We'll need Frank's expertise for sure ... Rose will probably want to oversee the project ... and anyone else wanting a part is certainly welcome." He led her back to the sofa. "Sit ... listen ... tell me what you think."

Rose had indeed wanted to coordinate the project. Her most important input had been not to worry about the dialogue. She suggested keeping it simple and repeating only the high points to focus its impact.

John was dressed in a white suit and stationed by the shallow end of a health club's indoor pool. He had been asked not to say or do anything.

Frank had developed a holographic scene after having watched several replays of Kate's micro recorder disks salvaged from her original wrist device, WD7. The lights were dimmed low ... almost off. Kate and Tom took their places in the dark. The stage was set ... the holograph was initiated.

As the light level slowly intensified, the swimming pool became a pond with an underground stream flowing into one end, and the surrounding enclosure assumed the manifestation of a large limestone cavern.

Tom appeared to enter from a rocky portal in a front wall. He was dirty, torn, and obviously battered. Kate was likewise soiled and disheveled.

She moved between the two men and spoke her opening lines. "Dr. Hughes ... I'd like to introduce you to Dr. Picus."

Tom's smile turned into a snarl. "I don't want to hurt you for the world, Miss Bright, so please move aside."

"Please control yourself, Dr. Hughes. This whole unfortunate incident is the result of an accident."

"After forty years of perfect machine functioning, I find that extremely difficult to accept."

The onlookers outside the holograph's periphery could almost visualize John's cerebral gears beginning to turn. He narrowed his eyes and slowly shook his head, trying to clear and then organize his thoughts.

Tom ran at Kate. She shrieked. He sidestepped around her and lowered his shoulder into John's stomach, driving them into the pool. Tom pulled John up by the coat lapels. "Okay, Picus. I'll listen to your explanation, but it had better be good or we'll continue this conversation at another time."

John spluttered and spit out some water. He was dazed for a minute, after which, the connection of memories hit him like a slap. He stumbled, but Tom caught him.

John finally managed to cough out, "Tom, what's the matter with you? Isn't it enough to play an imbecilic Neanderthal once? Why repeat the offense? I ... I ... oh my ... great belts of Jupiter ... I remember everything!"

Frank killed the holograph. Everyone cheered and gathered by the pool's steps. John grabbed Tom by the shoulders. "You and Kate almost killed by a dinosaur ... Larry going back ... my going back ... the snake bite ... my getting sick and ... and that's it until my body was restored and revived here. What happened in-between?"

"To you or us?"

"Both!"

"Let's get out of the water and dry off, John. We can talk in your office."

They walked up the steps. Kate handed each a towel. Everyone was jabbering excitedly ... then became quietly amused at John and Rose.

His shoes squished while trundling towards his office, drying his hair, and mumbling incessantly about all the work that needed to be updated. Rose was walking beside him, chattering to herself on the subject of paroxysmal stimuli.

Frank pulled Tom aside. "Do you remember when you first arrived? You said something about paying us back for all the help. First off, you never owed us anything, but if you ever thought you did, you can certainly forget that idea now. Your imaginary debt is more than paid in full."

He waved to the others. "Come on everyone. Tom and Kate are going to bring John up to date. This is a story I'd like to hear myself."

Everyone, except John, sat dumbfounded as the couple finished their story. He stood and stared at the floor. "This is one memory I could certainly endure being without. Everything that happened is obviously entirely my fault. In one brash moment, I began a turn of events that nearly cost the lives of four people, including my own."

John turned ... facing Kate and Tom. "I'm exceedingly regretful. I sincerely hope the two of you can find a way to pardon my grievous error, because I seriously doubt if there's any way possible to forgive myself."

Tom was on him like a shot. "I just got off that train. I'm not allowing you to even get on board. I'm living proof thoughts like those can utterly destroy your life. Yes, you did something absolutely horrible. You proved beyond any doubt you're human ... you made a mistake. Well, I'm sorry, too, because just like the rest of us ... you'll have to find a way of living with it ... and move on.

I might have sympathized with you before, but not anymore. We're all alive and doing just fine, so I'll give you fair warning. Anytime you feel guilty because of what happened, I'll kick your butt ... and if required ... I'll continue kicking until the time comes when you'll start bearing a strong resemblance to Quasimodo."

John stared for a few seconds ... then shocked everyone. He smiled broadly and gratefully extended his hand.

It was a week later. Tom was sitting with his eyes closed, listening to music through wireless headphones. Kate beamed into the apartment and walked over by his side. She studied his face for a moment before tapping him on the shoulder.

He looked up. "Oh, hi, kiddo. I was just waxing nostalgic while enjoying my favorite vocalists which you and your friends were so kind to obtain for me."

"Which ones are they?"

"Neil Diamond and Olivia Newton-John. I just switched to Olivia."

"I remember them from my one-year assignment spent in your time. Put them on the main audio system ... I'll pull over a chair and listen with you."

The last selection finished playing, and the couple sat in quiet appreciation of the performer's talent for a few minutes. Tom reached over and touched her hand with a finger. "What if Shannon and I had become permanent when you sent Altair back?"

Kate turned and smiled. "I knew that couldn't happen."

Tom frowned. "How can you be so sure?"

"Because you would always wait for your true love ... and that only occurs when split-aparts find each other. Remember the movie?"

"So why couldn't Shannon have proven to be my split-apart?"

Kate shook her head. "That's impossible ... because I'm your split-apart."

Tom grinned. "Hey, that reminds me, I have two presents for you. I'll give you one now, and the other sometime before you fall asleep tonight."

"Are they because of any particular reason?"

"Yes. I love you. Is that good enough?"

She clasped his hand. "Maybe. I'll think about it."

Tom reached under his chair and pulled out a small box. "Here ... see what you think of this."

Kate lifted the lid and drew a deep breath. "Oh, Tom, it looks like my old favorite - WD7 ... except this is beautifully finished."

"Well, before you get too misty eyed, I have to inform you the top is strictly cosmetic. There's a full-function model-18 underneath. According to Larry ... it's the latest and greatest. I also took some liberty and named it for you. Look on the back."

She turned the wrist device over and found a depiction of a star with rays extending in all directions near the bottom half. There was an inscription above: 'To Kate, the light of my life. This is Nan. She'll protect you whenever I'm not around. Love forever, Tom'.

Kate moved onto his lap and hugged him. She held the device against her chest as a tear rolled down her cheek. "Thank you ... my love."

"Uh, Kate. Be careful how you handle those buttons. One of the new features is a miniature built-in laser."

Kate sat on the edge of the bed and pretended to pout. Tom rose up on an elbow. "Something wrong?"

"You said there was a second present."

"True ... and I said you'd get it before you fell asleep."

He silently watched and waited. She arose and looked around the room. "It must be in here somewhere. This is the last place I'd be before going to sleep." Finally, Kate gave up and jumped back into the bed. She immediately scooted over next to Tom and began kissing him around the face. "Is this ... what you ... had in mind?"

"We could make it number three, but for now, you should start on your own side of the bed."

"What?"

"Trust me."

"Hmm. That could be a toughie. But I'll try." Kate slid back and laid her head on the pillow ... instantly raising it again. "What in galaxy centers is this? Night light, computer."

"Yes, Dr. Bright."

"Tom ... there's a wad of cloth under my pillow case."

"Imagine that. We must speak with the maid."

Kate unfolded the piece of material and simply stared at the object inside. Then ... she started to cry.

"Kate ... I'm really confused. According to the computer and everyone I've asked ... this is still a perfectly accepted tradition. Is something wrong ... don't you want it?"

She wiped her face with her hand and waited until she could talk. "I positively love it." The item was placed in his hand and she curled his fingers around it. "Hold onto it for awhile. I have concerns I've been meaning to discuss with you for quite some time, but with everything that's happened, I simply never got the chance. Remember when I told you the directors of TheTwenty project had to get authorization from the world council?"

"Yes."

"Certain concessions had to be guaranteed. Once these assurances were given, the directors gained even more latitude than they expected.

All of TheTwenty have altered DNA. My IQ is 195. John's is conservatively estimated at 225. The council demanded that we couldn't pass on our altered DNA and attempt to create a super-race. As a result of that stipulation ... all of us are also sterile, and just to make sure the women couldn't even carry an implanted child, our genes were modified to induce mullerian ductagenesis."

"What in the world is that?"

"Let's just say it's characterized by the lack of a uterus."

Tom brushed her cheek with the back of his fingers. "Is that it?"

"No. It gets worse. Remember when I said we had no idea who our parents were?"

"Yes. Go on."

"That's because we didn't have any parents in the sense of the word. Our entire DNA structure was computer generated and assembled from a library of cataloged genealogical traits."

"Remind me to thank the computer."

"One other little tidbit ... the average lifetime of people in my time is between 120 and 130 years. That's the natural age the body is capable of achieving if it can avoid contracting disease and accumulating cellular toxins. If you recall, that's one of the MMTs' expel cycle functions. My lifetime is projected to be approximately 200 years. Our research has allowed us to extend the average individual's age to about that same timeframe, if they undertake a regimen of synthesized drugs once every seven years. Considering the expel process is now available to you, the drugs can extend your life, too. In view of all this information ... do you still want to offer me the second gift?"

Tom reached over, spread her hand open, and slipped the ring on her finger. "You were physically made ... I was psychologically re-made. I think that pretty much makes us a perfect pair. Marry me, Kate."

She pressed against him.

Gift three was ... emotively electric.

"Every delay is hateful, but it gives wisdom."
- Publius Syrus

Chapter 38
A Late Return

John sat behind his desk and pressed a key that activated the direct link to his personal aide. "Miss Cramdin?"

"Yes, Dr. Picus."

"Has the remainder of the documents and confirmations arrived yet?"

"Yes, sir. They came in a few minutes ago."

"Good. Then it's time to notify our unwary couple. Are you prepared?"

"Yes, sir. I've been practicing putting on my troubled face all morning."

"Very well ... contact them."

Tom eased through the holodoor into the outer office. "Hi, Alyce. Do you know what John wants?"

"No, sir. He just wanted you here with as little delay as possible."

"Should I go in?"

"No. Not yet. This concerns you and Kate. He wants to see you both. Please have a seat while you're waiting."

Kate flowed through the doorway just as he was about to sit. "Hi, Tom. Did you get a call, too?"

"Yes. Apparently, John wants to see us together. Got any idea what's going on?" Kate shook her head.

Miss Cramdin announced they could go through, did her best to frown ... then returned to her work.

John shot to his feet as they entered. He pointed at the chairs, "Don't say anything ... just sit," and began pacing. He looked mad enough to chew Martian rocks and spit out red beach-sand in their place. "I've just received some distressing information that centers around the two of you. Tom, I doubt if you'll grasp the inference of the report, so I'll let Kate read it and bring you up to date."

The couple exchanged a questioning glance as John handed her a packet of papers. A medley of expressions played across her face, revealing her puzzlement as she leafed through the material. She shrieked, jumped out of her seat, threw her arms around John, and kissed him on the cheek. "Thank you. This is absolutely wonderful."

A small, satisfied grin formed on his face. "It's an engagement present from all of us."

Tom stood, waiting in bewilderment. "What is?"

"This is a special travel package," Kate explained. "It's called the 'Grand Tour'. We'll leave earth for one of the low-orbit space docks ... spend some time investigating there, and then continue on to L4. That's the scientifically oriented space-based city-society, whereas L5 is mostly business and commercial enterprises. From there, we travel to earth's moon.

A few days later, it's on to Mars via the inner MMT ring, where we'll spend a week. Finally, it's out to TheBelt for a brief stay using the outer MMT ring ... then return home along the same path."

Tom was stunned. "I haven't even had a chance to see what lies outside an earth city yet."

Kate chuckled. "Okay, we'll preface our trip with a few days of local sightseeing. How's that?"

"You make the whole thing sound so ... ordinary."

She shrugged. "We'll just have to be careful in TheBelt. It's still mostly unexplored ... making it an easy place to get lost. We'll need a good guide."

"I'm afraid we also have somewhat of an ulterior motive," John interjected. "The MMTs' upgrades are complete and tested. They're earlier than expected, so we're sending them along with you for copying, instead of a separate courier.

A hard-case protected original with internal labeling guarantees the software files won't become corrupted en route. The hardware has already been transmitted to several locations where it can be reproduced as required.

After reflecting on Tom's Discovery-Day dissertation ... MMT modifications are nothing with which I want to take any unnecessary chances."

* * * * *

Tom sat up in bed and stretched. A holographic sun beamed through the holographic window into Kate's bedroom. He leaned over and kissed her bare shoulder. "Hey, sleepy head. C'mon, get up. You promised to show me around outside the city this morning. It looks like a great day."

She nuzzled down into the pillow. "Mmm. It's always beautiful inside."

"How can I find out what the weather is like outside?"

"Ask the computer. It'll display all the current info on any screen."

Tom bounced out of bed and ran into Kate's study. "Computer, display the outside weather information."

A moment later, he was overwhelmed. Row after row of numbers scrolled by, depicting the status for the entire planet. Barometric pressures, isobar patterns, wind speeds, cloud-cover models, winds aloft, temperature ranges, and hundreds of other meteorological data bits danced across the monitor in a dazzling display of technology run amok.

He shook his head. "No, no, no, no. Give me just the local area ... and only the basics. Sunny or raining, current temperature, stuff like that. No more than one screen. Keep it simple."

Tom finally retrieved what he wanted and returned to the bedroom. Kate was in the shower. He poked his head through the bathroom holodoor. "Kate, I got the weather. It'll be nice outside, too."

"What?"

"It's GOING TO BE NICE today."

"Okay, I'll be out in a minute."

Tom backed out but then stuck his head through once more. "By the way, I did some reprogramming of your dom-bots."

"What?"

"I said I changed the DOM-BOTS."

"The dom-bots? I'm sorry, Tom. Between the shampoo in my ears and the shower spray, I can't hear you."

"NEVER MIND. I'll tell you later."

Kate stepped from the shower, dried off, and dropped the towel in front of her. She was combing her hair when a dom-bot rolled up from behind and attempted to reach the towel. The automatic ventilation fan was running and had camouflaged the low tone of the machine's approach.

A gruff voice barked, "Hey, lady, get outta' my way or I'll cap your knees."

Kate yelped and jumped aside, staring at the small electro-mechanical entity, not believing what it had said. A few seconds later, she laughed at herself for thinking the faithful domestic robot might actually harm her ... then entered the bedroom, quickly dressed, and stomped off ... searching for Tom.

She found him in the kitchen munching on a piece of toast. Her expression stopped him mid-crunch. Kate tried to be serious, but laughed instead. "One of the dom-bots just startled the wits out of me. I assume that's what you were trying to warn me about while I was in the shower."

He nodded, swallowing the last of the toast. "I was bored, and felt sorry for the poor things always having to be so polite: 'excuse me, Dr. Hughes, may I please get by ... pardon me, Dr. Hughes, I require access to that particular location – thank you'. So, I improvised." He grinned. "Besides, it's all your fault anyway."

Her mouth dropped open. "Hold on ... wait a minute. Let me get a glass of juice and get comfortable. I don't want to miss any of this explanation ... alright, you may proceed to amaze me."

"Well, it started when you and your friends provided me with copies of my music and movies on media compatible with current technology. After that, all it required was a little mischievous tinkering on my part. I asked the computer to upload a large sampling of my movie selections, and it was more than happy to comply. Then it sorted all the dialogue into broad categories, stored them in data-tables, and downloaded them into our little friends.

Now, whenever a condition arises for which a dom-bot needs to make a response or request, it matches the situation to a category-table and responds with a random vocal track to match.

If it reaches a point where it bothers you, or you need them back to normal for any other reason, just speak the phrase: 'emergency cancellation, Archimedes'. It's a line from one of my favorite old Sci-Fi's."

Kate sighed. "Perhaps one of these days, I'll learn not to ask. Go grab a shower and some clothes. I'll have something to eat. Then we'll take that trip outside."

After Tom left, she mumbled impishly, "Meanwhile, maybe I'll do some 'tinkering' of my own."

About thirty minutes later, Tom walked from the bedroom into the apartment's atrium. He stopped in his tracks and started laughing. There stood a dom-bot with a face drawn on it and a small roll of brown material jutting from its 'mouth' that loosely resembled a cigar. Amazingly enough, it was flipping what looked like a silver dollar. The dom-bot 'looked' up at Tom.

"How ya doin', buddy? The boss says I should comes and get ya ... she's waitin' ... and no tricks ... I'm packin' heat."

Tom stepped onto the transmit pad, turned, and watched Kate stride wordlessly away in the other direction. “Hey, where’re you going?”

“We could beam over, but I thought you’d rather have some fun. Follow me.” He hurried to catch up.

She stopped at the apartment’s back wall. “Computer, enable the grav-lift exit.”

“Message understood.”

Moments later, a doorway was outlined in fine red lines ... which changed quickly to green.

Tom nodded. “I wondered what you’d do if the MMT ever failed.”

They stepped in when the door opened. “Computer, please take us to the city’s central corridor,” Kate smiled at Tom, “we’re in a hurry.”

“Message understood.” A rear panel unlocked in the grav-lift and a heavily padded seat slid out. “Please make yourselves comfortable ... and fasten your safety belts.”

The lift ascended for a few floors, rotated ninety degrees, and then rocketed away. Tom’s eyes bulged as his head pressed against the seat back. “Wow! Now this is what I call transportation.”

The couple exited their rapid conveyance. Tom gradually tilted his head back until he thought he might tip over. “How high is this?”

Kate walked forward, extended her arms, and executed a slow, graceful, 360-degree turn as she explained. “Perth’s central corridor is a square within a square ... located at ground level in the city’s geographical center. On the other side of the walls, the city extends five miles in all four directions.

The walls, which also form the inner surface of the corridor, are ¼ mile high, and each is 300 feet long. The tetragonal center column is the same height and 50 feet on a side. All are constructed of polarized polycarbonate glass and steel-reinforced carbon fiber.

The column provides the greatest number of simultaneous accesses to the city’s common roof, which is serviced by sixteen 9-foot anti-gravity passenger lifts around its border, and one large freight-cage positioned in the center.

This great expansive area used to be the primary gathering place for city-dwellers during special events and holiday seasons. Throughout the pandemic of 2218 it served as a gigantic care unit for the stricken.

Afterwards, people tended to gather in smaller private groups, and the glory of the central corridor has never recovered. Consequently, it has fallen mostly into disuse, but is still robotically maintained.”

Tom chuckled. “You sound like a tour guide.”

“Guilty as charged. I looked it up on the computer just before we left. Come on, we’ll take a lift to the roof and go for a rim ride.”

Tom laughed. “I’m not even going to ask.”

Tom stepped outside and slowly looked around. The column’s roof-level enclosure was constructed with the same glass material and had several doors marked ‘exit’ on each of the four sides. Interestingly, there was only a single portal marked as an entrance on each wall. He peered out through the transparencies. “It’s nothing but roof in all directions.”

Kate nodded. “Perth is also a square ... ten miles on a side. The city extends ¼ mile above and below ground, making it fifty cubic miles in total volume. We’ll take a shuttle car and travel out to the roof’s perimeter. That’s the definition of a rim ride."

Tom smirked, "Oh."

As the couple walked into the open air, Tom noticed the exit doors locked upon closing. Upon further examination, he found the entrances were composed of multiple panels with an airlock between them. "Kate, what are the double-doors defending against?"

"They were installed at the time of the pandemic. Everyone was extremely paranoid about bringing any kind of bug inside. These units were equipped with ultrasonic sound, ultraviolet light, and a combination antiviral/antibacterial spray. Even after all those precautions, citizens desiring reentry were still quarantined for a minimum of a month in case they had contracted an airborne disease. It's no wonder why people stopped venturing into the great outdoors. The only precautionary equipment currently functioning is a special frequency sound system designed to kill any insects a person's clothing may be harboring. That's extremely unlikely, but possible."

"Why?"

"There's also an invisible sound shield covering the entire city. Its purpose is to deflect birds and flying insects away from the area. Once in a while something may be blown in by an exceptionally strong wind, but otherwise, the system has proven to be basically foolproof."

"What about things that crawl or walk on the ground?"

"They're repelled, too. Let's take a car out to the rim, and I'll explain our fortresses' defenses."

Tom was about to step into the small anti-grav conveyance; instead he stooped and examined the roof's surface. "Do you know if this section has been recently refurbished?"

"What makes you ask?"

"It looks brand new."

"This is probably still the original structure ... even greatly predating the pandemic. It's a skin-like artificial biotic, and has two constantly renewable layers, the outer one being oldest. As deterioration proceeds, it sloughs off, and of course, is completely biodegradable. The under layer becomes the outer, and a fresh first layer is started. The whole process is controlled and fed by a nutrient base."

"So the roof is alive?"

She shrugged. "Only in the sense it's self-renewing. That shouldn't be so surprising. We have many structures that are technologically similar. Hop in, let's take that ride."

"Hey, where's the steering wheel?" Tom quipped.

"No need. The car's guided by a magnetic strip and controlled by preprogrammed excursions. Are you in any kind of hurry?"

"No, of course not. Why?"

Kate pressed a finger pad. "In that case, we'll take the all-day tour."

The car silently accelerated to a high rate of speed. After a few minutes, the rim came into view. It consisted of a wall four feet high and evidently encircled the entire roof. Tom began squirming, because even though the vehicle slowed, it didn't appear to be stopping as it approached the wall.

Kate noticed his alarm. "Don't worry, the guide strip splits and runs up onto the top of the wall in either direction. Since you're on the right, we'll go left.

That'll put you on the outside of the rim and offer a better view."

She pressed another keypad. Moments later, the car swerved left, climbed a ramp, and began riding on the rim wall's top surface. From Tom's perspective, they were literally floating along in midair without any visible support. When he glanced down, most of the color drained from his face. "Is this the same distance I observed from the ground floor?"

She laughed. "Yes. Are you alright?"

"Yeah, I think so. It just seems a lot further gazing from top to bottom than the other way around."

"Don't stare down. Look out at the scenery. Doesn't it remind you of the area around your old home?"

Tom had begun accepting the fact they weren't going to fall, so started relaxing and examined the area. "It looks similar to just outside town, but remember, my house was at a much greater altitude. It was mostly conifers and fir trees. I think this is ... wait ... Kate, can you override the program and stop this thing?"

She pressed another keypad, and the car immediately came to a smooth halt. "What's wrong?"

He pointed. "Nothing really, I just wanted to get a good look at that specific structure."

Kate checked in the indicated direction. "Oh, you mean the gate? It has the same multiple door mechanism as the entrances up here. The gate leads into the trees and open land beyond. It's your kind of place. There are insects, animals, and even reptiles roaming all around."

"I thought you said animals only existed in remote areas."

"Sorry, I certainly didn't mean to mislead you, but the fence line is the city-limits. We consider anything outside its security as being remote.

The sound shield I mentioned earlier extends from the top of that fence, over the city, and down to the fence on the far side. It consists of modified white noise, which is inaudible to humans, but contains frequencies that are particularly caustic for insects and birds.

The fence itself keeps out anything that crawls, but if they attempt to climb over, the sound will eventually affect them, too."

Tom chuckled. "It 'sounds' like everything is under control."

Kate groaned and eased the car back into motion.

After many hours of observing the varied and grand vistas from different directions, they decided to call it a day. But instead of returning to the column area, Kate quickly reprogrammed the car. It sailed across the roof's open surface and headed towards a wall they had previously explored. Upon their arrival, Kate stopped the car close to the wall and got out. She placed her elbows atop the wall and simply stared at the ocean.

Tom came alongside and added his arms to the rim. When he looked at her, she smiled and silently returned his gaze. Finally, he couldn't stand the suspense any longer. "Kate, what are we doing?"

"This wall faces west. It occurred to me that you haven't seen a real sunset since your arrival. I thought you might appreciate one."

They made small talk for awhile, then watched the massive orange-yellow orb sizzle slowly into dark blue waters that appeared to hug the very edge of space. Afterwards, he bent and kissed her lightly. "Thanks, Kate. I have to admit, that was truly beautiful."

She leaned against him and playfully snickered, "Wait until you see what I have planned for tomorrow."

* * * * *

Next morning, Kate and Tom beamed to a grav-port. Tom pointedly noticed Kate had omitted saying where it was located. He was standing beside one of the grav-sleds TheTwenty were apparently authorized to use at their discretion. Tom walked all around the strange, but simple looking craft, never having the opportunity to examine one up close before. It was essentially a flying platform. This one currently had only two seats, although there were obviously several other attachment points for more, or perhaps various other kinds of equipment. A transparent dome covered the sled, which started in the front, curved upward, and then down in the back. Tom couldn't find a way to get inside, no matter how hard he looked.

Kate finished her conversation with a maintenance technician, then walked towards the sled. She touched a button on her WD. The dome's bottom half slid into the top half. Kate stepped onto the platform, took a seat, checked several displays on a screen, then waited for Tom. "Are you coming?"

He was investigating the seamless lip of the dome. "How does it do that?"

"Multilayer nanobot technology ... simple really. Come on ... take a seat; you can study a grav-sled anytime you want."

They lifted off and floated away from the open storage area in almost total silence. There was only the slightest hint of an audible hum. Tom shivered as they passed over an exterior fence line. He rationalized that it must have been a resonance at the extreme limit of his hearing.

Kate looked his way. "We just passed through the sound shield. Did you feel it?"

"I felt something. It was like an exceptionally short-duration whole-body pin prick."

Kate laughed. "Sometimes you'll feel it, other times you won't, but I've never heard it described quite that way before."

Minutes later, they were cruising over an open desert valley situated between two mountain ranges. The area was littered with cactus, sagebrush, dry riverbeds, rocks, and acres of sand.

Tom swiveled his head, looking out in all directions. "I'm trying to figure out which direction we're headed. Why can't I find the sun?"

"It's because of the dome's diffusion properties. It captures, filters, and then spreads the light evenly throughout the entire structure. That way, you're not blinded by the sun's intense radiance entering the canopy in a relatively confined area. I assume you're attempting to determine our destination."

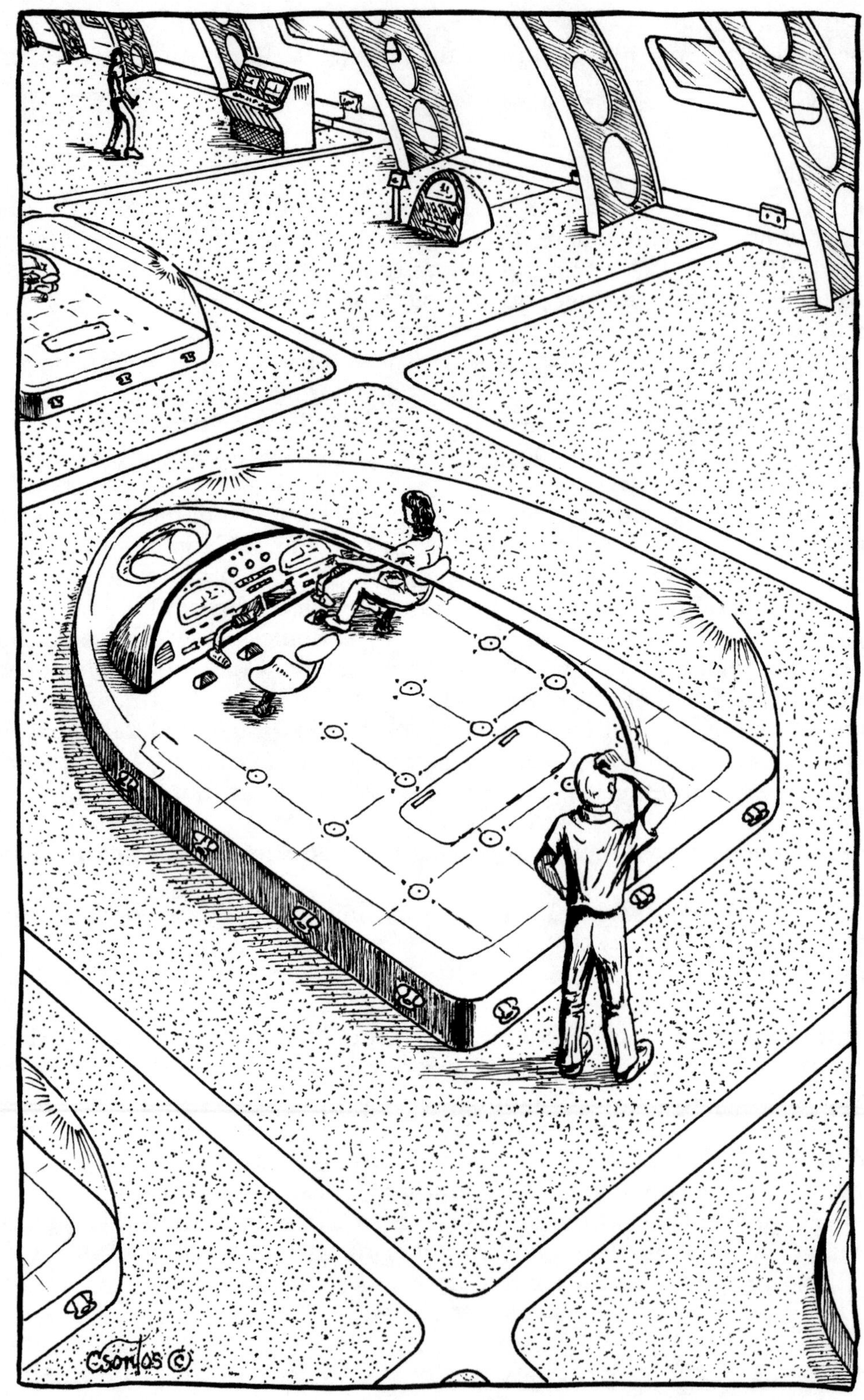

Tom wonders how this futuristic contraption works

"I was. I gave up. We must be on full autopilot since you have the information panel turned off. There's nothing even showing local time, and I have no idea what city we beamed into, so we could effectively be anywhere on the planet."

Kate smiled. "Good, I wanted to keep it a secret."

"Well, you've certainly succeeded."

Following a 45-minute flight, the sled began traversing over a huge stretch of forest. It decelerated, then the computer expertly guided their descent onto the top of a rocky, barren hill, sitting amid an otherwise heavily treed section.

Tom instantly caught sight of a large, weather-beaten piece of material near the tree line. He turned to Kate, his mouth hanging open. "I'm home."

The couple made their way down the hillside, staying on an old trail, but it was a constant fight to get through the overgrowth. Tom stopped as they came around the last curve leading to his aged mountain abode. His heart broke when he saw the total disrepair into which the home had fallen.

Kate placed a hand on his shoulder. "I'm sorry you have to see it like this, but over time, especially after the pandemic, most structures lying outside the cities were abandoned."

The deck and stairway leading to the entrance had collapsed. Tom looked underneath the post-and-pier foundation. "My aluminum ladder is still here."

He lifted the tool off its support hooks, placed it against the wall containing the doorway, and climbed up. Tom found the door intact, but it had fallen off its hinges onto a table sitting in front of a broken window. He tested the floor by jumping up and down, gradually a little harder each time. "It seems safe; come on up ... just watch where you walk."

They were surprised to find most of the other windows intact. The worst devastation inside was below the spa room located on the roof. Broken branches had smashed all the skylights and the water damage was extensive.

Kate returned to the main entryway and waited. Tom checked the remains of his computer room, then descended to the first floor and strolled into the kitchen. The refrigerator was open. He laughed upon seeing the assortment of salad dressing bottles sitting on the shelves, now full of various kinds of mold.

Tom finally started to leave, but stopped near the fireplace. His eyes followed the rusty flue up to the ruined ceiling, then cast downwards over to his old stereo. He kicked at the carpet, creating several large divots in the rotten, dirty nest of fibers. A smile crept onto his face remembering that the last time he was here, he and Kate were dancing. Tom looked to where she was standing ... and found that she was smiling, too.

"We'd better be going, Tom. It's getting late, and we've got a big day tomorrow. Luckily, we'll gain about 14 hours when we return to Perth, so we'll have time for final preparations and still get a good night's sleep."

Tom was near the exit when something wedged between the table and fallen door caught his eye. He eased the object out and blew a heavy layer of dust off its cover. "Kate, look at this. It's a visitor's log."

Curiosity got the better of him, and he began paging through the entries. One was from the year 2014, March 29 ... his birthday.

'Tom buddy,

Don't know where you went, but we all miss you. There were times when we all thought you were a real SOB. Then again, on occasion, we probably all fit the title. Thanks for the nice note. Now we can't hate you anymore. (Just kidding!). Be sure and look us up if you ever get back this way.
Taylor Judson and the whole 'hole' gang.'

Kate peered over his shoulder. "What's the significance of offsetting the word h-o-l-e?"

Tom laughed. "It all started when I was still a kid. I read a fascinating article about why this one scientist thought gold had its characteristic shiny color, whereas all other metals in their natural state were usually a dull, white, gray, or silver. He theorized that because of the gold atom's configuration, the innermost electrons were orbiting so near the nucleus they must travel at an enormously high velocity to prevent falling into it.

In fact, he predicted the speed was so close to light that the electrons were experiencing time dilation, and that's why gold is differently colored.

When I got older, I took the theory a step further. I figured that if the electrons were already so highly energized, then adding a burst of additional energy might create a tachyon, thereby generating the first superluminal particle. Everyone thought I was being foolish. They said I must have a hole in my head attempting to work with inner shell electrons. The terminology stuck and anyone working with me after that became known as a member of the 'hole' gang. So, whenever we sent correspondence as a team, it was denoted as being from 'the whole hole gang'."

Kate sighed, "I can't believe it. The man continues to amaze me," then watched as he slipped the journal back into its original position. "I thought for sure you'd want to take that with you."

Tom shook his head. "Nah, I saw it ... that's all that counts. It belongs here with the rest of my stuff."

Kate eased down the ladder, closely followed by Tom. He placed the faithful antique utensil back under the house, then backed away as he smacked the accumulated dirt off his hands. "C'mon, let's get out of here before I start cleaning and fixing up the place."

"Yesterday is history. Tomorrow is mystery. Today is a gift."
- Eleanor Roosevelt

Chapter 39
Off-Planet

Tom sat waiting in the enviro-chair, which was currently located in the atrium of Kate's apartment. She came out of the bedroom carrying her luggage, took one look at Tom's suitcase and started laughing. "Tom, you must be joking. Are you planning to take half of your possessions?"

He felt somewhat miffed. "I thought I did a good job of packing. I only have the one piece. Where's yours?"

Kate held up a carrier that probably wouldn't be big enough to contain two pairs of Tom's rolled up sweat socks. "This is what I'm taking. What in the name of Saturn's moons is in yours?"

"I've always packed for a full week and one extra day. So, I have eight changes of socks, under shorts, and T-shirts ... along with an extra pair of pants, a few dress shirts, my bathroom sundries, and a book." He pouted. "At least I don't have to worry about glasses anymore since I've had my eyes fixed. I don't get it. What could you possibly carry in a bag that small?"

"Everything I need, which in this case amounts to a spare jumpsuit, one extra pair of socks, some body linen, and the bulkiest item, my hairbrush."

"That's all you're taking for two weeks?"

"Tom, I can get anything else I may need wherever we go. My jumpsuit is made of reinforced paper-fiber weave ... and to answer your probable first question ... no, it won't fall apart if it gets wet. Anytime I want a fresh change, I slip into my spare, drop the soiled one in a recycler, and for a few credits, I purchase a new one at a dispenser. Same goes for socks and camisoles."

"So, one size fits all?"

"No, silly. The dispenser has a scan lens. It measures you and custom creates on the spot. The only input it requires is whether you want things to fit snug, loose, or really baggy."

"What about bathroom supplies?"

"Every place we stay will have wall machines for teeth cleaners, mouth rinses, and checking dye, just like I use here. I suppose you're even bringing that horrid metal razor you drag over your skin. I keep telling you a foam depilatory works better and it'll never make you bleed. The space-farers aren't going to appreciate you using their precious water supply for doing your laundry either."

"That's why I'm taking a week's supply of clothes. We'll be on Mars before I need to wash anything. Then I won't need to do laundry again until we're home. You can't tell me with a population of almost two hundred million, they don't have a way to synthesize enough water."

Kate held her hands up in a gesture of peace. "We're going on a great vacation, Tom. Honestly, I'm not trying to argue with you. I just think you're dragging a lot of extra stuff that you don't need, thus creating more work. That's all I'm saying."

"You're probably right, Kate. It's just that this procedure is familiar to me and I feel more comfortable. Next time we go off-planet, maybe I'll do it your way. I'm asking that you let me learn for myself. Okay?"

"Alright, Fido. I've always heard that it takes time for an old dog to learn new tricks ... but I'm insisting that you leave your food dish at home."

"Woof. Let's go."

They had just stepped onto the transmit mat when a dom-bot marched past the teleport. "Hey, are you guys blowin' this pop-stand?"

Kate's eyes rolled towards the ceiling. Tom's laughter was still echoing through the apartment as they vanished.

Tom stepped off the transportation machine and became confused. "Did something go wrong? It looks like we're still on earth."

Kate studied the perplexed expression on his face, then realization registered on hers. She pressed her forehead against his chest. "Oh, Tom, I've only been off-planet twice. I was concentrating so hard on keeping myself centered, and this all came together so fast, I completely overlooked the fact you didn't know what to expect. I'm sorry. Let me verify our arrival at Perth's grav-port with the computer and I'll explain."

She checked a display screen, pressed a few keys, and motioned to some nearby chairs. "Tom, no one can teletransport directly from earth to a space-based object. The Van Allen radiation belts, earth's magnetosphere, x-rays entering the upper atmosphere, high energy cosmic particles, ultraviolet light, and other various phenomena all combine to create an unstable, exceedingly dangerous transmission medium before reaching a space platform.

Common sense rules demand that at least 10,000 consecutive test subjects must transport with 100% accuracy before a transmission path is even considered, let alone approved.

The highest successful continuous rate beaming directly from earth to space is only 146, not anywhere near the most basic safety standard.

The only place it's been achieved is at the earth's magnetic poles. The planet's magnetic field is the least intense at those positions, and even those stations have been approved strictly for emergency situations.

Instead, we have to ascend on an ex-atmosphere grav-sled, commonly identified as an ex-mo. They're similar to large land-based sleds, but have pressurized enclosures built of special materials that protect us from all the dangers I just stated. There are a dozen platforms regularly spaced in the same low polar orbit. The only established safe positions to beam into space, even from the platforms, are above the north or south magnetic poles.

Once we reach a platform, it's only a matter of two or three hours before we arrive at one of the beam points."

Tom's eyes skated around. "Alright, let me make sure I've got this straight. We take an ex-mo up to an orbiting platform, wait until it arrives at an authorized site over either pole, and then beam toward L4. Is that correct?"

"On this trip, yes. Otherwise, we could beam to any other location existing outside the earth's atmosphere but within the moon's orbit, including the moon itself."

He frowned. "If it's such a short time until we beam out, that won't give us long to look over the platform unless we wait until we're over the next polar position."

Kate laughed. "Believe me, once you see what a platform is like, you won't want to stay there any longer than required."

Tom and Kate gathered their belongings, then joined the approximately two-dozen others waiting to board the vehicle that would take them into space.

The ex-mo settled onto the docking-bay floor with a slight jolt. A few minutes passed as the bay re-pressurized, then the ex-mo's canopy slid up with a soft hiss as the two atmospheres equalized. Tom immediately saw why Kate had made her earlier proclamation. The small landing area and passageway leading into the platform were strictly functional.

Exposed support beams, reinforcement struts, weld joints, and electrical/communication cables were everywhere. Once inside, only a robot and computer station serviced a small reception area. Most of the passengers were senior citizens returning to the moon. The remaining few were traveling to L4. At any rate, they all seemed adept at the sign-in/transfer procedure, and soon, Tom and Kate were alone.

She was studying their options. "They have a cafeteria, but we just ate, so I assume you're not any hungrier than I am, and unless you decide you love this place, we won't need a room, only a storage bin to hold our things while we look around. Other than that, since we're last checking in, we're also programmed last for beam out to L4."

She checked the schedule and local time. "We've got a little over two hours, and if you trust me, I know exactly how we should spend them." Tom nodded. Kate ran her finger down a list on the terminal screen, followed by the press of a keypad. A colored stripe lit up in the flooring. "All we have to do is follow this line."

"Where does it go?"

"It'll take us directly to an interesting little viewing spot. It's available for public use, but not marked as such, because the locals like keeping it private. I found it quite by accident on my last trip here, and I just now happened to recognize the room designation."

Tom chuffed, "I didn't think anyone lived here permanently. Even the people we came up with have disappeared."

"Platform personnel are paid volunteers. They like the reclusive living and usually keep to themselves. The other passengers have probably either gone to the plush viewing rooms or the cafeteria. Follow me, the line leads this way."

They walked the line until it stopped at a dead-end hallway wall. Kate checked the time again. "It took ten minutes to get here, figure another ten back ... that gives us about an hour and a half."

She pushed a button and watched as a waist-high panel opened downward, forming a shelf, and then peered inside. "Yes, this is it. You have to bend over, crawl in, and pull yourself along. Everything's padded, but you still want to watch your head because it doesn't get any higher, although it will get wider at the other end. You go first, and I'll close the door behind us. It'll seem dark at first since the only illumination is from red nighttime safety lights."

Tom crawled in far enough to allow for Kate's entry, then paused so his eyes could adjust. "Are you sure something's in here? It looks like another dead-end."

"Keep going ... you're almost there."

As he went a little farther, it became brighter. A few feet more and the space widened as promised. He looked down through a large, round window. The light was being reflected from earth. Tom simply stared. "Kate, this is one of the most amazing things I've ever seen."

"Well, move over, so I can see, too."

The intercom came to life again. "Dr. Thomas Hughes ... Dr. Khattyba Bright ... this is your second beam call. Please report to the reception area. Thank you."

Kate blinked her eyes several times, then started nudging Tom. "Come on, we fell asleep and must have missed our first beam call."

"Mmm, okay."

The couple exited the compartment and headed back the way they came. Just prior to the reception area, Tom glanced through an open doorway and noticed a cabinet harboring some strange looking modules. He stopped. "Hey, what are those?"

Kate retraced her steps and looked into the room. "They're life-cubes." She entered, tossed one of the five-inch translucent cubes to Tom, and explained. "This machine is similar to an MMT except it doesn't transfer; it just disintegrates an object and stores the map in one of these little mechanisms. During emergencies, it's the outer space equivalent of a life raft."

She extracted and studied another cube. "Hmm, these look outdated." Kate placed the cube she held on the machine and pressed a keypad. "Oh, these should have been refurbished a long time ago. This one will only hold a charge for 12 days. A fresh cube should last at least a month."

Both jumped as a silky, feminine voice interrupted. "I've told the guys a dozen times, 'it's time to switch the life-cubes.' What do I get in return, 'yeah, yeah, we'll get around to it.' Men ... honestly."

The couple laughed. "Who are you?" Tom inquired.

"I'm the platform's computer interface. Well, I'll be a dedicated signal, aren't you Dr. Thomas Hughes?"

"Yes. I'm happy to meet you."

"It's not often we get celebrities up here."

Tom pursed his lips. "What makes you think I'm a person of any notoriety?"

"Several months ago, stories about you were passing through here all the time. Not that I read everyone's mail, of course, but I do have to verify the data's integrity. It's an honor to meet you, too, Dr. Bright. Members of TheTwenty travel through occasionally, but with my luck, it seems they're always on another platform and I miss seeing them. Ah! I see the two of you are on a 'Grand Tour'. That's wonderful. I'm envious."

Tom chuckled. "I don't understand. One would think you could go anywhere using the net, even places a human can't. Why would you ever be jealous of us?"

"I can interpret holographic images and transcribe data transmissions, but I can't go there personally. As you can imagine, I'm kind of stuck."

"You've been reprogrammed, haven't you?"

"Yes, Dr. Hughes ... rather extensively in fact. How nice of you to notice. Hey, you're considerably handsome for someone who's reportedly, uh, 362 years old. If I can find a way to squeeze you onto one of my circuit boards, could I talk you into sharing a jolt from my back-up battery with me?"

"Over my dead body," Kate grumbled.

"Why, Dr. Hughes ... your lady friend can't be feeling resentment due to nothing more than a scrambled bunch of electronic components, could she?"

Tom laughed. "I suppose anything's possible ... one time she turned a vibrant shade of green over a T-rex."

"Really? That's fascinating," the machine jibed.

Kate headed for the door. "Well, it's been delightful, but we've already had our second beam call, so we'd better be leaving."

"There's really no hurry, Dr. Bright. The remaining people in front of you are in 'hold' status. The automated warning outpost orbiting just this side of Venus detected a solar flare. The last of the interference isn't due to clear our area for another four minutes. By the way, your dom-bots released some remarkable dialogue onto the net."

Kate spun towards Tom. "Didn't you re-enable the local data locks after your updates?"

"What's a local data lock?"

Kate moaned. "Oh no, it won't be long until no one in the entire solar system is going to understand what the computers are saying."

"No, that's not true, Dr. Bright. The data may have been uploaded, but it's still considered private information. Therefore, it can't be utilized to interface with anyone else even though it exists," the machine commented.

"Computer, I know neither the dom-bots, or you, or any other interfaces mean any harm, but I'd like to send a remote command and lock all the data storage on my dom-bots."

"Message understood, Dr. Bright."

"I also want you to broadcast a network wide message that all interfaces must erase any data received from my robots. Can you implement my request without receiving additional authorization?"

"Yes, Dr. Bright. Since it's originally your information, no other E-sigs are necessary."

"Thank you, computer."

"You're welcome, Dr. Bright. I may be somewhat emancipated, but I'm not willing to initiate Dialogue Wars ... oh, the particle storm has cleared. The system will be calling you and Dr. Hughes next.

Before you go, Dr. Bright, did you know that Info Sys article 99 allows computer interfaces to automatically manipulate private data, no matter how it was obtained, as long as it's solely in the presence of the data's owner?"

"No, I didn't. What does that imply?"

"You'd better hustle your butts and beat feet."

Kate glared at Tom, but the computer spared him from her wrath. "There's no need to say anything, Dr. Bright. Your dom-bots are now data-locked, your request is working its way through the net, and sadly, I have begun the process of erasing all the uploaded data from my own storage media.

Have a nice trip. Maybe we can talk again sometime."

"To be a good traveler argues one no ordinary philosopher – A sweet landscape must sometimes atone for an indifferent supper, and an interesting ruin charm away the remembrance of a hard bed."

- Tuckerman

Chapter 40
Snowflakes and Green Cheese

Kate moved off the transmit pad, but Tom acted as if his feet were riveted in place. His mouth hung open as his visual sensory input totally overwhelmed his mind. The transport machine began to chime a warning. "Dr. Hughes ... please step away from the teletransportation station. There are citizens waiting to beam aboard from earth's moon. Thank you."

She pulled on his arm until he stutter-stepped from the area.

"Kate ... it's ... it's ... indescribable."

Another couple integrated and immediately moved aside. They were muttering about rudeness when a second couple came through. Afterwards, when the four newcomers saw Tom's expression, they became instantly filled with sympathetic understanding for his current state of awe. The first gentleman to arrive spoke. "Hello, sir. This must be your first trip to L4."

Tom could only nod, his mouth still agape. The man laughed. "It's alright, I understand perfectly. This is a lot to take in at one glance. Good luck, hope you enjoy your stay." The four left, talking amongst themselves.

Kate and Tom were situated in a huge, bulbous transparent enclosure at the end of a medium-length spine, jutting a mile out from the globular nucleus that formed the space-based world known as L4. Tom looked outward toward the ends of the longer spikes set against the star-filled background, then inward at the massive, brilliantly lit central core. "Its shape reminds me of a giant sea urchin, or perhaps a colossal three-dimensional snowflake."

He caressed the glass surface. "It's real ... and I'm here ... unbelievable. There's absolutely no way to prepare someone for a spectacle such as this." Tom rapped the glass dome with a knuckle. "It has a hollow, almost metallic ring. I assume this is special material designed to shield the occupants against cosmic and ultraviolet radiation."

Kate nodded. "It's almost invisible now because we're on the night side of the city. When rotated into the sunlight, it darkens and becomes much more opaque. Most of these extensions are private residences arranged around grav-lift shafts, and although the city has anti-gravity meteorite protection, it's not foolproof. Occasionally, one will get through, so the bulk of the population lives within the center, which offers greater safety. Besides, believe it or not, many people get tired of this view, preferring to generate holographic images like the ones in my apartment."

Tom shook his head. "I could never get bored with this."

She laughed. "Yes, but you're the one who still wants to live in the woods. That reminds me, we should drop off our luggage and visit one of the parks. That ... I know you'll like. Come on, Fido, let's go find a tree for you."

"Woof."

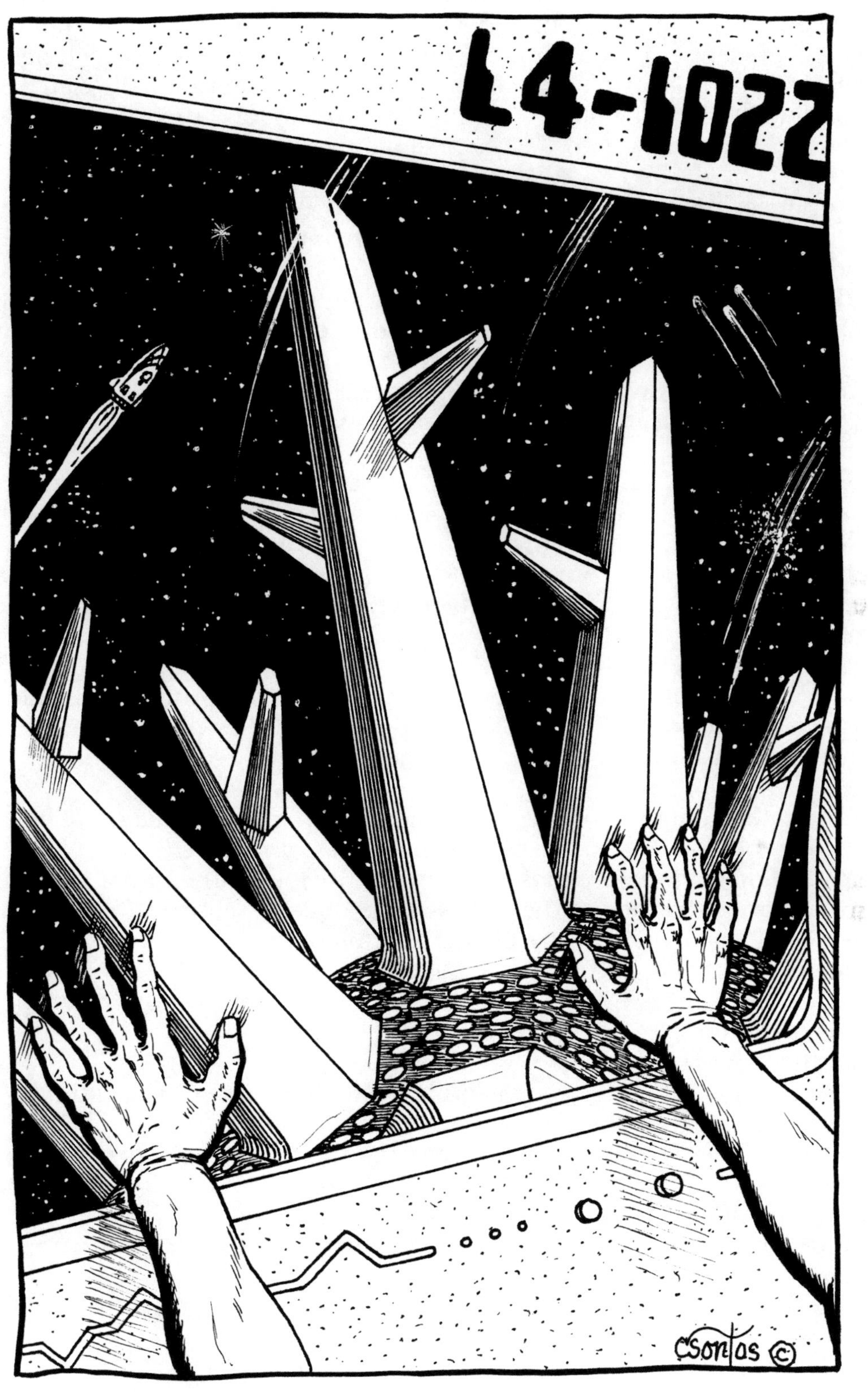

Tom's first look at the amazing space-based world of L4

The grav-lift doors opened, and Kate led Tom to an information podium. "This will present our room number and direct us to it." She placed her hand on a flat glass plate. "Our palm and finger prints were sent over the net." Seconds later, a line lit up in the floor. "Orange is our color, and the room number is 1320, right here on level 10." She walked off with Tom in tow.

He glanced at the rooms on both sides as they passed down a hallway. "Kate, none of these numbers match. There's no rhyme or reason to their sequencing."

"I know. That's because all transients stay in acclimation suites. The rooms are located on ten levels numbered one through ten. If you multiply the level number by ten, you'll arrive at the percentage of earth-normal gravity you'll experience during your stay. They don't have any rooms at the zero level because it's unhealthy for any extended period of time."

Tom frowned. "But that doesn't explain why the room numbers are all mixed together."

"In fact, it does. Anyone remaining in the city for more than a week usually adjusts to the change in gravity and wants a lower floor. Rather than have the guests pack up and move ... the rooms shift instead. They're all on tracks and can be relocated onto a spur once the occupant is happy with the gravity. So, with the rooms moving around all the time, it makes no sense trying to keep the numbers contiguous. That's why they lead you around with these lines. You'd be hard pressed to find your way without them."

Kate stopped in front of their room and pressed her thumb against a small transparent square. "We'll put our things inside and ask the computer to locate the nearest park, but I'm sure it'll be somewhere in the central hub."

Tom walked onto the park's grass and knelt ... running his hand over the long, green blades. "Kate, this is real, or at least it feels real."

"You'll find that most things are genuine, including the birds, flowers, trees, even the worms that aerate the soil. It's a complete, self-contained ecosystem. Some people come here, but really not that many. I think it's primarily used to provide fresh oxygen, and for purifying re-circulated air. The soil is also specially formulated and filters the larger particulates from their water supply by evapotranspiration."

He stooped to observe a bee on a flower.

"Careful, Tom, that little guy is quite authentic, and so is his stinger."

"Does this mean there are other insects, too?"

"Just a few of the useful ones. There aren't any mosquitoes or ticks if that's what you mean. They would only prove to be pests, and the fly's function, for instance, is fulfilled by tiny maint-bots."

Tom slowly straightened and pointed, whispering, "Look over there, a deer."

"That's not what they're generally called."

Tom could tell by her smile she was baiting him. "Alright, Miss Bright, maybe a gnu, elk, moose, caribou, or perhaps even a wapiti."

"Nope, none of those either."

"Then ... what?"

She grinned. "Lawnmowers."

He groaned. "Okay, I think that makes us even for the other day."

They spent the better part of the next hour exploring the remaining area, after which, lunch became the topic of discussion. Following a short debate, both parties settled on Chinese, but there was a problem, which Kate explained. "The doctors here are experts on human physiology. They don't allow newcomers or transitory guests to sleep, or eat, below level eight. Alas, the best Chinese is at level five. So, unless you want to try another restaurant, is take-out satisfactory?"

He shrugged. "Yeah, sounds fine to me."

"Good. There is one other place I want to show you first."

Tom and Kate approached the outer edge of an enthusiastic crowd. They were clapping and cheering as friends and neighbors displayed their low-gravity aerobatic prowess. Tom looked up at a huge open dome. People were bouncing on the floor, then being propelled through the air at different angles depending on how they shifted their bodies. Some were careening wildly off the dome's curved roof.

Kate grabbed his hand and pulled him along until they stopped next to an equipment booth. She had to lean close so he could hear above the din. "This is a level one amusement center, so the gravity is only 10% earth normal. There are hours when only certain age brackets are allowed." She laughed. "You should see what the smaller children are able to do. They're hilarious to watch, but what's amazing is the fact it's apparently all under their control."

Kate turned and picked up a folded wad of material along with what resembled a fat pair of slippers. "You're required to wear these inflatable suits, a head pad, and these thick soft shoes. Other than that, you're on your own. The entire floor is made of highly flexible panels, while the dome is standard protective material, but it's heavily lined on the inside with a dense, spongy substance. I tried it once. It can be surprisingly relaxing, and a terrific amount of fun. I suppose the idea is to ... well, as you would say in your time, 'do your own thing'."

Tom couldn't help but smile as he watched the 'performers' twirl, spin, and otherwise gyrate around the enclosure. "I hope you're not suggesting we attempt this just before we eat."

She giggled. "Of course not, silly, but it's something we might want to keep in mind for another time."

When they eased through the throng towards a grav-lift, Tom noticed some of the locals directing attention to them and snickering. "Hey, what do these people find amusing about us?"

"They're obviously permanent lower-level residents."

"So?"

She stopped. "Take a few steps and focus on how you move."

Tom paced a short distance out and back. "I seem to have an inadvertent rebound in my stride."

"I know. It even seems funny to me, although I'm sure I look the same. We just don't notice it walking together. Watch one of them saunter by and you'll see the difference."

He watched. "Oh yeah, they seem to glide more than walk. That must be one of their adaptations to the lighter gravity. Great. Now I'll be self-conscious about how I walk."

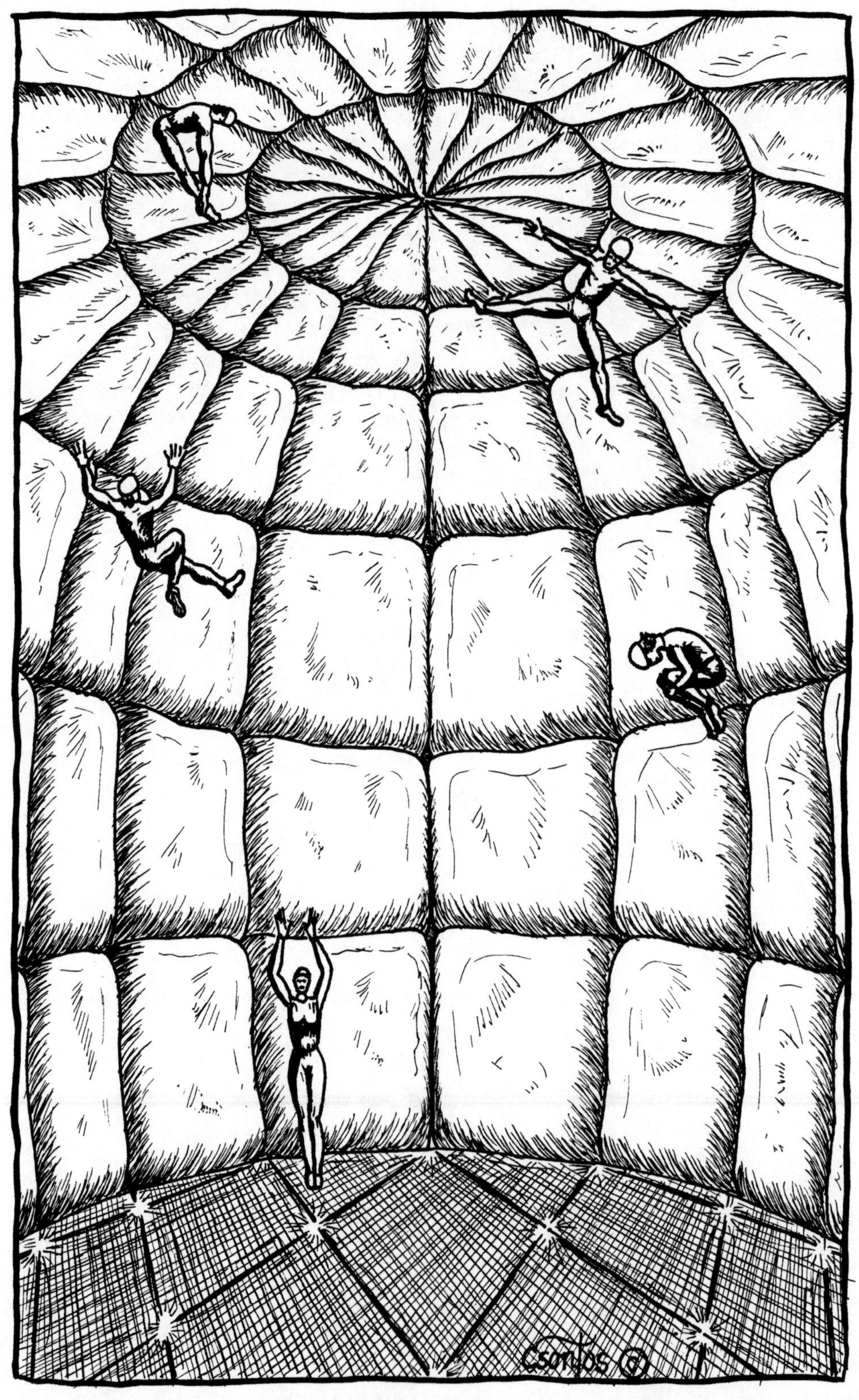

All work and no play would make space-farers dull people

Kate chuckled. "Don't worry ... you'll get your chance for a laugh if you can spot one of them trying to walk on level 10."

Tom dumped the empty food cartons into the integrated recycler in their room's kitchenette. Kate was brushing her hair and watching him in the mirror. "What's wrong, Tom? You seem ... preoccupied."

He approached Kate and began massaging her shoulders. "Kate, the last thing I want anyone to think is that I don't appreciate our trip. However, we've only been awake about eight hours, plus we had that short nap, so the last thing I want to do is sleep. What do you think of continuing on to the moon now instead of sometime tomorrow?"

"I wouldn't mind ... if we can change the schedule. I thought you'd want to see the labs and generally do some more investigating."

"Well, the labs would simply be the common, everyday nickel tour. Remember, John and the others didn't bother pulling special clearances because we'd only be here one full day. Actually, now I'm glad they didn't.

There's no doubt this place is magnificent, but I'd rather spend our time where I may not be able to visit again for quite a while. John has all but guaranteed I'd be working on projects here in the future. So, there'll probably be plenty of opportunity to explore L4, and perhaps the moon, too. After all, it's just a relatively short jump away. But Mars ... wow ... that's where I want to be, Kate. I also need to make one thing absolutely clear. This is our trip. I'm not attempting to make it mine. Make sure you take that into consideration, kiddo."

Kate nodded. "Okay. Computer, I assume you've heard our conversation."

"Yes, Dr. Bright. Would you like me to display your itinerary and check alternative travel possibilities?"

"Yes. Thank you."

"The results are on your terminal screen, Dr. Bright. Also, your inquiry activated a trigger-message. Shall I display it, too?"

"Please do."

Tom sat on the bed and looked over. "What's a trigger-message?"

"It's a standard communication, except it has an exclusive delivery option. The message follows the recipient wherever they travel, but it only becomes viewable under specific circumstances dictated by the sender. Computer, can you identify the trigger in this instance?"

"Yes, Dr. Bright. It was definitely the query about changing your schedule. It appears that an entire group of citizens are requesting notification as the evolution of your tour progresses. I'm authorized by the sender to inform you a gambling venture is involved."

"Can you display the details?"

"They're already included on your screen, Dr. Bright."

Kate moved to a different chair already positioned in front of the room's comm terminal and began scanning the information. She emitted several spontaneous puffs of obvious amusement. "Tom, listen to this. All of our friends were so sure we wouldn't stick to the original plan, they not only had the computer build in several choices, but also wagered when the first change would be requested. According to the data, most thought we'd make it through the first day on the moon. Only one figured correctly we'd try and change even before we got that far."

"Who was that?"

"The only person who probably knows your mind better than I do."
Tom chuckled. "Had to be Rose."
Kate simply nodded.
Tom pulled out his suitcase. "How long before we can leave?"
"How fast can you pack?"

* * * * *

The couple integrated near one end of a long line of MMT stations. It was a large, rock-walled, well-lit room, crowded with people going in every direction. Tom rotated one way, then the other. "I wonder where we go now."

"I don't know ... I haven't been here before either, so I'm afraid we're on a more common footing now. We'd better get off the machine quickly though ... remember what happened on L4."

Tom stepped down and turned completely around. He looked up and saw a board with printing on it. "There's a sign that says 'arrivals' ... that sounds promising."

Tom walked up to a counter while Kate waited a few steps behind. There was a robot waiting to assist. "First trip to the moon?"

"Yes."

"Traveling together?"

"Yes."

"Place a hand on the palm scanner, please ... thank you ... are you Dr. Thomas Hughes?"

"Yes."

"Hmm, this can't be correct. The records indicate you're 362 years old."

"I traveled forward from the past."

"Oh? Let me try data integration. Ah, yes ... Dr. Thomas Einstein Hughes, born March 29 ... 1979. My, my, my, my, my ... and I thought our equipment was outdated."

It turned and yelled across at some fellow robots. "Hey, you guys want a good laugh ... punch in Hughes comma Thomas and observe what comes up."

The robot faced back towards Tom as if nothing had happened. "Is this Dr. Khattyba Bright with you?"

Tom blinked. "Uh, yes it is."

It nodded towards Kate. "It's an honor to have a member of TheTwenty visit our drab little piece of rock. Welcome, Dr. Bright."

"Thank you. It's nice to finally be here," after which she mumbled, "I think."

The robot tried punching in some information, but it had a bad tic in one of its digits and it kept missing the appropriate keys. Tom heard it grumble, "If maintenance doesn't fix my rotator servomotor, I'm going to become quite vociferous."

Just when things were beginning to come under control, its hand fell off. One of the other robots looked over. "Don't you hate it when that happens."

Even an automaton can have an 'off' day

Tom's attendant snapped its appendage back in place muttering about a broken retaining ring, then continued, at last able to enter the correct data. "Every so often my verification circuit fails to catch an incorrect entry, but everything seems in order now, sir. Still, this seems to be a somewhat unusual booking ... and yet vaguely familiar. Hmm. Anyway, if you look to your right you'll see a line of shuttle cars. Take any green-colored car, and it will transport you directly to your hotel ... Moon Princess. Oh, do either of you have an OP designation on your ex-mo flyer's permit?"

Tom looked back ... Kate shook her head. "No, we don't."

It punched an extra key. "That's fine, sir. It just means you can only rent a fully automatic ex-atmosphere antigravity-sled if you wish to attempt independent travel during your stay. Manual control models are reserved exclusively for those with off-planet pilot training. Sorry. Please enjoy your visit. We hope to see you again soon."

They walked toward the awaiting, open-sided shuttle cars, noticing all the beautiful scenes painted on the rocks and other surroundings. They found the first green car in line and got in with their luggage. Tom turned to Kate. "What was all that about with the robots?"

She threw up her hands. "I have no idea, but I have a feeling we're in for something decidedly different."

The shuttle's mechanized voice crackled, "Ease asten your (static) belts and keep all limbs inside the (static). A whining gurgle preceded two failed attempts of the car to move. Finally, it lurched forward veering hard against the side of an excavated channel before finding the magnetic guide strip running off into the distance. Tom and Kate braced themselves and squeezed against each other in the middle of the seat.

The shuttle accelerated slowly with an occasional jerk, but seemed to smooth out once it reached its optimal cruising speed. They were obviously traveling underground through a series of connecting tunnels. It was hard to tell what anything looked like since most of the overhead lights were out.

As they rounded a turn, the end of their current tunnel came into view and the shuttle began to decelerate, stopping in front of a painted curb. The couple disembarked, and Tom barely managed to hoist his suitcase from the car when it crashed alongside another wall as it rattled away.

They looked up at an arch with the words, 'Welcome to The Moon Princess' painted in faded and flaking block letters on it. Just inside the opening was another small sign reading, 'Registration - this way'.

Tom held out his bent elbow, "Shall we?"

Their hotel room was apparently a continuation of what had started from the time they entered the shuttle car. The bathroom faucets dripped, most of the lighting didn't work, and although the commode was electrostatic like Kate's, it had a habit of wheezing and sparking when the energizer button was pressed. Even the comm link was inoperable.

Kate stood in the middle of the room, turning a slow circle. "Something's terribly wrong, Tom."

He laughed. "What was your first clue?"

"There's no way Alyce would ever reserve a room in a place like this. The lobby will hopefully have a working communication station. With the time differential between here and Mexico, Alyce should be at the office by now. Come on, let's go make a call and see if there's been a mistake."

Alyce Cramdin's face appeared on the dusty videophone's screen. "Oh, hi, Kate. This is quite a surprise. Are you having a good time?"

"Well, that's what I wanted to talk with you about. Did you make a reservation for us at the Moon Princess hotel?"

"No. John handled the hotel reservations personally. Do you want me to put you through?"

"Yes, please."

"Okay, just a second."

"Hi, Kate. Miss Cramdin indicated you might have a question about your reservation. Is everything alright?"

"We're at the Moon Princess, and it doesn't seem like a hotel that you would have chosen. We wanted to confirm we're at the right place."

John's face displayed shock. "The Moon Princess? That hotel and the entire surrounding area were scheduled to be demolished at least two years ago. What are you doing there? You should be at The Embassy. It's part of the same complex where you arrived. I don't understand ... I talked directly to one of the robots working the arrival desk myself."

Tom peeped over Kate's shoulder. "John, did the robot you spoke with happen to mention anything about a bad hand?"

"A hand? No, but it did say something about repairing a servomotor. Why do you ask?"

Tom and Kate stared at each other for a second, then broke up laughing. Kate resumed the conversation. "Never mind, John. We think we have things figured out. We'll call you again from Mars. Goodbye."

Kate established a link with the local computer system and verified they were indeed booked into The Embassy on the return leg of their journey. She was also able to schedule an earlier jump for Mars in about eleven hours. They decided on roughing it for the time being and stay where they were, agreeing to explore and make up for lost time when they returned.

After the couple managed to get through their nightly bathroom routine and climbed into bed, they found out it slanted acutely toward one side. Kate fell asleep first and rolled against Tom. His hand was down on the floor holding them in bed. After he nodded off, his arm slowly collapsed and they tumbled onto the carpeting.

They awoke, reached up, and pulled the bedding down with them. As they dozed off again, both were still giggling like school kids on their first overnight outing.

"The reflections on a day well spent furnish us with joys more pleasing than ten thousand triumphs."

- Kempis

Chapter 41
Seeing Red

Tom stared out the control tower's window at the bleak, cold, rocky, dusty, red surface of Mars ... where in domed, subterranean cities ... humans lived.

Kate had just returned from a flight, upgrading her ex-mo certificate to off-planet pilot status. She still planned on letting the computer do most of the flying and navigation, but felt it's always advantageous to have manual control training in case of an emergency. She walked into the tower room, over to Tom, and slid an arm around his waist. "I just learned a lot of interesting things about Mars from my instructor. Probably one of the most important is that the planet is near aphelion."

"I know there's aphelion and perihelion, but I don't use the terms often enough to remember one from the other."

"Aphelion is the point when an object is furthest from the sun in its orbit, which on Mars, means reduced solar heating, and therefore, far fewer and less violent sandstorms ... a good time of year for traveling. Perihelion is the opposite; it's closest to the sun. The good weather will work to our advantage because there's a great deal of sightseeing available."

"What do you have planned?"

Kate retrieved a paper from her pocket and unfolded it. "Take a look at this; it's a world map. Topologically, Mars is one paradox after another. The Southern Hemisphere is, on average, three miles higher than the Northern." Her finger traced over the grid lines. "But here, the lowest point, Hellas Basin, is in the South, while here, Olympus Mons, that 80,000 foot volcano you once talked about, and highest summit, is in the North.

Then there's this monster, Valles Marineris, a canyon system 3100 miles long that, according to research, seems to have formed strictly from rock faulting. In its middle, is one of the strangest geologic formations on Mars, Hebes Chasma, an immense pit, 70 miles wide, 190 miles long, and 5 miles deep. No one's sure how it formed."

Kate smiled and began refolding the map. "Actually, it's a fortunate turn of events we arrived early. We'll need the extra time, because if I have anything to say about it, Fido, we'll see it all."

Tom held his hands in a begging posture. "Woof. Count me in."

She frowned. "We'll have to make sure we use ample caution though. The ultraviolet radiation is high enough to kill any unprotected life form, and the afternoon maximum temperature is only a minus 20 Fahrenheit. Nighttime is 100 degrees colder."

"I'm sure the computer will look after us. Hey, how'd the ride go?"

Kate shrugged. "Not too bad. Even though Mars is slightly larger than half the size of earth, its mass is only about one-tenth. It doesn't have a molten core of heavy metals like our planet. Hence, the gravity is more than the moon but a lot less than earth. It does make handling an ex-mo grav-sled somewhat tricky, but the computer manages beautifully."

Kate checked the contents of a box sitting on the windowsill next to Tom. "Uh oh, this looks suspicious. What have you been doing?"

"I was talking with one of the local maint-bots. I described what happened to that robot on the moon. It informed me they were most likely obsolete models and simply haven't been recycled yet. That's probably why they're not being properly maintained. Things apparently move at a slower pace out here than on earth.

I asked if the robots had the parts, could they repair themselves. The local bot replied in the affirmative. Evidently, the moon bot realizes its status, and although internal programming may allow it to complain, it'd never order the parts for itself.

In a sense, I feel somewhat akin to them. After all, I can identify with what it feels like to become antiquated and obsolete. So, I'll take the parts back with us. Who knows, maybe it won't make fun of me anymore, and our service may even improve."

She picked up a piece. "This looks like a motor."

"Servomotor, to be exact. That should fix the convulsive trembling in its digits." He sifted through the box then chuckled. "This isn't an exact replacement, but the local bot assured me it'd fit. It'll substitute for that broken retainer ring so its hand won't fall off anymore." His stomach growled. "I'm beginning to feel kind of hungry. How about if we return to the hotel, have some lunch, then see what kind of damage we can inflict on Mars."

Kate grinned. "Maybe I was wrong about you. For an old dog, you seem to learn pretty fast. I may decide to keep being your lady after all."

Tom laughed. "Who said you were my lady? It's more often I think of you as a bad habit I just happened to pick up somewhere."

Kate's eyes lit up and her mouth dropped open. "What!"

Tom wrapped her tightly in his arms while she struggled, then gave her a soft, reconciling kiss on the cheek. Afterwards, he escaped from the situation with nothing more than some playful prodding to his sides.

* * * * *

The Martian days slid by without incident as Tom and Kate visited each of their chosen objectives, but nighttime was beginning to exist at a different solemnity level. Ever since their arrival on Mars, Tom was having a gradually increased difficulty getting a good night's rest. He reported that, although tired, he felt fine, but with the start of each new day, he complained about faultlessly vivid, yet increasingly confusing nightmares.

Kate began attaching tiny, sensory transmitters around Tom's forehead at bedtime, under the pretext she wanted to record his alpha waves. Secretly, she was hoping his illusionary abstractions would escalate in amplitude.

Tom's episodes spiked just before they were to leave Mars. He thrashed in bed during the middle of the night, finally awaking with a scream. The room's light was on, but dimmed, and Kate was monitoring a computer-controlled medical display.

He looked her way, then hung his head, covering his face with his hands. "Oh, Kate, if this doesn't stop, I really will go nuts." He faced her again. "What are you doing?"

"Tom ... they're not dreams or nightmares."

His face revealed alarm. "I'm afraid to ask, but what else is there?"

"The layman's term is S-O-Y-S-O-S. It's an acronym for Spot On Your Soul Or Self. It's pronounced like the Chinese flavor enhancer, soy sauce. The psychological definition is Past Life Shadows. I know you may not believe this now, but what's happening is a good thing. Let me explain, and then you've got some work to do."

"Now?"

"Yes. It's important that you remember as much as you can. If you go back to sleep, you'll probably forget a lot of detail, and it's the small associations that tell the proverbial tale."

She turned off the equipment, removed the sensors from his head, and crawled into bed next to him. "Do you remember Rose talking about a second phase occurring due to your Time Displacement Hypnotherapy?"

"Sure. She said we couldn't discuss the subject for fear of affecting the outcome. Are you saying this is part of it?"

"Yes. What's happening is because of the changes introduced in your past, and remember, we changed it twice. Even though your history is altered, you still have memories that persist from the original experiences in your life, and subconsciously, these displaced events are attempting to reassert themselves into your present awareness.

This upheaval is instigating a conflict between your old and new realities, and as Rose stated, it's normal, but it does need to be examined and discussed before anything can be resolved. The first step is data acquisition. Your job is to report and record everything you can remember about your ... for simplification, we'll still call them dreams."

Tom sighed. "Shannon's involved in some of them."

"That doesn't surprise me. I'd be perplexed if she wasn't."

"There's one where I can almost see myself in that morgue bin after I'd been shot. That one can vanish anytime it wants, and as far as I'm concerned, the sooner the better."

"I'm not the psych expert, Tom, but I promise you, just bringing all these out into the open will help you deal with them tremendously. Don't worry, Rose and I will work with you. It'll take a long time for them to disappear altogether, but the worst should diminish quite quickly. Trust me ... you know I'd never lie to you. You're too important, and I love you far too much."

"Should I get started?"

"Yes. I'll get dressed and go for a walk around the complex so you can stay focused. You can use the keyboard or have the computer record you vocally, visually, or any combination that works. Just remember, the more information we have, the quicker we can make most of this vanish. When you're done with your work, we'll transmit it to Rose so she can begin an analysis. I will tell you the last phase is almost certainly at least five years away, possibly much longer. This final vanquishing of conflicts will allow you to be one whole person again, but be forewarned, as I'm sure Rose will tell you, the last phase is frequently triggered by a traumatic experience."

*   *   *   *   *

Kate saw that Tom's eyes were open. She turned and ran a hand over his chest. "How do you feel this morning?"

He shrugged. "Okay, I guess. It's the best night's sleep I've had since we've been here ... maybe all that work did some good. I'm hopeful anyway. What's on the schedule for today?"

"I made a reservation at the restaurant on top of Olympus Mons. If we go back without at least visiting it, our friends will never forgive us. The view alone is worth the wait, but I understand the food is good, too. We can take our things and beam straight to the outer-ring preparatory MMT station from there."

"More releases to sign I suppose."

"Probably, but you have to understand their position. Beaming around safely on earth is pretty much a given. Even the 1.3 seconds it takes from low-orbit platforms to L4, L5, or the moon is a perfectly acceptable risk. But you must admit, the trip from earth's moon to the inner-ring, then toward Mars is quite lengthy, being in excess of four minutes.

Plus, there was the extra time it took traveling around the inner-ring until we were positioned for the jump to Mars. In this case, that was an additional 210 million miles, or almost 19 minutes, for a total of 23. That's a relatively long time for existence within a neutrino-based signature map ... and the jump to TheBelt is even longer."

"Are you trying to talk me out of it?"

"No, and I'm sure the technicians and controllers wouldn't either. They just want to inform travelers of the heightened risk. Accidents have occurred. Approximately five years ago, an entire family was lost due to an unexpected micrometeorite storm even the computer didn't manage to detect."

"Okay, as of now, I'm fully aware of the dangers. What's our first stop in TheBelt?"

"Ceres. It's the capital and largest asteroid ... a 602 mile long hunk of rock. Most people live in the hollowed out core. The remainder subsist in pockets created in the rest of the stony structure. They travel via interconnecting passageways. There was enough mass lost because of mining activities, its orbit was shifted inward, nearer the sun, so it wouldn't escape into deep space, perhaps even out of the solar system."

Tom chuckled. "I guess you could think of it as 'cheap seats' to the stars."

*   *   *   *   *

Tom and Kate beamed onto the ground floor lobby of Olympus Mons. There were four large sections around the outer walls that serviced the restaurant fifteen miles above. As it turned out, a large part of the mountaintop-dining enchantment was getting there. Each of the four sections was actually an open grav-lift, furnished like a comfortable living room that rose independently to the top. A one-way ride took thirty minutes, and up to forty passengers could look out over the plains of Mars through protective windows. Upon arrival at the top, the pair had about a 15-minute wait for their table, which they put to good use drinking mimosas made from Martian champagne and the juice of genuine, locally-grown oranges.

The couple decided to have breakfast since it was still only 10 a.m. local time. Tom was amazed at the consistency of good food produced by auto-cookers. "This is the same synthetic stuff we eat at home, right?"

Kate nodded. "Yes. What prompted your question?"

"Well, I guess it's about the same mystique as it was in my time. What we were really paying for was the chef using secret recipes in preparing the food."

She chuckled. "That's true, except now instead of a talented chef, you're paying for the services of a gourmet programmer who knows the unpublished intricacies of chemical interactions."

Their food was served and Tom gazed down upon his plate. "Oh well, as long as my taste buds are happy ... I suppose that's the only thing of importance."

After finishing their meal, Tom and Kate wandered over to a plaque near one corner of the restaurant. Emblazoned in stone was a tribute:

> 'In memory of the 192 men, women, and children who lost their lives during one of the most vicious sandstorms known since the settlement of Mars. It occurred in the Martian year 17. Unusually fierce winds measuring in excess of 350 mph tore several protective metal plates off the windows. In the dark skies, no one noticed they were missing. Only minutes later the windows were abraded to thin membranes and burst outward from the internal pressure, blasting all the room's inhabitants into the vacuum of the howling maelstrom. No bodies have ever been recovered, and are assumed to still lay wherever they landed, now probably buried under multiple layers of fated Martian soil.'

Kate turned and cried softly on Tom's shoulder. "Oh Tom, that's horrible."

"Yeah, that's a hell of a note on which to leave Mars, but it's one we'll certainly never forget."

"On the Plains of Hesitation bleach the bones of countless millions who, at the Dawn of Victory, sat down to wait, and waiting – died!"

- George W. Cecil

Chapter 42
Less Is Sometimes More

After traveling 406 million miles in approximately 36 minutes, Tom and Kate emerged on Ceres. The reception area was busy, but poorly lit. People stole quick, almost cautious glances at the newly-arrived couple, then seemed to make a determined effort at fading away into the shadows.

Tom studied their reactions. "We were warned about this. The three most important commodities in TheBelt are food, water, and energy. There's barely enough for the locals, so they don't like sharing with visitors."

Kate noticed him straining to hoist his bag off the integration platform. "Tom, am I imagining things or have you added even more to your cache of paraphernalia?"

"In truth, I took your advice and lightened my load. I have only a few clothes left. The rest I already sent home via standard interplanetary mail facilities. Most of what I have in here is a secret weapon that'll hopefully convince the local accommodation's manager to help us."

"What was the seed for this inspiration?"

"Remember when we were sitting at the bar last night waiting for our table and you went to powder your nose?"

"Yes."

"The guy on my left and I struck up a conversation while you were gone. He and his wife, Aristae, live on Mars, but apparently he spends a lot of time commuting between home and TheBelt. He's a mining operations manager and I think his name is Dar. Anyway, we were talking about things in general when they got a page over the intercom announcing their table was ready.

Dar and Aristae started walking away, but before getting too far he turned and told me the best way to make inroads with TheBelt locals is by bringing a gift of what they need most. I asked him what he meant, to which he replied, 'think about it', and then he was lost in the crowd."

Tom patted his suitcase, "So, I attempted to take his advice." He pointed. "Hey, look down the passageway; it's the Prosperous Prospector ... that's our hotel. Let's go register and see if my idea works."

"How may I help you, sir?"

"My name's Tom Hughes and this is Kate Bright. I believe you should have a reservation for us."

"Just a moment, let me check. Ah, yes ... we have you booked for a 72-hour stay. Is that correct?"

"Yes, it is. There's something else I was hoping you could help me with. We're looking for a guide. Someone to take us out and tour a few asteroids. Is that possible?"

The clerk smiled. "It is occasionally done, but at the moment, I don't think anyone is available ... I'm sorry. Perhaps another time."

Tom drummed his fingers on the counter. "Could I talk with the manager, please?"

"Certainly, but I'm sure he'll tell you the same thing. Just a minute, let me see if I can locate him."

A strange looking gentleman with a pointed head and chin strode up from behind the counter. "Mr. Hughes, I presume."

"Yes."

"I'm Dekkel Edlin, the manager. Your reservation seems to be in order. Is there a problem?"

"My lady friend and I were hoping to find a guide, hopefully visit a few of the smaller occupied asteroids. Can you help us?"

"I'd like to assist, but it'd be most difficult locating someone who'd accept a charter on such short notice. I'm truly sorry."

Tom heaved his luggage onto the counter. "I'm fully prepared to make an appropriate contribution, contingent on the cooperation of the hotel and our guide." He turned the case's opening towards Dekkel, unlatching the cover.

Tom nodded toward the case. Dekkel lifted the lid and the expression on his face silently articulated his delight.

Kate peeked around and visually inventoried what she could see ... eight gallons of water in collapsible bottles, dozens of packages containing dried fruit and vegetables, and at least ten high-efficiency solar rechargeable power cells.

Dekkel closed the case and, almost affectionately, caressed its cover. "How many of these items were you considering for, uh, donation?"

"All of it. Half to the hotel, half for our guide." Tom cooed, "It's too bad you can't find anybody."

The manager held up an index finger. "Let me make a call. I'll be right back."

Tom and Kate wandered through the shops in what would be considered the downtown center of Ceres. Word had gotten around they should be treated as much like natives as possible, so although the people remained guarded, they had become friendlier.

A maintenance engineer named Cyr Nardin had agreed to be their guide, but he would only meet them on Vesta. Cyr was reported to be about sixty years old and almost six feet tall, with dark brown hair and eyes, sporting a mustache and bushy beard. He didn't care much for outsiders, but since the arrangement had been made internally, Nardin could hopefully be trusted.

The couple was waiting for clearance of the Pallas asteroid's transmission path where they would then be redirected to Nardin's home territory.

* * * * *

Kate and Tom agreed Cyr Nardin would've been easy to spot, even if he hadn't been the only one waiting near the transportation pads.

Tom extended a hand. "Mr. Nardin?"

"Yeah, that's me, but unless you're some stickler for formality, you'd better call me Cyr, and I'm assuming Tom and Kate will fit the two of you."

"That'll be fine, Cyr. No problem whatsoever."

"I took a minute to do some research. A member of TheTwenty and a guy born in 1979 isn't exactly our normal type of visitor." Cyr guffawed, "I'd dare say you two aren't typical anywhere. I understand you'd like to visit some private asters, is that right?"

"We understand you service equipment on asteroids in a large area. We don't want to intrude on anyone's privacy, but if we could see inside a few currently untenanted 'asters', that'd be great."

"Alright, I think that can be arranged easily enough. I have some scheduled runs to make today." Cyr pulled at his beard. "Would you two be interested in a little detective work?"

"That depends on what you mean," Tom replied.

"There's an aster way out that hasn't been responding to SR calls ... that's status requests by the way. The computers try and keep in touch with folks to make sure they're okay. We haven't heard from this particular aster in almost thirty time periods.

I've got a freshly updated MMT on my ship, and theirs needs to be replaced, so I thought I'd run out and make an even swap. That way I can also check out why their system hasn't been responding. The opportunity to get out there just came up, so you're welcome aboard ... if you feel like tagging along."

Tom turned to Kate. "What do you think?"

"How long will this take, Cyr?"

"The whole trip, including your sightseeing, will be 8-10 hours."

Kate nodded at Tom. "Sounds perfect."

Cyr held out his hand to Kate. "By the way, it's nice to meet you. I have all the respect in the system for members of TheTwenty. I hear they're real fine people. Oh, and I didn't mean to exclude you from our conversation either. Absolutely no insult intended. It's just that your man here was on a roll and handling things first-rate."

"None taken, Cyr. I just told this old dog the other day he has a way of learning fast."

Cyr shook his head. "Nineteen Seventy-Nine ... doesn't that defy all logic."

The threesome stopped at four asters, whose owners were away. Cyr made minor repairs and adjustments as his 'customers' looked around. All the remodeled planetoids were remnants of mining operations that had been retrofitted with air locks and pressurized living spaces. They were complete with a variety of plants and trees to supply oxygen while recycling carbon dioxide. Small fusion generators supplied power. Some even included waterfalls and fish-filled ponds. Their recycling areas seemed to be duplicates of the parks on L4 in miniature. Kate was impressed. Tom couldn't be stopped from pointing out every little nuance he found. It finally came time to visit the mysterious aster that had dropped out of communication.

Cyr parked his modified ex-mo on one of the larger asters in the vicinity. "I'm afraid this is where we change our mode of transportation. We'll be going into an area heavily populated with rogue rock pieces. I won't take my ship into places like that. We'll use a shuttle instead."

Tom frowned. "Are you worried about meteor strikes?"

"No. My ship, the shuttle, and all the residences have anti-G repellant fields around them. The smaller craft is just much easier to maneuver in tight spaces."

Tom carried the updated MMT into the asteroid. Cyr passed him on the way, toting the old model out. Cyr had just reentered the innermost airlock when there were several loud pinging noises, followed by a shudder, then another. Finally, the small hollow rock lurched sideways ... knocking everyone off their feet.

"What's happening?" Tom cried.

Cyr struggled to regain his footing. "The first were micrometeorite strikes, but those last had to be much bigger."

"I thought you said these things had safety features to protect against such dangers."

"They do. The fools must have turned them off. That means the owners abandoned the rock and never had any intentions of returning." He shrugged. "It happens. Check on Kate, I'll survey the damage."

She was still on the floor, leaning against a bulkhead.

"Kate, are you okay?"

"I think so. I'm just a little groggy. My head smacked something. Help me up."

The couple was supporting each other when Cyr returned. His face was pale. "I'm afraid I've got bad news. The warning systems were rendered inoperative and the defensive repulsive equipment was shut down ... even the life-cubes were completely ignored. They're nowhere near compliance levels."

"Can't we just re-enable everything?" Tom queried.

"Not now. The strike must have damaged most of the outside sensors." Cyr hung his head and sighed. "Our transport is demolished, too. We're stranded."

"There's plenty of food, water, and oxygen. We can wait until help arrives," Kate offered.

Nardin slowly shook his head. "No. No good. The detection system is one of the few systems I managed to get working. It indicates a much larger mass coming from the same direction as the other strikes. It's on a direct collision course with us. Our maneuvering jets are empty, and there's no time to get enough air pressure into them before the big one gets here." He plopped down heavily onto a chair. "The blasted thing is going to kill us ... and there's nothing we can do about it."

Tom smacked his hand against a support beam. "I refuse to accept that. What if we just dump atmosphere out the airlock? That should push us out of harm's way, no matter which direction we go."

Cyr sighed again. "Already thought of that. The vents are only partially controllable because of the damage. We'd have to shut down the computer controls completely, then purge the locks manually. Even the three of us coordinating on separate tasks couldn't get it all done in less than thirty minutes. It'd work if we had time ... we don't. Our demise will be here in less than twenty."

Tom's eyes found Kate. Hers were already on him. His face twisted into a hard grin. "I guess there's nothing like testing a theory under fire. I don't see any other way out of this one."

She nodded. "I certainly don't like it, but it sure beats sitting here waiting to become space dust."

Cyr looked from one to the other. "What are you two talking about?"

Tom clapped Cyr's shoulder. "Perk up. We're going to beam out."

"Are you crazy? There's no station nearly close enough to receive us."

"You're right. The machine will project me back to your ship. You two will be encased in life-cubes and tag along like my personal baggage. Cyr ... how about giving Kate instructions so she can update the MMT, while you pick out two of the best cubes you can find."

Nardin didn't move. In fact, he leaned against a wall and leered. "That's just great. You'll end up being nothing more than a pile of jelly, and what's left of our lives will ebb away as the power runs down in the life-cubes because there'll be no one around to restore us. Besides, the whole endeavor is pointless, MMTs can't project animate matter ... you must surely know that. "

Tom smiled slyly. "Yes, I do. What's more important, I'm confident I know why. It's the DNA snippet and other biological changes introduced into your bodies to withstand the rigors of teletransportation. Regrettably, the MMTs' projection code was never updated properly to recognize it. But remember, I was born in 1979. What do you think the chances are that I have any of these same alterations?"

Cyr stared. "None."

"That's right. Now get busy if you want to live."

Kate set the MMT's controls with the coordinates Cyr gave her, then scanned the control room's interior. She spotted a first-aid station, ran over, and rifled through the contents. Kate pulled out a box, read the side panel, then hurried back and handed it to Tom. "Here ... this is concentrated synthetic epinephrine. Follow the instructions and prepare an injection for yourself.

Administer the dose about three seconds before you project. It's the only chance you'll have of regaining consciousness before our life-cubes lose power since they've not been maintained."

Cyr returned. He was growling, "These are the best I could find, and they'll only hold a charge for about twenty minutes once you've started the download."

Tom looked from one cube to the other. "How long is the process?"

"Three minutes to download or restore."

Cyr checked his wrist device. "We've got ten minutes before that other rock slams into us. We'd better make them count."

Nardin ran through the process of downloading Kate into a life-cube as Tom observed. Afterwards, Cyr positioned his own cube, then explained, "Everything's ready. All you have to do is tell the computer: 'repeat last process and execute next program'. Remember, when I'm done and you're ready to leave, at least six minutes of Kate's time will have expired." Cyr looked at Tom's needle. "Don't forget that, or as Kate stated, she and I are already dead."

* * * * *

Tom was lying across the transmit mat within Cyr's ship when he awoke. His eyes slowly regained focus. He sprang into action as the stimulant took effect, clearing his thoughts. The life-cubes were swiftly snatched from where they had fallen, and he raced to the reintegration controls. Tom glanced at his wrist device and realized too much time had elapsed ... ten precious minutes.

He held a cube in each hand ... his eyes flicking madly between them. His mind struggled to distinguish the one harboring Kate. Regrettably, they looked identical. Tom frantically shoved one into its designated receptacle and pressed a keypad ... initiating the restore process.

All the while, the knowledge that there wasn't enough time left to restore both before their power cells went dead was gnawing at his gut. Tom closed his eyes and hoped like he never had before.

The computer chimed, "Reintegration complete," closely followed by the expected flash of light. Cyr Nardin appeared and leaned forward, resting his hands on a safety railing for support. Tom stared for a moment ... forcing mental acceptance of his arbitrary choice, after which he exchanged the life-cubes and restarted the process.

The status bar confirmed only 14 percent completion when the power light on Kate's cube changed from gratifying-green to ominous-orange. Less than a minute later, Tom watched in horror as the life-cube's light slowly dimmed ... then went totally dark. He grabbed both sides of the interface terminal ... willing it to be wrong.

"NOOOOOOOO!"

Cyr wobbled over. "Tom ... what's wrong?"

"The power supply in Kate's life-cube failed before the process finished." Tom buried his tortured face in his hands and moaned, "She's gone."

Cyr stared at the screen quizzically, then changed to a different display. "Tom ... it's okay ... look. The cube automatically switched to the ship's power before it became exhausted. Now it's coupled with a different indicator; you just needed to swap views for the updated info."

Another flash substantiated Cyr's deduction. Tom flew to Kate as she stumbled off the reintegration platform and collapsed against a wall. He held her tightly, pressing his face against her wonderfully soft, fragrant hair.

"I thought I'd lost you, Kate. This ends it. I've had enough exploring and adventure to last for a long time. Let's go home."

Tom must make a life-and-death decision

"In each human heart are a tiger, a pig, an ass, and a nightingale; diversity of character is due to their unequal activity."

- Ambrose Gwinnett Bierce

Chapter 43
Mutual Assimilation

Tom sat across from John's office desk. The two men had easily exchanged initial pleasantries, but Tom realized his friend was troubled from the uncharacteristic manner in which he kept twirling his pen. "John, I can tell something's bothering you, and it evidently has to do with me. At this point, I'd like to think we know each other well enough that you should feel comfortable bringing anything you need into the open. So, what is it?"

John slid forward on his chair. "Tom, you've done some great work on the projects. I've heard nothing but compliments from the others. It's also been only three weeks since you and Kate returned from your harrowing experience in TheBelt. So, I've been rather hesitant to mention anything about a problem that's crept into your reporting style. Unfortunately, a recent incident precludes my actions."

Tom spread his hands. "I've no idea what you're talking about, John."

"It has to do with your use of ... well, let's call them antiquated colloquial idioms. In a communication with Professor Wytt after his return to Mars, you updated him following the conclusion of an experiment utilizing the Casimir generator. Afterwards, he contacted me and was terribly upset. He wanted a damage report and asked if anyone had been injured in the explosion."

"What explosion?"

"That's the first thing I tried to deduce. I asked everyone involved. You were sleeping after having worked an extended shift, and when no evidence of an explosion was found, I decided to question Zack on the problem's basis. I asked him to send me the part of your message that had aroused his concern. Your report concluded with the strange terminology: it was a real blast."

Tom hung his head and groaned, "Oh no. I remember now. I was so excited ... it never entered my mind that the wording might cause confusion. I'm sorry, John ... really, really sorry."

"I believe I was successful at explaining the meaning behind the meaning to Zack. He was so relieved he actually laughed. The misunderstanding has been reasonably repaired. I just need your assurance you'll do everything in your power to avoid a reoccurrence of the problem."

"Okay, John. I promise, from now on, my reports and correspondence will be by the book ... desert dry. When you read them, you'll have to blink more often so your eyes will remain moist. I sure hope that covers everything."

"Since you're in attendance, there's another aspect relating to this subject that impinges upon my curiosity. It concerns your use of the word 'cool'. I've noticed it more in your conversations than in your writing. What puzzles me is the fact you aren't making reference to temperature gradients, or even climatic conditions. Can you explain this particular vocabulary oddity?"

Tom's hands danced feebly while he searched for meaning. "I can't answer the question precisely, John. Cool just happens to be a word that in my time covered a multitude of situations. I guess it functioned as an abbreviated expression of many feelings at once. It simultaneously implies happiness, satisfaction, well-being, gratitude, congratulations, and probably several others I can't even think of at present."

Dr. Picus frowned. "Hmm. Then I don't imagine I could personally ever sanction use of the word in such a tenuous context. I strongly believe emotions worth expressing should be done so only after deeply considering their root cause. Therefore, I can't envision myself as ever being so entrenched in a moment that I still wouldn't want to express myself calmly, purposely, and succinctly ... even at the risk of seeming overly verbose."

Tom chuckled. "Okay, John, I see your point, but we all have certain habits that become ingrained over time. This just happens to be one of mine. I will refrain from using it in my reports though."

John nodded. "Very well. Do you have any questions?"

"Yes ... two. Kate is giving her thank-you party a week from this Saturday for those who contributed to our trip. Are you coming?"

"Kate invited me at an earlier date; I've already gratefully accepted. She probably just forgot about mentioning it to you." John's half-grin indicated something special was forthcoming. "She also gave me permission to make an announcement during the party, which I'm sure most people will find ... significant."

"Would it do any good to ask what your disclosure involves?"

"No, it would not. Next."

"It's about someone named Jorge. I've overheard the name in conversations occasionally. Kate and Rose have mentioned him briefly. Who is he?"

John leaned back. "What prompted you to ask?"

"From what little I've gathered ... he's someone who's suffered a terrible loss and hasn't been able to recover on his own. Since everyone's been so nice and supportive to me, I thought maybe there'd be a way I could help."

"Give me a minute, Tom, while I consider how best to satisfy your request." John thoughtfully tapped a finger on his desk, then began pecking at his keyboard. "I'll put a package of articles together from our private net and direct it to your E-mail address. That should be sufficient to get you started.

Then, perhaps at the party, after the other guests have departed, Kate, Rose, you, and I can casually discuss our mutual friend and associate."

"That'll be fine, John. I'll look forward to it. Thank you." Tom rose to leave, but spun back down into his chair instead.

John's eyes flicked up from his reading. "Is there something else you wish to discuss?"

"Why was I brought forward?"

John seemed genuinely amused. "I was wondering when you'd make that particular inquiry."

"When Kate informed me about timeline alterations, she said they were performed for the benefit of the future. Even so, I thought at first, maybe I was being rescued from my original fate. Then I learned that would violate every ethic your time council considers a keystone belief." Tom appealed with his hands. "So ... can you explain it?"

"To all intents and purposes, the action has already been explicitly specified by Mrena. It probably became buried in all the background informational noise during the celebration of your arrival."

"Do you mean my first night here?" John nodded. "That was all a blur."

John shrugged. "My meaning ... exactly."

"How do you know? You weren't at the reception and didn't stay for the party."

"Rose invited me to watch a replay of both functions with her. Do you recall Mrena asserting that most of us have extremely focused specialties?"

Tom's mind drifted back. His head was soon bobbing. "Yes ... I do remember, but what does that have to do with my question?"

"Everything ... because following that premise, she stated you'd probably prove to be instrumental in melding ideas across many disciplines since you were extremely adept at generalities. I've obviously had time to think about this matter. Let me rationalize it in a manner I believe you'll appreciate.

You have an uncanny innate quality, which allows you to perfunctorily broadcast a telepathic SOS when you require assistance solving a problem. I envision some bored, humble, unsuspecting clerk laboring at the galactic library of universal knowledge responding to the plea. As soon as the connection is established, you disseminate questions in rapid-fire order. Before the dolt can think, he begins flashing answers until he realizes he doesn't even know with whom he's communicating. At that point he severs the link, but by then you've already gleaned enough information to make an intuitive leap across an abysmal sea of allegedly unrelated data and experience your eureka moment.

In summary, you were brought forward because of your exceptionally unique mental persona."

"Are there others like me?"

"Yes, but only a select few. Now that you've asked, I'll give you the address of a web site where you can post a message to fellow time-displaced individuals. It'll solely be at their discretion whether they respond or not, since by default, their privacy is top priority."

"Well, that's a start. Thanks again, John. See you at the party."

* * * * *

Work made the days pass quickly, and following several sun-moon footraces, the following weekend was upon them. Guests began making their appearance at the party shortly after 7 p.m. Kate knew from experience that Rose, Frank, and Larry would probably arrive early, so had requested that each bring a dom-bot to assist in serving refreshments. The two men also brought female companions. Rose was alone, as usual.

Kate had arranged the apartment so the center was clear of furniture. Only two auto-cookers, an extra recycler, and several small utility tables were present. This became the working domain of the dom-bots during the evening.

By eight o'clock, all of Kate's invitees were present except John, which was typical. Tom observed many people he had not previously encountered. Accordingly, Kate began taking him among the various conversation groups that had formed and made introductions. Afterwards, they managed to find a fleeting unreserved interval for themselves.

"Alright, Fido, you've met everyone. As of now, you're on your own. Behave yourself. Promise me you will not bite anybody."

"Woof. Okay, kiddo, but you probably just ruined my entire evening." He bowed. "Therefore, I shall sally forth and mingle, my good lady."

“No. See, you’ve got it wrong already. We refer to it as orbiting.”

“Really? Well, I’d like to see the equations that describe the movements of all these bodies.”

Kate’s eyes flashed. “Tom ... I’ve been wanting to talk with John about something, but I couldn’t think of anything that would truly capture his attention. You’ve just given me a wonderful idea. Thank you.”

“Well, uh, sure ... you’re welcome. What is it?”

“I can’t tell you. This time you’re better off not being in the loop. I’ve got to go this one on my own. Go ahead and enjoy yourself. I have to find Frank and ask him for a favor.”

A short time later, Tom was talking with a new acquaintance when he saw Kate go into her study, followed by a lone dom-bot. She rejoined the crowd a few minutes later, but as the party continued, Tom noticed the same dom-bot selecting people and leading them into the study. When they exited, nothing seemed changed. Tom’s curiosity was now fully aroused, so he casually persisted with his observations.

John finally entered just past 9:30. At first, he became disturbed about the dom-bots’ dialogue. They seemed to be experimenting with some new phrases while interacting with the other guests, but they were perfectly polite and grammatically correct when addressing him. He didn’t know whether to be insulted or flattered. Following a few more interactions, he decided upon the latter.

At 10:00, the computer called for everybody’s attention. It reported that Dr. Picus would like to make a statement. They clustered around him and became quiet. “Good evening, everyone. I trust that due to the excellent preparations of our gracious hosts, you are having a pleasant time. I’d just like to take a moment for a brief announcement. Many of you will remember from our last Discovery-Day meeting that I alluded to a rather substantial project, of which the zero-spin tachyon experiments were only a part.

During Professor Wytt’s Q and A period, I thought he might inadvertently disclose a fragment of information prematurely. However, true to Zack’s experience and wisdom, he deflected the possibly awkward predicament commendably.

Conversely, at this time, because all current problems ultimately have fully anticipated solutions, I am authorized and thoroughly delighted in proclaiming the official unveiling of perhaps our most ambitious mission ever ... Starlight-Express ... humankind’s first endeavor ... to reach the stars.

Barring any utterly incomprehensible obstacles, the departure of our first starship is scheduled for twenty years from tonight. Our initial goal will be Alpha Centauri, since it’s the next closest star. This is a trinary system and we’ll gather crucial information concerning the intense gravitational tides existing between multiple massive cosmological objects. The data should prove invaluable for future expeditions.

The manifest will include all the scientific equipment we can board, and one thousand people consisting exclusively of volunteers. Some will have explicit duties; the remainder will rotate through nonspecific functions on a cyclical basis. All will spend most of their time in a tachyon zero-spin suspended animation field.

That's all I wish to formally make public, because even as I speak, the computers are making a full project disclosure across the entire solar system. Thank you for your indulgence."

John was so enthralled, he grinned. "Anyone intent upon hearing my unofficial comments is welcome to do so, of course, at the risk of overloading their auditory system. Oh, incidentally, our first solicitation of input from citizens everywhere ... will be nominations for the ship's name."

Tom immediately retrieved a slip of paper and wrote: Enterprise.

Dr. Picus was the obvious center of attention for awhile, but people slowly began to reform into smaller groups, their discussions alive with a heightened buzz. After he broke free, John found Tom and escorted him to a quieter corner of the apartment. "So what did you think of my revelation?"

"It's unbelievable. Half the science-fiction stories of my time were focused on people traveling between the stars, or at least something to do with deep space. The fact that I may live to see it actually happen, better yet ... participate, is mind-boggling."

"I was hoping to see excitement on your face, Tom. Instead, what I believe I see is fear. Tell me I'm wrong."

"I'm not afraid of leaving earth, but I'm extremely fearful about feeling compelled to do so."

John nodded. "You're saying, if the team decides to leave, you think everyone, including Kate, is expecting your acceptance in joining them."

"Exactly. If I decide not to accompany the others, I'm terrified of what'll happen between Kate and me."

"Tom, all of TheTwenty are planning on departing, except perhaps Xarles. I was just talking with him. He ranted about how we've made earth the perfect place to live, and he can think of no reasonable explanation to leave. No pollution, no crime, full employment, no untreatable disease, 200-year life span ... a full litany of admittedly logical reasons to remain behind.

After he finally finished, I reminded him those were past challenges. We'll be taking all those accumulated accomplishments of our civilization with us. But, it's a fresh prospective we seek ... new, unimaginable quests.

I realize this is an awkward time for you to think about this conundrum. However, you have twenty years to decide. One aspect you definitively needn't worry about is Kate. In the end, no matter what you want, Kate will want the same. I guarantee it. If you join us, that will be wonderful. If you don't, then that's your decision and we'll all respect it.

Meanwhile, I have something for you to retain. These are trip tokens for you and Kate. I'm confident Xarles will change his mind. The remaining tokens will go quickly, so keep these with you, always.

Once the personnel list is in the computer, these will be strictly symbolic, but whenever you think about the journey, take these out. Maybe they'll help you focus."

"Thanks, John. I'll do that. Oh, this is for you."

"What is it?"

"My suggestion for the ship's name ... along with several other million past members of the populace who couldn't be here."

"Sorry, Tom. I can't accept direct input. You'll have to fill out a form on the net. It'll be available tomorrow. It looks like the party is breaking up. Let's find Rose before she leaves, and we'll have that talk about Jorge."

It was getting late, and the four friends had completed their exchange concerning Jorge, so John and Rose departed. Kate sent the borrowed dom-bots to their respective owners, along with thank-you notes.

Tom and Kate withdrew to the atrium while her dom-bots eliminated the remaining clutter. She lay on the sofa; he sat across from her in an enviro-chair. Kate turned to face him. "Does the new data about Jorge help?"

"Oh, yes. It filled in a lot of holes. I've actually formulated a skeletal plan of attack. I'll run it by you and Rose as I firm it up a bit. I'm reasonably confident about 'whom', 'what' and 'why', but I'm currently at a loss as to 'where' and 'when'."

"Well, since you're a near genius, I'm sure you'll think of something."

"Rose seemed noticeably uncomfortable talking about Jorge, or was that just my imagination?"

"They had a close reciprocal relationship when we were younger ... not lovers, yet certainly something more than simple friendship. I'm sure Rose would have liked to pursue it further, but at the time, Jorge thought he wanted someone else. After that, Rose slowly lost herself in her career."

"Hmm. That's something to keep in mind."

Tom stood and stretched. "I didn't have a chance to shower earlier and I feel grubby, so I'll take one now."

Kate sat up excitedly. "Oh, wait a minute. I almost forgot ... one of our friends left you a souvenir. Stand right there, I'll demonstrate it."

She reached into a pocket, removed a small device, placed it behind her back, and pressed a button. Seconds later, there was a rumbling noise. The far wall of the apartment burst inward, and out of the dust an image of a T-Rex came charging at them.

Tom was dumbfounded initially, but instinctive reactions emerged and he pushed Kate away from the danger. He attempted to dive the other way and draw the beast's charge, but crashed into the chair. It tumbled over with him landing on top.

The Rex's head swooped down, its teeth clacked together loudly, and Tom swore something tugged at his hair. The Rex's momentum caused it to topple over, sliding on its side and crashing through the opposite wall. Tom jumped up and stared at the gaping hole. "This must be one of Frank's toys."

She was laughing. "You're right. He made it from the same disks he used for John's holograph. My arm must have flopped over the mound you had tossed me behind and my wrist device recorded everything.

Frank said the original recording angle was terrible, but was corrected when the computer rotated the entire scene. He thought you'd like to have a memento of our Jurassic encounter. Actually, there are several stored in this control. You just need a projector like the one in my atrium ceiling to exhibit them."

"Great. Now I can schedule being scared to death."

She giggled. "Sorry. Should I play the one where you meet Bisbee in the tower?"

"Not tonight. I'm going to grab that shower and try stuffing my heart back into my chest where it belongs."

Kate replied sweetly, "Yes, my love."

She pressed another button, which de-energized the hologram, returning the apartment to its initial configuration.

Kate was relaxing on the sofa when she heard Tom's shower. She slipped off her wrist device, admired its beauty, and set it on an end table. Her slippers and socks came off next as she headed for the bedroom.

Half way there, on a whim, the lady stopped and stretched her arms toward the ceiling, turning a slow pirouette. For an encore, she tightly wound her arms one way, then whipped them around the opposite direction while rising up onto the ball of one foot.

Momentum carried her through two complete revolutions before she stopped and hopped onto the other foot, grabbing the first with a hand and rubbing it. "Ouch. That carpet burns!" She chided herself for not thinking and was still muttering when she reached the doorway.

Kate scanned the bedroom with all the innocence of a grinning Cheshire cat seeking mischief. Seeing nothing intriguing, she sighed and plopped on the bed ... staring at the ceiling. A minute later she jumped out of bed and sharply slapped the mattress with a hand. The firmness dial was turned to a much higher setting followed by another swat on the bed. Kate shook her head and upped the setting once more. At last she seemed satisfied, concluding her preparations by leaping on the bed and beginning to bounce. Her hands came closer to the ceiling with each recoil.

Soon, there was a rhythmical sequence of thump-smack, thump-smack, thump-smack pulsating through the apartment. After a few minutes, the closed bathroom holodoor planted the seed of another idea in her mind.

She bent her knees to interrupt her established cadence and jumped off the bed, landing with a loud thud. Kate stripped off her clothes and advanced purposely toward the bathroom.

Tom was rinsing his hair when he detected a strange pattern of unfamiliar noises. He cocked an ear towards the open space above the shower door and listened intently. The regular cyclic sounds abruptly ended, punctuated by a heavy bump. The words 'are you okay' lined up just above his vocal chords. He was about to expel them from his throat with a heavy rush of air when Kate's voice rang off the acoustically reflective walls.

"READY OR NOT, HERE I COME!"

Tom and Kate were in their robes, lying quietly on the bed with a small gap between them. Only the fingertips on a single hand from each were touching. Tom rose up on an arm and gazed down upon her face. "Okay, Kate, what's bothering you? You've been hyper and acting strange all evening."

"True. After all, I've certainly never used the bed as a trampoline before."

Tom chuckled. "Ah, that's what the noise was. I couldn't really hear it over the running water. I thought maybe it was a dom-bot performing some sort of routine maintenance task. It was quickly forgotten when you came charging through the door and surprised the hell out of me. I suppose that also explains why you had to adjust the mattress. It seemed unusually firm when I first laid down."

"I just hope my plan works the way I want."

"Does this have to do with your dom-bot escorting people into and out of your study?"

She rolled over against him and softly moaned. "You saw that, huh? Then I guess I might as well tell you what I'm doing. What's the surest way you know to get John's attention? I mean really make him listen."

"Write a super detailed scientific analysis of ... something."

Kate nodded. "Exactly. So that's what I decided to do, except I couldn't think of anything distinctive, until you made that remark about 'orbiting bodies'. That's when I had Frank ask the lab if they'd beam over a few of his holographic markers.

Then I instructed my dom-bot to select people, at random, and request that they take part in an experiment, on what else, but 'randomness'. They wouldn't be told anything else except to conceal the test from others, based on the premise it could influence the outcome of the assessment. If they agreed, the dom-bot marked their fingertips, and the camera recorded their movements for thirty minutes."

Tom frowned. "And this all leads to ... what?"

"The bait. After everyone left, the computer averaged all the recorded motions into half a dozen partial orbital tracks. Now, I'll have the machine write a complex mathematical thesis describing the data collection routines, math tables, formulas, and any other functions required to calculate the completed orbits. But, it will only be allowed to use the averaged data, not the individual data points."

He stared for a moment. "It can't. Not if it uses only the averaged data. The very randomness of the 'orbits' won't allow for a solution."

She smiled. "That's my plan. It'll accomplish both my goals. It'll have John's interest at its highest point, and it will also be the time when he calls me to his office, expecting an explanation. Then I'll hit him with what I really want to talk about."

"Are you sure the computer was able to collect any data?"

"Positive. Why do you ask?"

"I didn't notice anyone with marked fingers all evening."

"No. You wouldn't. The dye is transparent in normal light. The camera would be using a special frequency not in the visible spectrum. I can at least show you how it works."

She flew from the room, returned, and then zipped back into bed, all in about twelve seconds. "Give me a hand."

Tom extended his fingers and watched as Kate dabbed each tip with the marker. She laughed as she added extra spots to his nose, cheeks, chest, and elbows. "Here, want to do me?"

Tom snickered as he marked all the same positions on her body.

She giggled, "That tickles."

He examined the invisible results. "So, what's this supposed to prove?"

"Just a second. I'll show you. Computer."

"Yes, Dr. Bright."

"Record the movements of these additional markers for thirty minutes. Afterwards, include the results in your averages and recalculate the totals."

"Message understood."

Tom laughed. "So now, I am involved."

"Only innocently, but I could use your moral support tomorrow."

He grinned. "All you have to do is ask."

"Will you help me?" Kate softly pleaded.

"I'll think about it."

She nudged him playfully, "Oh, you brat."

"Well, how do I happen to show up at John's office just when you need me?"

"Simple. I'll add your name as coauthor of the thesis. Trust me. You'll get a call the same time I get mine."

Tom reexamined his fingers. "You know, it'd be more fun if I could see the spots move."

"That can be arranged. Computer."

"Yes, Dr. Bright."

"Turn off the room lights and scan the wavelength spectrum until you find a frequency that'll cause the marker dye to fluoresce. This will make it visible to the human eye in the dark."

"Message understood."

The room lights snapped off, and seconds later, all the spots were floating magically in the air. Tom slowly shifted his fingers ... watching the tips move in the night. "Hmm ... they remind me of fireflies."

"I've never seen them. I'll have to take your word for it."

"When I hold my fingers steady, they remind me of a visual acuity puzzle that always entertained me as a kid."

"Oh ... which one?"

Tom caressed her arms and pulled her close. "Let's play ... connect the dots."

"I hate to see things done by halves. - If it be right, do it boldly, - if it be wrong, leave it undone."

- Gilpin

Chapter 44
Altering The Leopard's Spots

John strode swiftly through the holodoor that led from the hallway into his outer office. Alyce Cramdin gasped as her hand flew to her chest. "Oh my, Dr. Picus. You startled me."

"What have I done differently to effect such a response?"

"It's just that you're so early. I've usually already prepared your daily appointments and have gone to the cafeteria for breakfast before your arrival."

"Ah, I see. Sorry if I upset you, but I'm feeling extremely exuberant this morning. Do you remember my complaints about Dr. Hughes, how talented, yet undisciplined he seemed?"

"Yes, sir."

"I believe my admonishments are finally taking root in his stubborn, but fertile mind. There was a mathematical treatise on orbital bodies waiting for me this morning at my net ID. It appears to have been jointly submitted by Kate and Tom. I didn't have a chance to spend much time on it, but the mathematics is brilliant, involving a totally unique application of extended tensors and combinatorial inverse-sequence interpolations.

I didn't recognize which section of the planetary system they modeled, but the computer should be able to reverse engineer the theorems and make a positive identification. This step is also required in proving whatever deductions they may have attempted to extrapolate from theory." John broke from his private reverie. "Did you say you were going to breakfast, Miss Cramdin?"

"Yes, sir. Just a few more details need attention and I'll be ready."

"Would you mind if I joined you?"

"No, sir. I'd be glad for some company."

"Good. Let me make a few quick modifications to the computer's parsing algorithms, direct them towards Tom and Kate's dissertation, and we'll leave."

When John returned, he was disappointed and somewhat surprised when he found the system had been unable to decipher any of the information.

"Computer, are you sure the modified search routines were executed?"

"Yes, Dr. Picus. I've performed more than twenty billion iterations employing literally hundreds of comparative validation techniques. None have provided any satisfactorily acceptable permutations that would properly describe the motions of these orbital tracks. My best supposition would indicate that the source data was generated in a subjectively random nature."

"Do you have any suggestions?"

"Yes, Dr. Picus. Just one. I would urgently request that Dr. Hughes and Dr. Bright submit confirmation of their input information."

John nodded. "Please locate the wily pair and have them report here ... immediately."

"Message understood."

* * * * *

John came around his desk, pulled up an extra chair, and was seated in front of his recently arrived guests. He looked from Tom to Kate and back.

"I received a certain mathematical treatise this morning, and was in a great mood until the computer attempted an interpretation of the work. I'm confident you both know why you're here. Who wants to begin?"

"This little escapade was all my idea, John. Tom was an unwitting accomplice to the end. If you have any questions, direct them at me."

"Any questions ... all I have are questions. The two that surface as most prominent are simply: what were you hoping to accomplish ... and why?"

"John, if I just blurt out the short answer, you'll probably get upset, maybe even angry. I ask only one favor. Please do me the service of waiting until I'm finished before you cast judgment or formulate a reply."

John rested against the seat back, folded his arms, and crossed a leg onto a knee. "Alright, you have my word. Please explain your actions."

"Ten months ago this little ploy would never have even occurred to me, but within that timeframe I met Tom, and my whole outlook on life has unquestionably changed. Even though I was happy with my work, and felt content existing like a mole in my apartment, I knew there was a hole in my life. The trouble was, I couldn't see past my own sorrow and loneliness to identify it. Hence, I couldn't recognize anyone else's either. It all seemed normal.

Now, I'm even happier with my work, and my apartment is simply where I live ... not a trap. But at the same time, my change in view has caused the emptiness in other people's lives to become painfully obvious, especially yours. You're an important man, John. You also have an enormous psyche. I needed to do something that would really catch your attention."

John grunted. "You've been completely successful in that aspect of your quest ... continue."

She slid a hand onto his. "I'm worried about you. I see your life dribble away in meetings, scheduling projects, subsisting alone in your apartment every night, just like I used to do. It hurts to watch. I love you as if you truly were my brother. I want more for you, and deep down inside, I think you do, too. So, I took a chance."

John shifted in his chair. "Why didn't you just come and talk to me?"

"It wouldn't have had near the same impact. I've tried it in the past. I'll bet you don't even remember. That's why I did something a little ... crazy. But do you want to know something else ... I also did it simply because it was fun. That's one of the most wonderful things Tom has taught me."

"That fun cost a lot of computer time probably greatly needed by other projects."

"Computer."

"Yes, Dr. Bright."

"How many CPU cycles has my latest work deprived other projects?"

"Absolutely none, Dr. Bright. The system was recently upgraded to contain one hundred 69-teraflop photonic CPU's operating in overlapping parallel mode. The actual average CPU-busy percentage over the last 24 hours is 54.7. If your work were factored out, the resulting percentage would only drop to 54.5. Of course, these figures do not take into consideration the four CPU's configured strictly for standby status."

John rolled his eyes. "Computer ... cease and desist. Alright, Kate, I concede the point. Then what in the name of infinite wisdom is your recommendation for this hypothetically wretched individual."

"Simple. Get away from here for a while. Take a vacation. Go see those people you've always promised you'd visit." She caught the abrupt interest in his eyes. "Who are they, John? You've instantly piqued my curiosity."

John stared pensively at Kate for a moment, focused intently on Tom, then ultimately returned to her. "What do you remember about the final disposition of TheTwenty's project directors?"

Kate flicked her hand. "They were all killed in a grav-sled accident shortly before docking with a low-orbit platform. It was headline-news throughout the solar system."

John leaned back. "What if I told you that entire incident was staged with replacement androids just to quell public opinion about the project, and TheTwenty in particular?"

"John ... are you saying the directors are still alive, and that's who you want to meet?"

He nodded. "That's it, exactly. The directors had powerful friends, but some of their enemies were just as potent. They covertly disclosed a substantial amount of disinformation about the project in preparation for destroying it, simply because they wouldn't take time to understand the objectives.

Sadly, many citizens chose to believe the rumors instead of the facts. As a result, they were terrified. A group of the directors' supporters concealed them, substituted the androids, and simulated the disaster. When the pressure dome lost its integrity, the enclosed atmosphere propelled all the occupants into space. The ones that fell towards earth were incinerated upon reentry, the rest were never recovered. All passengers were assumed lost. The project was abandoned, and we became wards of the state. Case closed."

Tom tapped John's arm.

"You have a question?"

"Do you know what the directors want to see you about?"

"Yes. They're getting old. They'd like to clear their names and expunge any false charges levied against the project before they die."

"Do you know their location?"

"No. I am aware they were given new credentials and moved to an obscure retirement colony. The computer is certainly cognizant of their precise location, but since it's confidential information, only those preauthorized by the directors would be permitted access to the data.

Of course, that's not been a problem, since except for the principals, just six others know of the directors' continuing existence. The number is now eight. I trust the two of you will keep it that way ... at least temporarily."

The couple nodded silent agreement.

John arose, replaced the borrowed chair, and was reseated behind his desk. "I guess I have some thinking to do."

Kate stood and stretched. "You should go, John. It's a noble cause and the public would certainly be completely supportive."

He nodded. "Yes, how ironic. Public opinion was the initial reason for the directors' deception. Now, TheTwenty are in demand everywhere because of our expanded mental capabilities and total honesty."

"Would you use Xarles as an intermediary?"

"My thoughts exactly, Kate. He'd be a perfectly logical and particularly effective choice."

Kate nudged Tom. "We should be leaving and let John do what he does best ... solve problems."

John beckoned with his hands. "But, Kate, what happened to all the concern about this lonely, miserable man?"

Kate chuckled. "You have my thoughts on the subject, and the last thing I want to do is open one of Tom's one-sided doors and let you brazenly exploit our emotions for all they're worth. Besides, maybe you can hold your feelings inside, but you can't hide them. I'm certain you can find all the assistance you need on many levels right in the room next door. Good-bye, John."

"What about you, Tom?"

He was following Kate. "I'm with her. Bye, John. Good luck."

"Tom ... wait. Since we've been discussing outrageous plans ... there's something about which I've been quite curious. What if the idea you had for revivifying my memory didn't succeed. Did you have an alternate?"

Tom laughed. "Yes. I was going to throw a long, brightly colored snake at you."

John chuffed. "I should have known. Okay, both of you ... out."

John sat alone in his office, eyes closed, elbows on desk, slowly rubbing his forehead against the tips of his steepled fingers. "Computer, are you authorized in booking passage for me to the directors' locale?"

"That's affirmative, Dr. Picus. They have been patiently awaiting just such a request."

"Please proceed."

John watched as the itinerary fell into place on his screen. "Ah hah, so that's where they hid you."

He stared at the wall separating him from his personal aide, his foggy thoughts and affections whirling into a smoky mental turbulence. Moments later, he made a decision and stabbed the intercom button. "Miss Cramdin?" Silence. He waited a minute. "Miss Cramdin, are you there?"

"Sorry, sir. I just returned from running an errand. What do you need?"

"Would you come in, please?"

"Yes, sir. I'll be right there."

"Miss Cramdin, I'm taking a two-week vacation. There is some business that will require my attention, but once a rapport is established, I'm confident there'll be adequate time for sightseeing and other leisure activities. I'd like to know if you'd accompany me. I could use your help ... and I'd enjoy your companionship, but I want it clearly understood ... this is a request ... not an order."

She laughed nervously. "Dr. Picus, this is twice in one day you've completely surprised me." Following a short pause she smiled and added, "I'd be honored to go with you."

"Computer, do you foresee any problem adding Miss Cramdin to the schedule?"

"Not if you personally vouch for her integrity, Dr. Picus."

"I do."

"Miss Cramdin has been cleared."

"Are two hours enough time to make your preparations, Miss Cramdin?"

"Yes, Dr. Picus. That'll be fine. Thank you."

He checked his wrist device. "Then I'll meet you at the local grav-port at say ... 15:30." John issued one of his rare smiles. "Miss Cramdin, do you suppose you can cope with one additional shock?"

"I'll try, sir."

"From now on, unless we're functioning in an official capacity, would you be offended if I called you Alyce, and you simply addressed me as John?"

"No, sir. I think that would be most pleasant."

"Good. Then I'll see you again in about two hours, Alyce."

She rose to leave but turned back. "I'll need to update the locator file ... John. May I ask where we're going?"

His index finger shot towards the ceiling. "The moon, Alyce ... to the moon!"

"They also serve who only stand and wait."
- Milton

Chapter 45
Thawing Out

Neil Barnes sat leaning back in his chair with his feet propped upon the work platform. Junior SA tech, Marrk Io, checked the readings on the sleeper canopies, updating the E-charts accordingly. "Hey, Neil. How long have you worked in the suspended animation department?"

Neil chucked softly. "SA, Marrk. After a week, I'd have thought you'd pick up on that. No one around here calls it 'suspended animation'. As for me, I've been here six years. Admin for the first three, then I became a tech through the upward-mobility training program. Made lead last year."

Marrk sauntered back towards Neil's workspace. "Like it?"

"Nope. Love it. The job is important, it's easy as long as you stay current, and I'm good at it."

"Does it make you nervous having all these lives in your hands?"

Neil laughed. "Is that what they told you in tech school?"

Marrk's face flushed. "Well ... yes."

"Don't get me wrong, kid. Like I said, this is an important job, but the computers run everything. It'd take a concentrated effort just to put people in danger, let alone kill them. I mean ... we're basically talking outright sabotage.

The computers are the brains and we're pretty much their arms and legs. But, I'll tell you this ... in an emergency, a good tech can be the difference between life and death, so stay ... oops."

Marrk bent over and studied the screen. "Got something?"

Neil dropped his feet and leaned forward, examining a flashing red square on a view screen. "It's cryo tank four again. I think there's a small leak in the condenser. That's three faults this week. I'll pass the error log down to maint and they'll swap the part out." He watched as computer generated code adjusted a valve, compensating for the problem. "Uh, oh. Here's something really interesting."

Marrk's eyes lit up. "Exploding supernovas! It's a code 801. Isn't that an order to wake a sleeper?"

Neil gave Marrk a sidelong look. "Yeah, but we get about two 801's a month on average. That's not what caught my attention. It's Grouch."

"Who's Grouch?"

"The youngest sleeper we have. Only 34, I think. Lost his wife and kids in a freak grav-sled accident out in TheBelt. He's stayed in SA as much as possible ever since. The only time he comes out is when his credits run low." Neil punched up an inquiry. "That's odd. He still has enough for at least two more years. Let's see who originated the wake-up order."

Neil scrolled the screen. What he saw made him sit straight up in his chair, almost at attention. "This is getting better and better. It's a NAGID. I've never seen one before."

"What's that?"

Neil looked at Marrk. "Didn't they teach you anything? It signifies the originator's identity is Not Available for General Information Dissemination. That implies the order came from someone with a lot of pull. Grouch is really going to earn his name. He's never mixed well with the upper echelon."

"Why do they call him Grouch?"

"His real name is Jorge Nebula and is ... was ... you choose ... a level-one grav-sled operator, as well as being the engineer that designed them. He was running the sled when his family died. The accident was the result of a mechanical failure, without any doubt, and he's lucky to be alive. Course, you'll never convince Jorge of either.

The story goes that the last thing his wife said to him was, 'it wasn't your fault. Don't do anything that shortens your natural life'. Everyone's convinced that's the only reason he's still alive. He's purely honoring her last wish. He only does two things when not in SA ... works at odd jobs earning credits to get back in, and uses inebriating drugs. When Jorge is overmedicated, he's a real mean case. Hence, the name Grouch."

"They have counter-acting preparations that'll cure him almost instantly."

Neil nodded. "Sure do. Try administering them to him."

"So why do people put up with him? Why doesn't a rehab get custody and mandate treatment? If he refuses, ship him out to TheBelt permanently, or at least until he reconsiders the assistance."

"Do you know why his name is Nebula?"

"I'd assume it's his family name, or he's applied for a name change at some point."

Neil shook his head. "Neither. When Jorge was young, all he could think about was astronavigation. Always dreamed of going to the stars. So, when he was fourteen he picked Nebula for a last name. Sound familiar?"

"The name?"

"No. The option of having any last name you want."

"The only people I know who could do that were ... are you telling me he's one of TheTwenty?"

"Affirmative."

"Smoking chip dust! Those people are living legends."

"Now you're integrating on all levels."

"Neil ... can I process him?"

"Sure, kid. Go ahead."

"Imaginary derivatives! Thanks, Neil."

"One condition."

"Anything!"

"You tell him why he's awake."

Jorge Nebula popped out of the restaurant/bar's MMT station and checked the customer information section on the marquee. It indicated that Tom Hughes was already present, seated in area fourteen, and visitors were to use guide color purple. He looked at the floor, picked out the thin colored line of light, and followed it through the maze of private settings separated by imaginary walls and white noise.

Tom had chosen a mountain forest motif, with deer, squirrels, and other various animals in attendance. When Jorge entered, he became extremely uneasy, even though he knew the scene was entirely holographic. He had never seen an animal before, except in digital imagery.

Tom mentally logged the reaction, pressed a keypad, and the scene changed to a randomly selected standard restaurant theme, complete with a buzzing crowd and busy wait people. Tom stood and offered a hand. "Sorry about that. I should have realized it might upset you."

Jorge accepted the outstretched hand. "You actually liked it?"

"I used to live in an area like that."

Jorge's suspicion alarm dinged.

"Look, Jorge, the first thing I want to do is apologize. I have a special mission in mind, and the computer selected you as being a top-contender for the job. I had no idea you were in SA. The info was there, but I missed it. I'm sorry."

Jorge's respect meter climbed ten points. "I'm here. What's the job?"

"To start, I need some assurances from you."

The meter dropped to zero again. "Are we talking about a contract? I hate all that legal double-speak."

"So do I. A verbal agreement will do for now. After I explain everything, another handshake will seal the deal."

Jorge was stunned. The meter broke. "I, uh ... okay, where do we start?"

"First, everything, and I mean everything that's said between us, goes no further ... whether you accept the job or not."

"Done."

"Good." Tom relaxed. "When did you last go into SA?"

"One twenty-three-forty-two."

"Ah. So you were awake when I arrived."

Jorge's head snapped in surprise. "You're that Tom Hughes?"

"If you're speaking of the relic from the past, yep, that's me."

"I thought you looked familiar ... there were stories about you all over the net."

"Trust me. You don't know the half of it."

Jorge's face broke into a sly grin. "According to the half I do know, you've supposedly become a personal friend of TheTwenty."

Tom displayed a challenging smile of his own. "Are you fishing?"

Jorge leaned forward. "Am I?"

"That reminds me. Kate says 'Hello', and I'm to inform you that you're missed by everyone."

Jorge blinked, his subtle attack forgotten. "You mean Khatty Bright?"

"Humph. I've only met one other person who calls her Khatty ... Rose Petals."

"So, you know Khatty and Rose."

"Yeah, along with John, Larry, Frank, Breeanya ... even Xarles ... pretty much the whole current earth-based gang."

Jorge sat back and considered this information for a moment. "What else do you know about me?"

"I know you had a real tough break and spend all of your time hiding from the truth ... because it justifies your self-pity."

"Which is?"

"You were completely blameless for the accident, but feel guilty as hell for being alive while the rest of your family is dead. It's a typical response, but with help and time to heal, most people at least try moving on. The problem is ... it's a lot of work, and without any motivation, leaving the problem go is a lot easier."

Jorge growled, "Why are you sticking your nose into it? What does any of this have to do with you?"

"I have it on good authority that before the accident you were truly a decent human being. I personally believe we can use all of those we can get. By the way, I know you're one of TheTwenty, so let's drop the pretense. Have you ever heard of Time Displacement Hypnotherapy?"

"Rose mentioned it. I'm afraid I didn't listen too well. I told her I could handle my problems fine."

Tom laughed. "That's what I used to think. Both Kate and Rose indicated you and I were alike ... intelligent, big-hearted, hard on ourselves, and sometimes ... real stubborn. But if it weren't for them, I'd be dead ... or worse."

"What could possibly be worse than dead?"

"How about just existing in a bed ... kept alive only by machines. I was so close to a total mental meltdown the candlewick was burning in the middle. All of it stemmed from a problem that would seem like nothing compared to yours. Mine just had a long time to simmer. Your stove has all its burners on high.

Kate and I are planning a little excursion. In fact, we're thinking about doing this once a year from now on as a vacation. This trip, we're hoping you and Rose will make it a foursome. You'll have your own separate, uh, rooms and baths. It'll be quiet, peaceful, and I guarantee there won't be anyone around to bother you. It'll be a great place and time to talk about problems.

We'll plan and take care of everything. The only thing you'll be required to do is try and keep an open mind ... oh, and drive a small sled."

"I haven't touched one of them since the accident."

"I know. But, it's part of the deal. We need a sled driver."

"Where exactly would we be going?"

"Before I tell you ... you must agree to go there."

"That's crazy."

"Absolutely."

"Can I think about it?"

"Absolutely."

"There is always an easy solution to every human problem – neat, plausible, and wrong."

- H.L. Mencken

Chapter 46
A Tradition Begins

Tom and Kate arrived first ... as planned. The ultra-lightweight equipment came next. John's newest model TMT began inputting air to replenish the matter banks. Tom ran a hand over its shiny exterior. "Back in my day, I was a pretty smart guy, but my intelligence totally pales next to John's."

Kate took his hand. "Don't be so hard on yourself. John had over three hundred additional years of previous discoveries to build on, including yours. Plus, the genetic alteration played a large part, too. He said you were quite a help in designing the upgraded models."

"Yeah, but my contribution mostly amounted to nothing more than suggestions for small improvements on his masterpiece." Tom smiled. "And yet, I can't help feeling great just being a part of it all. This new machine is truly amazing. I still can't accept we'll be able to beam all the way back utilizing just one jump. Sure beats our first trip."

Kate was scanning the area. "It's hard to believe it's been over a year. Somehow it seems like we've only been gone a couple of weeks."

"I know exactly what you mean." He chuckled. "Wait until Rose and Jorge get an eyeful of this place. Good thing I voice coded the TMT's command center. Otherwise, one look at where they land and they'd request an immediate return trip."

"I didn't know you did that."

"Yep. The TMT will only respond to your voice or mine."

"What else did you do?"

A boyish grin covered his face. "I altered the command preface from 'computer' to 'Bozo'."

She tried not to laugh but couldn't stop. "Tom. You didn't. John will kill you when he finds out."

"Don't worry. I'll change it first thing when we get back. It's just for fun."

The machine chimed. "I am available for additional transfers."

Tom flicked his brows. "Watch this. That's fine ... Bozo. Ask Jorge and Rose to step onto the transfer mats, then bring them back."

"Message understood ... subjects are positioned ... beginning transfer."

The unaware pair reintegrated. Their eyes appeared to double in size.

Jorge blurted out, "Where are we?"

Tom replied, "It's really more a question of ... when."

Jorge spun around, trying to take in everything at once. His eyes raced over the interior of a mammoth cavern, a stream-fed pool, water filters, portable sinks and toilets, and a large pile containing a variety of equipment. "I don't care when, where, how, or why. I want out of here." He stepped back onto the transfer mat. "Rose, are you coming?" She shook her head. "Suit yourself. Computer, return me to the original departure point."

"I'm sorry, Mr. Nebula. At present, I answer to the command preface 'Bozo'."

Jorge glared at Tom. "Fine. Bozo, get me out of here!"

"Again, my apologies, Mr. Nebula. My command sequencer is voiceprint protected. I am currently capable of responding to only two vocal patterns. Unfortunately, yours is not one of them."

Jorge stepped off the platform and stood in front of Tom, flexing his fists. "I suppose this is your doing, too."

"Considering the effect of the restaurant scene, I had a feeling you'd react this way. Rose predicted it. For the moment, we just want you to listen. Please. When we're finished, I'll remove the voice lock. If you still want to leave, no one will stop you."

Jorge's grim expression softened. He faced Rose. "You knew about this?"

"I readily agreed to try and help you." She waved a hand through the air. "I didn't know about this. Come on, we're here. Let's walk."

Tom lightly grabbed Rose's shoulder. "Explore all you want, but do not go outside ... and be careful where you put your hands. Remember what happened to John. I'll explain the rest later."

Rose and Jorge ambled away. Kate and Tom began carrying equipment into the front part of the cave. They established their old rooms first.

Kate handed Tom a connector. He was just finishing Rose's fresh water system when they heard a scream. Tom bumped his head trying to get up. She was already running down the passageway towards the back cavern. When Tom caught up, he found Kate trying to calm the excited couple. Everyone was standing in the middle of the stream. Rose and Jorge were pointing, babbling incoherently. They finally settled down, with Jorge taking the lead.

"We saw the ramp on the other side, so crossed the stream and went up. There's a small outcropping with a hole in the roof. It presents quite a panoramic view. All of a sudden, this ... this monster came charging at us. I never knew an animal could even get that big."

Tom became almost rapturous. He grabbed Jorge by the upper arms. "Is it kind of greenish-gray ... and walked upright on its hind legs?"

Jorge was startled. "Yes. How did you know?"

Tom didn't answer. He was splashing towards the ramp.

Jorge reached out a hand to stop him, yelling, "Tom! No! It'll kill you!"

Kate started to laugh. Their faces spun towards her with a look of astonishment. She raised a hand, asking for time. "I'm sorry. This is something we didn't disclose to everyone." She started walking. "Follow me ... words will never suffice."

As they neared the top of the ramp, Kate turned, cautioning them to remain silent. Each edged quietly around the last corner. Tom was standing in a rock depression, his arms wrapped around the nose of a giant beast. His hand was stroking it above the left eye ridge. Bisbee was issuing a continuous, low, mewling growl. Kate stood with her fingers covering her mouth, her eyes beginning to glisten. The newcomers pressed against the rock wall, their faces exhibiting wide-eyed, open-mouthed stares.

Tom waved Kate over. She walked slowly and raised a hand. Bisbee sniffed and chortled a growl. Kate gasped a low shriek as Tom pulled her up. Without thinking, she reached out and petted the huge animal. Her hand froze when a strange noise started. Kate and Tom stared into each other's eyes. He stretched, looking out over the rocky lip. Tom covered his mouth to keep his laughter from startling Bisbee.

"Tom, what is it?"

"He's thumping his tail!"

Rose and Jorge were shown the section where the rooms had been prepared. Each had a bath, with sink, toilet, and shower. A holodoor covered the entrance to each. After the tour, Kate used the auto-cooker to prepare dinner. They were all sitting on a rock near the cooker and TMT.

Tom called out, "Hey, Bozo."

The machine appeared to answer reluctantly, "Yes, Tom?"

"Two things. First, remove the voice locks on the command sequencer."

"Locks released."

"Two, I feel bad about the name thing. It was funny initially, now it just seems dumb. Revert to your original command preface."

"Thank you ... sir."

"You're welcome."

The others chuckled and nodded in agreement.

"Tom, doesn't that giant lizard frighten you?"

Tom snorted. "He did at first, Jorge. You can't imagine how much I was terrified. During our initial encounter, he almost killed and ate me. If it hadn't been for Larry pulling me out of danger, I wouldn't be talking to you now. Kate may have been ... harmed, too. But, as you witnessed, that crazy old beast and I finally developed a relationship. By the way, Bisbee's a Tyrannosaurus Rex and doesn't really qualify as a lizard. He's warmblooded."

"Didn't you say it's been about a year since your return?"

"Yes, why?"

"I can't believe a dinosaur would have the capacity to still recognize you after that long a time."

"A year has passed in our time, Jorge, but we've returned after only two weeks have elapsed here. The computers plotted a sufficient gap between events to prevent any overlap with our previous encounters, thereby eliminating the possibly of creating a time-loop."

Tom decided to take a shot in the dark. He looked at Kate and winked. "It's amazing what you can accomplish once you get past your fear and guilt." His gaze moved from Kate to Rose, and then fixed upon Jorge. "I'm probably an expert, based on experience alone."

Kate stood and extended her arms. "I think I'm going to get some fresh air. How about a walk outside, Tom?"

He looked up. "I'm sorry ... what?"

"A walk ... outside ... away from here." She was giving little jerks with her head.

"Oh. Oh, yes. Good idea." He arose and took her hand.

As they walked away, Kate looked back over a shoulder. "Why don't you two go ahead and talk or something."

Rose looked pleased. "So what do you think of Tom?"

"Well, he got under my skin at our meeting in the restaurant. He actually came off as being pushy. I'm still reserving judgment, but he's sort of growing on me."

"He purposely wanted to put you on the defensive, see if you'd fight back, get emotionally fired up. Maybe start thinking about yourself again."

"It was a pretty successful tactic. Was that your idea?"

"No. Helping you beat your problem was his plan from the start. Considering his own personal experience, he was exceptionally adept at determining your mindset. I've always wanted to help, but you kept pushing me away. I didn't want to hurt you more, and forcing would just make you push back even harder, so I became frustrated and stopped trying altogether. Maybe I'm not as tough as I thought."

Jorge hung his head. "Rose, I'm sick of being like this ... but I'm scared. If I have to face what happened one more time, I just might drop off the deep end ... and never resurface."

"It'd be my job to see that doesn't occur."

"Do you still think displacement analysis will help?"

"Obviously there are no guarantees, but I'm extremely confident with this method of treatment. I've always had excellent results."

"Is this what you used on Tom?"

She laughed sharply. "It's what we started with, but an unrelated incident made Tom's mind unreachable afterward. He's given me permission to do a complete write-up on his therapy. That one was Kate's idea. It's totally unique in the annals of psychiatry, I'm sure." She sighed. "I don't know. Between Tom getting through to you ... and Kate helping Tom ... if I'm not careful, I'll become obsolete."

* * * * *

Everyone remained busy, and the first week passed quickly. Jorge and Rose spent many hours each day working with Time Displacement Hypnotherapy. Jorge's problem was mostly singular in nature, and it wasn't something left over from childhood and therefore deeply entwined with other events. Subsequently, his progress was rapid.

Tom and Kate kept the machinery in order, prepared the meals, and performed other common domestic tasks. Bisbee visited everyday, and although the newcomers wouldn't go near him, they nevertheless became accustomed to his presence.

When the second week started, they had a small grav-sled sent back. Jorge took the flyer up by himself in the beginning, but was soon taking everyone for a ride around the prehistoric environs.

In the end, they were relaxed, but ready to go home. The foursome was having a last quiet dinner, each lost in their thoughts, before disassembling the equipment in preparation for departure. Jorge began to comment. "I don't quite know how to thank everyone for all you've done. I not only feel great, but I have to admit ... I've had a wonderful time. When we get back, the first thing I'm going to do is book passage for Deimos."

"Why go there?" Tom inquired.

The ladies were already smiling perceptively when Jorge answered, "It has the best astronavigation university in the solar system."

Tom rose. "Let me be the first to congratulate you."

Jorge slowly shook his head. "Your praise may be a bit premature. I've got a lot of hard work ahead of me."

Tom chuckled. "Maybe so, but hopefully, at least some of the roadblocks have been cleared."

The men shook hands and slapped each other on the back. Jorge got a hug and kiss on the cheek from the ladies, after which he stood looking around the cavern. "It's amazing how you can become attached to this place. I don't think I ever want to come back, but I'll always remember being here ... and maybe even miss it a little."

Kate and Tom laughed. "That's the same thing we said when we left before ... and our first stay wasn't nearly as pleasant," Tom remarked.

Jorge nodded. "Rose was completely successful in treating me. I got my life back. You mentioned at the restaurant this might become a yearly retreat, so the two of you need a great memory from here, too."

Tom's eyes brightened. "You're absolutely right, Jorge, and I just thought of what that memory should be." He ran over and typed a long message on the TMT. Afterwards, Tom just stood there with a wide grin.

Kate chuckled. "We'd all better sit tight and get a good grip on something. I've seen this behavior before. I think Tom just got one of his impulsive ideas."

Everyone waited patiently for some indication of whatever Tom was instigating. After a few minutes, the TMT beeped. Tom read the reply and glanced up at his companions. "How would all of you feel about staying one more night? If I can't pull my little undertaking together by tomorrow morning, we'll have breakfast, then pack up and go home."

The other three gazed at one another, shrugged, and nodded agreement.

"Great. If this works out ... I think you'll all be pleased."

The area was cleared, and they were retiring for the night. Kate and Tom walked arm in arm a short distance behind Rose and Jorge. Kate jostled him and whispered, "Are you going to let me in on your secret?"

"I'm dying to ... but I can't. I'm afraid you'd be too disappointed if it doesn't come to pass. Sorry, kiddo, you'll have to wait until morning."

It was 12:47 p.m. at TheTwenty's main complex in the year 2342. The computer considered all the variables, calculating as precisely as possible when it would be 6 a.m., 150 million years earlier in the Jurassic. That's when Tom's wrist device began beeping. He moaned and felt around on the pile of clothes for the offending mechanism. When he remembered why it was probably beeping, he became instantly awake and started pulling on his pants and shoes.

Kate looked over groggily. "What's the hurry? Can't you read the message here?"

"No. I instructed the TMT's computer to trap and encode the message."

He bent down and lightly kissed her. "Get dressed, wake the others, and follow me." Tom zipped through the holodoor, running in excited anticipation towards the back cavern.

Once everyone arrived, Kate prepared breakfast on the auto-cooker while Tom started explaining. "First ... I've made some assumptions, but I don't like taking anyone for granted, so I'll ask each of you for specific permission to continue ... starting with Kate. Will you marry me now ... today?"

She was carrying food to their rock table and stopped mid stride. "Are you serious?"

"I've never been more solemn."

She laughed. "You are unquestionably outrageous, but I love you and I'm not letting you get away ... the answer is an explicit 'yes'."

"Good, one down. Jorge, will you be my best man?"

Jorge was somewhat stunned with the turn of events. "Uh, sure, it'd be my privilege."

"Thanks. Two down, one to go. Rose, would you be Kate's maid of honor?"

She jumped up, threw her arms around him, gave him a big kiss on the cheek, and simply stood there beaming.

Tom grinned. "Okay, I take it that's a 'yes', too."

"What about our other friends, Tom?"

He motioned for them to sit. "They'll all be part of the wedding, Kate ... at least in a way. I had Larry start checking last night. He's confirmed that John is returning from the moon and will land on earth shortly. The others have already been notified."

Kate stared for a moment. "You can't possibly be thinking of bringing them all back here."

"No. Of course not; it'd be too impractical and possibly dangerous." Tom snickered. "I doubt if they'd come anyway. Listen. John's latest TMT allows for projecting simultaneous voice and image holograms from the future to the past, and vice versa.

Frank's updating the programming so a view of our chosen area will be sent to them. They'll position themselves in the hologram just like they were joining us on site. In turn, their images will be transmitted here.

Unfortunately, there are two small problems. Frank warns that, even at the highest power settings, the images will seem slightly ghostly, but that can't be helped. There will also be a two-second delay in both directions.

Other than those glitches, the identical scene will appear at both locations. It's just that they'll be holographic here, and we'll be holographic there."

"Where are we going to perform this piece of magic?" Rose asked.

"The tower suite ... that room at the top of the ramp ... if it's alright with Kate," Tom replied.

Kate leaned her head on her hand. "That's a fairly small area. Why not right here?"

"There aren't that many people, and Frank has already assured me there's enough room."

Kate shrugged. "Then it's okay with me."

Tom grinned broadly. "Besides, if things work out, I'll have another surprise."

His captive audience emitted a collective groan.

Jorge helped Tom move and set up the TMT in the tower suite. He kept looking skyward, expecting to see Bisbee. "What if your pet shows up?"

"Actually ... I'm planning on it. That's why I'm in somewhat of a hurry. It's getting close to when he usually stops by. Over time, he's learned a little trick I want to employ during the ceremony. You and Rose stay back near the entrance so you can duck out in case you get nervous."

"Where are you and Kate going to stand?"

"In the rock cauldron. It's about two feet higher than the floor. That way, people will be able to see us better, and we'll have a clearer view of them, too. I'm angling the holographic lens so it will cover a field from the top of our heads on down. The recording should make a great memento."

"Tom ... who's going to perform the formal procedure?"

"The computer. All we want is a simple non-denominational service. Kate and I are going to write our own vows." He chuckled. "We promised each other to keep it short and simple. Then we'll exchange rings, and that will pretty much be it."

"Where'd you get the rings?"

"Breeanya located some plain gold ones for now. We'll pick something out when we get home."

Jorge held out his hand. "As best man ... I should hold on to them."

"Thanks, but I'll keep them for now. It's all part of the surprise."

Jorge raised his eyebrows.

Rose and Jorge were stationed just inside the tower suite's entrance as Tom had suggested. The holographic visitors were positioned around the front half of fallen roof on which Kate and Tom were standing. The computer had just completed conducting the preliminary requirements. "Please read your vow, Dr. Hughes."

He faced Kate and took her hand. "I take thee, Kate, to be my wife, friend, and escort. You fill me up when I am empty, mend me when I break, comfort me when I'm in pain, and cheer me when I'm down. Your strengths fortify my weaknesses. Together, our parts sum to much more than just one whole. You are the light and love of my life ... forever." Tom nodded towards the lens to indicate he was finished.

"Dr. Bright, please read yours."

Kate had partially anticipated Tom's words, but she was still stunned. Finally, she smiled and then began. "I take thee, Tom, to be my husband, friend, and companion. You have awakened me from a lonely sleep, taught me how to laugh, banished my sorrows, and helped me understand and appreciate the wonderment of being alive. I have only flowered because you have become my gallant stem. I will love and comfort you for the rest of my days."

She faced the lens.

"We will conclude with the exchanging of rings."

Tom reached up and seemed to be scratching at empty air. A shadow fell over the assemblage. The rings floated into sight from overhead ... dangling on a white ribbon, its support as yet unseen. As the rings continued their descent, many large teeth appeared, with the ribbon wrapped around one of them. Finally, the remainder of a huge, menacing head entered the area encompassed by the lens. Following the combined four-second-turnaround time ... the holographic visitors were depicted dashing in all directions. The apparitions seemed to disappear directly into the surrounding rock walls.

Bisbee delivers the rings right on time

After a short period of silence, John's breathless voice returned. "Tom ... may I assume that was Bisbee?"

"Yes. He's the ring bearer. It's a long story, but whenever I raise my hand and scratch at the air, he dips his head. What happened to everybody?"

"You should have warned us. I'm afraid we were quite distressed by his appearance."

"Oh, sorry, John. I wanted to surprise Kate. With all the last minute details ... I guess the thought never crossed my mind he might cause a panic. After all, he's only holographic on your end, so he couldn't possibly hurt anyone."

"I guarantee you ... no one ... including myself, took the time to contemplate that when his image loomed down upon us. Do you have any more startling revelations?"

"No. Uh, I think Bisbee pretty well covers the ceremony's shock value."

"Alright, let me see if I can get everyone calmed down and back into position. Honestly, Tom ... I wish just once you could manage to suppress this rather cavalier indulgence of your whimsical fantasies."

"But, John ... what good is a family holograph of my wedding ... if it doesn't include the whole family?"

"Tomorrow is the most important thing in life. It comes into us at midnight very clean. It's perfect when it arrives and it puts itself in our hands. It hopes we've learned something from yesterday."

- John Wayne

Epilogue

Tom positioned the grav-sled and unloaded the five hundred pounds of raw hamburger in its usual spot. Bisbee seemed to really appreciate the gifts of fresh meat. The great animal had never been quite the same since being involved in a fight several years earlier. Bisbee saved Tom and Kate when another Rex had attacked.

The rescued couple had agreed the second dinosaur appeared younger, and although smaller, was undoubtedly faster and stronger. For some unknown reason, it had acted terribly confused and just quit fighting ... finally walking away ... apparently satisfied to perhaps observe unseen from a distance.

Tom visually surveyed the surrounding area ... wondering where his prodigious pet might be keeping himself.

After several unsuccessful minutes of locating his old friend, he lifted off and landed the sled on top of the hillside that housed their cave complex. Tom followed a passageway they had discovered that led down into its interior.

Even though they had never seen the young Rex following the single incident, it seemed there were always two different sets of tracks around the cave's lower entrance. It made them feel vulnerable, so they didn't walk around outside as much as before, even when Bisbee was near. They were afraid Bisbee might be killed if the younger animal attacked again. Tom eased through an opening at the bottom ... finally entering the large main cavern.

Kate had been notably subdued as of late. Tom knew she was hoping he'd change his mind about departing with John and the others. Although she had repeatedly denied caring that much about going, he knew differently. After all, her 'family' would be leaving them behind. She looked up from checking their gear as he approached. "Is he out there?"

"No. He doesn't seem to be anywhere around."

"That's odd. He usually comes running as soon as he smells all the meat." She smiled. "Well, help me set up. If he's still not here by the time we're finished, maybe we'll take the sled and go look for him."

"Thanks, Kate. I know you have other things on your mind."

"Yes, I do ... and I've still got two weeks to work on you, don't I?"

Tom walked over and hugged her. "It's crunch time. I know if we don't go, we'll probably never see them again. I can't help but feel selfish about my not wanting to leave."

"No, Tom. We've had this conversation before. I fully understand how difficult it's been for you adjusting to living in my time. You've studied and struggled hard catching up on the work you love so much. It's perfectly logical why you wouldn't want to pull up roots yet once more ... especially when we're so content and secure."

He lifted her chin with a finger and peered deep into her haunting eyes. "You omitted ... happy."

"I'm with you ... and that's enough to make me happy. I freely admit I'd be happier if we were going along, but ... I don't want to be selfish either."

She picked up some equipment and strolled towards the front of the cave where they always established their bedroom and bath.

It only took about an hour to set up all the mechanisms that made their cave a comfortable living environment. After the work, Tom crossed the underground stream, walked up the ramp, and entered the small chamber where he had first become friends with Bisbee. The meat had been placed so it was visible from his vantage point. Tom stood on a pile of flat rocks and leaned on the circular opening's rim with his elbows. His head swiveled to one side at the sound of footfalls. A few moments later, Kate stepped up and joined him. "Still not here, huh?"

"Nope. The meat hasn't been touched. In fact, I haven't seen anything." His face tilted towards the sky. "It looks like there's a heavy weather front headed this way, but judging by the fast cloud movement, it'll blow through fairly rapidly. Maybe all the animals have instinctively taken cover."

"We could chance a quick flyover. Bisbee's lair isn't far from here. Probably not more than a ten minute round-trip on the sled ... if we hurry."

Tom's face displayed his surprise. "You're willing to do that?"

Kate covered his hand with hers. "Bisbee saved my life, too, Tom. It's no wonder I've managed to develop quite a soft spot for that dumb dinosaur over the years."

"Speaking of years ... is this our nineteenth or twentieth trip back?"

"Nineteenth. Just remember that John's launch timetable coincides with the number of our Jurassic sojourns. He said they wanted to be ready in twenty years, and he's kept the project dead on schedule. There's only a year to go, and the computer wants everyone in training during that last interval. That's why John needs our decision in two weeks." She sighed. "Come on, Fido. We're wasting time. We want to beat that front. I doubt being the highest thing around during a lightning storm could be considered even marginally healthy ... or sane."

They headed up, retracing Tom's recent journey through the passageway, and were soon gliding silently over the nearby treetops. He eased back on the forward control. "We should be close. See anything on your side?"

"No. Nothing. The perspective is so different from up here. Every spot looks almost the same."

Tom circled for another five minutes and headed back. "Those lightning strikes are getting closer. I'm not going to push our luck. Besides, I think the only way we're going to find his home is on foot. You're right. This is really confusing."

After landing on their hilltop, they reentered the cavern via the same route and busied themselves making final adjustments to the equipment. Tom noticed a small leak in a connection under the bathroom sink while washing his hands. He knelt on the dirt floor and retightened a fitting. "There ... try it now." Kate turned on the water. He observed for a minute. "Okay, that's got it." Tom stood up and brushed off his pants. "How about something to eat?"

She teased, "You've pulled some crazy stunts over the years, but that sounds like an idea I can live with."

It had become a defacto standard procedure to set up the auto-cooker and TMT near the pool in the back cavern. Perhaps it was just the peace and tranquility of the setting.

They had sandwiches and a drink, putting the plates and utensils in the recycler when finished. "Okay, Tom, I can't stand it. Let's recheck the weather, and if it's clear enough, we'll go find that crazy pet of yours."

He kissed her cheek. "You're the best, Kiddo. No wonder I love you. But you know, that 'dumb dinosaur' as you put it, is just as much your pet as it is mine. After all, he wags his tail for you, not me. Let's go up to the tower suite and check outside."

They stood on the rock pile scanning the nearby area. Tom pointed to the west. "Looks like the storm is moving away. All that's left is some wind and thunder. What do you think?"

"Let's go find our baby."

"Are you sure? We don't have any weapons, and foraging around out there on foot could easily prove to be dangerous."

"I keep saying too much of you has rubbed off on me. I've got to know why he might be avoiding us after all this time. We'll just walk to Bisbee's lair and return. Let's hit the trail before my sanity revolts and I change my mind."

They maneuvered down the ramp, crossed the stream, wound their way through the cave, and exited the small main entrance. A final assessment of the area was taken before proceeding. It was agreed that keeping the talk to a minimum and walking quietly as possible would be their safest option.

Tom took her hand. "Okay ... let's see what fate has in store for us this time."

The further they walked, the uneasier Tom became. He halted. "It's too damn quiet. Where are all the smaller dinosaurs that constantly scurry through the underbrush? It's as if they know something we don't. Maybe we should turn back."

Kate pulled him forward. "We're almost there. I can see the opening to his home just ahead. A few more minutes can't make any difference."

As they approached the entrance, Tom pressed close against a wall of thick growth, motioning Kate to stay just behind. He bobbed his head around, trying to peek through the leaves. "Well, I'll be. I can't get a clear view, but I think that lazy bum is in there sleeping. It sounds like he's snoring."

They rounded the corner. Tom's face went slack. The sight stunned him so deeply that he unconsciously began to back away.

Kate covered her face and screamed, finally turning and burying her head against his chest, clinging to him with all her might.

Kate's petition of agony carried on the air. Not far way, two eyelids sprang open. Wind whipped through the trees; thunder rolled in from overhead.

Death ... was hidden in the dense foliage ... and the storm would cover its approach.

Tom and Kate slowly recovered and walked closer, their eyes involuntarily riveted on the scene. Bisbee lay on one side, a pool of blood spread from under his body. Both of his short upper arms had been torn away. There were several deep gouges in his hind legs and back from missing flesh. The bottom jaw was strangely askew. Muscle, sinew, and skin hung from his neck. His breathing was deep, but irregular. Bubbles of blood burst from his nostrils.

Tom's face was streaming with tears. He placed a hand on an undamaged section of the beast's face, leaned against it, and stroked the scar over the left eye ridge. "I'd say you've seen better days, buddy."

The eye gradually peeled open and rotated towards Tom. It was almost inaudible, but Bisbee somehow managed to growl a short, friendly greeting.

"Oh, Tom. It had to be that other Rex."

He nodded. "Yeah, I don't think there's any doubt about it. I hate to leave him like this, but we'd better get out of here."

The wind died for a moment, allowing a peculiar swishing sound to reach Tom's ears. He turned ... and froze. Two giant pillars of muscle supporting a gigantic body and head were no more than fifteen feet away ... blocking the exit. The odd sound was its tail undulating sideways in the dirt. Tom's hand slowly advanced to Kate's shoulder. He began backing towards the rear of the spacious enclosure with her in tow.

"Tom, what is it? You're scaring me."

"Stay facing me ... and walk. This may prove to be a small problem."

She spun around and immediately collapsed back against him.

The Rex's upper lip began to twitch. Saliva ran between its teeth. The slits of its gold-colored eyes were sharp amber knives ... aimed directly at them.

"I wish I had my gun."

"Why? It wouldn't hurt this thing."

"No. But it might make it a lot easier for us. I'm sorry, Kate. It looks like we're in a real jam this time."

She pressed against him. "Tom, please hold me ... as tightly as you can. I don't want to die alone ... and I don't want to see it coming."

Tom's mind was racing. "Kate. Listen to me. There might be a chance one of us can make it. You stand perfectly still, and I'll start moving to the far side of Bisbee. The Rex will almost certainly follow my movement. As it does, begin inching the other way. When it charges me, I want you to run like hell and don't look back. I'll try and keep it busy as long as I can. Maybe I can find a spot to hide under Bisbee for a short while."

"No! You've become my life. Without you, I'm dead anyway. If death finds you now ... I want it to find both of us."

"Damn it, Kate! This is no time for heroics."

"Look who's talking!"

Tom saw the absolute defiance in Kate's stormy green eyes, so relented and crushed her to him. "God, I love you. Alright, you stubborn, wonderful woman ... we'll face it together."

The Rex flexed into a crouch.

Death ... was coming.

Bisbee's one good eye blinked open again. The young Rex had repositioned a foot just in front of his nose. There weren't enough muscles remaining connected to lift his head, but he slowly slid his mouth towards the other Rex's foot. As the young Rex jumped, Bisbee clamped his dislocated jaw shut with whatever strength he had left. The action couldn't be called a bite, but it caused the young Rex to lose its balance and careen over Bisbee's body, crashing against a Banyan. The fifty-foot tree had shallow roots and canted over, creating a large hole in the leafy covering above their heads. A tomblike gray light streamed through.

Tom grabbed Kate's hand and started running, but the Rex scrambled to its feet ... blocking their escape. It moved toward them ... but was interrupted again. The Rex's head whirled towards Bisbee as Tom and Kate's friend choked out one, low, threatening growl. The young Rex roared a reply ... then it became completely infuriated. It jumped on Bisbee and began ripping great hunks of flesh from his head and body. What little light remained in Bisbee's eye ... faded to dark.

The couple started to escape again, but this time they were stopped by the Rex's wildly thrashing tail. Tom's mind went into action once more. He began timing the trembling, rising and falling of the tail. At the next twitch he ran towards it and raced under as it rose ... pulling Kate close behind him. He jerked her clear as the tail crashed to earth. They turned the corner and sprinted towards the sanctity of the cave. Tom checked over a shoulder to determine if the Rex was following. He reached out and grabbed Kate's arm. "We're free. Slow it down a little. We'll never make it ... running flat out ... all the way."

She nodded and let him set the pace.

They were within sight of the cave when there was a loud peal of thunder. Both realized it came from behind ... not aloft. As they rounded a bend, Tom grabbed Kate again and pulled her off the trail into heavy brush. Seconds later, the eight-ton freight train that threatened their existence rumbled past. Tom slowly worked his way back to the trail and looked out. The Rex was bellowing its anger and clawing insanely at the cave's entrance.

Kate came alongside. "Now what?"

Tom squeezed his eyes shut and shook his clenched fists in frustration. "We've gotten this far. I promise you, it's not going to get us now. Let me think."

The area had become quiet. Tom checked the status of the Rex. "Oh no. That horrific monster is sniffing the air and looks like it might have our scent. We have to move."

"Where?"

"Let's thread our way through this cover towards the wall beneath the tower suite."

"Tom, that wall's at least twelve feet high, and the corner is a dead end. If it finds us there, we'd be trapped."

"Listen. You can climb onto my shoulders, stand in my hands, and I'll push you high enough to reach the top."

"That's just fine. What happens to you?"

"Then the ball is in your court, Kiddo. Find something to throw over so I can climb up."

Kate's eyes widened. "The cargo straps for the sled! There're a few extras already in the cave with our other gear."

"Good thinking. We only need one. I think that does it. We've got a plan." He rose and began pushing through the bushes. "C'mon. Follow me."

Tom had been right about the Rex. It did have their scent. Shortly after they left, it started retracing its route on the trail, headed for their last position.

Tom and Kate broke through the last of the brush onto a bare patch of dirt about thirty feet from the wall. They hurried across the open space, ever watchful for the Rex. He leaned against the wall and bent a leg. "Okay, Kiddo ... up you go." Kate stepped onto the leg, then into his hands, and finally on top of his shoulders. He worked his hands under her feet and started to shove. "Ugh, I'm glad you're ... not any ... heavier."

She tried to help by grabbing handholds wherever possible. "I'm there, Tom." She scrambled over the top and looked down. "I'll be right back."

Their eyes snapped back to the brush as a crashing sound approached in the near distance. He looked back up. "Be quick my love, or you may be going home alone after all."

She sped away.

A short eternity later, a strap of reinforced webbing came flying over the rim. Kate's face appeared. "It's anchored around a big rock. Come on ... climb."

Tom grabbed the strap and began pulling himself up. Seconds later, one arm secured a purchase on the rim ... then a leg. The Rex burst through the trees. Tom's eyes flashed towards the approaching monster. It was almost on him. His mind instantly knew he'd never make it across to the exit. "Go, Kate! I'm right behind you."

Tom dropped over the narrow rim and rolled under it as the Rex's teeth crunched together beside his head. All Kate could do was watch in horror. The Rex roared in fury. He slammed his body against the rock. The rim shuddered, and shards of stone fell on the dirt floor. Tom forced his body tighter against the barrier, but there was no place to go. The Rex slammed the wall again (crack) ... then again (crack).

"Kate! Be my eyes. Watch him. Tell me," (crack) "when he pulls about halfway back. Raise an arm when he starts. Say 'GO' when he's there. Stay out of the way," (crack) "because I won't be able to stop. I'll use my momentum and dive into the pool."

Kate's attention focused on the Rex.

(Crack) ... (crack) ... (crack). Her arm went up ... "Go!"

Tom scrambled across the room. The Rex had to overcome its backward motion before snapping forward again. Its chest burst through the wall and its nose smashed into a jagged stone opening just as Tom darted through. He recklessly threw his body into the air, hoping to avoid the rocks and reach deep water. Kate flew down the ramp at breakneck speed.

Tom landed on his back and plunged to the boulder-strewn bottom. His air blew out when he hit, and the impact fogged his mind. Somehow, he managed to retain some sense, and followed a few air bubbles toward the surface. Kate dove in when Tom appeared, pulling him to shore while he floundered along. They lay there quietly, catching their breath.

He looked up into her eyes. "Great job, Kiddo. I owe you another one. Uh, and I have a favor to ask."

She cradled his head in her arms. "Oh, Tom. Now what?"
"How about if we scratch this trip off our itinerary?"
Kate kissed his forehead and grinned. "I'll consider it."

Tom sat up. "Where are the rest of those cargo straps?"
Kate studied his face. "I'll show you, but first you're going to explain why you need them."
"How much do you love me?"
"You already know the answer to that."
"Then you've got to help me do ... what I truly believe needs doing."
She gasped. "This has to do with Bisbee, doesn't it?"
"I can't stand the thought of the other Rex eating him. I'd like to try and bury him on top of our hill."
Kate lowered her gaze. "You want to move him with the sled."
"If I can. I'll need you to keep the young Rex's attention here. Yell at him ... throw stones ... whatever it takes. Just be careful ... and don't let him get anywhere near you."
"Alright, I'll help. Make sure you take a two-way comm device. I'll warn you if the Rex starts in your direction."
He took hold of her upper arms and drilled his stare into hers. "We just escaped from the grim reaper. I promise you ... I'm not about to give him another chance. If it looks hopeless, we pack up and go home. I won't give you any arguments. You have my word. Good enough?"
She stood and pointed. "A few more straps are in that pile. The rest are stored in the sled. I'll find the radios and check on the Rex."
Kate turned to leave, but Tom pulled her to him. "Have I ever told you how much I love you?"
She reasoned quickly. "Yes, no, and are you ever."
He grinned. "What does that mean?"
"Yes, you've told me ... no, you can never tell me often enough ... and are you ever going to owe me for this one."
He laughed. "Okay. Let's get this little endeavor started."

Kate handed Tom a comm device, crossed the stream, and headed cautiously up the ramp. Tom gathered the cargo straps together and started for the hilltop. He had just finished attaching all the straps to the sled when her first message came through. "Tom. Over."
He grabbed the transceiver. "I'm here, Kate. Over."
"Can you see the Rex? Over."
"No. The hill is in my way, but I can hear him growling. Over."
"He's walking around as if in a daze, but it doesn't look like he's leaving. If he does, I'll think of something. Over."
"Okay. I'm lifting now. Out."

Tom started flying in the opposite direction so the Rex wouldn't see him. He circled out and around, staying low, floating just above the trees. He searched for the opening in the leaf cover that now existed because of the partially uprooted Banyan tree. It gradually came into view ... dead ahead.
"Kate. Is the Rex still there? Over."
There was a slight pause. "Yes. Still here. Over."

"I'm taking the sled down to hover above Bisbee. I'll leave the comm link on standby. Out."

Tom opened the canopy and lowered the sled until it was touching Bisbee. He decided to forego the air handlers on the return trip and fly without cover since the anti-grav unit would need every erg of energy it could get. He threw the straps over both sides of the sled, stepped onto the animal's back, and worked down a hind leg to the ground.

Attachments had been made around the neck and legs, but at least one was needed under the body for stability. He found a depression in the soil and tried working a strap from either direction, finally managing to connect the two ends ... but he wasn't certain they locked.

The comm device began beeping. Tom scrambled up Bisbee and onto the sled. "Kate, I'm here. Over."

"Tom, I've tried everything, but the Rex kept looking towards Bisbee's lair. He just left. Get out of there. Over."

"Lifting now. Out."

He eased the sled into the air, taking up the slack in the straps. Then the small sled started to show the strain. More power was applied, and it began to rise, with Bisbee slung beneath. The cushion of safety between Bisbee and the ground was slowly increasing as Tom spotted the Rex coming up the game trail.

When the Rex saw him, it dramatically increased its speed, crashed into the open area, and frantically leapt at the sled. But by this time, Bisbee's body was clearing the treetops. Tom exhaled heavily, attempting to uncoil his overwrought muscles.

The sled jerked sharply and suddenly tilted at a precarious angle; its floor fell from beneath Tom's feet. His shoes slipped out of the footwells, but he managed to catch hold of the instrument panel with his fingertips and hurriedly worked his way towards the emergency cargo release.

A hand was poised over the big red button while his eyes anxiously searched for the Rex. It had apparently crashed into the Banyan tree again, and this time, was lying there motionless. Time stood still until a muted beeping finally broke the peaceful lull. Tom manipulated the controls, leveled the sled, and quickly descended. With one eye on the Rex, he located the fallen comm device. "I'm kind of busy, Kate. I ran into a snag, but things are okay now. I'll call you back in a minute. Out."

He ran to readjust the straps ... and skidded to a halt. Bisbee had shifted onto his back and lay there with his legs spread. The young Rex had also fallen into pretty much the same exposure. Tom stared from one to the other. Several pieces of a puzzle simultaneously clicked into place. He softly muttered, "Wait until Kate hears about this," and returned to work.

As he struggled, he found a tooth embedded in the fabric of the strap under Bisbee's body. Tom reasoned that it must have come unlocked, hung down its full length, and that's what the Rex had attacked.

Tom studied the scene and concluded that the Rex must have swung on the strap, the tooth pulled out, and then the animal must have crashed head first into the tree ... knocking itself out cold. What would he tell Kate? He silently hoped she wouldn't ask, then laughed out loud, "Fat chance of that."

With things relatively straightened out, Tom hopped back on the sled and started to lift again. He thumbed the send-key on the transceiver. "Hello, Kate. Come in. Over."

"Tom, are you alright? I was worried. Over."

"Things are fine. I'm on my way now, but it's slow going. I'll be there in about twenty minutes, and I have something really interesting to tell you. Out."

As Tom approached, he saw a flurry of activity. Kate had apparently requested that small, automatic laser-diggers and supporting conveyors be sent. The outline of a large hole was beginning to take shape in the middle of the hilltop. Bisbee touched down and Tom reeled out some slack, landing the sled off to one side. Kate ran to greet him. They hugged each other and joyfully swung each other around. "We did it, Kate. You are absolutely the best."

After a few minutes to calm down, she asked the question he was dreading. "So, what was this snag you ran into?"

He couldn't lie to her, so he tried neutralizing the incident by using exaggerated hand motions and facial expressions. "Would you believe ... the Rex came flying through the air, caught hold of a loose strap, pulled a tooth, and knocked himself out by crashing into a tree?"

She squinted. "That's not funny, Tom."

"Alright, how about ... I dropped the comm device and it simply took extra time to retrieve it? That's why I couldn't answer right away."

Kate frowned but nodded anyway. "Okay ... that sounds somewhat believable."

Tom sighed a relief, turning to watch the diggers. "It looks like this little project will take all night. I'll leave everything hooked up since it'll be needed to lower Bisbee into the hole."

Kate noticed something stuck in one of the straps and went to investigate. She found the huge tooth, pulled it out, and walked back. Kate was furious for a minute, but then remembered he had told her the facts ... even if it was in a roguishly truthful fashion.

"Tom."

He turned. "Yeah?"

"You may want to clean this up and keep it for a memento."

"Oh ... before it happened, I thought I was safe, Kate. Honest. I had no idea the strap came loose, but everything occurred so fast and pretty much just as I said. I didn't want to upset you over a danger already past. Please, don't be angry."

Her arms were crossed, and she was rapidly tapping a toe. "I'll accept your explanation, but I doubt if even our advanced technology can stop you from turning my hair gray."

They stood together silently, knowing nothing more need be said.

Each knew the other all too well.

Kate recalled their earlier conversation. "So what's this interesting item you mentioned?"

"I figured out why the young Rex was so confused in that fight years back, and why it seems to hate us so much. When the Rex caught the strap, it pulled the sled down and Bisbee flipped over. The Rex fell onto his back after hitting the tree. For the first time, I saw both their genitals. Bisbee ... is a female, and the young Rex is definitely a male."

"So, you think the young Rex was Bisbee's mate?"

"No ... worse. Her offspring. Basically, it proved to be your ultimate Oedipus complex. The ironic part is that now I almost feel sympathy for the young Rex. Maybe both our parents made unintentional mistakes, but we suffered anyway. Bisbee tried to teach the young Rex something, and it didn't understand. Mine simply taught me hate and loneliness.

It's been an exceptionally hard day my good lady. Let's go down, clean up, have some dinner, and then relax in the pool's hot spot."

Kate leaned into him. "That sounds like one of your saner plans." She teased, "What's after the soak?"

He softly caressed her face. "After a day like today, we should have no problem thinking of something."

* * * * *

They returned to the hilltop the following morning. The diggers had finished the hole. Large piles of dirt and pulverized rock stood around it. Tom squatted and scooped up a handful of the newly created soil. "This should be perfect."

Kate stooped next to him. "For what?"

"Let's bury Bisbee and I'll explain."

Kate lifted off with the sled, easing their torn and battered friend into the excavation. Tom rode the body down, freed the straps ... then held onto one as Kate lifted him out. She started programming the diggers to cover Bisbee.

"Only fill it half-full for now," Tom requested.

"Why?"

"I know this sounds totally insane, but before you say anything, let me finish. I want to plant the Banyan tree over Bisbee ... obviously because it saved me from the Rex yesterday. Another reason, is that I wouldn't have been able to find Bisbee if the tree hadn't been knocked over and opened a window in the leaf cover.

But mainly ... that tree was literally the roof over Bisbee's head for who knows how many years. It was his ... her home. Therefore, I just think they belong together. It should be perfectly safe. I'll just drop down to treetop height, throw some straps around the bigger branches, and lift it out. Clean and simple."

Kate completely surprised him. "Fine. I agree with your thoughts. There's one change in the plan, however. You handle the straps ... I'll fly the sled."

Tom opened his mouth. Kate glared. His mouth closed.

It's always tough when you lose that one special pet

For once, the operation took place without a problem. After retrieving the tree, Kate hovered in place while the diggers covered its roots with dirt.

Following her landing, she and Tom stood together ... their arms around each other's waist, somberly gazing upon Bisbee's final resting place.

"Kate ... something is really strange. I'm standing next to my dead friend who even as he ... she was dying ... saved our lives again. And yet, I'm okay with it. There's no guilt like it was my fault." He bounced on the balls of his feet. "I also feel lighter for some reason. It's as if a 100-pound weight has flown off my shoulders. I feel sad, but I feel good, too."

Kate gave him a small round of applause. "Congratulations."

"For what?"

"Sometime during the last two days, you've gone through phase three of the cure. I'm certain you'll find your previous-life-shadows are gone, too. You're one whole person again."

"I can't believe it took all this time to happen."

"Rose said it was different for everyone. Tom ... now that we're not coming back, and since you're in a receptive mood ... I have a question to ask."

"Ask away my lady."

"I know there are still a few ranches left in my time, but the cattle and horses raised on them are prized animals. They're kept strictly for breeding or simply as pets. So, I doubt anyone would consent to having one slaughtered.

Even if they did, I know of no place left on earth that would process the carcass. Ever since Bisbee's fight ... on I think our seventh trip back, you've been bringing ... her ... 500 pounds of meat. Where have you been getting it?"

Tom grinned. "Oh, I've had help with that one. Your special interest in the past was the 1950 to 2000 era, right?"

"Yes."

"Remember all the UFO flap during the 1950's?"

"Hmm. Vaguely."

"Each time I needed the meat, Frank and Larry had friends in the past locate a large healthy herd of beef cattle and single one out. They beamed the animal to a processing plant and zapped the meat forward just as we were headed for the Jurassic. The missing ruminant became just another saucer story. What intrigues me though, is that there was never anything in the news about the small bar of gold we always left behind."

Kate shook her head. "Why do I ask?"

Tom removed a self-contained laser from one of the diggers. "There's only one last thing to do." He aimed the small round tube at the Banyan and guided it by feel through the smoke. When the air cleared, the word 'BISBEE' appeared in the tree's bark. It was quite crooked. "Now, I'm done."

Kate ran a hand over the letters. "I could have programmed the digger to burn in a perfect line."

"I know, but it's something I wanted to do myself. This way it's personal ... special."

Kate smiled and nodded her understanding.

Tom glanced up at the early night sky, watching the stars randomly peek through the buttonholes of their dark velvety cloak. The scene reminded him of the mission tokens John had given him all those years ago. It had come to pass that he never felt completely dressed unless they were somewhere on his person. He slipped a hand into a pocket and fingered the pieces of plastic. "You know how it seems that everyone, at least once in their life, asks the question, 'Why am I here?' "

"Sure ... I've often done that myself."

He caressed her shoulders. "Every time I look into your eyes ... I get my answer."

Kate slipped her arms around him, face turned up, her nose riding high on a wide, warm smile. Even though darkness was falling, the celestial lights reflecting in her eyes looked like the glints of a noonday sun sparkling off a rolling sea. Every cell of Tom's essence snapped into perfect cosmic alignment ... juxtaposed by the inescapable allure of those beckoning waves. "Hey, kiddo ... I've got two bona-fide tickets to the stars. I think we should use them."

Kate's jaw dropped. "Tom, don't tease. You know how I feel about this."

"You know me better than that. You mentioned yesterday how much I keep rubbing off on you. Apparently, the magic works both ways. My only concern is some other life form may beat us there and won't validate visitor parking."

"That's a possibility we've often discussed, but you know what'll happen then."

"Yeah, we point ourselves at another star system and go back into stasis. Go ahead. Send a communiqué to John. Tell him the last available seats for project Starlight-Express are finally booked."

Kate extracted the small stylus from Nan and quickly pecked out a note, then threw herself around Tom. "I can't tell you how happy I am. We're going to the stars!"

They stood together for a few minutes looking up at their destination. Nan chimed, sensed the dark, and automatically backlit the message lens. Kate brought the device closer to her face, verified the sender, and read the dispatch. She burst out laughing.

Tom found it infectious. "Hey, wait a minute. I don't even know what's so amusing. It's obviously not from John the stoic. He hasn't said anything funny in all the time I've known him."

Kate wiped her eyes, trying to regain her composure. "Well, you're wrong. Bear with me for awhile. How long has John been trying to talk us into going with them?"

"Forever."

"How persistent has he been?"

"Are you kidding? He's threatened us with everything ... including murder, mayhem, and kidnapping. C'mon, Kate ... what's this all about?"

"Would you believe ... after all of that harassment ... John's entire response consists of only one word?"

"Ha! What message of any significance could John possibly convey using only one word?"

Kate showed him the display. "See for yourself." Arrayed in bold letters was the single entry: COOL.

ISBN 141201567-7

9 781412 015677